THE SEER'S DRAGON

THE LEGACY OF THE TIME STONES TRILOGY, BOOK #2

BRITTANY FICHTER

Iilaedin
The Northern Mountains
Lady Seren's Fortress
Solva Breghan
Richlien Mountains
The Walled City
Mhaedin
Rangvald's Fortress

1

Eirin let out a relieved sigh as the sun finally sank below the western horizon. She was thankful, of course, that she and her companions had escaped from the mountain unscathed. That was more than they could say for the SgaethOirs, the elite guards who had tracked her escape from Torbaine. Their demise had not been pretty.

It was unfortunate, however, that the escape tunnel she and her friends had used led them out onto a ledge on the west side of the mountain. It had been safe enough that morning when there were still shadows to hide in. But from late morning on, there was no natural respite from the sun until it was gone. They had been forced to build a tent quickly to keep from frying beneath the sun's afternoon rays.

Even now, though the sun was down, she could still feel the sharp heat it had left behind. Its beams had spent all afternoon threatening to make it through the tent she and her friends had hastily erected upon escape. They had pitched their tent with multiple layers, just as they'd been taught in their rigorous warrior training, finishing just moments before the sun had reached them that morning. Still, her skin stung a little as she stood and stretched.

Her companions were sprawled out on the floor, lying on their sleep sacks instead of inside them, and a pang of guilt pricked her. They looked so tired. Their escape had only taken place that morning, and their moments of quiet rest would be few for a while yet. They wouldn't be on the run at all if it wasn't for her. Not that she had much choice in the matter either.

Drystan and Thane snored softly. Nuru slept silently in the far corner, as far away from Eirin as she could possibly get. Not that Eirin was about to argue. She might believe Nuru really did want to begin again, away from her poisonous mother's influence. Elder Na'ilah was a viper in the flesh if ever there was one, no matter what kind of Atharrach she might be. But just because Eirin had agreed to let Nuru come didn't mean she was ready to trust the girl completely.

Qeb's corner was empty, but he had insisted on staying in the shade of the tent to watch for more pursuers.

With everyone else still asleep, Eirin reached into the pack her mother had given her before she fled. In it were the few belongings that mattered. Lady Seren, their Dragon hostess, had given them all they might need before they left her fortress, but Eirin's mother had added a few things as well. A blanket, the map of Solevar her father had made, several small bundles of food... Eirin frowned at these. Her family didn't have enough food as it was. She wished her mother hadn't sent them.

Then her hand rested on what she had been looking for. Slowly, she pulled out her mother's letters.

They were written on her father's map-making parchment, and they had been sealed with his red wax. Eirin stared at them for a moment, her hands shaking slightly, before breaking the wax seal and reading them in the dying light.

My dearest Eirin,

I have entire tomes of knowledge I could write about what you need to know. Unfortunately, the knowledge I believed I would have time to pass on to you as you grew up was cut short by the king's plans, and I was never afforded the years I thought we would have. But what I can share now I will tell you quickly.

Your great-great-grandparents had always wanted to return to Iilaedin. But that was difficult, unfortunately, with the unrest Torbaine suffered in its early years. Guards were posted at entrances and exits, and they knew very soon that if they left the mountain city, they wouldn't be able to come back. As they had a young daughter, they felt it would be unsafe to leave when she was so young. Which meant they never left. So their daughter had a daughter who eventually married and had me. And to my great shame, none of us went before you.

The only blessings I can glean from this shame are twofold. First, the stone was never lost. It's been passed down through our generations in the hopes that someone would one day seek to return to Iilaedin to fix the Time Stones. From what I understand, the Time Stone Circle is quite large, and finding the missing stone piece would be difficult without it.

Second, we have not forgotten the truth as everyone else here has been forced to. We know what the world outside is like and who the Time Keeper is. We've also passed down the hope that the Time Keeper, in His mercy, will provide a way. For if the Seers know anything, it's that the Time Keeper orchestrates the minutest of details, even those that seem irreparable. This is your heritage. It's been passed down for your benefit and for the world's, and if you remember nothing else, cling to this.

It seems hypocritical to tell you to be brave and not to fear. But you seem to have been chosen for this task, and there is no other. So be brave, my girl, in the way you always were. Find trustworthy helpers and go to Iilaedin. Don't worry about us. We'll keep well enough. We always

have. As you go, know that you have our love always. As the ancient blessing says, may the Time Keeper keep your way.
  In love,
  Mother

Eirin put the first letter down to open the second.

Eirin,
  I forgot in the first letter to include a warning that I think you should be aware of already, but I'm including it none-theless. Do not, under any circumstances, allow anyone else to touch the Time Stone. It was made for Seers' hands only and will most likely kill the first person who comes into contact with the stone itself. And their death would be the least of our problems. The world was thrust into darkness when a prince and a Seer tried to take power that wasn't theirs. I shudder to think of what might happen if another tried to use it as well.

Eirin's hands trembled as she read the letters repeatedly, memorizing them as best she could. Her mother had said to burn them when she was finished, but her chest grew tight when she thought of destroying them. They were one of her last connections to her mother. If she let them go–

An explosion threw her to the ground, where she landed unceremoniously on Thane's legs. She struggled to push herself up, but a second explosion knocked her back down two seconds later. Nuru was on her feet immediately, sword drawn. Drystan was also alert and instantly at Eirin's side, his double-bladed staff in hand.

"What in the blazes..." he muttered, lifting Eirin off of Thane with his free arm. Then his eyes widened. "Where's Qeb?"

"He went out to watch the tunnel entrance," Eirin said, stuffing the parchments back in her bag. Then she ran to the front of the tent and knelt to unbuckle the ties at the bottom of the tent's opening as fast as her fingers could manage. The others stood ready with their weapons.

"Wait, he went *back* to the tunnel?" Drystan snapped. "I thought he was done there!"

He was outside before she even had the tent door completely open. He didn't get far, though. The air outside was filling rapidly with dust so thick she could barely see ten feet in front of her. Drawing her own sword, Eirin took a few steps to follow him, but Thane yanked her back.

"I don't know what's going on," he said, "but before she freed us, Alys made it clear that *you* are not supposed to be anywhere *near* danger."

Eirin frowned. Leave it to her best friend to tell everyone else she was a delicate flower.

Even if she was...somewhat delicate, comparatively speaking. It was still annoying.

Before she could quibble with Thane, however, Qeb emerged from the tunnel from which dust was still pouring. He wore the kind of thick, black cloak and hood they all had, which had been designed for those who might accidentally come into contact with Solevar's poisonous sunlight. And he was grinning.

"What did you do?" Drystan asked, coughing as Qeb met him. "Blow up the whole mountainside?"

"Close," Qeb said, still smiling as he rubbed the dust out of his dark hair. "I destroyed the bridge."

"You're not supposed to go out in the day," Nuru snapped, as though this hadn't been drilled into them all since they were old enough to walk. "I thought you were just going to guard from the tent's edge."

Qeb just shrugged and held up his arms, which were draped in the thick black material. "It was only to run between here and there."

He pointed from the tent to the tunnel opening. "Now they can't follow us. Not this way, at least."

Thane whistled. "What did you do?"

"Just some powdered kaekyi. I sprinkled it over the entrance into the tunnel from the lower tunnels and then again on the bridge."

"Alys gave you kaekyi?" Thane protested. "That's not fair! I only got regular weapons."

Qeb strode over to the tent and pulled out his sack. He dug something out and then held up his hand to reveal several small parchment packages, each about the size of his thumb and tied with string. "Guess she trusts me more," he said with another rare grin.

"Remind me not to let you light any fires while wearing that," Drystan murmured with a small smile.

"Did you see anyone while you were in there?" Eirin asked.

Qeb shook his head. "I think they expected their SgaethOirs to pursue us, so it could be a day or so before they realize something went wrong."

"Except," Nuru said with a frown, looking back at the smoking tunnel, "you just alerted the entire mountain. If they didn't know something was wrong, they do now."

"It doesn't matter," Drystan said as he straightened and looked around. "We need to get as far from here as we can. We'll walk tonight, stop before sunrise, set up the tent, and eat." He looked at Eirin, and she held his gaze.

What was he thinking?

Finally, he turned to the others. "I don't know how much Alys was able to share," he continued, "but we have a lot to tell you."

"Perhaps we should talk while we're eating in the morning," Eirin suggested. Drystan was right. There was far too much to share while they were here, just a stone's throw from the tunnel's entrance. The bridge may have been destroyed, but at least half of the SgaethOir seemed to have wings. Eirin shuddered delicately.

"And how do we know where we're supposed to be going?" Nuru asked.

"I have a map." Eirin held up her bag.

"Good," Drystan said. "We'll need it." He frowned back at the tunnel. "But if we're on the northernmost mountain, and Mhaedin is due south, I think we can safely make our way south for one night without consulting it. I'd like to put as much distance between us and the SgaethOir as possible."

The others had no objection to this plan. Nuru, Qeb, and Thane, despite being promised freedom by Torbaine's city Elders, had been locked up after returning from the outside world. It was for their own protection, they had been told, so they could be watched for Sun Sickness. But they knew that wasn't true, as Alys's father had easily gotten her out of her imprisonment. If they returned to Torbaine now, they wouldn't be receiving heroes' welcomes. Eirin would be captured and forced to try to break Solevar's curse without any of the helpful training she hoped to find in Mhaedin, and Drystan would most likely be put to death.

They all had very good reason not to argue.

And yet, after they had packed up the tent and set out, Eirin's heart still throbbed. Every step was taking her farther from everyone she loved. Her father and mother and little brothers. The unborn sibling she might never meet. Alys, her best friend who had sacrificed herself so they could all escape. More than once, Eirin was thankful for the dark of night as they walked because it hid the number of times she had to rub her stinging eyes.

Then there was the dread. That she knew of, there were only four remaining Humans in all of Solevar, and that included herself and her mother. The other two were a father and son who had helped hide her during her first journey away from her home city of Torbaine, back before she'd known most of the other people in Solevar were anything but Human.

A shadow much larger than hers drifted toward her as they made their way south under the light of the stars. She turned and glanced up at Drystan. His eyes had returned to their usual shade of bright blue. Or at least, she guessed they were. It was hard to tell in the dark. All she knew was that none of the glowing amber flame that had burned from within him that morning remained.

She shivered again, a little more violently this time, as she remembered what he had become. She had known he was an Atharrach, a shape-shifting creature, for a while. All Atharrachs had a Human form in which they could communicate with all other intelligent beings. But each had a true form as well, the form the creature took depending upon the color and location of its magic within its body.

Eirin didn't recognize many of them yet, but she had learned a few. Elves, like Mistress Alanna–Drystan's late mother–had violet magic that ran from their shoulders down to their fingertips. Griffins had orange magic that ran on each side of their body from their shoulder blades to the base of their necks. And Dragons had gold and blue that pulsed around their hearts in flames.

Drystan was a Dragon.

The memory of his Dragon form bursting forth from his Human form still made her shiver. She glanced up at him, and examined his Human face, which shone white in the moonlight. He must have sensed her gaze because he looked back down at her.

He held her gaze for a long moment. Unfortunately, as it was dark, she couldn't read his expression, and she almost wished once again for his Dragon eyes with their blue and amber glow, just so she could better see what he was feeling. And as they walked in the cool of night, she was reminded of the heat that had rolled off him in the cave, when her face had prickled at his approach, and the air around them had shimmered. His scales had glistened, and his claws had clacked against the stone floor.

She was also reminded of her fear. When Drystan had first looked up from killing Gerard—the Fae who had tried to capture her–there had been no sign of the Drystan she knew in the Dragon's eyes. There had been fire and bloodlust. He had been deadly. Deadly and beautiful with his glittering blue scales that shone like a freshly polished shield, and eyes where the familiar, icy blue fought with the foreign amber fire. Those eyes had been void of recognition when he'd turned to look at her, but with each step he had taken toward her, she'd seen the battle within. And she had dared to touch him.

She'd expected his scales to singe her fingers, so her first touch had been feathery light. She couldn't really say why she had touched him. She'd simply felt the need. His shining scales, the same blue as the sky at twilight, had beckoned to her. And though they were warm, as she'd expected, they didn't burn.

Her touch had sent a ripple down his body. He shivered, then his scales melted into warm, soft skin. Her hand had still been on his face when he took her own face with his Human hands and leaned his forehead against hers, breathing deeply and closing his eyes as though he were using her as an anchor.

Her heart fluttered at the memory of his touch. Which was ridiculous. He'd touched her a million times before, usually to yank her out of the way of something dangerous or, as he had done only months earlier, to train her for physical combat, most of which had involved knocking her to the ground. This touch, though...his fingers had trembled, and his breath had come in and out in uneven gasps.

She glanced at him again now. He was walking beside her, but his eyes were on the mountain path they followed. His dark hair, grown somewhat unruly during their travels, blew slightly in the wind, and though he was unusually tall and was covered in muscle, he looked every bit Human. Could he recall every moment of that short time as she could? Had it meant anything more to him? Or had he simply needed someone to hold him, to keep him from falling?

The others walked just as quietly as she and Drystan did, though she couldn't tell how much of their silence was from their stealth training at the Citadel or simply because they were trying to absorb everything that had happened to them as well.

"This should be a good place," Drystan announced hours later. Eirin looked up from the rocky terrain, which seemed determined to trip her, to find they were on a smooth, slightly wider ledge than what they'd been traveling on for the past few hours. Even better than the flat nature of the ledge, however, was that there was a cottage-sized boulder that would provide some shadow for them the following morning if they pitched their tent just beside it.

"Qeb," Drystan continued, "you and Thane make sure we're alone. Nuru, you'll help me pitch the tent. Eirin, you make the fire."

Everyone set to work as though they made camp on a mountain-side every day. They might as well have been. Their Instructors at the Citadel had forced them to practice survival skills for years so that every skill was second nature. A useful gift, considering how they'd all been forced to flee.

"This area seems pretty desolate," Qeb announced when he and Thane returned several minutes later.

"But not too desolate," Thane said cheerfully as he sat down beside the fire. "There are all sorts of little creatures around here. I even smelled a skunk."

Nuru, who had been rebraiding her long, dark hair, made a face. "And that's good why?"

"Obviously, because it's one of the top predators around." Thane leaned over and tapped Nuru on the nose with his finger. "Rejoice, love. It means we're less likely to be eaten by something big in our sleep."

"Touch me again," Nuru hissed, "and *I* will eat you in your sleep."

"Alys outdid herself," Drystan said, a little louder than necessary. "She even got us meat."

Nuru got the hint, but she continued to glower at Thane. Thane, however, was always happy to be distracted.

"Oh, what kind?"

"Hampig," Eirin laughed. "What other kind could we have?"

"I was hoping for a few dead chickens." Thane pulled a bundle of cloth out of his pack. "You know, the ones that are too stupid to stay away from the sunlight." He grinned as he unwrapped a slab of dried, salted hampork. "They're half-cooked by the time you find them." He then sliced a chunk off with his knife and bit into it. "So," he said between bites, "does anyone want to explain why we're on the run, and our Elders are trying to kill us?"

Eirin and Drystan shared another long look. Eirin's first instinct, of course, was to tell them as little as possible. But the days of hiding were over now. They were no longer under the king's orders. Their friends–though calling Nuru a friend was a bit of a stretch–had fled Torbaine with them, and their lives now depended on what Eirin and Drystan knew.

Drystan nodded as though sharing her thoughts. In the light of the fire, the dark circles beneath his eyes were accentuated, and she thought back to how haggard he'd looked after shifting back to his Human form from the Dragon. But when he spoke, his voice was as clear and calm as ever.

"It goes back to the curse of Solevar," he began slowly. "To something my great-grandfather did. Something my grandfather and then my father have been trying to fix since."

"Your father died, though," Nuru said, frowning.

Drystan swallowed and looked down at his food. "No. At least, not as of two nights ago."

"Wait, but…" Nuru looked around at the others, who all looked down at their food as well. "How do I not know this…history, and the rest of you do?"

"We found out after you and Alys were taken by your mother," Eirin murmured. "Alanna told us before she died."

"And how did *she* know?"

"Because she was my mother," Drystan said in a heavy voice. The circle was quiet for a moment before Eirin picked the story back up.

"The curse wasn't an accident."

"You mean, like the Solevar curse?" Thane interrupted.

She nodded, then paused. There was so much they didn't know. So much that she barely knew. She tried again. "Apparently, when the Time Keeper–"

"Who's He?" Nuru demanded.

Eirin sighed. So much information. "The Time Keeper is the one who created the world."

"Wait," Nuru said. "Do you mean the cult figure–"

"Would you like to hear what she has to say or not?" Qeb snapped. "Because if not, the rest of us would."

Nuru huffed, but Eirin sent him a grateful look. "So when He was creating Solevar, the Time Keeper imbued magic into all of the world. Into everything. Everyone." She drew in a steadying breath. "Everyone except for Humans."

"Which we are not," Thane said slowly.

"Everyone," Drystan said, "except for Eirin."

There was another long pause. This couldn't come as too much of a surprise to her friends. And yet, hearing it confirmed was still so strange. Finally, Thane turned to Eirin, his face perfectly solemn.

"So you *are* a Human then."

She nodded.

He glanced back at Drystan. "That…explains so much." Shaking his head then, he chuckled. "No wonder you're horrible at everything."

Drystan frowned, but Eirin just laughed with him. "That would be why."

"So why is everyone after the Human then?" Nuru asked, seeming unable to stay silent.

"Hold on," Eirin said. "There's more. So it seems that when Solevar was created, each creature had its own purpose. That's why different magical gifts were given to different races. But there were two groups that were necessary for the preservation of all the others."

"Let me guess," Nuru said dryly. "Humans were one of them."

"Yes," Eirin said, refusing to let Nuru rouse her ire. "And the other was the Dragons, who were made to rule."

"Rule who?" Thane asked.

"Everyone else," Eirin answered. "Some ruled smaller provinces as the lords and ladies. Others had even more power. But there was always a high king. And the next high king was chosen...somehow from his sons." She frowned. "It seems that the last king...King Faradoon was dying. Or dead. I'm not sure. But before a new king could be chosen, the high king's three sons began to fight about something. And one of them..." She drew in a deep breath and glanced at Drystan. "Prince Kamon, did something foolish. He broke the Time Stones, and as a result, brought down the curse upon Solevar."

"What are the Time Stones?" Qeb asked.

"It's... they're hard to explain." Eirin picked up a stick and drew a circle in the sand. Then within the circle, she began drawing little rectangles, some facing north to south and others facing east to west. "When the Time Keeper created Solevar, He included a way to determine truth and to record the kingdom's history more accurately than any scholar could do. Each of these stones," she poked at one of the rectangles, "holds a...a sort of memory from a particular time and place. We've been told that the Time Keeper continued to add the stones after creating the original Seers' Circles. But when Kamon convinced a Seer to help him try to insert a stone of his own creation–one he hoped would change the course of fate–the stones stopped moving. The curse fell, and the magic in Solevar began to die."

They were all quiet for a long time. So long that the sky began to gray in the east. Finally, Nuru shook her head.

"So Humans…"

"We're called Seers. And we're the only race that has no magic." The word for her own kind still felt strange on her tongue. "But we can See it and feel it, and we're impervious to its direct attacks. According to Lady Seren and my mother, we can read these stones and See what memories they were assigned by the Time Keeper." She looked down again. "Apparently, only a Seer can fix the stones. Seers were created to watch them, to be judges, record keepers, and witnesses. They were meant to touch the stones and see what truths the Time Keeper had recorded for them."

"So why did the Seer break the stones then?" Nuru asked.

"I… I'm not sure I understand everything yet. But it seems he thought that they could somehow alter fate by putting their own stone into the circle," she continued. "They knew it was a mistake right away, though. After the Seer shoved Kamon's stone into the circle, he tried to remove it, but only a piece of it came out. The other part of the foreign stone is still lodged in there. Now a Seer has to remove it from the Seers' Circle, or Solevar's magic will die completely."

"So why is everyone so intent on you going?" Thane asked. "I don't mean to offend, but you're not exactly an expert on all things Solevar." He looked around. "None of us are."

"That's true." Eirin nodded. "Unfortunately, it seems nearly all of the other Humans are dead."

Everyone except for Drystan froze.

"You mean…" Nuru's voice shook slightly. "That *you* are our last hope of surviving this curse?"

Eiri gave her a dry smile. "Sorry to disappoint. But I'm afraid you're stuck with me. Again."

"No. No, this makes sense, though!" Thane cried, jumping up and beginning to pace. "All those times you saw things, and we thought you were going crazy. And when you didn't fall prey to the Tsuchigumo's lie!" He let out a short laugh. "All this time, we thought you were—"

"Were what?" Drystan growled.

Thane seemed to swallow his words. "Nothing. Just…We always wondered why she was…" He gave a nervous laugh. "Sorry."

Eirin gave him a bemused smile. "You're not wrong."

"But that still doesn't explain why our Elders lied to us and forced us to use bruthsi root," Nuru said, shaking her head.

"The cowards liked being in charge," Drystan said. The others stopped and stared at him.

"But…in charge of *what?*" Nuru asked.

"Dragons were meant to rule," Drystan said, his voice still gruff. "That's why Kamon was chosen as king when they fled the curse and made it to the mountain. The city Elders were originally representatives of their various races. When the races began to fight, though, they began using bruthsi root to suppress the people's magic. Then they used another herb mixed with magic to clear their minds, making them forget they ever had magic at all."

The others sat in stunned silence. Even Nuru.

"So…they stole that from us…but kept their places anyway?" Thane finally asked in a quiet voice.

"The Elders quickly decided they liked being in power," Eirin said gently. "They decided it would be best if they took power instead of allowing the king to hold his place as well."

"Not to sound…stupid," Thane said, "but since Kamon was the one who brought down the curse upon the people, wouldn't it make sense to let someone else make the decisions?"

Eirin spoke before Drystan could. She got the feeling that whatever Drystan had seen while they were separated in Torbaine was fueling his anger now, and that it had something to do with his father. The last thing they needed up on the ledge was an angry Dragon.

"I can't answer as Lady Seren would," she said, wishing sorely that the great Dragon was with them now, "but it seems that our kings did *try* to break the curse. But with each generation the Elders have taken more power until they began preventing the kings from leaving the city at all."

"They think the curse will leave them alone in the mountain," Drystan said, still sounding annoyed. "It's as if they haven't even noticed the food shortages. They hide, and they lie to the people, taking the easy way out when death is on their doorstep."

"So what are we doing then?" Nuru asked. "Besides running away from the people who captured us."

"We...I need to go to Mhaedin because Lady Seren says there are people there who can help me learn how to fix the Time Stones." Eirin's hand hovered over the part of her shirt where the small, broken rectangular stone hung from her neck—the very shard of stone that Kamon's Seer had tried to force into the Time Stones.

But that should probably stay a secret for now.

"I need to try to remove the rest of the broken stone," she told them, letting her hand fall to her lap. "Only Seers can touch the Time Stones. And it appears that I'm one of the few left who can even try."

Drystan's head snapped up. He'd caught her slip. But she did her best to ignore him. As far as he knew, she was the only one left. Well, she and her mother. She hadn't shared the Humanity of two other individuals they'd met during their first journey into Solevar, and she wasn't about to tell him now in front of all the others. Mannish and his father had protected her secret, and she wasn't about to divulge theirs.

"So you need protection," Qeb said.

Eirin nodded. "We were actually much closer to the Time Stones when we were with Lady Seren. They're in Iilaedin, where the Emerald Palace is." She opened up her pack and pulled out the map her father had given to her months ago, unaware at the time that she would ever truly need it. "Here." She pointed to the northwestern corner of the map. "Right next to the water. Apparently, that was the royal city where all the Dragon kings lived. This is where we were." She pointed to a spot near the northernmost mountain in the Rich-lien Mountain range. "But she said we needed training and knowl-edge before venturing out."

"And she couldn't provide that?" Qeb looked skeptical.

"I suppose not." Eirin shrugged. "She was...very old."

"She thought that the people in Mhaedin would know best how

to travel safely with a Human," Drystan said. "She says they'll know how to get Eirin to the stones alive."

"She seems to expect a lot of danger for such a short distance." Nuru squinted at the map.

"Oh, there is," Eirin said. "Seers have been hunted by various groups for years." She shivered.

"Hunted?" Qeb asked with a frown.

"Not hunted like you would hunt an animal," Eirin said. "Chased down and dragged to the Time Stones."

"So if they're not hurting the Seers themselves," Nuru said slowly, "why are the Seers dying?"

Eirin looked out over the valley below. She couldn't see well in the early gray of morning, but enough was visible to view various land levels beyond the mountain. "The curse is poisonous to all living creatures," she said. "Animal, Atharrach, and Human. But it's especially deadly to Humans because we have no magic to protect us."

"So most of you...Humans...die because of the land?" Thane asked.

Eirin nodded, and a shiver ran up her spine. Here they were, speaking so casually of the death of her people because there was no other way to discuss it. "Many made the journey across Solevar to the stones, but none survived long enough to fix them."

"And what if we don't?" Nuru asked, looking at Eirin and Drystan in turn. "Then what?"

"Simple," Drystan answered. "Everyone dies."

They were all silent for a moment.

"So if you're the great-grandson of Kamon..." Thane finally said, staring at Drystan. "What's your part in all of this?"

"At the risk of sounding simplistic, I'm trying to fix what my great-grandfather broke by escorting Eirin to the Time Stones." Drystan looked at Eirin. "And being a Dragon gives me an advantage."

Qeb smiled. "So you are something big." He looked at Thane. "Pay up."

"You can't assume he's big," Thane told him. "You've not even seen him. Maybe he's like a dwarvish Dragon. Or a Wyvern. Or a Lizard."

Qeb only grinned more widely.

Thane rolled his eyes, but he pulled a hunk of his hampig out of his pack and tossed it to Qeb. "I want that back if he's miniature."

"There's no such thing as a miniature Dragon," Drystan said dryly.

"*Any*how," Nuru snapped, "How did you hide your lineage from everyone? The whole point of choosing the Heir by strength was to keep the king from getting married."

"How do you know that?" Thane asked.

Nuru's eyes darkened. "My mother told me."

Elder N'iliah, Nuru's mother, was one of the scariest women Eirin had ever met. Disagreeing with her was like pulling a cat's tail. You might be right, but the encounter would end in scratches and bruises and blood.

"My grandmother was a crafty woman," Drystan said with a dry smile. "She was the one who suggested the next Heir be chosen for his strength."

Thane's eyes grew wide. "Which meant you would win! Because you were a Dragon! And Dragons are the strongest–"

"And there you have it." Drystan nodded.

"Look, I don't mean to be the naysayer," Nuru said, standing and dusting the crumbs off her trousers, "but how do we expect to succeed where everyone else has failed?"

Eirin gave her a sad smile. "We have to try." Then she took a deep breath. She could share this without sharing everything. "And we have something else. Before we left, my mother gave me special instructions about the Time Stones. Instructions passed down for generations in our Human line. Because while the Elders used magic to remove the memories of our ancestors, we didn't forget."

"Why?" Nuru asked.

"Humans are immune to magic. So we remember, and I hope to use that knowledge when we finally reach the stones."

The sun was close to rising, so the group agreed to continue this discussion at another time. Thane put out the fire as everyone else squeezed all of their things back into the tent. The silence was so heavy that Eirin finally spoke when they were all inside again.

"I know you all weren't expecting or even wishing to get caught up in this," she said, suddenly unable to look at them. "But King Egan sent us out into Solevar the first time so we could discover what the Elders had lied about. If any of you wish to leave, though, you're… you're free to do so."

"I'm going with you two," Qeb said without hesitation.

Thane laughed. "Have you ever *not* gone with him?"

Nuru grimaced. "We're being chased at home," she snapped. "I don't think we have anywhere else we *can* go."

"Which, I think," Thane said, still chuckling, "means we're all coming."

Eirin breathed a deeper sigh of relief than she had since they'd left the caverns. She and Drystan wouldn't be alone. Solevar would be just a little less lonely after all.

"If you're a Dragon," Thane said, turning to Drystan, "can't you just fly us to this…wherever we're going?"

Drystan scowled. "Absolutely not. The shift was violent, and I'd probably kill whoever was trying to take a ride." He stretched uncomfortably as though it still hurt.

"So then…" Thane said, drawing his words out, "not to sound as though I'm panicking…because I'm not, but what about the rest of us Atharrachs?" When everyone looked at him, he held up his hands. "There's bruthsi in my bag, but not much."

They all looked at one another as the weight of his words settled upon them.

Eirin suddenly felt nauseous. Drystan was suffering. She could tell that much by looking at him. And he was their strongest fighter. What were she and Drystan supposed to do with the rest of them when their bruthsi ran out? They'd be immobilized and vulnerable at best. At worst…

She shuddered, remembering the feral emptiness that had filled Drystan's eyes after his shift.

"I think," Drystan said slowly, "that you should all take as little as possible to make it last until we reach Mhaedin. If they can help Eirin, they can probably help you too." His eyes darkened as he stared down at his hands. "What I went through in the cave…I wouldn't wish that on my worst enemy."

Eirin nodded, her chest swelling with relief. "That's right. They all shift. So they should know how to make it better."

Qeb raised his eyebrows. "You shifted *in* the cave?"

Drystan nodded but didn't say anything else.

Qeb seemed to take his best friend's hint and stood. "I'll take first watch."

"No, you had it last night." Thane stood and stretched as well. "Get some sleep." He turned to Nuru and grinned. "Ready for one last moonlit stroll with me, love, while we search the premises for villains?"

Nuru rolled her eyes, but for the first time that night, Eirin saw the corner of her mouth quirk up. "Yes. But only because I don't trust you to actually look. And call me 'love' again at your peril."

"So…" Eirin said, unable to help smiling. "You are all coming with us then?" It seemed too good to be true. She'd feared that once they'd heard what they were up against, the others might decide the risk wasn't worth it. Well, except for Qeb. Qeb would have to be physically cut from Drystan's side.

"I mean," Thane said, "I could go wander the wilderness, but heading to a city, which most likely has some lovely ladies in it, sounds much more promising." He ran his hand through his pale hair with a grin.

Nuru elbowed him in the side.

"Careful how hard you roll those pretty eyes," Thane told her as they picked up their weapons. "They'll roll right out of your head."

"Eirin."

Eirin turned and jumped a little to find Drystan's face just inches from hers. "Yes?"

"We're taking the shift after theirs."

She nodded. "Very well."

He leaned in closer. "We need to talk."

2

Only seconds after she'd closed her eyes, there were a few bumps and low curses from Nuru. Eirin rubbed her eyes to realize that it hadn't been seconds since she'd fallen asleep, but hours. The sun was already on its afternoon descent, though, to her great relief, the large rock they'd built their tent beside kept most of the tent in the shade, including the entrance. Nuru and Thane were trying to pick their way around Qeb's hulking form to find the same corners they'd slept in the night before, though it looked like Nuru had accidentally stepped on his hand, which Eirin guessed had brought on the cursing. Drystan was nowhere to be seen.

"Drystan's outside," Thane whispered, answering her questioning look.

Eirin nodded and stood. Her whole body was sore from sleeping on the ground, but she felt far more rested than she had the night before.

She made her way carefully around Qeb's other side before slipping silently out of the tent.

Drystan was sitting against the shaded side of the rock on the sparse grass that covered the higher mountain ledges. His eyes were closed, and he looked almost to be sleeping. So she sat beside him and laid her weapons in her lap without saying a word.

"Distract me," he whispered without opening his eyes.

Eirin blinked at him. "From what?"

"The pain." His jaw clenched. "It's been here ever since the shift."

"You've done a good job hiding it."

He took a slow, deep breath. "I had a distraction."

Oh. Eirin thought for a moment, then glanced at the tent. There were several sets of soft snores coming from the inside. The others must be exhausted. So she pulled the leather cord from her neck and held out the broken, rectangular stone. "I can show you this."

He opened one eye. "Is that what I think it is?"

She nodded.

He studied it for a moment longer. "Where did you get it?"

"My mother gave it to me before I left." She studied the broken stone. Aside from its smoothness and perfectly angled rectangular cuts, it looked absolutely ordinary, like any gray stone one might pick up on the road. "Apparently, it was my ancestor's."

His eyes were trained on hers, so intent that they did strange things to her stomach. So she looked back down at the stone and went on. "She says my great-grandfather knew the Seer who worked for Kamon and forced the stone into the Time Stones Circle. The man died, and this was lying beside him. So my great-grandfather took it and ran." She frowned slightly. "He meant to go back and try to fix it, but, apparently, the curse fell into place, and he…he never did."

Coward. Although a quiet voice in her head wondered if it really made any difference. As it was, nearly the entire Human race had been killed trying to do what he hadn't.

"I saw it earlier when it fell out of your shirt," Drystan said. "You need to keep that better hidden." His words were rough, but there was a strain to his voice. She was supposed to keep distracting him.

"My great-grandparents were both Humans, and they served at the palace in Iilaedin," she continued, babbling for lack of anything better to do. "They fled the curse when it fell and escaped with Kamon's caravan. And when the Elders chose to give everyone the magic that erased everyone's memories, they simply pretended to forget, along with everyone else. My grandmother was their only child, and my mother was an only child as well."

"And none of them ever tried to fix the stones?" Drystan frowned.

Eirin's face flushed. "My mother meant to. But she said she was angry at her parents about something and rushed off and married my father to rebel. Then I was born, and…" She shrugged. "She didn't want to leave me."

"Hey." Rough fingers touched her face and gently turned her face to him. When she finally met his gaze, he was giving her a sad smile. And despite all the more important things they were discussing, the feeling of his fingers on her skin was highly distracting. She had the ridiculous desire to place her own hands on them to keep them there.

"You don't need to explain," he continued. "You're speaking with the great-grandson of the man who accidentally masterminded the curse." His smile became bitter.

"I think…" Eirin's breath ran out, and she had to take another deep gulp of air. "I think this stone is the key to breaking the curse. At least, my mother thought so. It's been passed down through the generations for whoever would return." She looked down at the stone, about the length of her thumb, in the palm of her hand. "My mother says I can find the stone's other half and pull it out because I'll know what to look for, something none of the Seers ever had." She couldn't imagine not being able to find a hole in the circle of stones, but there must be a reason the others hadn't fixed them yet.

"At least," she finished, "this stone is something none of the others had."

"I think we also have something else that the others never had," Drystan said, the corners of his mouth turning up as he gently tapped her nose.

Eirin's face heated, but she couldn't help smiling a little. Then his eyes moved back to the stone. "Keep that secret, though. Don't tell the others even. Not yet, at least."

"Why?"

He furrowed his brows. "There's a reason your mother kept it secret all these years. And if they accidentally let some hint drop…" He shook his head. "Let's just say I have a hunch that that stone might have the ability to change everything...for good or for bad."

Eirin nodded and put the leather cord back around her neck, tucking it carefully beneath her shirt. Then she turned back to Drystan. "I...I know we didn't have much of a choice in all of this. But... thank you."

He said nothing, but in the quiet afternoon light, he found her hand and gave it a gentle squeeze.

3

The remainder of the day passed without incident, much to Drystan's relief. Unfortunately, as night fell and they began packing up their supplies, they all got the distinct feeling they were being watched. It was immediately agreed that silence was prudent, and so with Eirin just behind him, Drystan led the way south along the mountain's continuing ridge.

The silence was not only useful for stealth, but it also allowed Drystan to mask his fear. The potency of it was startling. Drystan wasn't used to feeling fear. Not even during his final moments with his father had he felt this shaken. But then again, he hadn't shifted yet at that point. And he hadn't been a refugee making his way to a city of strangers who would most likely toss him out as soon as they learned who he was. And banishing him would be the merciful response.

But that was the crux of the problem. He wasn't even sure who he was anymore.

Drystan had never wondered about his place in the world. At least, not before all of this. But now that he was running for his life, the facade of easy confidence was gone. And though he was leading a band of runaway renegades, they weren't even his to command. No one was. Because he wasn't the king he'd been raised to think he would be. He was the distant descendant of a fool who had happened

27

to be the youngest prince of three. The man who had also happened to have plunged the world into darkness and death.

The death of his parents didn't help. But no. Drystan wouldn't think about losing them. That was a door that needed to stay shut. For now, at least. Because if it opened...

It needed to stay shut.

Overshadowing it all, though, was the residual pain of Drystan's first shift and the terror it still roused within him. He'd only shifted into a Dragon for a few minutes, but even a day and a half later, his bones hurt, and his muscles felt shaky and unreliable. And tired. Drystan couldn't remember the last time he had felt so exhausted. But this seemed all wrong. He'd seen many shifters in recent weeks, and they'd all seemed to shift without a second thought. So what was wrong with him?

Even worse than the pain, though, were those few terrifying moments in which he'd forgotten who he was...and who Eirin was. For a brief, eternal moment, his strongest desire had been bloodlust and death, and when he'd spotted Eirin, his instinct had roared for him to indulge in both.

Then he'd seen the fear in her eyes. Her fear had been what returned him to his Humanity. She'd looked terrified, and her widening eyes had recalled him to his senses, as if he was fighting his way back to the surface after drowning. But if he hadn't returned to his senses...

He didn't want to even consider that.

Drystan looked back at his little band. As usual, Eirin was soldiering on. He smiled slightly at her thin frame taking larger-than-usual steps to try and keep up with him. He slowed slightly, though he didn't dare insult her by mentioning it. She would simply scowl at him if he did. He wished he had her determination and resilience. She was the most vulnerable of them all. And yet, as she always had, she carried herself as though she were untouchable.

They continued on that way for days. As soon as the sun faded in the west every day, they were up and throwing everything back into their packs. Then they walked the length of the night, wolfing down food and water just as the gray of morning appeared in the sky again. And after a few days, not even this stopped them, for they realized that they were close enough to the mountain that the sun wouldn't touch them until halfway through the morning.

Even if they had felt comfortable talking, however, the wind would have prevented many conversations. It blew incessantly, each gale threatening to push them off the cliffside if they got too close to the edge.

And, as always, there was the danger of their ever-dwindling store of bruthsi root. While Drystan knew very little about the world they were sojourners in, he did know that he did not want to be alone with Eirin and three Atharrachs as they writhed in pain, helpless and vulnerable. So, three weeks into their walk, he called Qeb to him after breakfast.

"I don't know how much longer it's going to be," he said in a low voice, glancing back at the others. As usual, Eirin's watchful gaze was on them, but the others seemed absorbed in their own thoughts as they ate. "And I'm afraid we're not going to make it before we run out of bruthsi."

Qeb, ever honest, nodded. "I've considered that."

"I was thinking perhaps we should induce the changes sooner than later," Drystan said slowly. "If we found a sheltered cave or someplace similar where we wouldn't be in the open, we could try to facilitate your first shiftings, one at a time."

"Have you seen any caves?" Qeb asked.

Drystan opened his mouth to answer, but he was interrupted by the sound of Nuru, Thane, and Eirin's weapons being drawn. He and Qeb immediately drew their own weapons. Turning, they found everyone else staring up at distant figures in the sky. His heart nearly stopped.

"Wyverns," Eirin breathed.

Sure enough, a group of Wyverns circled in the sky not far to the north. Drystan counted seven. Far too many to face off without...

Without an Atharrach of their own.

Drystan's friends were well-trained. It was the only reason they'd survived in their Human forms so long. But they'd never had to face Wyverns before.

While not as large or strong as Dragons, and with thinner scales, Wyverns were wily, and they traveled and fought in packs. They also lacked the forearms Dragons had. That didn't mean they were by any means weak. Even with his limited knowledge, Drystan knew precisely what damage the talons at the end of their wings could do.

Fear leaped up in his chest as he sheathed his sword.

"Back up!" he called, moving toward the cliff's edge. "Stand against the wall!"

Nuru, Thane, and Qeb looked at him like he had lost his mind, but Eirin understood. She grabbed Thane and Nuru by the hands and dragged them back with her. Nuru tried to shake her off, but Qeb, seeming to understand, grabbed Nuru's other arm and dragged her back as well, succeeding where Eirin had failed. Then he pulled out his battle axe and stood in front of Eirin.

Just as he had every day of his life, Drystan wondered how in the world he could have found such a friend. But as he turned back to the figures in the sky, which were growing larger by the second, he realized he had a new problem.

Drystan didn't know how to shift. Not on purpose, at least. His shift in the cavern had been instinctive. Eirin had been in danger, and in that single second, his whole purpose in life had become being her protection. Closing his eyes, he tried to focus on the fire within. It was there. He could feel it burning inside. But accessing it? He held his breath and tensed.

And nothing happened.

"They're getting closer!" Nuru called, her arrow trained on the front Wyvern. It was close enough now that Drystan could see that it had green scales, even in the still gray of pre-dawn. About Eirin's height, it was very much like one might imagine a miniature Dragon to be, though its claws were on its wings rather than on dedicated forearms.

Try again!

And yet nothing. Drystan's breath came in and out too fast. He had only been a Dragon once. If he couldn't do this now, Eirin would–

The fire within him seemed to burst in every direction, and he was briefly eaten from the inside out as the flames pushed into every corner of his body. He cried out as he felt his bones expand and harden. Relief and disgust filled him as he looked down and saw not his feet but scales and claws. Relief for the change, as the Wyverns had nearly reached them. Disgust because bloodlust was already coursing through his veins. The disgust, however, was easy to ignore as he spread his wings so they shielded his friends.

The first Wyvern landed on the ledge and tilted its head to the side, its large yellow eyes studying Drystan with what looked like... Was that amusement?

"What family is this one from?" a second one hissed as it landed beside the first. "Do you see a mark?"

Dragons had marks?

"Can I help you?" Drystan growled.

"That depends," the first one said as two more landed to his right. "Why aren't your friends shifting?"

"That's not your business."

"Oh," said the second. "But it is." He smiled and glanced around Drystan's right wing at his friends, more of his friends landing behind him. "Because if they can't shift, that means they'll be easy supper. But if they're Human..." His eyes glittered. "That would be even better."

A small one, the seventh, having landed on the outermost edge of the group, tried to skitter around Drystan's outstretched wing. Drystan snarled and let forth a burst of gold and blue flame. The Wyvern leaped back and squeaked, and her companions stopped laughing.

"A son of Oreck," the second one whispered, his eyes widening.

"It's not Karolus, nor is it Rangvald," the first replied. "Which can only mean one thing."

"It means you can leave," Drystan growled again. In truth, he didn't feel nearly as fierce as he was acting.

"Something," the second continued as if Drystan hadn't even spoken, "has drawn a son of Kamon out of his hiding place." His eyes flicked to something behind Drystan. Drystan had been trying to shelter his friends from their view, but there were seven of them, and he could only do so much. "Which means," the Wyvern continued, "that he has something precious enough for which to risk death."

As if a command had been given, the seven Wyverns, including the young female, fanned out until they formed a semi-arc around

Drystan and his friends. Drystan tried to puff himself up to be larger, but there were too many of them to make a great difference. He was far larger than any of the Wyverns, but he couldn't put himself in seven different places at once.

Make that nine. Two more landed beside the others.

"Notice how they still haven't changed," the fourth muttered. "Even though we're clearly a threat."

"Which means either they won't shift," the second said, "or they can't." A smile spread across his scaled face, his pointed teeth glistening with drool.

"Yes," said another. "They draw their weapons, but they make no move to change forms."

"And notice," the first continued, "how they hide that little one in the back."

The mention of the "little one" had Drystan's bones on fire again, and this time, he didn't warn or hesitate. He simply flamed.

It was probably a foolish thing to do. In his very minimal studies at the Citadel, he had learned that a Wyvern's scales were thinner and less protective than Dragon scales. They were also unable to withstand fire, as they had none themselves. And the Wyverns had known this, of course. They must have. But to his surprise, they still leaped into the air as his flame came down upon them, shrieking and cursing to one another as if they hadn't expected the attack.

He flamed again at the group to his left. But as he did, one darted around his right wing, and two went over him. A guttural sound came from behind Drystan. He twisted his neck to see one lying dead near where Nuru and Thane were fending off two more. Qeb, likewise, had two of his own opponents. Eirin, sword drawn, was standing behind him, her back to the mountain.

One of the Wyverns had fallen under his second flame and didn't stand, and the other three were looking the worse for wear. But two of those were still edging forward even as he watched them. Instinctively, he swiped at them with his massive wing, sending one bouncing down the mountainside. The other ducked and flattened himself against the ground as Drystan flamed again.

Nuru and Thane were holding their own against their opponents, using techniques they'd been taught at the Citadel to guard one another as they fought, and Qeb ran his longsword through one of his attackers. The other, however, simply danced back.

"They're protecting the girl!" it shrieked to the other. "Get her!"

Drystan wanted to flame them all, but he didn't want to burn his friends. So he took advantage of their distraction to run his claws through the chest of Thane's opponent.

"There are too many!" the young Wyvern cried, falling back from Nuru's blade. "We can't!"

As though to confirm his fears, a flash of light lit up the ledge, and a deafening BOOM shook the mountainside.

Eirin had somehow grabbed one of the kaekyi packs and thrown it into the middle of the writhing Wyvern crowd, where more Wyverns had just landed. Only one pack, it seemed, which was not large enough to destroy anything the way Qeb had destroyed the tunnel, but it gave Drystan enough time to locate the leader.

He was about to flame again when he heard the sound of more flapping wings. He turned and looked, as did the others, at the sky.

A dozen more Wyverns hovered in place above them.

This was bad.

The Wyverns began to form a line in the sky, descending just as the others had done. Drystan flamed them as they dove, but most of them were too fast. Three fell into the chasm below, and three more fell screaming in the grass. There were still too many, though, and Drystan had to withhold his flames, as he feared hurting one of his friends by mistake.

Instead, he resorted to slashing and biting and clawing, tearing bone from flesh. And for a brief moment, the Dragon within him exulted. But then a scream jarred him from the trance he'd briefly fallen into, and he looked up to see two of the Wyverns rising into the air, each clutching one of Eirin's arms in its talons. The one on the right had blood dripping down its leg, which meant Eirin had probably stabbed it before it had grabbed her. But Drystan didn't pause to surmise any more than this. Instead, he launched himself up at them.

The one that was bleeding dropped Eirin's arm immediately at the sound of his roar, but the other hung on, Eirin crying out as her arm twisted in its grasp.

Drystan was just trying to angle himself so he could attack the Wyvern and catch Eirin when Thane threw a knife at its chest. The blade was well-aimed, and the Wyvern dropped Eirin as it cried out.

Drystan reached out to catch her. He did so but nearly missed, as his wings seemed to forget how to beat. Still, despite the near slip, he held her tight, turning so that his body took the brunt of the impact when they hit the side of the mountain.

Much to his relief, they landed back on their ledge. Unfortunately, even as they landed on the ground, Wyverns began to rush at them again, pulling at Eirin, trying to yank her from his grasp.

Had every Wyvern in Solevar made an appearance?

Drystan could hear his friends trying to hack away at the scaly bodies surrounding them, but they weren't fast enough, and Drystan was afraid the Wyverns would succeed in stealing Eirin out of his arms.

Anger coursed hot through his veins, and he let forth a burst of flame. The creatures squealed as they jumped back. Only when many of them took to the air, thinning the swarm, did Drystan realize how close he had come to killing his friends at the same time. They'd all been knocked flat by his flame, and signs of smoke showed on their faces.

Drystan laid Eirin down on the ground and leaped to his feet, ready to take on another attack. But instead of facing him, they began to scream at each other and turned to fly back in the direction they'd come from.

Were they fleeing from him? He doubted it. Though he hadn't been a Dragon for very long, he had been trained as a warrior, and he knew undoubtedly that this fight had by far been his worst.

"Look!" Eirin called, pointing to the south. Drystan turned to see why the Wyverns had truly fled.

The incoming Dragon was massive. Far bigger than he was. Its scales were a deep shade of purple, almost like the night sky, and it turned gracefully in the air while keeping within the protected shadow of the mountain.

"There's a second one!" Nuru hissed, pulling her bow taut as she spoke. "Not far back!"

As the deeply purple Dragon landed on the ledge just a little ways off, Drystan drew in a breath that tasted of burning metal. Before the first Dragon could make a move, however, the second Dragon, this one a far darker shade of blue than Drystan's own, landed between Drystan and the purple Dragon, its massive weight making the ledge shudder. Then the dark blue Dragon spoke. But to Drystan's surprise, it didn't speak to him. Instead, it addressed the purple Dragon.

"This is our territory, Rangvald," he said in a rumbling voice. If Drystan had been in Human form, he would have gaped. This was Rangvald. The one who had left a blood trail trying to find Drystan's little group the first time they'd ventured into Solevar, sending his henchmen Griffins after Drystan's party time and time again.

So if the purple Dragon was Rangvald, was the blue Dragon friend or foe?

"I have every right to meet them," the purple Dragon answered. "We both heard the explosion, did we not? Or am I banned from your land as well now?" The purple Dragon further surprised Drystan by shifting into his Human form. His eyes roved the faces of Drystan's companions. "I just need to see her," he said softly. "I didn't think it could be possible. Two Humans in one year."

Two Humans? Drystan's hackles rose. First of all, how did this man know what Eirin was? And second, what did he mean by two? But before Drystan could ponder this, the man took another step toward them, and Drystan let out a snort and lowered his face to the man's level.

"I don't believe you for a minute," the dark blue Dragon snarled, still talking to Rangvald. "Everyone knows you've been sending your Griffins into the mountain to bring the rumored Human back by force." He jerked his gigantic head toward them. "How do you know she's one of them anyway?"

"I was only seeking her to protect her." The man scowled. "You know what kind of filth lives in the mountain."

"So *you're* the one who sent scouting parties after us?" Thane called out, stepping forward. "And put bounties on our heads?"

"Not bounties!" Rangvald cried. "I offered a reward to the first party who could find and bring you safely to me. It was impossible to comb the entire mountain myself."

"Well, thanks to your reward," Nuru spat, "one of our friends died."

Rangvald closed his eyes. "I'm sorry," he said softly. "So sorry."

Drystan couldn't tell if the man was acting or not. If he was, he was good. He seemed genuinely repentant. Not that such would buy Drystan's trust.

"If she is one of them, she's under our protection now," the dark blue Dragon said impatiently. "You can return to your fortress, thank you very much."

"And who are you?" a soft voice called out from behind him.

Drystan closed his eyes and silently cursed. Was the girl determined to be found out?

The man and the Dragon looked at her in surprise, but the dark blue Dragon answered first.

"I am Karolus of Mhaedin." He looked down at the man beside him, his face showing a surprising amount of dislike for being covered with scales. "And this is Rangvald."

Eirin's voice sounded brighter. "We're making for Mhaedin!"

This made both Dragons share a surprised glance. How did they know one another? Drystan wondered briefly at their seemingly tangled past. He felt as if he should know. But he had more important things to figure out at the moment.

"What I want to know," Nuru said, stepping closer, spear still in her hand, "is why we've been tracked and cornered like animals."

To Drystan's surprise, both Dragons looked slightly apologetic. There certainly was a history there.

"The Lady Phaidra," Karolus said, "was notified that there was a party of warriors crossing the mountains. She sent me out to find your purpose."

They must be close to Mhaedin if they were being spied upon from it. Drystan heard a few sharp intakes of breath behind him, and he knew the others were thinking the same thing.

"I do not wish to force you into any course of action," Rangvald said, his voice surprisingly soft. "But I must know. Are you the Human?" His eyes beheld a deep longing as they rested on Eirin.

"We were sent by Lady Seren," Eirin said, ignoring his question as she came closer to Drystan until she was nearly touching his wing.

Good girl. "She gave us instructions to go to Mhaedin and seek assistance there."

"If Lady Seren has sent you, I will escort you all there," Karolus said. His eyes, however, lingered on Eirin alone. "I am from Mhaedin."

"I...I see you wish to continue unharassed," Rangvald said, clearing his throat. "And I will not attempt to dissuade you. But..." He paused. "Should you ever have need of my services," he nodded once in Karolus's direction, "they can tell you where to find me." He bowed low. "Always your humble servant." And in a motion so smooth it made Drystan jealous, he turned, and in a burst of flame, assumed his Dragon form, soaring through the air once more.

"What are your Atharrach forms?" Karolus asked Drystan's friends when Rangvald was gone.

Drystan turned to see his friends glance at one another.

"They don't know yet," he answered for them when no one spoke.

Karolus stared at them. "Don't know..." Then he closed his eyes and shook his head. "Come on. The sun will be rising soon. We don't want to get caught out this far without shade." He said the word as if it were dirty. Then he paused and looked back at Eirin. "But you. You're really Human?"

Eirin stared back at him for a long time, seeming to size Karolus up just as he was doing to her. Finally, she lifted her chin slightly and squared her shoulders.

"I am."

"In that case, wait here. I'll be back."

4

$\mathcal{E}$irin pondered what had just taken place as they waited for Karolus's return. She was inclined to trust Karolus. She would have liked to have trusted Rangvald as well. He seemed much gentler in person than she had imagined him all these weeks. But even if he had intended to protect her, his pursuit of them in the mountain had resulted in the death of their river guide, a kind Merman named Benjamin. And Eirin couldn't forget that.

"Do you think we can trust them?" she heard Drystan ask in a low voice. He was still in his Dragon form, talking to Qeb in hushed tones.

Qeb looked to the south. "If he is from Mhaedin, we have little choice." He paused. "Rangvald seemed to think he was telling the truth. And they weren't exactly on good terms."

Drystan looked to the south as well. "I guess we're about to find out."

A familiar Dragon's form was black against the gray sky, but this time, he was flanked by three other flying creatures.

"A Griffin, a Pegasus, and…" Nuru squinted. "Another Griffin." She looked at Drystan. "That makes four. You can fly, can't you?"

Drystan muttered something incoherent.

"What?" Thane asked.

"I said I think so."

Nuru's eyebrows flew up. "You *think* so?"

39

"I've only done it once!" Drystan snapped. The second time, launching up to grab Eirin out of the Wyvern's grasp, didn't really count, as he'd landed on his back.

"Well, you'll find out now," a deep voice thundered. The ground shook as Karolus landed on the ledge, followed by his companions. "Girl," he said to Nuru, "you'll be with her." He gestured with his head at the first Griffin, a female. "You," he said to Qeb. Then he paused. "You're bigger than I thought. You'll go with Vagan." He looked in the direction of the Pegasus. "That leaves you," he said to Thane, "to go with Gad." Thane and the Griffin looked at one another, and Eirin had to suppress a laugh. Neither looked enthusiastic.

"And you," Karolus said as he turned his Dragon head toward Eirin, "will be riding with me."

"I'll take her," Drystan said, stepping forward, but Karolus hissed at him. "You just admitted you're not sure you can fly. You would knowingly put your Human at risk?"

Drystan's eyes glowed slightly, but Eirin went over to him and put her hand on his front arm, as she couldn't quite reach his shoulder. He looked down at her, the orange circling in his blue eyes.

"We came to trust them," she said in a soft voice. "They can't help unless we let them."

"Listen to her," Karolus said. "She has good sense. And the dawn grows near."

Drystan glowered up at him but finally nodded. Then there was a flutter of activity as each member of Eirin's party was told how they would be carried. Nuru and Thane would be held tightly against their Griffins' chests, looking down at the ground below as they flew. Thane's eyes nearly popped out of his head, which made Nuru laugh out loud. Qeb would be riding the Pegasus as one would straddle a horse, holding onto his mane for stability. And Eirin would be sitting atop the Dragon's back, clinging to his spikes to stay on.

She felt a jolt of excitement as Karolus helped her up. He was far bigger than Drystan, big enough that she was able to sit cross-legged on the left side of his spine. His scales were metallic and smooth, warm to the touch. Not hot, though. Just pleasant in the cool breeze of morning.

She also couldn't help noticing the marking on his back. Its contours weren't easy to make out, and she didn't even know how to describe the shape. She could only say for sure that there was a definite golden shimmer on some of the scales on his back that she hadn't seen anywhere else.

"We need to go. The sun has already risen on the other side of the mountain," Karolus said in a voice so loud it echoed across the mountainside. "Dragon, ride to my right. You'll be looking for attackers."

Drystan had been sulking, but at the mention of attackers, he straightened and looked immediately out at the vast valley to their west.

"Baena," he said to the Griffin carrying Nuru, "you fly at the nose. Vagan, the rear. Gad at my left. Are we ready?"

The others called out in agreement, and Eirin's stomach quivered as the Dragon stood at the edge of the cliff, spread his wings...and let himself fall. But they didn't fall for long. His wings caught the wind, which pulled them into the sky. Her stomach lurched around, but Eirin decided immediately that she liked it.

The others followed his example, and in moments, they were high above the ledge they'd been standing on. The Dragon kept them low enough that the mountain still protected them from the sun's rays, but they were high enough that Eirin guessed a ground attack would be difficult.

"Where are you from, Human?" Karolus called back.

"Torbaine!" she called over the wind. "In the mountain!"

"That's what I thought," he said. "Look around you and see what Solevar holds."

Holding tightly to his spines, she dared to sit up on her knees and look to the west. And what she saw made her laugh and weep.

Trees. So many trees. Thousands. Millions of trees. They looked like tiny balls of green from above, much like her mother's broccoli had looked in her little garden. There were so many. And beyond the trees, there were rolling hills and fields, deserts and lakes. And though she couldn't see it from his back, she knew from her father's map that the sea, blue and glittering, lay beyond the horizon.

She didn't have long to look, though. Karolus called for her to hold on tightly and took a slight dive, and Eirin let out a stifled scream. But their descent was small, and when they were level again, she chose to stay on her backside, where she was less likely to fall off. But that was well enough with her. She could study the Atharrachs who carried her companions.

Atharrachs. It was still so strange to think that her companions themselves were Atharrachs. Magical, shifting creatures who could change from Human form to magical form and back again. All their lives, Eirin and her friends had been taught that such creatures were depraved and mad by nature. But now...

Now she wondered what they would become. What they already were.

That Drystan, the king's son, had transformed into a Dragon didn't surprise her in the slightest. His first transformation itself, though, had been a shock to both of them. He had changed just in time to save her from the Fae who had been trying to capture her and take her back into the mountain. But then he had seemed as feral as the stories she'd been told as a child. His eyes had flamed, and they'd moved over her like a hungry animal...

She shivered and shook the memory from her mind. Drystan didn't need any reminding of what she knew shamed him tremendously. So instead, she studied the creatures who carried her companions. None of them seemed even a bit out of control, which was of great comfort, considering they were keeping her friends from certain death right now as they soared through the sky.

The Griffins were what she had come to expect. Their magic pulsed orange, flowing down from their necks to their shoulder blades. They were muscular and a whole head taller than even Thane, the tallest in Eirin's group. Their eagle-like faces had sharp black eyes and beaks that could undoubtedly draw as much blood as any knife. Their wings were also like eagle wings, but their necks were covered in a ring of thick, long fur. Their bodies were also like those of lions with tails that flicked dangerously when they were standing on the ground.

The Pegasus was even more intriguing, as Eirin had never seen one of them before. He was built like the horses back in Torbaine, but a whole head taller. His body was thick and muscular, covered in a sleek white hide that was so white it was nearly blue. He was so muscular, in fact, that Eirin would have been surprised he could even leave the ground except for the length and elegance of his wings. Long and pointed in a triangular shape, almost like a hummingbird's, they flapped gracefully as he flew. They were blue like water. The Pegasus's eyes were like ice, and his magic was a similar icy blue. The magic ran from the rounded edges of his shoulder blades all the way to the tips of his wings. Instead of pulsing like flame, though, his magic zipped and zapped like miniature lighting that flowed through his body.

"There it is," Karolus called, snapping Eirin's attention back to their flight. "Mhaedin."

They had just cleared a ledge and were approaching a canyon. Eirin's breath caught in her throat.

In all her wildest dreams, Eirin couldn't have conceived of a city like Mhaedin. The entire city was in a deep, boxy canyon that faced the west. Thousands of homes ran up the foot of the mountain and up and into the mountain itself, and fields at the base of the mountain were filled with neat lines of vegetation. While the crops weren't exactly emerald green, they looked alive enough. Between the crops and the mountain were the buildings that jutted out from its side. Yellowed canvas covers spread over half of the houses and towers that climbed up the mountain's side. The canvas covers, hundreds of them, continued to unfurl as Eirin watched.

Most amazing, however, were the people. So many people. Humans—or at least, people in their Human forms—and creatures of all kinds roamed the streets. Some of the races she didn't even recognize. Most exciting, however, were the lights all over their bodies. Eirin couldn't wait to learn who and what they were.

"The sun is coming out soon," Gad called over his shoulder. "We'll have to land in the square."

Karolus nodded. "I'll lead. Baena, drop back." Then he looked at Drystan. "Have you landed before?"

Drystan paused before answering. "Once."

Karolus shook his head and then sighed. "Very well. You land after me. Watch what I do and try not to hit anyone. And Human," he called over his shoulder again, "Hold on." With that, he moved into a dive.

Eirin felt as though she'd left her stomach behind as he plummeted toward the mountain. And yet, there was a thrill that came with it, one she hoped she would get to feel again after this. She had crossed into a new world. She still ached for her family and her dear friend Alys. But for the first time since they'd set out, she finally felt as though she could abandon her doubts. This was truly where she was meant to be.

The marketplace, which was built into the side of the mountain, rose up to meet them faster than she could have imagined possible. She screamed a little as the Dragon landed and immediately reared up and threw her off. Just as quickly, though, he whirled around and caught her, holding her away from Drystan as he came in behind them.

There were several cries from the crowd as the people scurried out of the way. His left wing was high enough that it didn't hit anything, but his right wing clipped several stalls, and Eirin cringed as she heard glass break.

"Shift back!" Karolus shouted over his shoulder, still shielding Eirin from Drystan's landing. "The sun will be up any minute!"

Only then did Eirin realize that the two Griffins and the Pegasus were still behind them. Drystan let out a cry. A few flames ran down the side of his body then were snuffed out. He cried out again, but this time, much to Eirin's relief, the shift back was complete, making space for the others to land behind him. He fell to his knees as they hit the ground. Several people shouted all at once, and not a moment too soon as the canvas ceiling rolled out above the marketplace, blocking the sun's first rays.

Eirin ran to Drystan the moment Karolus let her out of his grasp.

"Are you all right?" she asked, taking his arms in her hands and forcing him to meet her eyes. He gave her a wry smile.

"Me? Yes. But I'm not sure I'm going to survive this venture with my ego intact."

"That was exhilarating!" Thane exclaimed, fairly dancing as he turned in circles, trying to take it all in.

"Stop it," Nuru whispered to him. "You're embarrassing me."

"Good!" Thane beamed. "You could use a bit of that."

Qeb, of course, was at Drystan's side the moment he had been put down as well.

"You know how to keep us holding our breath," a thin stranger said as he strode forward to meet them. With a smile, he addressed Eirin and Drystan. "By the way, I'm Hector."

He was in Human form, a slight man with sandy blond hair. There was nothing extraordinary about this form to make him memorable, but his light, or rather, his lights were like nothing Eirin had ever seen before. There were two on his head, almost where a deer might have antlers, and two more that covered the whole of each foot. Eirin had to concentrate for a moment before she recognized what he was. Hector was a Faun.

In a moment, Karolus was in his Human form as well, though only now did Eirin realize she hadn't yet seen his Human form. She'd only seen him as a Dragon. He had dark, shiny hair, similar to Drystan's, that reached the nape of his neck, where it turned out slightly. His high cheekbones were covered in dark scruff, and he was long and lean on the whole, though his shoulders were of an impressive size. His eyes, which were blue, looked oddly familiar.

"Hector." Karolus greeted the small man alone as if the crowd surrounding them didn't exist. "Tell Phaidra we have visitors."

Hector looked behind Karolus, and his eyes widened slightly, as though he hadn't realized the true size of their party, but he must have been used to strange requests because he merely nodded and turned to walk with purpose in the direction from which he'd come.

"Follow me," Karolus said to their little party. "We have some things we need to discuss."

Despite the lingering thrill of the ride, anxiety niggled at Eirin as she fell into step between Drystan and Qeb. The expressions of the people around them were mostly of shock, though a few looked downright annoyed at their appearance. There were few smiles.

She had little time to focus even on this, though. They were entering a large cavern. But less than a cavern, it looked like the entryway to one of the palaces in the books she'd read back in the Citadel. The granite walls, polished and smooth, were flecked with white, black, gold, and various shades of pink. Silhouettes of figures had been carved into the mouth of the cavern. The carved figures of Atharrachs and Humans seemed to pass judgment upon them even as they moved into the first chamber. Engraved filigree danced between the carved creatures, scrolls with ivy leaves and various flowers between them. The grandeur was surprising in its intricacy. These people were literally watching Solevar die, and yet they had seen fit to create painstakingly detailed beauty everywhere Eirin turned. Lights hung from chandeliers on the ceiling, which was also surprisingly high, making the sweeping entrance nearly as bright as the day outside.

The deeper they moved into the cavern, the closer Eirin's companions walked, Eirin at the group's center. As soon as she realized what they were doing, she felt oddly safe despite the dozens of people staring at them as they followed Karolus and the Faun.

About half the people surrounding them were in their Atharrach form and half were in their Human forms. Eirin wondered why so many would choose to remain in their Human forms, but she didn't have time to ponder this because they left the long tunnel and moved into a large antechamber.

It was funny. Now that Eirin saw her friends in comparison with the other people around them, she realized how tall they all looked as a group. Thane was the tallest, but Drystan and Qeb weren't much shorter. Nuru was tall as well. They all trod with confidence and grace, their many weapons clacking slightly against each other as they moved. King Egan had chosen her retinue well.

Then, of course, there was Eirin.

There were dozens of people in the antechamber, most better dressed than the people in the square. The room was bright with sunlight, but none of it was direct. Really, the design was quite brilliant. The distant ceiling had screens at the top, which dispersed the light into thinner beams. The beams were cast onto clean canvas sheets, much like the ones the people had rolled out to cover their homes and streets outside. And because the granite was of a light shade, the indirect sunlight that made it through the canvas sheets bounced around the room, keeping it bright while avoiding any injury to those below.

As genius as the light was, however, there were far more interesting things in the room that the scholar in Eirin longed to study. Painted portraits of various people and creatures. Dragons, more than any other. Stone podiums encircled the room as well, each one holding some sort of object. Eirin couldn't make them all out, but those she could see were all shapes, sizes, and styles. A painted vase with gold veins running through it. Remnants of colored glass pressed together to make a picture of a rose. A short sword. Jeweled rings.

"Karolus," called a low, feminine voice.

"Lady Phaidra," Karolus answered back.

Everyone turned to look at the woman walking toward them. She came to stand beside Karolus. There was no crown on her silky black hair, and her thin, white fingers bore no rings, but like Drystan, Karolus, and Rangvald, a fire whirled about her heart. Unlike theirs, however, her fire had no blue in it. Her age was difficult to decipher. She could have been in her early thirties or in her late forties. There were several lines that sometimes touched her face when the light hit it a particular way, but her dark eyes looked young, bright, and determined.

Her clothes, like those of the others in the room, were of better quality than what most of those in the streets had worn. While more intricately detailed, though, they were still reasonably practical. Eirin could see that the lady's midnight blue gown had been split up the middle, and beneath, the woman wore trousers of the same color. She wore no weapon, but doubtless, a Dragon needed no sword.

Eirin got the distinct sense that they ought to bow. She elbowed Drystan and Qeb softly and dropped into a polite curtsey. Taking her cue, Drystan and Qeb bowed beside her. Out of the corner of her eye, Eirin could see Thane bow as well. Nuru, of course, muttered something imperceptible, but to Eirin's relief, she curtsied as well. Instinct told her that this Phaidra was the person they would need to impress if they were ever to learn what they needed to finish their quest. Or maybe all those books Eirin had read in the Citadel had gone to her head.

"So," she continued in her low, rich voice, "are these the guests you went to receive?"

"They are," Karolus said, turning to face them. "And I know

nothing about them. Except that that one," he gestured to Drystan, "is a Dragon."

Lady Phaidra's eyebrows rose high. "Really?" she breathed.

"And that one," Karolus said as he pointed to Eirin, "is a Human."

Cries of exclamation went up from the crowd, which had grown very large. People spoke excitedly to their friends, and the sound went from a dull roar to nearly deafening when Phaidra held up her hand. Immediately, the room fell silent.

"You are Human?" she asked Eirin.

"Yes, madam." Why did her voice suddenly sound so small?

"And you." She turned to Drystan. "From what house do you hail?"

Drystan blinked at her. "I'm…sorry, madam. I don't understand you."

"You're a Dragon. Which line do you claim?"

Drystan looked down at Eirin, and for an eternal moment, she knew they shared the same thought. His line was one of royalty, it seemed. Possibly far higher than even what this woman could claim, according to Lady Seren, the Dragon lady they'd met in the northern region of Solevar. But royal as it might be, Drystan's line was not one he was proud to hold.

But what else could they do? Even if they wanted to lie, she was sure it would be impossible here, when everyone else knew far more than they did about the world in which they would now live.

"Perhaps," Drystan said slowly, turning back to face Lady Phaidra, "we ought to tell you our whole story."

Please, Eirin pleaded silently, *if you're there, Time Keeper, let them understand!* If Drystan wasn't careful, what he was about to reveal might get him killed.

Lady Phaidra nodded. "Very well." She turned and walked away. Karolus motioned for them to follow. The crowd parted for her, and when they neared the far end of the room, they could see that she had seated herself on a gilded chair that looked very much like a throne. "Now," she said, positioning herself comfortably. "Enlighten us."

Eirin quietly took his hand, and he squeezed back. Then he began to speak.

"My name is Drystan. These are my friends, and we hail from Torbaine."

More whispers went up, which were silenced by Lady Phaidra. "Torbaine? You mean you came from inside the mountain? All of you?"

"Yes. Though it was not without great cost."

Eirin briefly closed her eyes as Alys's face flashed across her mind. Her best friend had sacrificed herself so they might be free. How had Torbaine's Elders chosen to punish her, she wondered, for setting their most prized captives free?

"My father, Egan, was king of the city. He was allowed little chance to rule, though, for the city Elders kept a tight grip on what liberties the king might take with his people. And there were few." He paused. "Are you familiar with Torbaine's ways?"

"You mean their suppression of our natural forms and persons? Yes. Go on."

Drystan nodded. "I was training to take over for my father. Although, at the time, I didn't know that he was actually my father. I had been told that my real father was dead, and that only more distant relatives remained on my mother's side. And my friends and I," he indicated their companions, "were raised as warriors. We were meant to stay in Torbaine and protect it. That was our duty. The outside world was too dangerous to venture forth into. But after our city was attacked by Rangvald's army–"

The whispering started again, but Drystan ignored it.

"My father, against the Elders' wishes, sent us on a journey outside the city. None of us had left the city before–" He sucked in a short breath, and Eirin squeezed his hand again. When he spoke again, his voice was husky.

"Actually, one of us had been outside the city before. But she had been magically silenced by the Elders and could tell us little of the world we were entering."

"Who was this woman?" Lady Phaidra asked, not unkindly.

Drystan clenched and unclenched his teeth. Finally, he answered. "She was my mother."

Lady Phaidra's face softened. "I am sorry," she said.

Drystan nodded then cleared his throat. "She died on the journey.

But before she passed, she delivered us safely to the Dragon, Lady Seren, where we were told that everything we knew was a lie. She revealed my own heritage to me, something I'd not known up until that day. And she revealed that my companion here," he stepped closer to Eirin, "is a Seer."

At this, Lady Phaidra smiled.

"We were told we must come to Mhaedin, where we could learn how to best survive Solevar's dangers. So Eirin," he put his hand on the small of her back and pushed her slightly forward, "can fix the Time Stones."

When the crowd cheered this time, Lady Phaidra made no motion to quell it. Instead, she stood and walked down to Eirin, smiling at her.

"Two Humans in a month," she said, touching Eirin's hair gently. "We were sure our death was near. Then one came, and we were afraid to hope. But you, my dear... you've given us courage once again."

Eirin looked at Drystan, and once again, she knew he had the same question she did. *Two* Humans?

Eirin relaxed slightly as the cheering and laughter continued. Spontaneous singing broke out from somewhere in the room, and many joined in the happy tune that echoed loudly in the chamber as Lady Phaidra turned back to Drystan.

"You said Lady Seren made you aware of your line," she said, having to raise her voice to be heard. "What line is it?"

Drystan's blue eyes flicked to Eirin's. She could feel his hesitance. This was the moment they had truly been waiting for.

"I am Drystan, son of Egan, great-grandson of Kamon, seed of Oreck."

Eirin hadn't thought Drystan's voice was very loud. But the song broke off, and in its place, she felt the room grow chilly.

"Kamon?" Lady Phaidra breathed. "You...you come from Kamon?" She turned to Karolus. "And you didn't see this?"

"I didn't see his back," Karolus retorted. "We were on a ledge. There wasn't much room for me to give him a full inspection."

See his back? Eirin wondered if that had something to do with the kind of shimmering mark she'd seen on Karolus.

"You are *Kamon's* son?" a Giantess hissed. "And you had the gall to come waltzing in here, your blood as tainted as the land?"

"He had the gall," Qeb growled, "to come as the Seer's protector!" Though his voice was low, it reverberated through the hall. The Giantess sneered and ducked back out into the entry tunnel.

"It's true!" Eirin called out. "I was going to come alone. But he fought his way out so he could come with me. He nearly died so that I could escape Torbaine to come here!"

The silence was long and pregnant. It lasted so long that Eirin began to get annoyed. Really, this couldn't be so hard to understand. They were acting as if Drystan had been the one to curse them all.

"And if," she called out again, this time addressing the crowd, "you cannot accept him, then you will not have me!" She was about to stomp out when a door on the opposite side of the room opened, and a man looked out.

"Eirin!" he shouted, throwing open the door and sprinting toward her. "Eirin, you came!"

It took Eirin a moment to recognize him. But as he came to stand before her, she laughed as she finally understood. Two Humans.

Mannish, the young Human who had befriended and helped her on her first adventure out of Torbaine's walls, had made it to Mhaedin as well.

"You came!" he said again, throwing his arms around her in a massive hug.

"And you're walking! And running!" Eirin laughed, pulling back to look him up and down. "The last time I saw you, you were…"

"Not like this," he laughed. Then he turned to Drystan, as if he hadn't just pushed past Karolus like he wasn't there, and hugged Drystan too. One might have thought they were old friends. "You kept her safe! My father would have been proud."

Then something else dawned on Eirin, and her joy died as though someone had poured cold water on it. Two Humans. Not three.

"*Would* have been?" she asked. Where was Mannish's father?

"I see you are already acquainted," Lady Phaidra said, her left brow quirked up.

"Mannish's family helped us when we first left Torbaine," Eirin said as Mannish continued to exclaim over the rest of her friends.

"He and his family saw us for what we were when we didn't yet know ourselves." She smiled sadly at him, and he beamed back. "If it hadn't been for them, we would have been dead long ago."

The crowd had ceased its stony silence and resumed its murmuring. Karolus jerked his head to the side, and Lady Phaidra nodded.

"I think," she said, "that we should continue this little reunion somewhere more private." She turned and, motioning for them to follow, made her way back to the door through which Mannish had come.

5

$\mathcal{D}$rystan struggled not to frown at the enthusiastic Human as Mannish fairly bounced between the members of their party. On the one hand, Drystan was thankful. Mannish's recognition of them would add veracity to their story. On the other hand, though, Drystan was very aware of how often he turned to look at Eirin as they walked toward the door. Or how much longer he hugged her than he did anyone else.

Sure, maybe they were two of the only Humans left in the world. And granted, Mannish had helped save Eirin's life during a fight in the mountain tavern his family had run, the place Drystan's party had stayed during their first venture outside Torbaine's walls. But that didn't mean Drystan had to like it. There was something about the way he…well, the way he was that annoyed Drystan excessively.

They were led back through the door through which Mannish had come and into a smaller chamber. This one didn't have round, polished walls like those in the larger chamber, but they were painted white, making the little light that got in through another canvas-covered hole in the ceiling much brighter. There was a large, rectangular table in the center of the room with chairs surrounding it. Drystan shared a glance with Qeb. Back in the mountain, Torbaine had held few real chairs. They used too much wood and took too much time to build. Whoever these people were, they had far more resources than Torbaine had ever held.

55

And their Elders had told them that they were by far the most sophisticated, richest people left in Solevar. Once again, the Elders had lied.

"Sit, please," the woman said, indicating the chairs. Then she, Karolus, and Hector exited through a second door, and Drystan heard the lock click behind them.

"So tell me!" Mannish, who was sitting on Eirin's other side, whirled around to face the others. "What happened? I want to know everything!"

Eirin laughed. "What about you? The last time we saw you, you were limping on a crooked leg." Her smile faded. "And your parents?"

He looked down at his hands. A moment passed before he spoke. "My parents decided to leave as soon as you had gone. My father said it was getting too dangerous, especially after Rangvald began sending search parties down every few days. So we packed up what we had, left the tavern under cover of night, and made our way here."

"Where are they?" Eirin asked softly.

He sighed. "They didn't make it. My father..." He cleared his throat. "We were attacked by a party of Wyverns on the side of the mountain. They had him bleeding before they realized we were Humans. They would have carried us away with them if my mother's screaming didn't attract the attention of some of the patrolling Griffins. They have guards constantly circling the city here, you see. Anyhow, they saw and came to help." He shook his head. "But he died here. They couldn't save him."

"And your mother?" Thane asked.

"She died a few days later. They...the Nymphs...they do the healing here. Anyhow, they said it was a sticky lung. They thought one of the Wyverns might have punctured it while they were harassing us." He shook his head and sadly smiled. "I'm not so sure it wasn't from a broken heart, though."

"I'm sorry," Eirin whispered, and Thane echoed her. Drystan nodded. As annoyed as he was with Mannish's enthusiasm around Eirin, he couldn't begrudge him acknowledgement of the pain he was living every day.

"It wasn't all bad, though," Mannish said, taking a deep breath. "As you can see, the Nymphs were able to heal me." He gestured to his leg. "And I've learned so much. It's been less than two months since I arrived, but Eirin…" His eyes took on that annoying sparkle again. "Wait until you see what we can *do*. And this place." He held his arms out and looked up at the ceiling as if he could see what was beyond it. "They have all sorts of weapons and medicines and technologies I'd never dreamed of back in the mountain!" Then he leaned forward, reminding Drystan of an overgrown puppy. He just needed a tail to wag. "What about you? You said you weren't going to come! What changed your mind?" From the way Nuru rolled her eyes, Drystan could see he wasn't the only one who thought this.

So Eirin, along with help from Thane, relayed the events of their recent journey through the mountain, into Solevar, back into the mountain, their escape, and their journey here.

Just as she was finishing, the door clicked again, and Lady Phaidra, Karolus, and Hector returned and took their places at the other side of the table. Lady Phaidra sat at the end, and the two men sat on either side of her.

"We want to begin by saying," Lady Phaidra began, her words slow and measured, "that we are glad you all have come. I know it couldn't have been easy. Especially not knowing the world as the rest of us do. And telling us your lineage," she turned to Drystan, "took a great amount of courage."

Eirin frowned. "It's not as if he can help it."

"I'm aware of that," Lady Phaidra said placatingly. "But the truth is that having the great-grandson of Kamon here will be difficult for many of our people. You will have to prove your honor to them."

"But–" Eirin began again. Drystan nudged her leg with his, but he didn't have to, for Lady Phaidra held up a hand.

"We believe you."

Karolus grunted, but Lady Phaidra ignored him. Hector, however, looked as serene as he had from the beginning.

"You," Lady Phaidra continued, "have kept the Seer safe and brought her to us. That is proof enough for me. But…" she sighed. "The people of Mhaedin have long memories. Some are still alive who had to flee the curse when it fell. Accepting the great-grandson of the one who brought the curse upon them will be difficult."

"Beyond that," Karolus said gruffly, "is the fact that while your intentions may not reflect it, Solevar's Blood Fire Throne is still unclaimed. I can guarantee you that many of the people here will immediately assume you've come not only with a Seer who's inclined to be in your favor because you're her protector but that your ultimate goal will be to claim the crown once it's been restored."

"It doesn't work that way," Lady Phaidra said quietly.

"It doesn't matter. You know that's what they'll think."

Drystan's face flushed. Which was ridiculous, he knew. He wasn't responsible for his great-grandfather's actions. But he felt the shame anyway. Shaking those thoughts away, he took a deep breath.

"I promised to keep Eirin safe. And that is all I want to do. I don't want a claim to any throne. I just…" He looked at Eirin. "Eirin needs to break the curse. And I swore to help her do exactly that."

"And we are grateful," Hector said in a gentle voice. Drystan briefly wondered what their positions were in Mhaedin. Lady Seren had explained that the Time Keeper had made Dragons the rulers of the land. And the Dragons themselves were ruled by line of Oreck. But she had also said that Lady Phaidra and Karolus worked together. How did they balance the power without a struggle? Whatever their dynamic, Lady Phaidra was clearly in charge.

And as to Hector, Drystan had no idea where he fit in. But so far, he liked the Faun best of all.

"There's another problem," Karolus said, looking at Lady Phaidra and then at Drystan. "How long have you been shifting?"

This time, Drystan's face felt like it might catch fire from its flush. "Um, that was my second time."

The three stared at him. Finally, Lady Phaidra spoke.

"Your…second time?"

Karolus let out a curse and stood up to pace.

"The others haven't shifted yet at all," Drystan added quickly. "We've been forced to take bruthsi root since we were born. In fact, the others are still taking it."

"Lady Seren said you would be able to help them shift," Eirin said. "And I don't see what's wrong with Drystan's shifting twice."

Karolus shook his head and sat down so hard the chair protested. Then he leaned toward them, elbows on the table. "Dragons' shifts are incredibly violent. When your friend here shifted, he went up in a burst of flame that encased his entire body." His eyes met Drystan's. "Do you know how dangerous that is? You could have killed her without even being aware of it."

"None of us knew that," Qeb said in an almost growl.

"But both times he shifted, it was to protect me!" Eirin protested. "I don't think he even meant to!"

Lady Phaidra nodded slowly. "He would have burned any remaining bruthsi root out if he felt strongly enough," she said. Then she looked at Drystan. "Unfortunately, it's generally not wise to let a young Dragon near a Seer. Usually...young Dragons aren't allowed near anyone but other Dragons and their trainers."

"Because of the shifting?" Drystan asked, hoping he had misheard what she had just said.

"Obviously," Karolus said, crossing his arms over his chest and leaning back. "Too risky."

"So..." Drystan licked his lips. "What do you suggest?"

"We would assign a different protector to her," Lady Phaidra said. "I understand that you wish to have someone with her, especially after your incident with the Wyverns. It would be wiser, however—" But Eirin was already shaking her head.

"I said it once, and I'll say it again," she said in a slow, stubborn voice. "I'm only alive now because of him. And if he can't be with me, then we're leaving for Solevar. Now."

Lady Phaidra stared at Eirin, but Karolus waved his hand.

"No. It's too dangerous."

Lady Phaidra looked at him. "We've lost too many already. We need a new Dragon. Preferably, one to stay with her."

"But he's too young!" Karolus cried. "I'd have to start training him from the beginning!"

"I know it's not the same," Drystan said, hoping they both didn't turn on him for interrupting, "but I was trained in combat in my Human form."

"For how long?" Karolus snapped.

"Since I was three."

Karolus raised his eyebrows.

Until that moment, Drystan had never realized how insane that sounded. Who trained their toddler for mortal combat?

His family, that's who.

"My grandmother wanted me ready for the Citadel," he did his best to explain. "So she brought in experts to teach me the moment I was able to lift a wooden training sword."

"He's telling the truth," Eirin piped. "We were all trained. In the Citadel, where warriors are made."

Hector raised his eyebrows even higher. "Including you?"

Eirin nodded, and Lady Phaidra, Karolus, and Hector all looked at each other. Drystan knew that look. It was the same look of sophisticated horror Lady Seren had worn when she'd learned that Eirin, the fragile Human, had been subjected to the Citadel's brutal combat school for thirteen years of her life.

Lady Phaidra finally sighed and stood. Drystan forced himself to stay seated, despite having the growing desire to jump up and drag all of his friends out behind him.

"As much as I want you all to stay," she said, "it's only fair that you know the situation we're in. I am the master here because in the day of Solevar, Mhaedin was a little-known home for miners and mountain-dwellers. My family has ruled these foothills for nearly a thousand years." She held her hands up. "Yes, you can see now that we're full of people and, to an extent, supplies. But our food sources are shrinking. We've had some of our farmers, who live on the land they tend, beginning to show signs of the sickness caused by the curse, despite never being unshielded during the day."

She drew in another deep breath. "We were small and insignificant before the curse. Our supplies were never great before the curse fell, and as the curse creeps up the mountain today, we're harvesting less than ever before. We know we need to make the journey to the Time Stones once more, but countless Humans have died during past excursions, and we had to watch and learn the hard way what we were doing wrong. Those who did survive still died in the royal palace before they could figure out how to remove the stone." She paused for a moment then shook her head. "All that to say that we're on borrowed time. And with less food and fewer people, it's not going to be easy."

Eirin raised her eyebrows slightly, and her hand brushed her chest just above where Drystan knew her stone was hanging, but when their eyes met Drystan just shook his head, hoping the others wouldn't notice. Something told him that it wasn't time to tell the others all their secrets just yet.

Eirin nodded slightly.

Lady Phaidra, thankfully, didn't seem to notice. "We've tried every way we know of to protect the Humans who came to us to help. And toward the end, we did learn of ways to keep them alive longer."

"Is that supposed to be comforting?" Nuru asked.

"The last four we had made it all the way to the royal city." Lady Phaidra gave Nuru a knowing look. "We kept them safe through storms, ambushes, and poison from Solevar itself. If you attempt the journey alone, you'll face dangers you never imagined could exist. The sun has poisoned the earth itself. Much of the food outside what we manage to grow is inedible and toxic. Shifters can survive longer, especially in our Atharrach forms, but Humans are far more susceptible to the dangers." She paused and looked at Drystan.

"We had thought all the Humans were dead, to be honest. Then not one but two have shown up on our doorstep in the last month. And while this brings us greater joy than we can express, you need to know what you're up against. Because if you don't, you'll die." She looked hard at Eirin. "I would truly discourage you from any thoughts of attempting the journey alone. Because if you wish to save anyone you've left behind, you'll not do so by throwing your life away to prove a point."

Eirin glared sullenly at the table, but Drystan knew Lady Phaidra's words had done their work. Eirin might be loyal to Drystan, but she would never purposefully abandon her family to death in the mountain. Not if there was any way she could help it.

"I ask instead," Lady Phaidra continued in a slow, thoughtful voice, "that you let us do what Lady Seren wished for us to do. We can't stop the curse, but as I said, we've learned enough that we *can* get you safely through Solevar."

"What will you do differently this time?" Drystan asked.

Lady Phaidra gave him a small smile, her eyes seeming to grow brighter with each passing second. "We'll show you if you're willing to learn."

"What if," Hector said in his soft voice, "we agreed to wait a little longer before setting out? We had planned to leave one more time with Mannish." He nodded at the young man. "But if you give us a chance, we'll teach you what we know. And in the end, the two of you have a better chance of breaking this curse than any Human ever has before."

Karolus, who was standing in the corner, looked less than thrilled. Or maybe that was his everyday face. Eirin, meanwhile, looked around at her friends. And her eyes said what Drystan was thinking. They didn't really have a choice.

"Very well," Eirin finally said in a soft yet clear voice. "You will teach. And we will learn."

6

ady Phaidra turned to Hector. "Please have their rooms prepared," she said before turning back to Drystan's little group, somewhat apologetically this time. "I'm assuming you would like your rooms all together?"

"Yes," Drystan answered before anyone else could. He glanced down at Eirin. "Actually, do you have any rooms large enough that could be shared? One for the ladies, of course, and one for us."

Eirin's eyes widened, and she glanced back at Nuru, who looked utterly bored, examining her fingernails as though she weren't about to begin the rest of their lives. Drystan knew why Eirin looked alarmed, of course. Just a few months ago, Nuru had tried to injure Eirin beyond healing. Much had happened since that day, though, and Nuru had all but pleaded to be allowed to come with them. In fact, it had been Eirin who decided she could come. And while Nuru had shown no sign of aggression toward Eirin since they'd begun their journey, a lifetime of enmity wouldn't easily be forgotten, and Drystan wondered if Eirin was regretting her decision. He would have to have a word with Nuru in private before they settled in. Having the two girls share a room wasn't ideal, but there was no way Eirin could be allowed to sleep alone.

"Oh, of course." Lady Phaidra nodded, though she looked surprised as well.

"I think," Hector said quietly, "that the fourth level on the central southern wall should do. Don't you, my dear?"

My dear?

Lady Phaidra relaxed and smiled. "Yes, that's perfect." She turned to Mannish. "Would you do them the honor of leading them there? Perhaps give them a tour of the city on your way to give us time to prepare the rooms?"

"Of course!" Mannish beamed and was on his feet again in an instant. "I'm sure you're hungry. We'll take Food Road."

"Food Road?" Thane echoed, his eyes brightening.

"It's the lower road where the best food vendors stay." Mannish paused. "They won't have any coins, Lady Phaidra."

Lady Phaidra frowned slightly. "True. Perhaps you could buy them something, and Hector will compensate you at a later time?"

Mannish's grin widened. "Perfect!"

With that settled, Mannish led the way, making sure to place himself beside Eirin.

"How does the currency here work?" Eirin asked as they made their way into the street. Everyone stared as they passed, but Mannish seemed oblivious. Drystan decided he would do well to follow suit.

"Many people had some Solevarian money when they came," Mannish said, leading them away from the main road they'd landed on and down another steep path. Drystan could see countless other such winding paths leading up and down the sides of the canyons.

"I don't know what they have in Torbaine, but a bind is about what you would pay for a potato." Mannish pulled a small, round coin out of his pocket. It was silver in color, and it had a small creature imprinted upon it, but it was too faded for him to see which one. Although…if the coin had been created before the curse, it probably was nearly rubbed off. "Ten binds make a bondar," he continued. "That will get you a small basket of potatoes, or half a bushel of grain. Ten bondars would equal a barrow. A hundred barrows, and you can buy–"

"A barrow bar!" Eirin exclaimed, laughing. "Just like at home!"

"It is? That's wonderful! One less thing for you to have to remember then." Mannish laughed along with her, making Drystan wish more than ever that he could wipe the enthusiasm off the young man's face. For some reason, it annoyed him more than he could say.

"Yes," Qeb said. "But we use different coins in Torbaine."

"I would think the number of people here would be too many to provide enough coins for, considering most of them came to escape the curse," Nuru said, looking narrowly at a man crushing herbs in a stall as they passed it.

"Well, there were, from what I understand. Shortages of coins, I mean. People had to barter and all when they first arrived. But eventually, Lady Phaidra used one of her scales to grant someone's wish of creating more."

"Her scale?" Qeb looked at Drystan. "Is she a Dragon?"

"I'll explain later," Drystan said in a low voice. "But in short, yes." Once again, Drystan wondered how exactly the two Dragons balanced the power. As a son of Oreck, Karolus shouldn't be subservient to anyone else outside the Oreck line. But if he had come and Lady Phaidra's family was already ruling over the vicinity, that might explain...

"Apparently, there's a lot you still need to tell us," Nuru muttered.

She wasn't wrong. Drystan and Eirin had told the others much of what Lady Seren had told them back when they had visited her castle in the valley north of the mountain. But there was simply so much to remember. In this particular instance, it seemed that he'd forgotten to tell the others that Dragon scales were more valuable than gold. Each contained a bit of the Dragon's power and could be gifted to grant a wish, should the Time Keeper see fit to use the magic within the scale to grant it. At least, that's what Lady Seren had said. Then, as the scales waned in number, the Dragon aged. And when the last scale had been given, the Dragon lost his ability to shift, and he could happily live out his days in peace, much as a Human would do.

Just as Drystan's father was about to do when Drystan had left him back in Torbaine. Although he hadn't lost a single scale to earn his death.

"Here we are!" Mannish cried, interrupting Drystan's morbid thoughts. They had come down several winding paths to the largest mountain road Drystan had ever seen. And despite his sour mood, the scents and sounds of sizzling meat made his stomach feel suddenly as if it might collapse upon itself.

They gratefully took their food from the first vendor Mannish suggested, and this time, Eirin wasn't the only one to sincerely thank him. They carried their roasted turkey legs over to a short wall and sat upon it, looking back up at the mountain. At least, what they could see of it.

Everything was covered in those white canvas sheets. They were ingenious, really. Thin and light enough to let the sun's light through without the painful effects of the direct beams. Even Drystan's thick black cloak wasn't nearly as effective as these at keeping the searing pain of the sun off his skin. He'd learned that in Solevar.

"So I'm going to ask the question we're all thinking," Thane said, wiping his mouth, having finished first as he always did. "How is it that you can all live out here, exposed to the surface and the sun, and not die from the curse?"

Drystan had actually been wondering if Mannish was always this annoyingly happy, but now that Thane had asked it, he realized he had been unconsciously pondering the same thing as well.

Mannish nodded and swallowed his food. "I wondered that too when we first arrived." He turned and faced the west, though this only brought them face-to-face with more sheets. "You can't see it now because of the protective coverings, but once the sun sets, they'll roll these up so we can see the west."

He adjusted his position, and his legs, which never seemed to sit still now that they could move, bounced up and down as if he were four. "It seems the curse was blown in on ash, or something like it. No one knows where it came from, but it fell on the land and settled there. And that, they think, is what poisoned everything and every-one. Here in the mountains, it's nearly always windy, so the ash never settled. At least, not the way it did down below. I hear it often blows in from the south, but because we're protected here in the canyon, we get less of it than most other parts of Solevar."

He pointed to the sheets. "We can't stand in the sunlight here, of course. No one can do that anywhere that we know of. But the death isn't so significant. At least...it wasn't." A slight crease formed between his eyes.

"Things have been getting worse in Torbaine as well," Eirin said. "Our crops are dying. Even our animals are suffering."

Mannish ran a hand through his curly hair. "That's what Karolus and Lady Phaidra are afraid of. They think we're going to pass the point of no return soon."

Qeb paused. "Which means?"

Mannish sighed. "The finalization of the curse."

They were all silent for a moment before Mannish shook his head. "And if these mountains will no longer hold us safely…" He shrugged. "Where else is there to go?'

"How does the power structure work here?" Nuru asked. "It seems Phaidra, Karolus, and Hector are in charge?"

Mannish stood and brushed the crumbs off his legs. "How about I tell you as we get something to drink?"

They stood and followed him up the street. Their party attracted no small attention, and though Drystan wasn't one to blush, he couldn't help noticing how the people's faces changed from wonder when they saw Eirin to undisguised loathing when they looked at him. He moved closer to Eirin and kept his eyes on the road.

"Lady Phaidra is the lady of the realm," Mannish said as they walked, seemingly oblivious to the stares they were receiving. Maybe he was used to it, having been the only Human here for the last month. "This was her family's domain. Hector is her husband." He smiled a little as though this amused him.

"What about Karolus?" Qeb asked.

Mannish looked at him with wide eyes. "Karolus is King Faradoon's grandson."

Thane stopped walking and gaped. "You mean he's–"

Drystan's mind raced back to what Lady Seren had told him of Mhaedin. He hadn't thought to tell the others what he'd learned there.

"The son of Kamon's older brother, Dimitrius," Mannish continued. "So I supposed that would make him…" He squinted thoughtfully at Drystan. "Your great-uncle."

Drystan blinked at him. This shouldn't be a surprise. Lady Seren had told him as much. But there had been so much to learn, and so much had happened since then that it had fallen through the cracks of his mind.

No wonder Karolus hated him so much. Then another realization hit him as well.

"Rangvald was the firstborn son of King Faradoon." He looked at Mannish. "Wasn't he?" He had met his only living relatives that morning. And he'd been so distracted that he'd had no idea.

"That explains the bad blood between them," Eirin said.

Mannish looked back and forth between their faces. "How about we get something to drink?" he asked hesitantly.

Eirin looked at Drystan, and he nodded. So she turned to Mannish and smiled. "Lead the way."

It turned out that water was captured in giant cisterns that caught snow runoff as it trickled down the mountain. These cisterns were filtered using thin cloths to catch the dirt and sticks and other runoff that might fall into the water on the way down the mountainside. Mannish picked up a wooden cup that hung from the side of the cistern and dipped it in the water, handing it to Eirin first.

For some reason, this only annoyed Drystan. Not that he would begrudge her the first drink. A Human would need sustenance the most after a long day of travel. But that Mannish was the one to do it...

Drystan shook off this distraction as everyone took turns drinking their fill. Mannish explained meanwhile how they had barrels higher up the mountain that they filled with water during the great spring runoff. They kept these for dry spells.

"Down in the fields, the Brownies gather water from wells and springs. They use this to drink or water their crops," Mannish said.

"So the Brownies are the farmers?" Thane asked. Drystan tried to remember what a Brownie looked like in Atharrach form. He vaguely recalled from his lessons a small, stout being that would come up about as high as his waist. Brownies weren't a species the Citadel had spent much time studying, though. They weren't likely to invade Torbaine, so they weren't considered worth the time.

"The Brownies are generally our farmers, yes. Though we do have a few others," said Mannish. "Let's turn here and go back that way. Your quarters will be up there." He pointed higher up the mountain on the southern side to their left, but Drystan couldn't see where he meant because of the protective sheets everywhere.

The noise of the streets made it too difficult to talk much as they walked, but Drystan was thankful for that. They had learned enough in one day to last him years to mull over.

There was more than enough to observe without talking. Stalls and other little buildings lined the streets that zigzagged across the mountain's lower face with a far wider variety of shops than there had ever been in Torbaine. But that was probably because there were far more people. A mix of Atharrachs in their shifter and Human forms filled the stalls. Many watched with a great deal of curiosity. Some called out to Drystan's companions to look at their wares. Others even offered samples of food or drink, all of which Thane happily accepted, making Nuru roll her eyes. But one thing was consistent as they went. Everyone avoided Drystan.

"Word spreads fast here," Drystan murmured to Eirin who was walking beside him.

She turned up her little nose and sniffed. "Ignore them."

Drystan smiled.

Soon they turned onto a new road, which began to climb. Shops gave way to houses that had been built either onto the face of the mountain or carved into the mountain itself. They weren't large homes, but they seemed sturdy and dry enough. Nothing grand, not more than a window or two and a door. Far more practical, though, than the traditional Solevarian homes found in Torbaine.

Every time Drystan wondered if they'd reached their quarters, they would come to another set of stairs. Just when he began to wonder if they were ever going to get there, Mannish came to a path that lined a new kind of dwelling. Stacked in rows, one above the other, were straight paths that lined about a dozen doors on each level. The doors were painted red, and beside each door was a window. Each path had an overhang to shield it from rain and a metal fence on its outer edge, probably to keep people from accidentally stumbling off and rolling down the side of the mountain.

"I'm sorry it took so long," Mannish said, smiling as they came to a stop in front of two doors that stood side-by-side. "I took the long way so you could see more of the city."

Nuru groaned. "Are you serious?" Qeb closed his eyes and shook his head slightly, and even Eirin's smile was strained this time.

"Oh," Mannish said, his smile fading. "I suppose you're tired. Well," he dug into his pocket and pulled out two brass keys. "I'll let you get some rest then, I suppose." He handed one to Eirin and pointed to the door on the left. "This is for you girls. And the rest of you," he said, handing the key to Thane, "get the other one."

Eirin opened her door first. She and Nuru went inside, and Drystan followed. So did Qeb. Thane, however, let himself into the men's room.

"Your things have been delivered," Mannish said from the door, pointing to the packs in the corner of the room. "And there will probably be more food sent up later since you don't have any money yet."

"Thank you," Drystan said, turning back to examine the room, hoping the boy would take his hint.

The room wasn't large, but it was still nicer than anything the girls would have gotten at the Citadel. There were two beds. The floor was made of smooth, flat gray stones, and the walls, while part of the mountain itself, had been smoothed and flattened as well. There was no wardrobe, but an ancient graying chest sat at the foot of each bed, and a table sat below the window with two stools tucked beneath it. An oil lamp hung from a peg on the wall between the beds. The window and door faced the northwest, and each, of course, had a roll of canvas above it that Drystan guessed could be unrolled at any time to block the sun. There were no colors or attempts at decoration aside from the door, but it all seemed clean, dry, and far better than the tent they'd all been squeezing into every night.

Drystan peeked over his shoulder. And there was Mannish, still lingering in the door, looking very much like he wanted to say something.

"I think this will do well," Drystan said in a voice slightly louder than it needed to be. "There's only one window, and the glass seems sturdy. You can bar the door too." He glanced at Mannish again.

Still there.

"It's perfect," Eirin said. Then she turned to Nuru. "What do you think?" Her voice was softer this time.

Nuru shrugged. "It will do." She unbuckled her sword and tossed it down on the bed farthest from the door.

"They want everyone?"

They all turned to look at Mannish, who was still standing at the door. A young woman was at his side, whispering in his ear. As soon as she finished, he nodded, and she left.

"It seems Lady Phaidra has requested that you all eat and rest tonight and tomorrow. Tomorrow night, they wish to help those of you who haven't shifted to find your true forms. You'll all be assigned mentors from your respective races." He beamed at Eirin. "And you'll be with me in the scholars' room." He paused. "Would you...you would like to come see it?"

Eirin's smile was suddenly as bright as Mannish's. "Yes! Yes, absolutely!"

Drystan really just wanted to go into his room and pass out for the next thirty-six hours, but he wasn't about to let Eirin go traipsing about the strange city unattended. With a sigh, he straightened. "Lead the way." He half-expected Eirin to protest his attendance, but to his surprise, she simply gave him a small smile and followed Mannish out the door.

———

By the time they left, the sun was high in the sky, and in the yellow light that made it through the canvas sheets, Drystan could see how the people had tried to brighten up their homes. Tiles painted with pearlescent paint covered many of the doorposts. The doors became more crowded as they made their way to the central part of the city on the east side of the canyon. In spite of himself, Drystan slowed to look more closely.

"Lovely, aren't they?"

Drystan looked down to see Mannish had stopped too.

"Oh, they are!" Eirin exclaimed as she joined them in looking. Each doorpost was covered in the clay tile pieces, which were shades of yellow, pink, blue, purple, green, and orange. Some doors were outlined completely with neatly lain rectangular tiles. Others were covered in broken pieces fitted into patterns and images.

"The Phoenixes do that," Mannish said. "When they're not helping Phaidra or training the Dragons, they're quite the excellent potters." He held up his hands and laughed. "Hot hands and all. They can cook the clay as they work with it."

But Drystan and Eirin were staring at him now.

"Working with the Dragons?" Drystan asked.

"Oh, yes. You'll probably meet yours tomorrow, actually, now that I think of it." Mannish frowned thoughtfully. "That's what they do best, you know. Young Dragons are often…" He glanced up at Drystan. "Well, the Phoenixes are the best equipped to handle them, you know."

"No," Drystan said, folding his arms. "I don't."

"Oh, well, it's just with Phoenixes being able to burst into flame and all, and then return as they were before." He shrugged. "Can't have other folks going up in flames. They don't recover so well." He laughed, though it had a nervous sound to it, and waved them on. "Let's go so we can get you back in time to sleep tonight."

Eirin glanced at Drystan, and he gave her a small shrug. *Dragons are often…* Mannish had said. Dragons were what? And how many were there here?

"Is Drystan considered a young Dragon?" Eirin asked, hurrying after Mannish.

Mannish threw a glance over his shoulder at Drystan. "Um, I'm not sure. I suppose Karolus will have to answer that."

Wise answer, Mannish.

Drystan was still pondering these things when they reached another red door that led straight into the mountain. The door was the same size as the ones that led to their rooms. But unlike their rooms, the little tunnel that led to the door had an ancient feel similar to the grand entrance of the throne room. Ancient symbols were carved into the door and cave walls around it, and they had been polished and painted as well. Eirin probably recognized them, with all the time she'd spent in the Records Keep with Alanna back at the Citadel. Sure enough, when Drystan glanced at her, she was tracing the symbols with her fingers, her eyes bright as she whispered something inaudible to herself.

"What does it mean?" he asked, watching her eyes rather than the symbol she was touching.

"It's...um, ancient Elvish," she said softly, her eyes sparkling. "Alanna...your mother said it meant life."

Drystan's throat was suddenly too tight to speak.

"I'll just need a moment to bring in some light," Mannish said as he unlocked the door.

They stepped into pure darkness, the light from the open door lighting nothing but the floor.

"Hold on," they heard Mannish call, then a slight curse as something bumped and clanged against the floor in the darkness.

The room burst into color a moment later as flames raced to ignite a thin path, flickering gently along the edges of the room. Drystan was relatively sure they used a ring of oil built into the wall, similar to the temporary trenches they dug in the dirt to surround their camp in the mountain.

Though he knew what little of it meant, Drystan could tell from Eirin's intake of breath that the room held countless treasures. It was really just a large, round cave. And though the walls weren't laden with white marble, the dark walls here were no less intricate. Perhaps even more so. Veins of silver cut across the dark stone, glittering in the light of the small flames that danced along the ledge that encircled them. Shelves of books filled the walls below the ring of fire, and more symbols had been cut into the walls and ceiling above it. As his eyes adjusted to the light, Drystan could make out constellations, familiar now after traveling so far in the night.

There were twelve waist-high pillars standing in various places around the room, each holding some sort of relic. Some were on pillows, but others stood on their own. A large square writing table stood in the center of the room, littered with parchments, maps, and books.

"What is this place?" Eirin breathed, moving slowly as though she were in a dream.

"I'm so glad you like it," Mannish said, his eyes as bright as hers.

She was staring at the walls and the books and the relics, but he was watching her.

"A few of the original Seers who escaped were able to bring books with them. From the palace, I mean, in the royal city, as well as from the private libraries of lords and ladies in other places." He pulled a book from the table. Its binding was simpler than some of the others', and there were no words on the outside. "Others wrote down what they could remember to try and replace the texts they'd left behind." He put the book back and ran his hand down a few leather spines.

"Is this...for *us*?" Eirin asked, finally turning to look at Mannish.

"It is." He beamed, then his smile faded slightly. "Lady Phaidra told me that it was built to replace the sanctums the Seers left behind when they abandoned the Time Stones. A place to remember and write." He shrugged. "Not that I write much, but I read as many texts as I can. And Hector has been helping me. Not that he's a Seer, of course, but it seems Fauns...because of their propensity for art and music, were often used in the old days–before the curse–to help the Seers immortalize their most worthy visions. Hector's father helped create this place for the Seers, and because Hector spent so much time with them when he was small, as his father was helping them, they told him their stories." Mannish paused. "I'm... I'm not really sure what I'm supposed to be doing here. It's quiet, though, and peaceful. And I try to learn as much as I can about the Time Stones and how they worked. And how curses worked and all that. So when we do go to Solevar, I'll be as ready as I can." He took a few steps closer and watched as Eirin reverently pulled out a large, leather-bound volume decorated with peeling gold paint.

"If you...if you want," he said softly, "we can look at it together."

Eirin just smiled serenely as she turned the pages, and Mannish pulled up a stool beside her so he could look over her arm.

They were a lovely picture together. Drystan gritted his teeth as he pulled out another stool and dragged it over to the wall so he could lean back against it.

No, this was not his ideal way to spend their first evening with real beds and a roof over their head. But he had promised to keep Eirin safe. And if sitting like an idiot in the corner was how he was going to do that, so be it.

7

$\mathcal{E}$irin paused on her way back to the entrance to spin once more in the middle of the room, just to take it all in. A door had been opened in her mind, and she felt as though pure, clean, safe sunlight was streaming through, chasing away the darkness she'd stumbled through before. There was so much knowledge here, so much history and understanding untouched. And it was all hers for the taking.

This was why Lady Seren had sent her to Mhaedin. Yes, it was farther from the Time Stones in Iilaedin. But it would bring *her* closer to fixing the Time Stones. She was sure of it.

"Eirin," Drystan called, holding the door open. "Are you ready?"

Eirin opened her mouth to answer, but then she stopped. The pedestal to her right held an urn, and the strange shine on its surface distracted her. At first, she'd believed it to be paint, but as she drew nearer, she realized the clay itself was reflective.

"What kind of clay is this?" she asked, leaning closer. "I've never seen anything like it before."

"Oh," Mannish said, coming near, but she didn't hear what he said next. She had reached up to brush its handle lightly with the tip of her finger.

What she meant as a light brush, however, thrust her out of the room she'd been standing in and into a new world altogether. A garden burst into view. Grass tickled her feet, and flowers

79

surrounded her, varieties she'd never even imagined could exist. She could feel the grass as it grew beneath her feet, which were suddenly bare.

Then it was gone. Eirin was back in the room with Drystan and Mannish, who were both looking at her with furrowed brows. Mannish was frozen where he'd been before the strange vision, but Drystan was beside her.

"What is it?" he asked.

"I...I don't know," she said slowly, shaking her head to clear it. The dream...vision...whatever it was had only lasted the briefest of seconds. But whatever it was that she had seen, it certainly wasn't here.

She looked back at the urn and then at her worried friends. "I am tired, though. And hungry." She laughed a little. "Perhaps I do need some rest."

Mannish began to protest, saying maybe she should sit down on the window seat and rest, but Drystan ignored his offers and simply guided her toward the door, his large hand gently grasping her shoulder.

"I'll see you tomorrow!" she called back breathlessly to Mannish, who was still looking bewildered.

"What was that?" Drystan asked as soon as the door had shut behind them.

"I'll tell you later," she murmured back, looking at the bustle of the street around them. "Not here." The sun had gone down while they were in the room, and it seemed everyone in the city was out in the streets now.

Drystan just nodded.

8

$\mathcal{D}$rystan glanced behind them several times, but when he saw Eirin's questioning look, he gave her a wry smile.

"Just making sure we're not being followed by an extremely helpful Human," he said. Eirin rolled her eyes and gave him a playful elbow to the ribs.

"He *has* been helpful." Even as she said it, though, she marveled a little at how things had changed between them. Not only had they run away from the only home they'd ever known into a world of danger, but she had gone from loathing him to teasing him.

As if to prove her point, Drystan put his arm around her shoulder and pulled her close. The sudden heat of his chest against her left shoulder took her by surprise, and she found herself wishing he would slide his hand down from her shoulder to her waist, the way a number of the other couples on the street were walking.

But why in the world would he do that? She pushed the unhelpful daydream aside as he bent and whispered just above her ear.

"What happened in there?"

Ah, yes. That was why he'd pulled her so close. He didn't want to be overheard. A part of her deflated while the other part attempted to think straight. She tried to keep her eyes straight ahead as they walked.

"I saw something."

"I'd gathered as much. What was it?"

She frowned. How to explain? "When I used to study with your mother in the Records Keep," she said slowly, "she would sometimes let me touch the ancient texts. And sometimes...every once in a while... Well, I wouldn't See things exactly. But...I would get the sensation that I was touching another world." She paused, then continued, keeping her voice low. "I can't put a name to the feeling exactly. I would just...I could sense something other. At the time, I didn't understand. I just thought it was wishful thinking." Not that she really understood now. The difference, however, was that this time, she knew she was a Seer. That much had changed at least.

"Was it different this time?" he asked, bringing her back to the present.

She nodded. "I saw something real this time. Only for the briefest moment, though. Just a flash."

"Could you tell what it was?"

"It was a garden. I don't know where, but flowers and grass were growing in the sunlight." She paused. "But the sun wasn't poisonous."

"Could you feel it?" he asked.

"Yes. Just briefly, though." She sighed a little. "It was deliciously warm."

They turned a corner, and Eirin stopped speaking. More and more people were watching them now. Drystan used his left hand to pull his hood over his head, though Eirin doubted that would keep people from watching. A new Dragon had arrived in Mhaedin. A Dragon, she got the feeling, that wasn't welcome.

"And?" he asked when they turned onto a street that was less crowded. They were nearly back to their rooms by now.

She shrugged. "That was it. It was all so brief. Like closing my eyes to blink and then opening them again." Then she sighed, letting her shoulders sag. "I wish my mother were here."

He squeezed her arm slightly, and she had to resist leaning into him. That *wasn't* why he was pulling her in close.

"She trusts you," he said quietly. "That's why she gave you the stone. She wouldn't have given it to you if she didn't believe you could do this."

"I think she gave it to me because she's pregnant and desperate." Eirin gave him a dry smile. "But thank you."

Drystan stopped walking. "She's pregnant?" he whispered. Then his eyes widened. "That's right!" he muttered to himself. "I'd completely forgotten!"

Eirin froze, realizing what she'd said. She hadn't meant to let on about her mother's pregnancy. But when she was talking with Drystan, everything felt so natural that she often forgot to be on her guard.

Then she realized what *he'd* said. "Wait! How did you know that?" She blanched. "*I* didn't tell you!"

Drystan sighed and shook his head at the ground. "Just before I ran off to find my father in the dungeon, I was required to attend a supper at which Gerard told the Elders that he'd suspected as much for a while."

"Oh fantastic!" Eirin put her face in her hands.

It was inevitable. She'd known it. Her mother knew it. Eventually, someone would have found out. Whether during the pregnancy or after, they wouldn't have been able to hide her sister's existence forever. But she had hoped that if they began their journey fast enough...

"I'm sorry," Drystan said, his voice strained. "I suppose...not that it will fix everything. But if it makes you feel better, my grandmother will be there. And if anyone can protect your mother, she can."

Eirin nodded but didn't respond.

"And..." Drystan paused, "I'm guessing you seem to think it's a girl?"

Eirin lifted her head from her hands and smoothed back her hair. "We do." At first, Eirin's mother had been sure it was a girl. And Eirin had hoped her mother was wrong. But after learning about Atharrachs' magic and Humans' lack thereof, the fact that neither her mother nor Eirin could see a light within her mother's belly was confirmation enough.

Drystan's eyes somehow grew wider. She could see understanding seep in as he stared at her. "Which means if we don't fix the Time Stones soon..." He let the words trail off.

Eirin nodded and took a deep, long breath. "Just another reason to succeed now instead of waiting for another generation." Instead of waiting for the Elders of Torbaine to get their hands on the child as King Egan had taken her.

She started walking again, making sure to keep her voice low. "We're here now. And there's more knowledge in that room than I had ever dreamed could be left in the world. So I'm going to be grateful."

He squeezed her shoulder again and then let go, as they'd reached the end of the row their rooms were located on. As he let go, she recalled yet another conversation they'd had in Solevar. On the roof of an abandoned Elven fortress, he had explained to her why he'd sworn off marriage and a family. He feared for their lives, and he didn't want their deaths or injury on his conscience.

But now... Everything had changed. He was no longer a prince being hemmed in on every side by Torbaine's Elders. The man who had sought to kill the women in Drystan's line was dead. They were no longer in the mountain. And Drystan, no longer crown prince of Torbaine, was a free man. For some reason, this made Eirin's heart beat harder in her chest.

"How do you feel about sleeping with Nuru?" Drystan asked.

Eirin gave a little start. "Sorry, what?"

"Sleeping with Nuru." Drystan nodded at their doors as they approached. "Do you feel safe?"

Eirin stopped before the door she was supposed to share with the only other female in their party. She knew she should assure him that all would be well. But if she was honest...

"I won't lie," she said slowly. "It will take some getting used to." After sharing a room with Alys since she was six, and then sleeping in large groups as their little company traveled in and out of Solevar and Torbaine, sleeping with the girl who had once tried to maim her would be...different. "But all the group travel lately has worn the shock off somewhat," she continued.

"But do you feel safe?" he pressed.

Eirin paused and considered this. "I wouldn't have believed it six months ago," she finally answered, "but I really do think Nuru has changed. I think...I think she feels lost. And she's too smart to jeopardize herself in a world that isn't her own." She smiled a little.

"Defense was always her strength. I don't think she'll be going on the offense anytime soon."

Drystan nodded as well. "Losing trust in her mother seems to have shaken her."

"It's true," Eirin said. Nuru's mother had been the meanest of all the Elders back in Torbaine. And while Eirin trusted few of them, there was none she'd disliked more than Elder Na'ilah. During their first journey into Solevar, Nuru had confronted her mother after betraying her companions to the Elders, and since then, she'd been a shell of her former self. Quiet and bristly as ever but...lost.

"Well," Drystan said, glancing up and down Eirin's person with a slight frown, "just remember that you can bang on the wall if you need anything. I'll come, and Qeb won't mind."

"Thane will," Eirin laughed.

"Thane sometimes needs his feathers ruffled." Drystan gave her a small smile, but it quickly disappeared. "I mean it. I promised to protect you. And I intend to keep my promise." He looked up at the sky. "From whatever decides to try its hand at you."

Eirin thanked him and then used her key to let herself inside. As she stepped in, she spotted a large bowl of fruit on the writing table. Nuru was reclining on her bed, eating a slice of pink melon Eirin had never seen before. She gave Eirin a brief look.

"The Faun brought this. There's some bread in the basket behind it too." She went back to eating, and Eirin let her. She focused instead on choosing a wide variety of fruits and several pieces of bread. Their fresh food earlier that day had tasted so good after weeks of eating the dry food they'd been able to carry in their packs.

The silence didn't last long, though. Just as Eirin laid back on her bed and took her first bite of bread, the door burst open, and Thane walked in.

"Drystan wouldn't like that," he said, a grin on his face as he took a bite of the apple he was carrying. "You're supposed to keep your door locked."

"And you're supposed to mind your own business," Nuru said without looking at him.

"Oh, what did you get?" Thane was already digging through their bowl of fruit. "We didn't get any of these." He held up a fuzzy purple fruit. "I'll be taking this, thank you very much."

A melon rind hit him on the nose. "I think not," Nuru said with disgust. "You'll be leaving that right where you found it."

"Nuru, you wound me," he said, putting his hand over his nose. Then he flounced over to her and knelt beside her bed.

"Save your breath," Nuru said, laying back and closing her eyes. "Whatever foolishness is about to come out of your mouth, I don't want to hear it."

Eirin grinned as Thane gasped. Before he could speak, though, the door opened again.

"Why wasn't that locked?" Qeb asked as he walked in, followed by Drystan. Then his eyes fell on Thane. "Oh, that's why."

"None of you has an ounce of romance in you," Thane said, standing. "Look at Eirin. She's laughing at you."

"She ought to do more than that after you waltzed in and left her door unlocked," Drystan said, locking the door behind him.

"Nuru said Hector came by while we were out," Eirin told him as he and Qeb leaned against the wall. Thane began to go through their fruit basket again.

Qeb nodded. "Yes. He told us to make sure our shades were drawn before late morning tomorrow. A bell will toll to remind us."

"He also said we will have tomorrow morning to rest," Thane said, sniffing a shiny yellow fruit. "Why hello, beautiful. What do we have here?"

"When Thane is done flirting with the fruit," Nuru said, propping herself up on her elbows to glare at him, "he might remember to give you the rest of the message."

"Oh, yeah. Only that after we're done resting tonight, someone will come fetch us so we can learn how to shift."

He said it casually, but as soon as the words were out of his mouth, the room's atmosphere grew stiffer. This was it. They would all find out what they were. Well, Eirin and Drystan already knew. But the rest...

Their days of pretending to be Human would be gone. The natural inclinations and instincts of whatever her friends were would be drawn to the forefront. There would be no going back.

Eirin had avoided thinking about it before, but now they were too close for her to ignore it anymore. She didn't know much about Atharrachs, despite having grown up surrounded by them. Even her father and brothers were Atharrachs. But the people she had grown up loving and learning from had cruelly had their true natures suppressed by the bruthsi root from birth on. She didn't really know what it was like for most Atharrachs to take their true form, or if they were any different while in their magical form.

From the little she had seen from Drystan since his Dragon nature had broken free, she could only gather that the Atharrach form—the magical form within—wasn't separate from the person, but it was part of them. And when that Atharrach broke free, the true nature of the magical creature within was magnified.

Her friends were united now. Together, they'd learned the truth and lost their homes. They'd saved one another's lives again and again, and had sworn to continue on together. But would they continue to want that once they found their true selves? Would they wish to keep their strange little band? Or would the calls of their ancestors be too strong for them to ignore?

She glanced at each one in turn. Drystan she had little worry about. He had made a promise to her, and if she knew anything about Drystan, it was that he kept his promises. If anything, his Dragon self seemed to accentuate his already strong personal convictions...with the small exception of the moments in which he'd forgotten who she was. But that had only happened once, and for that, she was more grateful than she could say.

But he wasn't the only traveler in their little band. There was Qeb with his warm, brown skin and his even darker eyes, hulking and watchful, ever at Drystan's side. Then there was Thane, who couldn't be more Qeb's opposite with his pale hair and even paler skin. Thin and wiry and yet taller and faster than Qeb, his easy laugh and dancing eyes gave the group life. Even Nuru, with her dark, guarded gaze and bristly personality, would leave a hole if she abandoned them now. Somehow, over the last few months, they had become a single unit, being to one another what their families could no longer be.

At least, they were one now. But would their loyalty last?

Thane broke the silence. "We already know Nuru's going to be a Hydra. Then she'll have more heads to snap at me with." As a reward for his little speech, he got an orange peel thrown in his direction, but he just laughed and took another bite of his stolen fruit.

"I'll take first watch tonight," Qeb said, turning toward the door.

"Do we need a watch tonight?" Thane groaned. "Isn't this supposed to be a safe place?"

Qeb shrugged. "Trust the strangers if you want to. I'll be taking the first watch either way."

"I'll take over for you in the morning," Drystan told his friend, following him toward the door. "Come on, Thane. Leave the girls be."

"I'm just waiting for you to leave so I can make my move." He wriggled his pale eyebrows up and down.

"I'm not sure who you're trying to impress," Eirin said, unlacing her boots. "You know I'm not falling for your charms. And I'm pretty sure Nuru would prefer to strangle you."

"Gladly," Nuru muttered.

But Thane wasn't perturbed. "So you think I have charms." He fell into a deep bow. "Then I shall not give up hope of winning a fair maiden's hand. Until then, my lovelies."

"Goodbye, Thane." Eirin shoved him out the door and then locked it behind him. She could hear him laughing on the other side and couldn't help chuckling a little herself.

She stopped, though, when she turned back, and it dawned on her that she and Nuru were really sharing a room. She had believed what she'd told Drystan outside on the balcony, that Nuru had changed. Still, her heart stumbled a little as she returned to her bed and sat down.

"I'm not going to kill you in your sleep if that's what you're worried about."

Eirin looked over at Nuru, who was lying on her bed, a scornful look on her face.

"I didn't say you would," Eirin said, trying to sound unruffled.

"No. But you were thinking it. And you're right. I could kill you. Easily."

Eirin arched an eyebrow. "Is this supposed to make me feel better?"

Nuru huffed at the ceiling. "If I wanted to kill you, I would have done it ages ago. But I didn't." She threw Eirin an annoyed look. "All I wanted was to leave my mother behind. And doing something stupid here isn't going to help me achieve that."

Eirin held her gaze for a long moment before nodding. "I can understand that," she finally said. "And I believe you."

"I'm also fully aware that you're wishing Alys were here instead of me," Nuru continued.

Eirin thought for a moment before answering. "I do miss Alys. You're right about that. But..." She took a deep breath. "I also think this place will be perfect for a new beginning. And if you want that, then I do too." She sent Nuru a tentative smile.

But Nuru just shook her head and blew out the oil lamp. Then she rolled on her side, facing away from Eirin.

It wasn't necessarily a friendly start, but as the light disappeared, Eirin was surprised to find that her angst went along with it. She was far from her home, but as she climbed under the covers, she found that the day's fear and excitement began to slip away. Suddenly, she felt as though she could sleep happily for a hundred years undisturbed. The mattress beneath her was softer than any bed she'd ever slept in before, and the blankets chased away her lingering fear. Who could be afraid when one was wrapped up in such perfect comfort?

Nuru gave a snort. "Things that seem too good to be true usually are."

Eirin thought about answering Nuru, but decided not to. Tomorrow she would worry about the cost of their actions, but for tonight...

She would sleep soundly tonight.

9

When he woke up the next morning, Drystan was forced to admit that it was the best sleep he'd had since being at Lady Seren's fortress. Even better, was the platter of food left at his door. With steaming bacon, rolls, and more fruit, it was possibly the best meal he'd ever eaten. Largely, Thane pointed out, because they hadn't had to catch or cook it.

After checking on Eirin and Nuru, Drystan relieved Qeb of his watch and sat quietly at the door. Despite the weight of the evening that was to come, Drystan found a certain peace he wasn't sure he had felt since his father had sent them away from Torbaine to find Lady Seren. Perhaps it was because he'd never gotten to sit outside during the day. Sure, he'd sat outside many times as they'd traveled the mountain. But he'd always been on alert, waiting for an enemy or an animal to appear. In Torbaine, it had been the Atharrachs. In the mountain, he'd always feared Eirin would be discovered. On the path to Mhaedin, they had been on the watch for…well, anything. Wyverns in particular. But here, with the guards and sentries, where Eirin was to be revered and protected, where the Wyverns couldn't come…

He might be on watch, as Qeb had insisted, but here he might… dare he think it?

Rest.

Not enough to send Eirin off on her own, of course. But for the first time in a long time, Drystan felt as though the world didn't lie solely upon his shoulders.

The canvases hid the sky, flapping lazily in the breeze. Sounds of people in the streets below floated up to him. The few words he could make out were mundane. They were oddly soothing, however, in their rambling tones. He'd spent countless days watching the people in the market in Torbaine, of course. But there had always been a fear there, one that floated in the air, permeating and polluting even the peaceful days like a disease.

Not that these people were unthreatened. Lady Phaidra herself had said that they were running out of time and supplies. And yet… there was a freedom here Drystan had never realized he lacked. These people were their own selves, free and unashamed. Some walked around in their Atharrach forms. Others wore their Human forms instead. But from the glimpses he had seen, no one seemed to resent anyone else for their choice.

His heart clenched. He wanted that.

Unfortunately, that might not be his lot here either. Not with the blood of Kamon running through his veins. Drystan wanted to curse the man's name. It all seemed so pointless. And for what?

More food was delivered not long after that, and soon Thane came out, by Qeb's urging, apparently, to take Drystan's place.

"Not that we've seen a single person come in or out of these doors since we arrived!" Thane called loudly, gesturing to the row of doors that stood down the length of the walkway. "I'm pretty sure most of these people have no idea we're even here."

Drystan thumped Thane on the back and went back inside the room to sleep some more. Then, when the bell chimed to announce that the canvases could be lifted, yet another platter full of food was delivered. And with it, a ridiculously excited Mannish.

"I was hoping that Hector fellow might be the one to fetch us," Qeb murmured to Drystan. "He's delightfully quiet."

"You and me both."

"It's nearly time!" The young man beamed up at Drystan from the walkway below. Drystan scowled down at him, his hunger going up in smoke.

Eirin and Nuru came out of their rooms, making Mannish's impossibly wide smile even brighter.

"I'm supposed to take you to the training platform!" he told Eirin, as if she was the one finding her true form. "Karolus and Lady Phaidra will meet us there with some of the other instructors."

"Instructors?" Thane asked. "Are we to be instructed?"

"Oh, lots of races use instructors," Mannish said. "Most do, in fact. Not all races gain their Atharrach form at the same time. Dwarves are born with their Atharrach forms, and so are Merfolk. Impundulu gain their forms when they're six years of age. But Dragons, for example, don't get their fire until they reach adolescence, which is a good thing." He met Drystan's hard gaze. "Fire, and all that," he finished weakly. "Doesn't go well with buildings."

Eirin scoffed and turned her head away, and even Nuru gave one of her rare dry grins.

"Anyhow," Mannish continued, speaking quickly, "many races have individuals dedicated to teaching the young members of their race how to fulfill their roles properly. Without causing mayhem and destruction, in particular. And it's a good thing too. I heard of one about a young Phoenix who set a whole town on fire once during a temper tantrum."

They started down the stone steps that led back to the main street toward the center of the city. People openly gawked at them as they passed by, but Drystan knew better than to dwell on the looks he received. It was better to pretend they weren't there at all. The sensation of peace he'd cherished earlier was long gone now.

"How will they get the rest of the bruthsi root out of their systems?" Eirin asked.

"I think it would be better to just wait and see," Mannish said with a grin. "It's kind of hard to explain." He opened his mouth again, but Drystan interrupted.

"Mannish, how old are you?"

"Oh, I just turned twenty-two." He sent another grin at Eirin.

Twenty-two? How in the world was he older than Eirin? He looked barely old enough to grow a beard.

Eirin sent him a warning look, but Drystan simply returned the look. For some reason he couldn't quite name, this happy man-child annoyed him beyond reason.

Qeb's expression bordered on a smile, and Drystan had to resist giving him a hard shove. As usual, his friend seemed to know what he was thinking. And, even more frustrating, he found it funny.

"Here," Mannish said as they left the main road and headed up another mountain trail. This one was steeper than their previous paths, and they didn't speak much as they hiked upward to a flat area at the top of the path. Drystan guessed it wasn't only the elevation that made the others quiet. Even Thane had stopped speaking. What they were about to do weighed heavily upon them all. Drystan could sense it, even though he wasn't the one shifting. And he hoped for his friends' sakes that they were happy with whatever their lots turned out to be.

"These are the training grounds," Mannish said as they climbed closer, sounding slightly out of breath. "Our defenses are made up of people from each race." He paused, and his next words sounded more subdued. "Unfortunately, they've needed more fighters as of late. Gangs and marauders have gotten worse since the food production has fallen. And Lady Phaidra and Karolus have had to ask the elders of the different races to put forth more people to fight."

"What is their end goal?" Qeb asked in his deep voice, sounding far less winded than Mannish.

"Lady Phaidra wants as many people as possible ready to accompany us on our final attempt to reach Iilaedin. But…we lost a lot of people the last time we tried to make it to Solevar." His face darkened.

"Wait, you've already tried to make it to Solevar?" Drystan asked. "Lady Phaidra didn't mention that."

"Oh, well, I'm sure it's because she was too excited about having all of you. And Eirin." Mannish gave them another smile, but for the first time, it didn't reach his eyes. "They're making sure our next trip goes better. So no need to worry."

Drystan and Qeb exchanged a glance.

When they reached the top, Mannish announced their arrival, as though the dozens of people standing around weren't already staring at them.

"They're all ready." He beamed. "And excited."

Nuru made a slight sound of disgust, and Qeb quirked a thick brow, but they didn't have time to balk at his words. Lady Phaidra was coming toward them.

They were standing on a large, flat circle made of stones laid together like one of Drystan's father's old wooden puzzles, one of the few toys brought from Solevar into the mountain. They weren't perfectly smooth, instead offering a number of different surfaces, probably to imitate different terrains. There were also boulders strewn about the circle, similar to the obstacles that had been placed in the training pits in the Citadel, where Drystan had trained growing up. Several lamps had been hung from poles that surrounded the circle, and now that he was higher up, Drystan could see at least six more training circles scattered across the mountainside nearby.

"Thank you for coming," Lady Phaidra said, clasping her hands in front of her. "I know this is difficult. It's hard for children and adolescents whose families have been preparing them for years, much less individuals who have no idea what to expect." She gestured at a small table holding three goblets. "We have prepared a drink for each of you to chase the bruthsi root from your systems." She grimaced slightly. "I'm afraid it won't be particularly comfortable, but you'll quickly burn the remains of the bruthsi off with your magic once you've imbibed the drink."

Thane and Nuru looked at one another, but Qeb stared doggedly at the drinks.

"I'm going to ask Eirin and Drystan to sit up there." She pointed at a ledge beside another training circle slightly higher up. "I'm afraid it's not safe for Humans when Atharrachs shift for the first time."

Drystan's face burned as he remembered the first time he'd nearly shifted. He'd been animalistic in his actions. Eirin had said his eyes had burned ember. And then again, when he'd actually found his Dragon form. He could still see the fear in her face, even in the hazy memory of that day.

No. New Atharrachs definitely weren't safe to be around fragile Humans.

"And thank you," Lady Phaidra said to Mannish with a somewhat reproving smile. "I sent Hector to fetch them, and he returned and said they were already gone."

Drystan wondered how Hector could have possibly gotten to their rooms and back so quickly when he realized the faun was in his Atharrach form. Ah. Hooves were faster than Human legs for sure, especially climbing uphill.

"I wanted to welcome them," Mannish said with a sheepish grin.

Lady Phaidra rolled her eyes, but she gave him an indulgent smile. "Well, get on with you then. You know better than to be here."

"But–"

"I'm only allowing Eirin because she's made it clear that she doesn't intend to be reasonable about this." She gave Eirin a wink.

Mannish looked crestfallen, but Eirin beamed, which made Drystan smile too.

As Mannish walked away, and Lady Phaidra moved in to talk quietly with her husband, Eirin leaned in close.

"What do you think?" she asked, her smile gone now and her face taut.

"About shifting?" Drystan asked.

She shook her head, a crease forming between her brows. "About them." She nodded down to their friends. "How are they going to take this?"

Drystan studied them without speaking for a moment. He knew what she meant. Eirin had always been…herself. Even back in the Citadel, when she'd been known as the weakest, most useless student the Citadel had ever trained, she'd never been afraid of being exactly who she was. But the others…

"I think Qeb will be happy as long as he's something big and threatening," he said, a small smile escaping. "Thane will be a show-off no matter what. He could turn into a hedgehog, and he'd think he still lucked out better than anyone else here."

Eirin was laughing now, and it was a sweet sound to hear, which earned her a disgusted look from Karolus.

"Get her up there," he barked at Drystan, jerking his head in the direction of the upper ledge Lady Phaidra had pointed out.

Once they were sitting on the ledge overlooking the training circle, Eirin frowned down at her friends again. "What about Nuru?" she asked.

"Nuru." Drystan shook his head. "I honestly don't know." The girl was a mystery. Sometimes, it seemed, even to herself.

"I'm not sure she knows who she is now in Human form," Eirin said. "Maybe this will help her start anew."

"I hope so," Drystan said with a wry chuckle. "For all our sakes."

"Welcome!" Lady Phaidra's voice rang out in the night, and despite their distance, Drystan could make it out clearly. He wondered if that was a Dragon thing. "I know most of you are familiar with what is about to take place, but for our newest members, I will explain what we're about to do." She turned to Hector, who handed her a goblet. She raised it high in the air.

"This drink has been concocted especially by the Nymphs with the purpose of chasing bruthsi root out of an Atharrach's blood. Obviously, it's not generally needed for such ceremonies, but as this is no average ceremony, we are thankful for the Nymph's help." She paused and turned to Qeb, Thane, and Nuru where they stood at the edge of the circle.

"An Atharrach's first shift is considered a sacred moment. Such moments are generally commemorated by the witness of family and friends and followed by a feast. Unfortunately, you have no family here with which to celebrate. We hope, however, that you'll consider celebrating with us, allowing us to be to you like those you bravely left behind." She gave them a warm smile. "No warrior should find his magic alone." She turned and addressed the crowd again.

"Tonight, they will discover the source of their magic. You three probably already have hints of it in your personality and preferences, but they will be tenfold once you have your Atharrach form. We will teach you how to protect your sources of magic, wherever they may be."

"What is she talking about?" Drystan whispered to Eirin.

"Each race of Atharrach has its magic in a particular location in the body." Eirin paused. "You can't see it, of course, but I can. And I can tell you that each magic has its own color and appearance."

"Why do they need to know how to protect them?" he asked.

Her eyes flickered to his chest. "Any injury to the origin of magic can be deadly." She frowned slightly. "Elder Gerard was a Sidhe, which is a particular brand of Fae. His magic was in his head." She was referring, of course, to her best friend's father, the Fae who had tried to drag her back to Torbaine as she was trying to escape. And Drystan had killed him for it.

"Yours," Eirin said in a softer voice, "is here." Her fingers brushed his chest, and though Drystan knew she was only pointing to his heart, his skin felt like it was on fire , even through his shirt.

Eirin softly sucked in a deep breath and turned back to the platform below. Drystan tried to follow her gaze, but his mind still felt pleasantly scrambled.

"Unpleasant as it is…" Karolus was speaking now. "You will need to learn to shed your Human instincts. Those will get you killed. And you'll be no use to anyone dead. Your magical form will feel foreign…animalistic. But you must embrace the creature within. Because that creature is the only thing that will keep you alive from both predators and Solevar itself." He paused. "Also, don't get too comfortable sleeping at night. We'll be doing much of our training out here after the sun goes down and before it comes up. The mountain, as you've noticed, gives us some shade in the early morning, but we don't want to take that for granted."

"Are you ready?" Lady Phaidra asked, holding out the goblet. "Who wishes to go first?"

10

"Bet you it's Thane," Eirin whispered to Drystan, giving him a sideways smirk. For some reason, that smirk made Drystan's heart lift. Eirin had a wickedly sharp sense of humor when she wanted to, but he'd seen far too much fear and worry in her eyes lately to enjoy it as much as he'd like.

So he smirked back. "Bet you it's Qeb."

After a moment of silence, Thane stepped forward. "Might as well get the best done first," he said, flashing a grin at Nuru, who gave him a dirty look.

"Excellent," Lady Phaidra said, holding out the goblet. Eirin bumped Drystan's shoulder with her own, and he quietly laughed.

Thane turned to the other two and raised it above his head in a mock toast. "To me." He winked at Nuru, who scoffed. Then he put the goblet to his mouth and drank.

"Think he'll spit it out?" Eirin asked.

Thane was looking rather pale, and he was taking longer to drain the goblet than Drystan had guessed he would. For a moment, he stopped drinking and squeezed his eyes shut.

"No," Drystan said. "His ego's too big, and Nuru's watching. He'll drink the whole thing in one go just to annoy her."

Drystan was right this time. Thane finally lowered the goblet with a violent shudder and wiped his face on his sleeve. Still trem-

103

bling slightly, he handed the cup back to Lady Phaidra, who was no longer smiling. Instead, she watched him with an intense gaze.

"That was..." Thane began to say, stopping to shudder yet again. But this time, his whole body seemed to ripple.

Lady Phaidra, who had handed the goblet to Hector, fell into a crouch, and with an ease that made Drystan jealous, shifted into her Dragon form, a line of fire consuming her Human skin and leaving copper scales behind.

She was beautiful, not as large as Karolus had been, but still larger than Drystan's Dragon form. Where Karolus had sharp spikes, though, hers were rounded. Her eyes, like his, had the fire-light of ember burning within them. Except hers were like molten gold rather than blue.

Not that any of that mattered, though. What mattered was that Thane was staring up at a Dragon, his mouth open wide, still in his Human form.

Drystan saw it before Thane did. Or perhaps, he felt it, the swell of fire within her fiery heart.

"Thane!" he shouted. "Shift!"

"How?" Thane yelled back, stumbling backward. For once, he'd lost his bravado completely. Instead, he leaped behind a large boulder just before she let out a stream of fire.

"She's going to kill him!" Eirin grabbed his arm hard.

But Drystan couldn't answer. He had remembered what he'd been trying so hard to forget, how it felt to be feral, to feel the monster within him writhe in exultant joy.

"Instinct, boy!" Karolus shouted. "Let it out!"

"I would if I could!" Thane called out as Lady Phaidra let out another burst of flame.

"I think she's trying to force him to let his instincts take over," Drystan told Eirin. Then he yelled down to Thane. "You have to face her! Fight!"

Thane sent Drystan a look that said Drystan had clearly lost his mind. But after another shout from Karolus, Thane jumped out from behind the boulder with his sword drawn.

It was clear Lady Phaidra wasn't trying to kill him. She could have done that within seconds of the match's start if she'd wanted to.

But Thane made the mistake of aiming a poorly planned attack at her arm, and in response, she scratched him hard. Thane let out a yell as blood ran down his arm.

Though Drystan was in Human form, he had begun to realize that some of his Dragon abilities remained enhanced, even while out of his scales. And unfortunately, scent was one of those that remained. The scent of blood filled his nostrils, and his body jerked hard.

He felt as though someone had ignited his entire body, like a flame to oil. Every bone and sinew practically quivered. Not with a hunger for blood. Not that, thankfully. But instead, he felt the nearly overwhelming urge to fight, to burst out of his weak Human bonds and fly down into the midst of the battle that raged below.

"Drystan?"

Her voice was quiet and wavered slightly. Turning to look at Eirin, he saw amber light reflecting in her wide eyes. Only then did he realize that his own vision was swimming in amber light.

He shook his head, and the amber light died, but he could feel her eyes on him long after he went back to looking down at Thane. He willed his eyes to stay there, and not on the girl beside him.

Thane was not doing well. He was hiding behind another pile of boulders, still clutching at his bleeding arm. He must have tried fighting several more times, however, because he was bleeding from his left leg and his shoulder.

Just when Drystan began to wonder whether Lady Phaidra's method of coaxing the Atharrach out might not be as effective with people who had been ingesting bruthsi root for years, she swiped the top of the boulder pile he was hiding behind with her tail. The top rock, about the size of Thane's head, wobbled slightly before rolling down toward Thane.

Eirin let out a small cry and covered her mouth.

Thane screamed. Once again, his body rippled, but this time, the ripple was so violent that when it was done, a Centaur stood where the man had knelt. The rock hit him just as he threw his arms up over his head.

Instead of knocking him to the ground, however, the rock shattered against Thane's forearms. The crowd, which had now swelled to well over fifty people, burst into applause. Lady Phaidra shifted back into her Human form just as easily as she'd shifted out of it, and when she was a woman again, she was smiling as brilliantly as a mother watching her son.

A large Centaur male came forward into the circle to welcome Thane, who looked exhausted but happy. His clothes had disappeared, as Lady Phaidra's had done with her shift, and now he was bare-chested, his pale skin darkening into a chestnut hide where his hips should have been. He stood on four muscled legs of the same color, and his hooves had a near silver sheen. His blond hair had been longer as of late, as they hadn't stopped to cut it during their escape, but now it ran all the way down his back, as wild as the rest of him.

"Look at Nuru," Eirin snickered, seeming to have forgotten Drystan's lapse. Drystan followed her gaze, only too happy to forget it himself.

Sure enough, Nuru's mouth had fallen open, and in spite of herself, it seemed, she was staring at Thane as though she'd never seen him before.

"Who's next?" Lady Phaidra asked as the older Centaur led Drystan from the circle, speaking to him in inaudible tones.

"Me," Nuru fairly snapped. As she spoke, she began removing her boots, which she then shoved at Qeb, who took them with only a mild look of surprise. Then she stomped out into the circle, muscles tense. Drystan had seen that look far too many times to count. Nuru had something to prove.

Karolus was the one to shift this time, but before he had even completed a full sweep of his spiked tail, aimed in her direction, she leaped into the air as a Human and came down as a Sphinx.

"For some reason, this doesn't surprise me," Eirin muttered with a slight smile.

Drystan could only smile and shake his head.

"Sly and silent with deadly claws," he recited from memory, knowledge he'd gained in his Atharrach class back at the Citadel before they'd known any of them were such creatures. "No, that doesn't surprise me in the least."

Nuru's face still looked like her face...but less than Thane's had.

Her dark eyes were just as bright as they'd ever been, but her body was now like that of a great, sleek cat. Her dark skin was covered with golden fur, and she had large, padded paws and sharp, blade-like claws. Her tail, long and golden, was held proudly in the air. Her face, however, was slightly narrowed, and like the rest of her body, had a golden sheen to it. Sharp ears stuck up one each side of her head, and they twitched the way Elder Zu's cat used to do. But unlike Elder Zu's cat, she also had a long, thin pair of wings that folded neatly along her back.

Just as had happened with Thane, an older Sphinx, this one a female, came out to greet Nuru and led her out of the circle.

"It's almost as if they knew what everyone would be," Eirin whispered. Then she gave a start. "I remember now! Her mother was a Sphinx! Back when they came to find us in the Elven fortress!"

"I try to remember as little about her mother as I can," Drystan said. Then he pointed to the varied faces and shapes in the Atharrach crowd. "It looks like there are instructors from most races here, so they're probably prepared no matter what race they end up being." But his eyes then returned to Qeb.

He wouldn't have admitted it to his best friend for the world, but Drystan felt uneasy about Qeb's shift. Since he had been accepted to the Citadel at age six, Qeb had been his shadow. Drystan had no idea really why or how they had become such good friends. They had always simply been. And while he knew the world didn't revolve around him, especially now that he was known to be the great-grandson of the disgraced prince, Drystan found himself hoping desperately that whatever Qeb turned out to be, it wouldn't hate Dragons.

Qeb drank the entire draught without flinching. And Lady Phaidra's attempt to unnerve Qeb took nearly as long as her session with Thane. Unlike Thane, however, Qeb didn't get hurt. Never once did Lady Phaidra get in a swipe of her claws or tail, nor was she able to pin him down with her flames. Qeb gracefully avoided every attack and even dealt out a few of his own, never drawing blood but making Lady Phaidra roar in protest. Only when Karolus shifted as well and began to stalk toward Drystan and Eirin did anything change.

One moment, Qeb was sprinting toward Karolus, his feet pounding on the stone floor. The next, great wings had exploded out from his shoulder blades, and his hands, now like gargantuan bird's claws, were outstretched as he flew straight at the back of Karolus's head. Karolus let out an ear-piercing scream as Qeb dug his claws into the back of the Dragon's neck and yanked his head around. Drystan was seconds from jumping off the ledge and into the circle himself when he realized it was over. Lady Phaidra and Karolus were both in their Human forms again. Qeb, however, had a head like that of a great bird, covered in white feathers with a sharp, yellow beak, and he stood at least two heads taller than Karolus. Karolus was scowling and rubbing the back of his own head, but Phaidra was grinning as everyone else once again broke out in applause.

Hector walked up beside Karolus.

"You owe me a bondar," he said with a smug smile. "I told you he was a Griffin."

Karolus just rolled his eyes and stomped off, still rubbing the back of his head. But Drystan didn't watch him go. Instead, he was staring in awe at his friend.

Qeb was a Griffin.

"Of course!" Eirin exclaimed. Drystan turned to look at her. She was laughing now. "It makes so much sense!"

"What does?" He frowned.

"Don't you remember from class?" She beamed up at him. "Griffins are loyal! So loyal that they seek out a soul they find worthy of protecting. They spend their entire lives protecting that person and their kin." She looked up at Drystan, her brown eyes sparkling. "Qeb is a Griffin. And he chose *you*."

Drystan stared down at her. "I'm not sure–"

"Drystan, don't be thick!" She shook her head and looked back down at the circle, where another Griffin was greeting Qeb. "A Griffin usually bonds with one person in his entire life." She arched an eyebrow at him. "Don't think I haven't noticed how the others here treat you." She nodded back down at Qeb. "That Griffin, with all the goodness in his very strong heart, found you worthy. Just remember that."

Drystan was still staring at her when Karolus's voice broke into his thoughts.

"Drystan!"

"Yes?" Drystan called down, tearing his gaze from Eirin.

Karolus scowled up at him.

"It's your turn."

———

Drystan sat straighter. "I already shifted."

"I'm aware of that. I want to see if your fighting skills are as lousy as your flying." He looked at Eirin. "You need to go."

Eirin glared at him as though he weren't a Dragon and she wasn't a very small Human. "I'm staying right here."

"I will stay with her," Lady Phaidra broke in, shifting even as she spoke and flying up to sit beside Eirin. Karolus gave Eirin another glower. Instead of arguing, thought, he just shook his head and turned away. Drystan gave Eirin a shrug and stretched his arms out to shift, but a shout from Karolus stopped him.

"You can't shift while you're next to her! Are you mad? Get down here first!"

Drystan swallowed back a retort and ignored the sympathetic look Eirin sent him as he marched back down the stone steps to the training circle below.

"*Now* may I shift?" he snapped when he reached the center of the circle.

Karolus gave him a sneer, changing into his own Dragon form as he did, his voice deepening mid-sentence. "If you can."

Drystan stretched his arms out and tried to shift. But it was hard. He was acutely aware of Eirin watching from above, as well as Karolus's mocking gaze.

On the third try, he did shift, but it was clumsy and awkward, and he nearly fell on his face when his back legs changed before his arms. The pain wasn't as intense as the first time, but it still hurt, the fire eating slowly down his body. He wasn't quite finished when something hard slammed into him from the left.

All his years of training at the Citadel urged him to leap up and face the threat, but when he tried, his new proportions and strange hind legs couldn't do what his Human legs could have. While his legs struggled to find their balance, his wings seemed to know what to do on their own, and he had lifted himself several feet off the ground before a spiked tail like a whip slapped him back down again. A claw followed quickly, raking down his back.

"Stop him!"

A girlish voice broke through the roars and grunts of the fight.

"He's only shifted twice! This isn't right!"

"Karolus is testing him," he heard Lady Phaidra's rumbling Dragon voice respond. "If he's to protect you, he has to be able to fight."

Drystan didn't hear what Eirin responded with because something white-hot ignited in his chest. Eirin. He was supposed to protect Eirin. And Karolus was making her unhappy.

Karolus's tail slapped his side again, but this time it only glanced him as Drystan launched himself forward. He crashed into Karolus's shoulder and knocked the older Dragon off his feet.

Karolus, though, while older, was faster, and instead of hitting the ground, his wings came up and caught the air like a sail, keeping him upright as he slid sideways. Before he had come to a complete stop, Drystan sensed the fire build within the other Dragon's chest. Drystan rolled to the left but got caught on his wing as Karolus's fire grazed his stomach.

Training. He'd trained all his life for this. He should know how to maneuver and evade and attack easily. But the animal in his head wanted to react instinctively, and the two natures clashed in his head the same way he and Karolus were fighting now. And just as with Karolus, one nature was far outstripping the other.

Drystan managed to retake control of his body just as Karolus began to build another ball of fire in his massive chest. It wasn't easy with Eirin's indignant exclamations still ringing in his ears, but he forced the animal down long enough to get his body to lay still on the ground.

For a moment, he wondered if he would suffer greatly for his gamble. Playing dead wasn't a technique he'd used much at the

Citadel. But at the Citadel, he'd been the biggest and the strongest. He was neither of those here.

But, it seemed, Karolus had bought his act. The ground crunched beneath the bigger Dragon's feet as he came closer.

Just a little closer.

Drystan flamed as he rolled onto his side, his tail snapping out and hitting Karolus in the face. He'd meant to catch him off-guard, but Karolus was faster. Using his spiked wing, he pinned Drystan back down. Eirin's scream echoed through the training yard as Karolus's jaws stopped inches from Drystan's chest.

They stayed frozen like that for what felt like eternity, but finally, Karolus let go of him and backed away, shifting into his Human form as he did.

"Disappointing." He scoffed as he turned and walked away.

The white heat in Drystan's chest that had been smoldering exploded, and the animal inside burst free from the chains Drystan had held him with. Drystan leaped to his feet, the move coming easily for once.

"Well, what did you expect?" he thundered. Everyone remaining in the training yard froze, but Drystan didn't care who heard him.

"You don't fight like a Dragon because you refuse to be one!" Karolus waved his hand at Drystan. "A child could see it! You use your head, not your instincts! How can you be a Dragon if you insist on clinging to your Humanity?"

"I've been burning from the inside as long as I can remember!" Drystan snapped. "But they wouldn't let me turn. They lied to me and kept me tame. But when I needed to shift, I did. I may not have done it well, but I did it! Alone! Without you or any of the people here. I was told to bring the Human here, and I did that, too."

"You've lived a pampered life," Karolus scoffed. "What do you know of hunger? Or cold? Or the curse? You and your fathers—"

"You hate me?" Drystan shouted back, the monster inside of him roaring, forcing the words from his mouth. He couldn't have stopped, even if he had wanted to.

He really didn't.

"If we're being honest, I do," Karolus growled.

"That's well enough," Drystan snapped. "Because you know what?

I hate myself. Everything I am and everything I'm not. But that won't be good enough for you either. Because nothing is. And nothing will be, thanks to the blood of a man who lived a hundred years ago."

"Drystan." This time, the voice was a woman's. Drystan turned to see Lady Phaidra hurrying toward him in Human form, Eirin trailing behind her. Eirin's face was white, and Lady Phaidra's was distressed.

"Son," she said softly. "Please. That's not what we want." She glared at Karolus and then turned back to Drystan. "We want to help you. Truly. And I'm sorry–"

"I'll stay," Drystan snapped. "But for her sake." He jerked his head at Eirin, who was standing wide-eyed beside Lady Phaidra now. "Not yours." He took a long look at Eirin, willing himself to calm down. He had to calm down, or he could hurt her. That much he instinctively knew.

And somewhat to his surprise, it worked. Slowly, painfully, he shrank back down to his usual size. As soon as he was steady on his feet, he marched over to a wide-eyed Eirin and wrapped her small hand in his. With Eirin in tow, he strode back toward the stairs.

"It's not safe for him to take her!" Karolus cried to Lady Phaidra, but Drystan felt Eirin's hand tighten around his.

"Forget the abductions," Karolus continued. "If he's only just shifted–"

"Let them go," Lady Phaidra said softly."

"But–"

"Or we might lose them both!"

"Fine." Karolus's eyes rekindled some of their ember glow. "You'll be here tomorrow night the moment the shades come down."

"Very well, then," Drystan replied, holding his gaze. "I will."

"Drystan–" Lady Phaidra began, but Drystan didn't hear anything else. He was too busy stalking away.

11

$\mathcal{E}$irin looked up at Drystan as they walked. His face was unmoving, like a mask of stone. It was concerning, to be honest, too much like the mask he'd worn at the Citadel for so many years. Too hidden to tell her what she really wanted to know.

What had happened back there? Her heart twisted as she played the words over again in her head, chewing on them like she was unable to swallow.

I hate myself. Everything I am and everything I'm not.

"Drystan. Eirin."

They turned at the sound of Hector's voice. The Faun jogged up to them, his hooves clopping against the road as he did. Eirin feared for a moment that Drystan might keep walking, but he seemed restrained by her hand, which, curiously, was still in his.

"I'll walk with you if you don't mind," Hector said with a kind smile. "I don't get nearly as much time to stretch my legs on that training pad as my wife or Karolus." He gestured to his legs and chuckled. "With good reason, of course."

Eirin couldn't help smiling back. His eyes crinkled kindly, and the little brown and silver pointed beard that ran a handspan past his chin reminded her of the one her grandfather had worn before he died.

Drystan gave him a cold look but nodded curtly before resuming their walk.

115

"Karolus is a good man," he said in a low voice. "Don't hold these last few days against him."

Drystan's jaw tightened with an audible click, but Eirin tried to look politely concerned. Karolus had been awful to Drystan, but that was no reason to take it out on Hector.

Hector's smile grew grim. "His son died," he said in a low voice. "Just a few weeks ago. The loss is still raw, and I'm afraid," he gave Drystan a sad smile, "that you have the misfortune of looking very much like your late cousin."

Drystan's steps slowed slightly but then picked up again.

"But," Eirin said with a slight frown, "shouldn't that make him more disposed to welcome Drystan?"

Hector smiled gently down at her. "We all mourn in our ways, dear." Then his smile faded. "Before you arrived, he'd been taking it out on us. I suppose your presence has given him a more acceptable place to punish the world for his pain."

"What happened?" Drystan asked. It was more of a grunt than a question, but that he was speaking was good. Drystan knew all too much the pain of losing loved ones.

Hector sighed. "It really was our fault, I'm afraid. His as much as anyone else's, but we meant well." He nodded at the market stalls they were passing. "You can see it in their eyes. In everyone's really." He reached up and rubbed the back of his neck. "When your friend, Mannish, arrived here, you can't imagine the rejoicing. We'd believed Humans extinct. It was all we could do not to admit to ourselves that we were simply waiting for the same fate. And though Mannish's parents died almost as soon as they arrived, the city was exuberant. For the first time in years, we had hope."

They turned onto another street, though Eirin only noticed this because a small Centaur nearly ran over them, his mother chasing him and shouting rebukes. Once they were out of danger of being trampled, Hector continued.

"We made a decision when we were emotional and desperate, and it was an expensive one."

Eirin sucked in a breath. "You tried to reach the Time Stones!"

He gave her a pained smile and nodded. "We did. We believed we had enough experience and numbers to make a successful trip without much planning." He indicated the crops at the foot of the mountain. "Our crops have been shrinking for several years now, and our population is growing. We were sure our determination could make all the difference."

"Our food has been failing as well," Eirin said, thinking back to her family's dwindling portions the last time she'd eaten supper with them. "In Torbaine, I mean."

Hector nodded. "I'm afraid it's widespread throughout all of Solevar. We have new people arriving every day whose families had been determined to survive the lower regions of the kingdom, despite the curse. There just isn't enough food anywhere these days."

"People without resources are dangerous," Drystan grunted.

"Exactly. And we feared news of the Human spreading fast as well." Hector's mouth tightened. "The curse isn't the only danger to Humans in Solevar."

"Mannish said it ended badly," Eirin said.

"Badly is an understatement." Hector let out a gusty breath. "We lost so many healthy young people. Only a few days into the journey too."

"What happened?" Eirin asked.

"A storm. An ice storm all the way from the Northern Mountains, of all things." Hector winced. "Violent and laced with magic, and we still don't know what happened. Then, as though we weren't weak enough, we were attacked by a group of vagabonds." He shook his head and blinked several times. When he spoke again, his voice was strained. "Many died, and it was a miracle that we got Mannish back here in one piece."

They reached the stairs that would lead them up to the fourth level of doors, where their rooms were located. Hector stopped beside them.

"I know you need to rest," he said. "But I do want to help you understand one more thing about Karolus."

At the mention of his uncle's name, Drystan's eyes hardened, but Hector either didn't notice or ignored him.

"The reason he wishes for you two to be separated is not a vindictive one." Hector stared at Drystan's face this time until Drystan finally met his gaze. "I have, of course, never personally undergone a

Dragon's shift. But I have been married to one for a long time. And we've talked about our natures enough for me to be very familiar with what happens every time you change."

Drystan glared at him, but Hector continued.

"Remember the flame, how it ate you up from the inside." His voice was suddenly low and urgent. "That's what Dragons do. They burn away the weakness of their Humanity every time they shift. Magic mixes with fire, creating an even hotter fire than the one in your heart. Especially," he paused, "for a son of Oreck."

Eirin's eyes immediately went back to the blue and yellow flames that constantly surrounded Drystan's heart. Her companions couldn't see them, of course. But now, she tried to remember how his fire compared to Lady Phaidra's. She'd been too busy at the training circle to do much comparing, but she made a mental note to look again the next time Drystan and Lady Phaidra were in the same room.

"Because of who you are," Hector went on, "your flame will burn even hotter. It's a seed of magic, passed down through the sons of Oreck over the years. All Dragons have fire, but none like the sons of the kings."

Hector glanced at Eirin, then back at Drystan. "Unfortunately, until you learn to control it the way Phaidra and Karolus have, you'll be likely to burn anyone and anything standing too near." He nodded at Eirin. "Including her."

Drystan's eyes widened, and he looked at Eirin questioningly. She could see the fear and uncertainty warring with his suspicion.

Was Hector telling the truth? She could only guess that he was. She'd seen Drystan shift three times now, and every time, it had been so bright it nearly hurt her eyes. And yet, something in her heart hissed at the idea of keeping her distance from him. And it went beyond the way she liked having her hand enveloped in his.

Perhaps it had something to do with the way she felt as though they were partners in all of this now. Back at the Citadel, Alys had been her safe place. But Alys was gone now. And she and Drystan had survived far too much together for her to be easy about their parting. Their friends had journeyed with them from Torbaine. But she and Drystan now bore a burden even none of them could completely understand. Lady Seren had tasked Drystan with getting Eirin to the Time Stones. And Lady Seren would also have been aware of the dangers of traveling with a young Dragon. Her decision to make him swear to protect Eirin had not been made lightly.

With a deep breath, she squeezed his hand slightly and gave him a small nod.

Drystan nodded back and turned to Hector. "I...thank you for explaining that," he said slowly. She recognized the official way he spoke as the tone he'd used with the Elders back in the Citadel. "But we're staying together. I swore that I would protect her, and I can't do that from afar."

"Your intentions are noble," Hector said slowly. "But I might ask that you consider this."

Drystan raised one dark brow.

"Consider whether or not you might need to protect her from yourself." He took a deep breath and then gave each of them a small bow. "I will take leave of you now. I'm sure you have much to talk about. And rest a bit more before tomorrow." He turned and began to walk up the street, but a few steps later, he paused and turned to face them again.

"I'm aware that you didn't have the most cordial greeting here. Hopefully, we can prove our intentions to you in the future. For all our sakes." And with that, he was gone.

12

They were quiet as they climbed the stairs and made it to their rooms. Drystan seemed lost in his own world, and Eirin felt little better herself. Hector's words still rang in her ears as they reached their doors.

"Think they're back yet?" Eirin asked as they hesitated. Why were they hesitating?

Drystan frowned at the door. "I doubt it. I can't hear Thane."

Eirin pulled out her key and unlocked her door. It was impressive that there were locks in such simple doors. They must have skilled smiths here to create such complicated mechanisms for guest quarters.

When she stepped in, however, she found Nuru already asleep on her bed. Eirin smiled a little as she realized that her companion was curled up like a cat. Eirin grabbed another piece of fruit and a roll from the baskets still on the table, then she paused to stare at her bed.

She should sleep. She was meeting with Mannish tomorrow. Who knew how long they might study? And then she would be going with Drystan to his training session, and that wouldn't begin until evening. She ought to sleep all she could now.

And yet, she knew she couldn't do it. There was too much swirling about in her mind for her to even doze off. So she took her food and went back outside to stare out over the balcony at the nighttime activities in the bustling city below.

On the south side of the canyon, where their rooms were located, other dwellings like hers ran up and down the mountain. There were other larger buildings closer to the center of the city, similar to the one they had gone to see Lady Phaidra in. One entrance in particular was so large that it dwarfed even the Throne Room entrance. She hadn't seen it earlier because of the canvas coverings, but there was light coming from the inside now, and it lit up the mouth enough to highlight its sheer size.

The north side was filled with doors as well, but its higher levels were also dotted with more of the training circles. She could see the bare outlines of distant Atharrachs moving around on them, and she wondered what kind of training they were engaging in. Was it anything like what she'd suffered for thirteen years?

To the west, of course, lay Solevar. The moon shone gently over the land, as though it were trying to undo the poison the sun inflicted daily. There were hills, sloping meadows, patches of farmland, thick forests, and so much more she couldn't even begin to name.

The sound of a door opening behind her made her turn, and she found Drystan softly padding out as well. He was barefooted and in a simple tunic and trousers. It felt strangely intimate, and Eirin was thankful for the dark, should she need it to hide her blush. She couldn't remember the last time she'd seen Drystan in anything but his royal robes at official functions or his warrior gear, which he'd been wearing since they first left Torbaine. It made him feel strangely...Human.

That thought made her smile.

"What?" he asked as he came to stand beside her, leaning out over the railing.

"Nothing." She shook her head. "Couldn't sleep?"

He shrugged. "Qeb's not back yet."

Eirin nodded. For other friends, that might require further explanation, but not Drystan and Qeb. They'd been together the vast majority of their lives. Of course, now that she knew what Qeb was, this was far easier to understand.

"So...you can See the magic within people. Correct?" Drystan asked.

"Yes."

"Why couldn't you tell what they were before the test? I mean, at least Qeb, for example, since we've seen lots of Griffins before this."

Eirin paused to brush a few strands of hair out of her face as a slight breeze came up. It was pleasant, both cool and warm at the same time.

"I think it's because of the bruthsi root. You stopped taking yours weeks ago, but they were still ingesting it even up through yesterday. I could See flashes of their magic, but not all of it for what it is. It all exploded into clarity as soon as they shifted for the first time."

Literally. There had been explosions within their bodies. That had been what was causing the ripples.

"And..." she continued, "even though I can See the magic, there was no book in the Citadel telling me where each Atharrach's magic is located or what color it is. Just because I See it doesn't mean I know what it is."

"It has color?" Drystan's eyebrows went up.

"Mhm. Remember how I saw the red when we were–"

"The Manticore. In the caverns." Drystan nodded grimly. "You were the only one to see it."

Eirin shuddered, remembering the bright red lights hanging from the cavern ceiling in the dark of pre-dawn. Drystan's mother had been right about many things. And one of those had been her claim that many Atharrachs had given themselves over to their animalistic sides. Of course, Eirin supposed even Humans could go to such lengths if they really wished to ignore their better instincts. There just weren't any sharp teeth or venomous spikes to aid in their efforts.

She glanced up at Drystan as he gazed out to the west. It was so strange to think that a year ago, they weren't even speaking. Well, that had mostly been because she was holding onto pain and resentment from years past. How silly her anger seemed now. He had gone from the distant heir to the throne to a lost man whose only purpose in life was to keep her safe.

What did that say about her?

He shifted slightly, his arm moving closer to hers on the railing, and even this felt slightly unnerving. Warmth radiated from him like the stone floor in the Citadel after the sun went down, old heat flowing from it despite the absence of the sun. He was so handsome and strong, like a marble statue on the outside, but so afraid of who and what he was. What he had become.

But then, had Drystan ever really seen himself the way everyone else did? That she couldn't say.

It was clear he hated the Dragon within. And, it seemed, he expected everyone else to hate it as well. How could she prove to him that, while she couldn't answer for anyone else, the Dragon didn't disgust or frighten her?

Well, it was a little frightening when his eyes glowed amber. But thrilling too. It was simply who he was. It explained so much about him, more than he had ever let on, probably even to Qeb.

"What was that?"

He was looking down at her, not a fleck of amber in his blue eyes now.

"You were about to say something. What was it?" he asked.

She just shook her head.

His gaze stayed on her, though, and she snorted. "What?"

"Is this what you want?"

Eirin blinked up at him. Their faces were so close. Like when he'd held her as she cried after escaping the Tsuchigumo.

"Um…" She scrambled to find her thoughts, which were currently scattered like her twin brothers as naughty toddlers. "What I want?"

"This." He gestured to the city around them. "If you think this is where we should be, then I'll stay as long as you want. But if you think we ought to go, just say the word."

Eirin felt heat rush to her cheeks at the kindness in his voice. She drew in a deep breath of the night air to clear her head.

"I'll admit, not everything has gone as…as smoothly as I'd hoped. But I think we can learn here. And," she laughed a little, "while I might have put up a good bluff yesterday…" Her laughter died. "We're not strong enough to venture out into Solevar on our own.

Not yet, anyway. We have to learn more first. If they failed in their last attempt as quickly as they did with as many resources and as much knowledge as they have," she shrugged, "I'm not sure how we're going to do any better."

He snorted. "It doesn't say much for them in their favor."

"I think it does. And I think it makes the situation that much graver. If they, who have survived trips to Solevar before, couldn't make it because of a storm, then we'll need to be that much more prepared before we venture out. With or without them."

"You didn't tell them about the stone," Drystan said softly, nodding at the little rectangular rock, which she had pulled out of her shirt and was clutching tightly.

"I was considering it," she said with a small smile. "But I think you were right, and we need to wait a while longer." She tossed her head. "I like the people, and I want to give them a chance. But I'd also like to hope I'm not naive enough to trust everyone we meet."

Drystan grinned. "There's the paranoid Human girl we all know."

She rolled her eyes but couldn't help smiling. Then she sighed. "Thank you, by the way. For staying. What Karolus did to you–"

He waved it off. "It's fine."

"Drystan."

He turned to look at her, and after hesitating for a second, she held her breath and took his face in her hands. He went perfectly still, as though he really were made of stone.

"I'm not afraid of you," she whispered, willing him to look her in the eye and accept it.

He gave her a long look. "Maybe you should be."

She leaned in, and his eyes widened.

"What are you going to do about it?" She quirked an eyebrow.

He broke into a grin. "Nothing, I suppose. There never was any talking sense into you."

She let go of his face and stepped back, though her instinct told her not to.

Her instinct was acting out.

Instead, she beamed up at him. "None whatsoever."

They went back to looking at the stars after that, their conversation turning to lighter topics, such as which new fruit was their favorite and betting on when Thane would get himself beat up for mouthing off to the wrong person. And even though the day had been less than stellar in many respects, Eirin went to bed an hour later feeling suddenly as if the day had been a game. And somehow, despite their setbacks, she had still won.

13

If Eirin had believed she would be given another day to sleep in, she was mistaken. A knock on her door sounded far too early for her taste, though when she listened, she could hear the bells chime the fifth hour of the evening.

Nuru rolled over and groaned. "They need to make up their mind. Day or night. Not both." She pulled the pillow over her head.

Eirin wasn't the least bit surprised when she found Mannish waiting on the other side of the door.

"Are you ready?" he asked, his eyes bright. He was holding a platter of fresh fruit and a new kind of bread that smelled like cinnamon. His hair, for once, looked as though it had been brushed, and he was fairly bouncing from one foot to the other. Though, when Eirin considered that he hadn't been able to bounce at all for most of his life, she couldn't blame him. She would want to move as much as she could too.

"Oh!" he exclaimed when he saw her. "Did I wake you?"

She waved him off. "Just give me a minute, and I'll be ready," she said, trying to stifle another yawn.

"Of course." He nodded, looking somewhat sheepish. "Whatever you need."

Eirin shut the door again and looked around the room, trying to wipe the sleep from her eyes. She frowned down at her clothes, which she'd accidentally fallen asleep in. To say they needed laundering was an understatement. Lady Seren had given her new clothes, and her mother had added one of her own work gowns to Eirin's pack before she'd escaped Torbaine. Unfortunately, Eirin was never in a position to wear gowns these days. And though she'd tried to wear her other outfits equally, they were all were very dirty and smelled strongly of campfire by this time. All they needed was a good washing, really, but Eirin owned that she wouldn't mind getting new clothes tailored soon. Something without holes would be ideal.

After throwing on her boots, rebraiding her hair, and washing her face, she opened the door once more. This time, Mannish was neither smiling nor was he bouncing. Instead, he and Drystan were sizing one another up.

"I, um, would have brought more food if I'd realized he was coming too," Mannish said, sending Eirin a pained smile.

"I told you I was coming along," Drystan said, looking down at the young man, clearly enjoying being a head taller than Mannish.

How Mannish could have forgotten Drystan, Eirin wasn't sure. But perhaps he'd thought their trainings would overlap.

"We can share," Eirin said with a smile, stepping between them. "I'm too excited to eat much anyway." She gave Drystan a slight poke in the ribs with her elbow.

Be nice. Annoying everyone who could help them wouldn't work to their advantage. And Eirin got the feeling that Mannish might be a powerful ally. The wishes of the only two Humans known in existence could probably be a powerful driver if push came to shove in the end.

Drystan grunted slightly but said nothing else as they made their way down the stairs and back to the scholars' room. When they arrived, Mannish led Eirin to the main table in the center of the room. It was cleaner than it had been yesterday. Instead of being covered in parchments and books haphazardly tossed in any open corner, there were several bound books and about a dozen scrolls unrolled and stacked neatly on one side. Clearly, Mannish had something planned.

"I thought," Mannish said, grabbing one of the scrolls and unrolling it, "that we might start with the Time Stones and all the known attempts that have been made so far to fix them." Using some of the books, he carefully weighed down the parchment's corners so it lay flat.

"Have there been that many?" Eirin asked as she stared at the list on the parchment.

Mannish winced slightly. "There have been a lot." Then he looked at the parchment he had just unrolled and pointed to the drawing in the top left corner. "See this?"

"The Time Stones!" Eirin exclaimed, resisting the urge to reach up and touch the stone that hung around her neck.

"Yes!" Mannish nodded enthusiastically. "There are three others beside the main one, but from what we understand, none of the lesser stones can be fixed. Only the original one in the Emerald Palace in Iilaedin, where the Dragons' Blood Fire Throne sits."

Eirin glanced back at Drystan. If he felt a reaction to the name of his ancestors' home, he showed no sign of it.

"Those are the Time Stones Prince Kamon broke," Mannish continued, glancing up at Drystan. Upon meeting Drystan's eye, however, he quickly looked back down at the image. "The others are spread about the kingdom. One is north–in your Lady Seren's castle, I believe."

Eirin nodded. "I wanted to see them, but Lady Seren said it would be no use without fixing the main stones."

Mannish nodded. "She was right. There have been a number of attempts to restart the stones by using the lesser circles, but nothing worked. We assume this is because the stone is stuck in the main stones." He frowned. "There were, however, a great number of deaths associated with those who tried."

"How so?" Eirin asked.

"A few Seers tried to destroy them."

"What?" Eirin gaped.

Mannish nodded. "They were all struck dead on the spot. Several Atharrachs tried to fix them, too, but they were also struck down." A crease formed between his brows. "It seems the Time Keeper is insistent on keeping the stones consecrated if nothing else."

"That can't be how most of the Humans died, though, can it?" Eirin asked. "Lady Seren said once that there were far more of us."

"Oh, there were. Just as many as any other species. In fact," his face grew red, "from what I understand, Humans were very..." He swallowed and glanced at Drystan.

"Very what?" Eirin asked.

"Um, good at reproducing."

Eirin felt a similar blush heat her face, though she couldn't say why. There was nothing to be ashamed of in a simple historical fact. And yet, she wanted to look at neither Drystan nor Mannish after that.

"Anyhow," Mannish said, shaking his head slightly, "the Seers... the Humans, that is, quickly concluded after several failed attempts that only the original Time Stones could light the others again. So they made their way to the capitol in wave after wave, trying to fix them."

"Trying to remove the stone," Eirin said softly. When Mannish gave her an astonished look, she shrugged. "My mother told me."

"Oh, yes. Well, she was right." He rolled up the Time Stones scroll and opened one of the books. It seemed to be a ledger. Each heading was a name, and beneath each name was a paragraph ending in a date.

"As the curse grew stronger, many cities and races grew desperate. They began dragging Humans back to the capital against their wills to force them to fix it. Unfortunately," he sighed, "the curse had grown so strong by then that most of them died along the way. And those who made it to the stones in one piece died there trying to fix them." His jaw tightened, and suddenly, Mannish didn't look quite so young anymore.

"You survived," Eirin said softly.

He ran a hand across his face. "Only because many died to make sure I survived the attack." He turned and stared up at one of the paintings on the wall, his hands on his hips. "I just...I don't understand."

"Why the Stones–"

"Why the Time Keeper isn't letting us fix them!" He shook his head. "We've been trying to fix it, to change what happened. Why kill us for it? Why bother to create us at all if He was planning to leave us here in squalor and death?"

Eirin looked down at the list of names as well. "We must be doing something wrong," she finally said.

"But there's nothing else *to* do! We've tried it all!" He ran a hand through his hair, ruining any attempt at brushing it that he had made earlier. Then he paused and looked at her. When he spoke again, his voice was slightly softer. "Why do you think so, out of curiosity?"

Eirin pursed her lips. "I'm...I really can't say for sure. Because I don't know. But something...something my mother said tells me that there has to be a way."

Mannish gave her a tired smile. "I'm glad you're here." He laughed a little. "I know I've been here just over a month, but it's been really lonely bearing this burden alone."

Eirin gave him what she hoped was an encouraging smile. "You don't have to bear it alone anymore."

Mannish's eyes grew round, and he opened his mouth. Before he could speak, though, a clanging crash made them both jump. They turned around to see that Drystan had dropped the platter cover on the ground.

"Sorry," he said, not sounding sorry in the least. "I was getting something to eat." Then he held the platter up. "You need to eat, Eirin. We'll be going to my training after this."

"Yes, eat," Mannish said. "While you do, I can show you on the map what they've tried."

So Eirin ate as Mannish unrolled a map of Solevar. It was similar to her father's rendition, though there were several new locations on this version that she hadn't seen before. Predominantly new cities and lakes and such. Mannish pointed out the different routes they had taken and what dangers had waylaid them each time. Some groups had successfully reached the Emerald Palace in Iilaedin while others had met with the same fate as Mannish's first journey, though usually, the Human was among those who were killed.

Eirin attempted to smile and nod and take note of each one. But deep down inside, she had to admit that she was terrified. Never in her life had she imagined that there were so many ways to die.

Finally, when the bell tolled half past the seventh hour, Drystan stood.

"We need to go," he said. Eirin nodded and stood as well,

thanking Mannish for his help that day.

"You don't have to go," he called out. "If you're not ready, I mean. I'd be happy to escort you back to your room when we're finished here."

"Thank you," Drystan said, his voice icy, "but I'll take her from here."

Eirin had begun to follow Drystan, but before she made it to the door, she came to the same urn she'd touched the day before. This time, however, instead of touching it, she studied it. "What is this?" she asked Mannish.

"Oh, that's from the Emerald Palace. It was one of the few special pieces that survived the journey here," Mannish said, coming to stand by her side. "It's inlaid with silver, if I remember correctly."

"What did they use it for?" she asked, frowning at it.

"I could be mistaken, but from what I understand, watering plants." He glanced at Eirin. "Why do you ask?"

Eirin knew better. She really did. If Alanna had drilled anything into her head while she was working in the records room in the Citadel, it was that there ought to be no handling of the artifacts. At least, not with bare hands. The oil on her fingers, Alanna had always warned, could damage the material. And yet, Eirin felt the need to touch, the desire that pulled her hand closer and closer until the tips of her fingers grazed the urn's cool, smooth surface.

She was thrust back into the garden again, but this time, the vision was so much stronger than it had been the day before. The transition into this other world surprised her with its violence, but that was nothing compared to the shock of finding herself standing in the shadow of what could only be the Emerald Palace.

The palace wasn't made of emerald as she had first supposed, but thin, clear lines of green sparkled from between the large white stones that soared high in the air in towers and walls and ramparts. The sun still shone as it had yesterday, and she could still feel its warmth. The world she now stood in wasn't perfectly clear, of course. It was still like looking through a dirty window. But the raw power in the world around her...it was astounding. Like the grass had the day before, the whole world pulsed and grew this time.

But the scene didn't stay that way. Even as she reveled in the potency of the life around her, she could feel it dying. The sun that beat down on her skin began to sting as the flowers and grass wilted and died. A strong wind whipped around her, ash getting in her eyes and nose and mouth.

Without thinking, Eirin threw her hands over her face. In doing so, however, she must have broken the strange connection with that otherworld because she was suddenly back in the scholars' room. And before her with their mouths hanging open were not only Drystan and Mannish, but Lady Phaidra, Hector, and several people Eirin guessed to be Lady Phaidra's attendants. And Lady Phaidra looked radiantly happy.

"I can't believe it!" she breathed. "You were having a vision, weren't you?"

Eirin swallowed. "Um, I think so." There was no ash in her mouth, but the memory was so strong that she felt there ought to be.

"Eirin," Lady Phaidra said, coming close and taking Eirin's face gently in her hands. "I don't know if you're aware of this, but I've known many, many Seers in my day. And I can promise you that only the strongest of Seers can have visions of the past by touching something other than the Time Stones themselves."

Eirin wondered if Mannish would resent Lady Phaidra's words, but he looked just as in awe as Lady Phaidra did.

"So," Eirin said slowly, "all those times back at the Citadel when I touched the scrolls and felt...something?" She looked at Drystan, but his eyes were wide as well.

"This is incredible." Lady Phaidra beamed at her attendants. "I must go speak with Karolus. We have things to discuss!" She turned her radiant smile back on Eirin. "We'll be seeing you shortly."

When they finally escaped back into the streets, Drystan leaned down to Eirin as they walked. "Are you well?" he asked in a low voice.

Eirin frowned. "I am."

He raised his eyebrows. "But?"

She shook her head. "I don't know. I just...something feels off." She didn't really know how to put it into words. Of one thing she was sure, though. The potency of the vision lingered within her. And with it the destruction it had wordlessly promised.

14

Drystan watched Eirin carefully as they made their way to the training circles. She seemed well enough after the vision, but he still felt uneasy about leaving her unattended. Fortunately, it seemed he would have no trouble with that. Nuru and Thane joined them as they left the scholar's room, and Qeb met them a few minutes after that.

"I thought you were sleeping," Drystan said as his friend joined them. "I've only been gone a few hours."

Qeb, in his Human form, was flushed and sweaty and carrying a small drawstring bag.

"Once he learned that I was already tied to you, my mentor asked if I wished to train sooner so I could attend your training as well," Qeb told Drystan. "I was much obliged to him."

"You also need sleep," Drystan murmured.

Qeb waved him off. "Oh, and Hector sought me out as I finished," he said, holding up the bag. "He's sent money."

"What for?" Nuru asked.

"He says that because we're going to be in service of the city, our labors will be compensated as such."

"I don't remember them asking us if we want to work in service of the city," Nuru snorted.

"Would you like to open a stall?" Qeb gave her a sideways look as they walked.

"I can see you selling something…" Thane rubbed his chin thoughtfully. Then he snapped. "I've got it. Hugs. You'll sell hugs! You can use all your winning people skills."

Nuru grabbed him and shoved him against the wall as Drystan, Eirin, and Qeb exchanged an amused glance.

"When you children are done," Drystan had said dryly, "Qeb can distribute the coins they sent."

"That's not a bad idea," Qeb said, stopping on the side of the road. "There are many food vendors here."

After Qeb distributed the coins, and Nuru and Thane began to argue over where they should buy food, Drystan pulled one of his own coins out and examined it. The coin was silver in color and about the same size as one of their coins in Torbaine, but the image engraved on it was different. A Dragon on one side and a man on the other. There were several other coins of various colors and sizes, but every single one was engraved with a Dragon.

"Does anyone remember how to buy a potato?" Eirin asked, studying his coins as well.

"It's the same as our currency at home," Nuru grunted.

"Yes, but the coins are different," Eirin said, still frowning.

Thane and Qeb joined them, staring at the coin.

"I'm pretty sure that's a bind," Qeb said.

But Thane shook his head. "No, it's a bondar."

"For the love of Solevar, that's a bind!" said a female voice.

They turned in surprise to see the woman in the stall nearest them. She looked to be in her mid-thirties and was selling spices. A baby was perched on her hip, and several small children ran around behind her, laughing. She just looked annoyed.

"A bind will buy you a potato. Ten binds get you a bondar, which will buy you a leg of ham. Ten bondars get you a barrow. A hundred barrows get you–"

"A barrow bar!" Eirin nodded. "Thank you. It's the same as at home. We just don't always remember which coin is which. They look different here."

The woman gave them a somewhat haughty look. "Torbaine reminted their coins then, did they? Shows what they think of the rest of us."

"I think their aversion to magic shows what they think of all of us," Thane muttered.

But Eirin simply thanked the woman...a kinder response than such a remark deserved, in Drystan's opinion, then they made their way up the street again.

"Word travels fast here," Eirin said, leaning close. "Everyone knows where we're from, it seems."

"So it seems," Drystan said, casting a wary glance around them. Qeb waved them on with an eye roll as Nuru and Thane continued to argue. He would catch up soon, Drystan knew. Nuru and Thane would meet with their mentors soon as well, and then perhaps the rest of them would have some peace and quiet.

With just the two of them, Drystan hoped he and Eirin would attract less attention as they walked. Unfortunately, however, they were still watched from every side. Nothing that would likely end any time soon.

"Still," Eirin said as they stopped to purchase two small meat pastries, "it's nice to have something in common with this place. Even if it is just money. It makes Mhaedin feel less foreign."

Drystan glanced down at her as they resumed their walk. "For being all dark and foreboding a few minutes ago, you seem rather pleased with yourself."

It was true. Despite her consternation just a few minutes before, Eirin seemed quite satisfied. Her brown eyes were bright, despite the falling dark, and there was an extra bounce in her step. She fairly glowed.

Eirin, noticing his studious gaze, laughed a little. "It's a bit embarrassing."

"What is?"

She shrugged, and her smile grew. "I've never been good at anything. " She held up a hand to cut off his protest, "not at the Citadel. Nothing they counted as useful, at least." She looked up at the city, which curved around them with the canyon. "There, I was scrambling just to survive. Mediocre at best. Here, I can be useful. I'm...good at something."

They were nearing the training circles now, but before they began the climb to the one where Karolus stood, Drystan stopped

Eirin. Taking her by the shoulders, he tried to ignore how good it felt to draw her close to him. Instead, he worked to steady his voice. "You were never mediocre."

She quirked an eyebrow. "You *do* remember sparring with me, don't you? Or did Karolus knock that memory loose too?"

Drystan made a face at her and mussed her hair. She squealed in protest and danced away.

"Do you plan on coming up any time soon? Or should I send your trainer to do something better with her time?" Karolus's voice boomed down from the edge of the training circle above them.

Drystan and Eirin sobered up immediately. "Coming," he called up.

"*Her?*" Eirin whispered behind him.

They quickly climbed to the top of the stairs to the lowest of the training circles. Karolus stood waiting for them, his arms folded over his chest, his eyes hard like flint. Beside him was a young woman.

Drystan had forgotten that he was supposed to be assigned a trainer aside from Karolus, and this girl's youth–she couldn't be older than Drystan–surprised him even more. But as there were no other people in the circle, he could only guess that this young woman was indeed to train him.

He also couldn't help being struck by her loveliness. She was tall and slim but not skinny, her long, lean muscles evident through her tunic and trousers. Her hair was fiery red even in twilight.

"This is Callispa," Karolus said, gesturing to the girl. "A Phoenix descendent on both sides, her father is the head representative of the Phoenix clan, and her mother's family was well sought after among Dragon nobility for their excellent teaching. Callispa, however, will be your trainer."

Eirin stepped forward. "Does every Dragon need a Phoenix train-er?" she asked, her voice slightly cooler than Drystan was used to hearing it.

"Dragons have...particular needs when they're young," Karolus said. "We don't usually shift until we reach our adolescent years, but Phoenixes shift as early as five. Their entire education is spent learning how to train Dragons."

Eirin stepped slightly closer to Drystan. "Why Phoenixes?" Then she hurried to add, "If you don't mind me asking."

Drystan gave her a wide-eyed side glance. When she briefly met his gaze before turning away, he had to hide the smile that wanted so desperately to come.

If Callispa was offended by Eirin's clipped words, she didn't show it. Instead, she smiled. "Young Dragons are unpredictable until they master themselves," she said, her voice low and smooth. "They're the most powerful creatures in the world, nearly too powerful for their own good." Her smile grew. "Or anyone else's. Phoenixes are the only creatures who can survive being engulfed in a Dragon's flames by accident." Her gaze briefly met Drystan's. "We've been training Dragons for centuries. So long, actually, that we're not even sure when it began."

Drystan tried to look attentive and polite as he listened, but the more she spoke, the more his heart began to sink into his stomach. Was he really that dangerous for her to be around?

...Engulfed in a Dragon's flames...

He looked down at Eirin. "Are you sure you don't want to go find Nuru–"

"No." She lifted her chin defiantly. "I'm staying."

Karolus scowled but seemed to expect her answer. "Go wait up there where you were last night." Then he looked around. "We'll need to find–"

"I'll keep her safe." Everyone turned to see Qeb appear at the top of the steps Eirin and Drystan had just climbed. He came to stand by Eirin's side. "We'll get along fine." He smiled down at her.

"She'll be safe up there," Callispa said kindly. "Besides, no one would be stupid enough to hurt her." She turned to Drystan. "Even if you weren't with her. Everyone knows better than to hurt a Human."

Drystan and Qeb exchanged a glance. Neither of them was convinced by this well-meaning speech. Still, Drystan did feel better with Qeb at Eirin's side.

Once Qeb and Eirin were perched safely up on the next level, looking down, Drystan turned his attention to his new trainer.

"Your first goal will be to seamlessly shift," Callispa said. "Eventually, you'll be able to do it without thinking. You'll have complete control over not only the speed of your shift but also your flames. Watch Karolus." She turned to Karolus, who was standing just an arm's length from them. In a flash of light, Karolus had multiplied his length and height. The flame was there, and then it wasn't. Then, just as quickly, he shifted back into his Human form.

"After that," Callispa continued, walking in a slow circle around Drystan, "you'll master flight. Taking off. Landing. Then we'll begin to practice maneuvers in the air, techniques for both feinting and fighting. Finally," she said, standing in front of him again, "you'll practice using your flame."

"Shouldn't that be one of our firsts?" Drystan asked. "Seeing as I'd like not to fry anyone by accident?"

"For most Dragons, it would be. But you're a son of Oreck. The magic in your fire is ten times as hot and just as potent." She shook her head. "We won't be practicing that until you have absolute control over every other part of your body."

Drystan drew in a long, slow breath. "All right. I'm ready." He absolutely was not ready. But that was beside the point. If he was going to get Eirin safely to Iilaedin, he would have to learn whether he wanted to or not.

Callispa nodded and beamed. "Perfect. Let's begin." She walked up to him, and to his surprise, began to physically adjust his stance. "Eventually," she said as she took his right arm in her long, slender fingers, "you'll be able to change from any position. But when you begin, it's easier if you start from something like a fighting position."

Drystan tried to pay attention to what she said, but it was hard to focus as she manually poked and prodded him into what she seemed to think was the perfect position. None of her touches were lingering or intimate in the slightest, but the constant physical contact was distracting. He dared a glance up at the ledge and quickly looked back down again. Eirin looked as though she was about five seconds from leaping off the edge and putting an end to the session. For some reason, this thought struck him as funny.

"Pay attention." A hand came out of nowhere and cuffed Drystan on the head. This time, it was Karolus speaking. "Your trainer just told you to shift, and you're standing there grinning like an idiot."

The Dragon inside Drystan growled savagely, but Drystan just managed to shove him down. Primarily for Callispa's sake. He didn't care a whit what his horrid uncle thought of him.

He did try after that. And after several tries, he began to shift on command more often than not. But it was difficult. Never did he look graceful or sleek the way Karolus or Lady Phaidra did. The change was always uneven and clumsy.

He knew one way to do it, of course. It would be effortless. All he had to do was unleash the Dragon. Give it full reign. Even as he considered it, the Dragon within purred with pleasure at the thought. But that was the problem. The animal inside wished desperately to take over. The same animal that had threatened Eirin more than once. If he gave the animal full reins...there would be no telling how far the creature might go, or what destruction he might delight in. Maybe it was Oreck's fire burning deep within him. Or maybe it was that the Dragon had been locked up for so many years. Either way, Drystan became aware that he feared little more than the creature that wished desperately to be let outside.

"You're thinking too much," Callispa said gently. "Just let your instincts take over." She gave him an encouraging smile. "Your body will know what to do if you just let it."

"That's the problem," he whispered tersely as he fought the beast back from within. "I'm afraid he'll know too well."

"Drystan," she whispered, leaning forward. "Just do it."

Drystan wanted to groan in frustration. But with everyone watching him, he sighed and closed his eyes. One. He would give the creature one glimpse of the night. Just a tiny peek. Then back in the cage it would go.

The second Drystan rolled back the cage door in his mind, the whole world exploded with light. And as Drystan felt himself contorting, stretching, and filling out, he wrestled back control. Unfortunately, the Dragon desired to return none of it. No, it wanted to fly free. He felt as though he were watching from afar, yanking on ropes that might as well be in pieces.

Even more horrific than the Dragon's desire to remain free, however, was the sight of Callispa below, going up in flames.

"Callispa!" he shouted, his voice now deep and rumbling.

The ball of flame that she had become collapsed into ashes. Eirin screamed at the blackened pile of dust below him.

He had just killed Callispa.

Strangely, Karolus looked utterly bored. Drystan wanted to rave and beat at him with his new claws and teeth, the Dragon within barely restrained by the new tether forged by horror that Drystan had put on him. But before he could say anything else, the pile of ash burst into flame. Flame that shot up into the night sky above him. In a burst of red fire, the silhouette of a large bird took shape. Then, Callispa's Human face and body appeared, only the great fiery wings remaining as they lowered her back down to the ground. When she landed, and her wings disappeared, she beamed up at him.

"That was brilliant, Drystan! Perfect!"

Drystan stared down at her. Was she mad?

She clapped and smiled. "Now, I want you to shift back to your Human form, and we'll do it again. Did you see how fast you changed that time?"

Drystan wanted to go to bed. He felt anxiety had aged him ten years in the last two minutes. But Karolus and Callispa were looking up at him expectantly.

Well, if that's what they wanted, let the games begin.

"Maybe," Karolus said, uncrossing his arms and making his way toward the steps, "there's some of Oreck's blood in you yet."

15

$\mathcal{E}$irin knew she ought to wipe the pout off her face when Callispa finally announced that Drystan's training was over for the night. The sky was beginning to lighten into a dull gray, and Eirin could feel Qeb's eyes on her more often than she was comfortable with.

It wasn't his fault that Callispa was Drystan's trainer. Or that she was beautiful with that ethereal mystique that Alys had always had. Nor was it Qeb's fault that Eirin… didn't have that.

Thankfully, Qeb was one of those people who didn't fill empty space with words unless he felt something actually needed to be said. So he remained mercifully silent as they made their way back down to Drystan's training circle.

"You did well." Callispa beamed as Drystan, back in his Human form, wiped the sweat off his brow. She lowered her voice. "And don't mind Karolus. He hasn't been the same since his son died. It's nothing you can help."

"Are you ready to go?" Eirin asked loudly as she and Qeb approached them. "I don't know about you, but I'm tired and hungry."

"Actually," Callispa said, looking at Drystan, "I was hoping to introduce you to a few other Dragons and their trainers." She glanced at Eirin and added quickly, "It should only take a few minutes."

Qeb's eyebrows went up. "There are other Dragons here? Besides Karolus and Lady Phaidra?"

Callispa nodded. "Not many. And their pedigree is nothing like Drystan's and Karolus's. But I thought it would be nice to know you're not the only ones."

Drystan shot Eirin a questioning look. She inwardly huffed like a five-year-old but nodded. Let it never be said she was holding him back.

"If you shift once more," Callispa said, "we can fly up." She nodded up at the training circles above them. The one Eirin and Qeb sat on had remained empty, but as the night had progressed, the sounds of training had come from many of the platforms nearby.

"We can do that," Drystan said.

"We'll be back," Callispa said with a bright smile before helping Drystan shift once again. Eirin stared after her, annoyance quickly growing in her chest, but when she turned, she found not a man but a hulking creature peering at her with his sharp, golden eyes. Qeb held out his clawed yellow hands and raised his great feathered wings. Despite her annoyance, Eirin smiled at the Griffin and went to him.

"I knew I always liked you," she said as he picked her up and lifted her with him off the ground.

Drystan and Callispa were already in the air, Drystan's scaled wings beating unevenly as Callispa hovered at his side.

Eirin's annoyance immediately doubled as she looked at the Phoenix in the early morning light. In all her time studying at the Citadel, Eirin had come across very little information about Phoenixes. All she knew was that they could regenerate after being engulfed in flames. She'd always wondered why a Phoenix would be engulfed in flames in the first place, as no sane creature she knew about would ever wish to be that close to a large fire. But now that she understood their role in this world—training Dragons—it made sense.

What the scroll hadn't mentioned, however, was the Phoenix's beauty. When in Atharrach form, Callispa's bright red hair burst into flame where it waved gently in the breeze. This made sense, as in her Human form, her bright orange magic covered her hairline. Two orange wings of fire had burst forth from her back. They were shaped much like hawk wings, and though Eirin was too far away to be sure, she was pretty certain the girl had fire in her eyes as well. Eirin slumped back into Qeb's arms. He sent her a curious look, but being Qeb, said nothing.

For that, she was very glad.

They followed Drystan and Callispa up several levels to a training circle that was four times the size of the one Drystan had been practicing on. Qeb brought them down to rest at the edge of the circle, where they waited and watched.

Not one but three Dragons were there, each with a red-haired Phoenix. Two males and one female Dragon, and two females and one male Phoenix. And every Dragon was smaller than Drystan.

"Good morning!" Callispa called in her low, velvety voice. "I wanted to introduce Drystan."

Eirin watched Drystan carefully. Would these Dragons reject him as most of the city had?

To her surprise, they all turned to him with wary but kind smiles.

"This is Lee and his wife, Priscilla," Callispa said, indicating the couple on the left. The male Dragon shifted into his Human form as Callispa spoke. "And that's Hu and his wife, Chloe." She nodded at the third couple, the female Dragon and the red-haired man. "And that's Ju and her trainer, Gregory."

To Eirin's surprise, the other Dragons moved closer until they and their trainers were all standing in a circle with Drystan and Callispa.

A circle, it seemed, that Eirin and Qeb were not invited into.

Drystan shifted into his Human form, though his change wasn't nearly as fast as the others' were. Still, no one here seemed to scoff the way Karolus had. Instead, they merely waited.

"Do you live here?" Drystan asked when he was finally in his Human form. "I haven't seen you since arriving."

"We don't." Chloe looked up and smiled at her husband. "We all live in smaller villages nearby. But Lady Phaidra allows us to train here."

"Are you going to be staying here as well?" Ju asked. Though

Callispa had introduced them as Dragon and trainer, Eirin watched as Gregory casually draped his arm over her shoulder.

"Well, isn't that cozy?"

Eirin squeaked and then turned to find Nuru standing on her other side. She was in her Atharrach form, standing like a proud house cat as she studied the Dragons and their trainers. Even in a seated position, her head nearly reached Eirin's shoulder. Her tail flicked sharply from side to side.

"Let us introduce you to our children," Priscilla said, turning and motioning to someone Eirin couldn't see. As the children ran up, Hu nodded at Eirin.

"Are you betrothed to the Human?"

Drystan's eyes briefly met Eirin's, and for some reason, she felt her face burn as he spoke.

"No. We came here together from Torbaine. I've promised to keep her safe while she makes her way to the Time Stones."

"She's smiling a little too brightly for my taste," Nuru said, narrowing her eyes at Callispa. Eirin followed her gaze.

Yes, she looked just a little too happy about that.

After several minutes of quiet talk and the introduction of Lee and Priscilla's three children, the group finally said their goodbyes and split up.

"Are you ready to go back?" Drystan asked Eirin and their friends, seeming unsurprised by Nuru's addition to the party.

Eirin nodded, but as they made their way down, Eirin didn't miss the lingering look Callispa sent Drystan before heading off in the other direction. It was…wistful, Eirin decided.

And far too full of hope.

16

$\mathcal{E}$irin was exhausted from the long night. They would need to get into a sleeping schedule soon, or she might lose her mind. Still, when she was finally back in her room and in her bed, she couldn't lose consciousness no matter how much she tried. Instead, she tossed and turned. Half-dreams and thoughts ran together until she was seeing a never-ending loop in her head of Callispa's flaming hair and Drystan's fire.

A knock startled her awake enough to realize that she must have fallen asleep after all. She didn't have time to even walk to the door, however, because Nuru unlocked the door and let herself in. She was carrying a bowl of fruit and bread.

"Apparently," she said as she shut the door behind her, "there's a dining hall for those who work for Lady Phaidra. You can get food there all day, though they've started limiting it lately due to constraints."

Eirin stared at the bowl. "If that's limited, I can't imagine what it was before the constraints were set in place."

Nuru shrugged and put the bowl on the writing table. Then she grabbed an orange and plopped down on her bed in silence. As she stared at her roommate's back, Eirin was once again reminded of just how much had changed in the last year.

How she missed Alys.

"I was talking to some of the other Sphinxes," Nuru said slowly as

153

she peeled her orange. "And, apparently, it's expected that Dragons will fall in love with their Phoenixes."

Eirin had just taken a bite of an apple. She choked as she swallowed and had to wait an embarrassing amount of time under Nuru's annoyed gaze to cough it all up.

"I'm sorry," she finally croaked. "Go on."

Nuru sniffed and turned daintily back to her orange. "At least half of the Solevarian queens were Phoenixes. The princes and their trainers spend so much time together that it's somewhat inevitable."

Eirin's apple suddenly felt mealy, and she fought the desire to spit it out and throw it away. She knew better, though, than to show that kind of weakness in front of Nuru. She'd already given too much away as it was.

Though really...what was she giving away? Eirin rubbed her eyes. She really needed sleep.

"It makes sense, I suppose," Nuru said matter-of-factly, daintily pulling a slice off.

"What does?" Eirin asked.

"Callispa. She watched him as though she was already naming their grandchildren."

Eirin wanted to groan. This wasn't making her feel any better. If only Alys were here. Alys would have known how to be properly affronted on Eirin's behalf. But Alys wasn't there, and Nuru, for all her faults, was. And, it seemed, she was trying. She'd gone out in search of information on Eirin's behalf...even if she then dropped that information on Eirin like an avalanche.

Callispa was beautiful in a way Eirin was not. There was no denying that. Not that Eirin thought herself bad-looking. But not being hideous wasn't exactly the kind of appeal to stir passionate, romantic desire.

And not only was Callispa beautiful, but she would literally be touching Drystan more than possibly anyone else. She'd already touched him all over for their first training session. Nothing to overstep boundaries or that was untoward. Every touch had been corrections to his stance or to shuffle him right or left. But Callispa had been touching him all the less.

Eirin wished she could be angry at Drystan. That would make

this all easier. But it had been her choice to stay in Mhaedin. She had even encouraged him to train. She just… hadn't known that training would involve a woman with the desire to marry him.

"So that's it? You're just going to stare off into the blue?" Nuru scoffed.

Eirin shook her head and looked at Nuru. "I'm sorry, what was that?"

Nuru rolled her eyes and flopped back down on the bed. "Forget it. I was just wondering if you were simply going to stare and pine away forever."

Eirin's face flushed. "I'm… I'm not sure what there is to say. He and I have never had any sort of agreement. I mean, there were times that…" her voice drifted off as she remembered when he had pressed his head against hers in the cavern after the first time he had shifted. And when he'd held her hand. And when he'd squeezed her knee. But what was that really? He'd told her once that he couldn't marry or have a family because being attached to him would put them in danger. His circumstances might be different now, but who was to say he had changed his mind? It wasn't as if they weren't out of danger yet.

"This is the problem with you," Nuru scoffed as she rolled over. "You think too much."

"I'm not sure what you want me to say." Annoyance flared up. "Drystan's a big boy. He can make his own decisions."

Nuru snorted. "I just thought you were more of a fighter than this. That's all."

Eirin had a smart retort on her tongue when bells began to toll outside.

"Agh! What is that?" Nuru yanked the covers over her head. "Does anyone ever sleep around here? Up all night for required training and then bells in the morning!"

Eirin stood and went to the door. Two women and a man–people she didn't recognize–had left their rooms and were making their way to the nearest set of stairs.

"What's happening?" Eirin called out to them.

They looked back and seemed surprised to be addressed, but one of the women answered.

"Everyone's being summoned to the Bastion. Something big must have happened."

Eirin turned around to find Nuru right behind her. Eirin squeaked.

"How do you do that?"

Nuru shoved her out the door. "Let's go, Human."

Eirin allowed herself to be moved outside, but she couldn't help snapping back, "Are you sure you want to spend more time around me if I'm that annoying?"

Nuru gave her a wry smile. "You might be annoying, but I'd like not to die. Can't have you getting crushed in the crowds." And with that, she shivered for a moment before beginning to shift. Once she was in her Sphinx form, she bent her front legs and lowered her shoulders and back.

Eirin stared at her. "What... I'm supposed to *ride* you now? You can't be–"

Before she could finish, Nuru bumped her hard enough to knock her over, throwing her body beneath Eirin and catching her as she fell.

"Fine then," Eirin said, glowering at the Sphinx as she righted herself. "But you'd better not drop me." She had barely straddled Nuru's back when Nuru shot forward, and it was all Eirin could do to hold on for dear life as Nuru made her way down into the crowd.

17

"Drystan, wake up."

Drystan sat up in bed so fast that he nearly fell over. "What is it?" he croaked, rubbing his eyes as he did his best to stand.

"There's something going on." Qeb was standing at the open door. "A call went out, and everyone's heading back into the city."

Drystan already had one foot in one boot and was fumbling with the second. This continuously changing sleep schedule might just do to him what the angry Fae had failed to do back in the mountain.

"Where's Thane?" he asked, glancing around. "Why didn't he wake us up?"

"He's not here." Qeb's deep voice was thick with disgust. "I woke up when I heard a door slam."

"The girls?" Drystan stood and grabbed his room key from the writing table.

"Gone." Qeb's voice was grim. "I would have gone after them myself, but I thought you'd want to come too."

Drystan joined his friend outside the door and locked it. "Which way do you think they went?" They would have either gone down the stairs to the main road or taken the path in front of their rooms to the higher road.

Qeb frowned. "Can you smell them?"

Drystan gave him an odd look, but Qeb just gave him a grim

159

smile. "Griffins have a terrible sense of smell, it seems. Not that I'm surprised."

Drystan frowned. He'd never tried to smell someone in his Human form...or in his Dragon form, for that matter. But now, he closed his eyes and focused.

At first, he had no idea what to even search for. He was sure Eirin had a particular smell, and that Nuru would as well. All people did. But he was surprised to find that he was able to identify them both much faster than he would have expected in his Human form. Eirin's was easy to pick out. She smelled faintly of roses and herbs. It was from her little bar of soap, the one he'd seen her washing her face and arms with on occasion. Nuru had a similar bar of soap, but hers had no roses, and she also smelled slightly of cat.

"That way." Drystan pointed down the path that ran in front of their rooms. He and Qeb broke into a sprint, but they were forced to slow when they reached the road. It seemed every soul in the city was making his way slowly to the center of the city. Drystan and Qeb wove their way in and out of the groups of people around them. Several cries of protest went up from those they cut in front of, but he couldn't have cared less.

"I would bet we're going to the Bastion," Qeb said in a low voice.

Drystan looked back at him. "Where?"

"My trainer showed me yesterday," Qeb said as they rounded a corner. "Griffins are usually used for protection, so he wanted me to see all the main parts of the city."

"But what is it?"

"It's a great cavern deep in the mountain, nearly as big as the one Torbaine is in." Qeb gave a withering look to a large woman sending them a nasty glare. "An arena was built there as a place where the city could host meetings and have discussions. But they also use it in times of danger. It's the safest part of the mountain."

Drystan pushed harder, and Qeb kept pace, but Drystan's mind went in circles as they walked.

It was unlikely that the whole city was being herded to the Bastion because of a threat. For while the people were moving at a steady pace, none were particularly apprehensive. With a start,

Drystan realized that he knew this because he couldn't smell their fear. When had he learned to smell fear?

"I'm losing their scent," he said in a low voice to Qeb. "There are too many people here."

Qeb nodded and stretched, trying to look over the heads of those around them. Both he and Drystan were taller than most of the crowd. Still, neither of them could see Eirin or Nuru. Eirin was short enough that Drystan somewhat expected this. But Nuru was tall, and her absence further concerned him.

"Nuru will take care of her," Qeb said quietly.

"I'll bet you my future coins that the boy has found them by now."

Qeb chuckled softly. "He's almost our age."

Drystan snorted. "Would you call him a man?" On appearance alone...perhaps. He was growing the beginnings of an acceptable beard. But the feeling Mannish emitted was too much like a puppy to think of him as anything else.

They weren't far from Eirin's scholars' room, and Drystan began to wonder if he ought to check there, when people began to squeeze together as they neared a large stone entrance, pinning Drystan and Qeb in line. Drystan hadn't noticed the cavern mouth before, but now it was impossible to miss. They passed through a short tunnel lit by torches before moving into an arena of breathtaking size.

Drystan couldn't see the rock ceiling for the darkness, but dozens of banners hung down from it, emblazoned with what looked like family crests, though they were difficult to see because of the number of flying creatures who hovered above, trying to find a place to sit. A large round dais stood in the center, circular steps leading down to the lowest level of stone benches. There were five more entrances through which poured more people. The stone benches, which had been cut into the walls and floor, were already filling fast. Lady Phaidra stood on the dais, talking quietly with Hector and a few other Atharrachs, three of whom were in their shifter forms.

"Do you see them?" Drystan asked, scanning the rows already taken.

"There." Qeb pointed down to the lowest level beside the dais. Sure enough, Eirin was sitting at the foot of the dais with Nuru on one side and Mannish on the other.

"The lowest rows are too full for us to sit near them," Qeb said, his brow creasing slightly. "We'll have to sit further back."

Drystan growled.

"Karolus is near her. He'll make sure she's safe." Qeb tugged on Drystan's shoulder. "I see some open spots in the eleventh row if we can get there in time."

Drystan let his friend drag him along, but he made a mental note to move closer to Eirin the first chance he got.

When they were about halfway there, Drystan caught a glimpse of a pale blond head. Sure enough, Thane was laughing with a group of young men who could only be Centaurs. They were all built tall, sleek, and powerful the way Thane was.

"So that's where he is," Qeb grumbled.

Drystan shook his head and focused on reaching their seats. He would have a word with Thane later. *Although...*a voice in his head wondered, *would Thane really listen?*

Drystan was no longer Thane's future king. They had merely been companions for weeks, traveling together to escape a dangerous past as they tried to save the future. Yes, Drystan had taken the role of leader. But there were no legal constraints binding Thane to obey him. And once again, Drystan was hit with the nauseating uncertainty that had plagued him since leaving Torbaine. Where exactly did he fit in all of this?

Eirin flipped her braid over her shoulder, and Drystan's eye was drawn to the movement as they slowly made their way over. When he saw her, the nausea died down somewhat. He was Eirin's protector. He could figure the rest out later. What mattered now was getting Eirin safely to Iilaedin. That was more than enough to occupy his thoughts and labors for a long time.

They eventually found seats about six rows behind Eirin and Nuru, which meant Drystan had an excellent view each time Mannish leaned forward and spoke with the girls. Nuru quickly bored of him, but Eirin kept her sweet countenance and had a smile and laugh ready for whatever dribble he uttered often. What had she been thinking? Had she and Nuru gone off with Mannish rather than waiting for him?

A hush fell over the arena as Lady Phaidra raised her hands and walked to the center of the dais. She smiled as she turned slowly in a circle.

"I called you here," she began in a clear, strong voice, "because we have reason to rejoice. More than one reason, actually." She paused, and the air hummed with anticipation.

"Not so long ago, we received an unexpected gift. A Human came to us after we'd believed them all dead. A sign, we believed, from the Time Keeper that we ought to try once more." She sighed and dropped her head. When she spoke again, her voice was low. "Unfortunately, we were arrogant in our zeal, and we pushed out before we were ready. And we paid dearly for it."

Drystan looked around. How did these people view their leaders' mistake? Did they, too, consider themselves a part of the problem? Or were they angry?

Karolus was angry.

Finally, after a moment of silence, a tall female Giant stood. She looked like the one who had taken offense to him in the throne room.

"You promised us success with our last Human's arrival," she said, her voice bouncing off the stone walls. "And we paid for your foolishness with the blood of our children!"

The room began to buzz with murmurs. But Lady Phaidra's face stayed open and sympathetic.

"You promised us salvation!" The Giantess began to cry, large tears spilling down her cheeks, "So why should we believe you now?"

Others began to shout, and a few stood up. Drystan met Qeb's eye, and he knew they were thinking the same thing. If it got much rowdier, they would have to whisk Eirin away. The last thing she needed was some sorrow-blinded Giantess accidentally stepping on her.

"I lost my child, too, Leah."

The crowd's sounds went silent, and Drystan's gaze snapped back to Lady Phaidra. But she showed no sign of tears. Instead, her eyes began to blaze with embers, and Drystan could feel the air vibrate even from where he sat.

"But the sacrifice wasn't in vain," Lady Phaidra continued, her voice growing louder and deeper with each word. "We learned a lesson that day. We will never rush out with such arrogance again. And now that we are wiser…" She looked at Eirin, and her face fairly glowed, "we are closer than we've ever been before.

"Ouch," Qeb whispered, nodding down at Mannish with a slight smirk. "Someone clearly has a favorite."

But Mannish didn't appear offended at all. Actually, he seemed nearly as delighted as Lady Phaidra. The partial smile Drystan could see from where Mannish sat looked as brilliant as Lady Phaidra's smile was fierce.

"Our new Human has proven today," Lady Phaidra continued, "that even though her powers are still young, she is what we refer to as a rare kind of Seer, one that's only heard of every few Human generations. The Elves called her kind the Thallahst."

Drystan's gaze was drawn to Eirin, who was sitting stone still. He couldn't see her face, but he could tell from the slightly hunched set of her shoulders that she was feeling vulnerable.

"Everyone," Lady Phaidra said, holding her hand out toward Eirin, "I would like to introduce you to our newest Seer, Eirin from Torbaine." She wiggled her fingers as if summoning Eirin up to the dais.

Eirin looked at Nuru for a moment before Nuru nodded. Eirin slowly rose from her seat, and even more slowly, climbed steps to the dais.

"She's a Dragon, Drystan."

Drystan looked at Qeb. "What?"

"You'll crack your jaw in two if you keep grinding it that hard," Qeb said. "I was reminding you that Lady Phaidra is a Dragon. If anyone can keep Eirin safe up there, it's her." He nodded further down. "And there's Karolus."

Drystan frowned. Qeb had a point. Well, two really. But that didn't mean he had to like it.

"Today," Lady Phaidra said, drawing Eirin gently to her side, keeping her left hand on Eirin's shoulder at all times, "Eirin proved that not only is she a Seer of the Time Stones, but she can See the memories of other objects, things outside of the Time Stones."

"How does that help us?" someone called out.

"It means," Lady Phaidra said, "that we have a stronger Seer than we have ever hosted before."

"So." A Fenris stood. Drystan was rather sure he was the head of the Fenris clan, but he couldn't be certain. "You speak of leaving again. How can we know that this won't be a repeat of what happened last time?"

"We can't." Lady Phaidra took a deep breath. "There is no guarantee. We could fail spectacularly. But I will also say that if we don't do something, there will soon be nothing left to save."

The crowd broke out into a roar of murmurs and talk, but Lady Phaidra raised her voice above them. It rumbled slightly.

"Our food is in depletion. We estimate that we shall not have enough to make it through this winter."

The noise of the arena became nearly deafening.

"But!" Lady Phaidra raised her voice again. The sound of it was closer to a roar than a shout, and the stone seats rumbled beneath them. Most of the noise stopped as she held the people in place with her glowing eyes. "But," she continued again in a lower voice, "even if we fail, we will lay our heads down on the last nights of our life knowing we gave our children every chance we could."

Movement drew his attention, and Drystan realized Karolus was on his feet, his eyes glowing embers as he glared at a darkened corner of the nearest arena entrance. There was a figure standing in the shadows, tall and powerfully built. And though he'd only seen him once before, it took Drystan only a few seconds to recognize Rangvald.

Drystan was halfway down the steps to the dais, cursing himself for allowing Eirin to stand up there alone as he sprinted toward her. Qeb followed on his heels. They arrived at Eirin's side as Lady Phaidra raised her voice.

"Rangvald. Welcome." Her tone was anything but welcoming.

Rangvald lowered the hood of his cloak and sighed. "You've no need to worry. I've only come to see her." His eyes rested on Eirin, and Drystan heard himself snarl.

Rangvald's sharp eyes moved to Drystan. "So the rumors are true, nephew." His voice was oddly gentle. "You do favor him, despite the generations." His voice dropped to a whisper. "You could be his son, and I wouldn't have known better. You have his eyes. And…" He waved a finger at his own temple. "Yes. The shape of your face." He gave Drystan a small, thoughtful smile.

Only then did Drystan realize that Rangvald had only seen him in his Dragon form before this. That would explain the reminiscing.

"What do you want, Rangvald?" Karolus growled, making Drystan and Rangvald jump slightly.

Rangvald drew in a deep breath and then sighed. "I want to come with you."

"After what you pulled last time?" Karolus snapped.

"I told you! That wasn't my fault."

Against his better judgment, Drystan couldn't help noting for a second time that Rangvald was very unlike the villain he had imagined. The man who had sent dozens of mercenaries to fetch Eirin to him after sending an army to attack Torbaine in search of her had seemed the most ruthless kind of man in Drystan's estimation. This man, however, was soft-spoken and gentle. Never once had he tried to force Eirin to come to him against her will. And now he was being kinder to Drystan than Karolus ever had.

It didn't make sense.

"Let me come with you." He turned to Lady Phaidra. "Phaidra, I want to help."

Lady Phaidra studied him warily. "The last time you helped, everything fell apart."

"My people are starving too." He held her gaze. "What do I gain by your failure?"

Neither Lady Phaidra nor Karolus answered him.

Scoffing, Rangvald shook his head and turned to Eirin. "I can see that you're surrounded by all sorts of help here," he said. "But if you ever decide you need me, I'll not be far off."

Then he turned his piercing gaze to Drystan. "I know their wealth and accommodations can be tempting, but don't believe everything here is as it seems." He nodded at Eirin. "Just as I told her, my door is always open to you." Then he turned and stalked out of the room.

As soon as Rangvald was gone, Drystan turned to Lady Phaidra and Karolus.

"We need to talk."

Lady Phaidra sighed and looked down at the ground before straightening and turning to her people, who waited, looking as though they'd seen a ghost.

"Go back to your day. We will let you know what has been decided once we've made more plans. But know this." Her eyes blazed once again. "We will be going back to Iilaedin. And the Time Stones *will* turn once again."

She whirled around and walked off the dais, her head held high. Hector, who seemed to appear out of nowhere, smiled and gestured for Drystan to follow. Drystan put his hand on Eirin's back and gently guided her to walk in front of him. He kept his hand there even when they were off the dais and exiting the arena behind Lady Phaidra. And to his surprise, she didn't shake him off.

Perhaps it was because of Rangvald's sudden appearance. Or Lady Phaidra's unspoken loss. Or the fact that the city's leaders had chosen to make plans without them. Whatever the reason, he and Eirin were both shaken. He could feel it from the others too. Nuru and Qeb drew closer to them as they walked. And as if summoned, Thane burst through the tunnel behind them and placed himself at Nuru's side as if he'd been there the whole time.

"What's happening?" he whispered.

"Well, look who decided to show up," Nuru snapped.

Thane gave her a confused look. "I was training when the bells went off." He put his hand out, probably to tug playfully on her hair, but Nuru only sniffed and moved up beside Qeb.

Drystan sent them a warning look, and the group was silent then as they wound through several smaller hallways and tunnels until they came to a door. Karolus removed a key and then paused, sending Lady Phaidra a questioning look.

Lady Phaidra nodded and turned to Drystan. "These are delicate discussions we'll be having." She paused and glanced behind him at Qeb, Nuru, and Thane. "Perhaps it would be better if we entertained only a…small party. We usually don't entertain even our clan heads at such talks."

Drystan shook his head. "We're in this together." He turned and gave Thane a pointed glare, which Thane had the decency to blush at. "All of us."

In spite of the exhaustion around her eyes, Lady Phaidra smiled slightly. "Very well. Let's talk."

They entered, finding themselves in the same small antechamber they'd sat in the first day they'd come. Had that really only been a few days ago? Drystan felt as though he'd lived a lifetime since then.

Lady Phaidra sat at the head of the table and waited for everyone else to be seated, but Drystan didn't wait to hear what she had to say.

"Before we talk about anything else, I need to know in truth whether or not Rangvald will be a threat to Eirin."

Lady Phaidra sighed. "I don't believe so."

After meeting him, Drystan was inclined to agree with her. But he had to ask. Satisfied for the moment, he pressed on. "And what did he mean about *last time?*"

Karolus, Hector, and Lady Phaidra shared a long look.

"Up until recently, we worked with Rangvald and his people on a regular basis."

"His people?" Eirin asked.

Lady Phaidra nodded. "When the curse fell, each prince was followed by his supporters. Kamon to Torbaine." She nodded at

Drystan. "Karolus here, and Rangvald to an old defensive fortress compound just southwest of here at the foot of the mountain."

Karolus grunted. "Not that they're protected from the real danger."

"What do you mean?" Eirin asked.

"It's the mountains," Hector said. "Much of the poison blows in from the southern dunes. The mountains block us from most of the poison as it blows north. It's why we're able to grow so much food here compared to everywhere else."

"The last time we set out for Iilaedin," Karolus said, "Rangvald promised to meet us on the way, as he always did. We'd worked together for years, as we'd found that we were more likely to make it to Iilaedin together than on our own."

"Wait," Eirin said, sitting up. "Lady Seren said that there was a rift between the princes when the curse fell." She paused. "Wasn't Rangvald one of those princes?"

Lady Phaidra nodded. "There was. But after the curse fell and Kamon disappeared, Rangvald and Karolus's father, Dimitrius, joined forces whenever they could to try to stop the curse. And after Dimitrius died, Karolus took his place."

"We'd worked together for years," Karolus picked up again. "And we were getting better at it. The Humans were finally starting to survive the journey there, and several made it weeks past arrival." His jaw hardened. "Then, about twenty years ago, the Humans disappeared. We began to believe all Humans were gone by then, and so did Rangvald. Then Mannish appeared out of nowhere."

Lady Phaidra sighed. "We were sure we could get him safely to the stones."

Karolus glared at his hands. "We called Rangvald, as we always had, and we made plans to join our forces." He paused and looked at Lady Phaidra.

"What happened?" Thane asked, glancing back and forth between them.

"He was supposed to meet us along the way," Lady Phaidra said slowly. "But he never did. Neither he nor his forces joined us at the agreed-upon location."

"After three days of waiting for them," Karolus growled, "we gave up and moved on."

"It's dangerous in Solevar to sit too long in any one place," Hector added quietly, his eyes distant.

Karolus nodded. "The next day, we were attacked by a group of angry Basilisks."

Drystan's blood ran cold, and he could tell from Eirin's expression that she felt the same way. "Basilisks?" he asked. "You mean the ones with the paralyzing voices?"

"In the times before the curse," Hector said, "they were often quite helpful. They can speak without paralyzing, of course. But they saved law enforcement from a great deal of bloodshed by paralyzing the criminals who tried to escape punishment."

"Unfortunately," Karolus said, his voice hard, "many have chosen to embrace their animalistic side since the curse fell. They came at us from the sides and from above. Anyone who tried to fly was paralyzed and sent crashing to the ground." He shook his head and sat back. "What made it even more suspect, though, was that while they acted animalistic, we knew there was a mastermind behind the attack."

"How did you know that?" Drystan asked.

"They tried to take Mannish."

Everyone was quiet for a moment until Eirin broke the silence.

"I thought you said there was a snowstorm."

"Oh, there was," Lady Phaidra said. "Though it might have been a blessing, I suppose, if you look at it the right way. The Basilisks were doing great damage to our forces when it began. Their attack stopped when the ice and snow were too thick to see through. But if it was a blessing, it soured quickly. There was little we could do but wait it out. Mannish, who had barely escaped being abducted, nearly died."

"How did Rangvald excuse his delay?" Qeb asked. "He claimed today that it wasn't on purpose."

Karolus stood and leaned on the back of the chair. "He arrived after the snowstorm, claiming that he'd been worried sick." Karolus rolled his eyes. "He said there had been a delay with his people. An illness had broken out among them that had prevented them from coming when they were supposed to. They arrived just as we returned to Mhaedin."

"Do you have a reason to disbelieve what he said?" Eirin asked.

"No...and yes," Lady Phaidra sighed. "There *was* an illness that had spread throughout his compound. But when we enquired about it, we learned that it was an illness suffered by children. Not adults. And there were certainly no children who would have come on the journey with us."

"So they stayed behind to nurse their sick children?" Eirin asked.

"They could have," Hector said. "But the illness itself wasn't a severe one. Nothing to remain home for." He shook his head. "You can see now why we struggle so greatly with trust.

"But what would he gain by your failure?" Qeb asked.

"Nothing," Karolus said. "And we might have believed him except that our Human was nearly taken."

They were all silent for a moment, and Drystan was glad. He'd guessed a history existed between the two older Sons of Oreck, and he'd been right. But Lady Phaidra was also correct. It was difficult to know what might have happened. That a group of Basilisks would have risked joining together to attack a well-stocked travel party... possible. That they would happen to strike the traveling party and then go after the Human? Unlikely. Just as it had been unlikely that the children's mild illness would have prevented an entire army from marching forth to save the kingdom from its curse. Particularly without any news from their leader.

"When Mannish came to us," Hector finally broke the silence, "we were thrilled. Long had we believed we would die a slow and painful death. But when we made our plans to go, we didn't realize what a large protective force Rangvald's had been. Even though we brought an even greater number of Atharrachs with us than we ever had before, it wasn't enough to make up for the difference." He sighed. "Traveling with a Human makes the entire force vulnerable. We didn't stand a chance."

"So what will make this journey different?" Drystan asked. "Why do you expect success this time when the last one ended in disaster?"

Lady Phaidra gave him an amused smirk. "Shouldn't that be obvious?"

Drystan and his friends stared at her, but her smile only grew.

"This time, we have another son of Oreck with us."

"With the exception of our last attempt, we have always taken two sons of Oreck," Hector said, smiling as well. "And now that you are here, Drystan, we have yet two again."

"Which means," Karolus said, turning his steely gaze on Drystan, "you have work to do."

19

*I*n the days and weeks after Lady Phaidra's fateful announcement, Eirin did her best to lose herself in her studies.

The ache in her heart for her family and her best friend sometimes threatened to consume her. When that happened, she would close her eyes and imagine her mother's arms around her. She would imagine all the things in Mhaedin that her father would wish to draw, and all the trouble her little brothers would get into. The few times when she was alone in her room, she would talk as though Alys were listening.

"It's a good thing you aren't here," she told Alys about a week after arriving. "You and Nuru would likely end up in some bloody duel. She gets up at the most random times and just leaves. It drives Qeb and Drystan crazy. And she returns in the same way too." Of course, Alys wasn't there to answer. But Eirin knew her well enough to know exactly how she would respond.

Which sometimes made it all the worse.

To her surprise, though, Eirin found quickly that she wasn't as alone as she'd first thought. Drystan was a surprising source of comfort. Not because he said many wise and meaningful things, but because he was there. Often hovering at her side, she felt his presence, even when focusing on other things. His magic was warm, the way the sun had been in her vision. She could feel it even from

177

across a room. And if she was ever tempted to wonder if he had tired of her or found her burdensome, the notion was quickly put to rest when she caught him watching her, his eyes alight with curious interest.

What he saw in her, she couldn't begin to imagine. But she liked having him there nonetheless.

The others were helpful as well. Qeb, though he was often training, stayed with her when Drystan couldn't. Thane, when he was present, though that was far less than Qeb, never failed to make her laugh. Even Nuru, despite her moods, was a source of stability, like the fourth corner of a room.

And then there were her studies.

Every afternoon, Eirin, Mannish, and Drystan went to the scholars' room, where Eirin pored over maps and books and scrolls and every other source of information she could get her hands on. Learning about Solevar and all its creatures was like eating after a period of starvation. Eirin couldn't get enough. Even Mannish teased her about it two weeks after her arrival.

"This is the fourth time you've read that story," he laughed after leaning over her shoulder to get a closer look at the book she had perched on her lap. "What's it about?"

Eirin could feel Drystan's glare from across the room and had to smother a smile. Mannish seemed to have very little sense of personal space, and it annoyed Drystan to no end.

"It's the ancient story of the first Will-o'-the-Wisp." She closed the book and ran her hand lightly over the gold-etched image on the cover. What would her father look like in his Atharrach form?

"I've read it before." Mannish crouched on the rug beside where she was curled up. "But I didn't find it nearly so interesting as you seem to. Now I'm even more curious."

Eirin frowned thoughtfully as she traced the book's carefully sewn binding. "I suppose it's the mercy."

Mannish's eyes widened. "The mercy?" He took the book and opened it to the page she'd been reading. As he did, his knee shifted close enough to touch hers. "I don't remember noting anything particularly merciful about a creature who was sentenced to losing his body for playing a trick."

Eirin shook her head. "Perhaps at first glance. But the Time Keeper could have punished him far more severely than He did." She took the book from Mannish, their hands brushing as she did. Sneaking a side-glance at Drystan, she half-wondered if it was possible for Dragons to spontaneously combust. Drystan had always been protective, but he'd hovered more than ever after Rangvald's visit.

Why he cared so much about Mannish, however, she couldn't quite make out. Mannish obviously wasn't a threat. This Human male was probably one of the few people Eirin could beat soundly in a fight, thanks to her years of physical training with the Atharrachs. Not that Mannish would ever put her in that position.

"More severely than revoking his body?" Mannish asked with an incredulous laugh.

"But it really could have been worse," she protested. "Instead of killing him on the spot or putting him through pain and agony, the Time Keeper took the Will-o'-the-Wisp's body and turned his Atharrach form into pure light. It was a punishment...and yet, it wasn't." She shook her head. "What he did really was deserving of death. The Will-o'-the-Wisp had forced a whole group of Brownies into a bog and left them there. They could have died."

She shook her head and sat back, still looking thoughtfully at the text. "By all accounts, he should have forfeited his life for the lives he tried to take. But instead of killing him, the Time Keeper took his physical form so he couldn't force anyone to follow him ever again. But at the same time, He gave the Will-o'-the-Wisp a new form that could travel over nearly any terrain in nearly any weather. He took away his power to harm others by force but also gave him the power to explore to his heart's content." She shrugged. "Mercy."

"Huh," Mannish said. "I never thought of it that way."

"My mother told me that it's a tradition of the Seers. Of my family, anyway. That we've passed down stories through generations of how the Time Keeper has always provided a way..." She paused. "Through mercy."

As she spoke, she felt that now familiar tug, the urge to touch the urn once more. To taste the life in that garden in the vision.

And, if she was telling the truth, the death she felt there as well. Why was there death in the garden?

She shook her head and began gathering up the books and scrolls that she'd scattered around the rug.

"Since coming here, I've noticed other similar stories as well. Many from the time when the Time Keeper still walked the earth."

Mannish chuckled and ran his hand through his hair. "I suppose you and I have a different definition of mercy." Eirin raised her eyebrows at him, which only made him laugh more. "I can see what you mean, though." Then he shook his head. "I'm not sure what it all signifies, though. I mean, how is any of this going to help us restore the Time Stones?"

"I...I can't say for sure," Eirin said, slowly stacking her books in a neat pile. The sound of someone clearing his throat across the room made her look at the window. "I suppose it is time to be going. I'll just pick these up first." She reached out to take her stack of books, but Mannish put his hand on hers.

"Actually," he said, "I think I'll look over some of these again. Maybe something will stand out to me that hasn't before." He gave her a grin. "Who knows? Maybe the student has now become the master."

Eirin rolled her eyes and smiled. Then she bid him goodbye as she followed Drystan into the streets. As they set out for Drystan's training, she wondered if Mannish was right. Was she seeing things that weren't there? Was she imagining the patterns she had spotted in history?

"What do you think it means?"

Eirin started a little. "I'm sorry. What?"

Drystan was peering down at her as they walked. His expression was as curious as Mannish's had been.

"So you were listening." She bumped his shoulder with hers. Well, his arm. His shoulder was higher than her head. "I thought you had decided to ignore all things Mannish."

He rolled his eyes. "I ignore his prattling. But this was your idea." He gave her another studious look. "You seemed to think the stories might help you with the Time Stones."

Eirin took a deep breath. "I'm... I'm not sure how to explain it, but I'll try. I suppose I keep seeing the Time Keeper's mercy in those early days. And even now, once you think about it."

"How so?" Drystan raised a dark eyebrow. "We seem pretty thoroughly cursed."

"We do." Eirin nodded. "And yet...if you look at all the awful things we've done. To ourselves and to each other. Even *since* the curse. We all deserve punishment. But... we're not dead. Not all of us. Not even close." She pulled her braid over her shoulder and began to unbraid it as they stopped to stand in line at one of the food vendors. The sun had gone down, and the evening air gently ruffled her hair as she brushed through it with her fingers. "I think that Kamon's attempt to change fate was perhaps the final straw. But as I said, we're still not dead. We have air to breathe. Food to eat. Family and friends." She eyed a woman laughing as her gaggle of children made silly faces at one another. "We think Kamon's foreign stone must be removed from the original Time Stone circle. But... I'm starting to think it might be more complicated than that."

"So...you think removing the stone alone won't fix it?"

"Not necessarily. I mean, I don't know for sure, of course. But I do think something will have to change. Eventually, the debt will come due. And that's what worries me." She accepted the stuffed bread Drystan handed her and began walking again, eating as they went. "I just...I feel like the better I can get to know the Time Keeper, perhaps the better I'll See how this can all be resolved."

"That sounds foreboding." Drystan stopped in front of the steps that led up to the training center and folded his arms across his chest. His eyes twinkled, but Eirin could feel the tension rolling off him in waves.

"Not foreboding, necessarily," Eirin said slowly. "Again and again, I see mercy. And I'm trying to find its origins. Why the Time Maker gives it at all and how to get more." She paused. "And then my mother told me–"

"Anytime, Drystan," Karolus called from above.

Drystan took a deep breath, and amber flashed briefly in his eyes before he turned and gestured for Eirin to walk ahead of him.

Eirin laughed and began climbing the stone steps. For all his brooding, which was what Drystan had been known well for back at the Citadel, he was an excellent listener.

When they reached the top, Eirin continued on toward the next set of steps that would take her to her perch. Qeb was already sitting there, waiting for her as he always was these days. And Callispa, Drystan's ever-helpful trainer, was waiting for Drystan with her usual beaming smile on the other side of the training circle. Eirin's smile seemed to melt from her face.

"Eirin!"

Eirin turned around to see Drystan walking backward as he spoke.

"What?" she called back.

"If you think that's what will save us, then keep searching."

Eirin sent him a wry smile. "I could be wrong."

"But then again," he spread his arms, "you could be right. You have been before." Then with a wink, he turned and headed for Karolus and Callispa. And Eirin, as she climbed the steps to sit beside Qeb, couldn't help beaming as well.

"Do you think Callispa saw that?" Qeb asked in a low voice as she joined him.

Eirin gave him an ornery grin. "I hope she did."

20

ou did it that time!" Callispa squealed, jumping up and throwing her arms around Drystan's long, scaly neck in a quick hug. Then she let go and started circling him, her bow slung over her shoulder, one arrow in hand. "Again!"

Drystan cringed inwardly as he prepared for the shift. It was slightly less painful each time. But that didn't make it easy. Moving from Human to Dragon to Human again was still tricky, and though it only took a few seconds now, it was far more awkward than any of the other Dragons' changes.

Ten seconds later, he was in Human form again. He stretched his shoulders and felt a satisfying crack.

"No dawdling," Callispa called, fitting the arrow and taking aim. "No feral Cerebus cares that you had a tragic childhood or that they stuffed you full of bruthsi."

"No Cerebus uses a bow and arrow either," Drystan replied dryly. Her red hair was getting slightly easier to make out in the early morning gray, and while her skill with the bow wasn't quite what Nuru's was, she was right. Five weeks of solid training had passed, and Drystan still wasn't nearly fast enough.

"Shut up and shift. You need to be able to do it between the time it takes me to loose this arrow and the time it hits you square in the chest."

Drystan grunted slightly, but he readied himself all the same. The arrows Callispa was using didn't have sharp tips. Instead, they'd been fitted with small bags of colored powder that would leave a mark on his chest if he let them hit him.

His sensitive hearing told him the exact moment the arrow was loosed. And he had less than a full second to shift once it was. But, unfortunately, as he had nearly all day, the arrow hit him while he was only half changed. It bounced harmlessly off his chest, but Karolus, who was standing at the back of the circle, had already seen.

"You're getting slower, not faster." His frown deepened, but he glanced up at Qeb, who had dark circles under his eyes, and Eirin, who watched them as though her life depended on it. "Morning is coming soon. Go sleep. Come back tonight."

Drystan nodded but said nothing. Better to be silent than utter the words that wanted to come. While Karolus didn't insult him to his face as much as he had at first, his obvious disappointment was possibly worse. And the disappointment was there, etched on Karolus's face, his disgust easy for anyone to see even in the early light.

A cool hand rested on Drystan's arm, and he looked away from Karolus to see Callispa giving him an encouraging smile.

"You are improving." Her smile grew slightly. "And you've learned in weeks what takes most Dragons years to grasp."

Drystan raised his eyebrows slightly. "You mean adolescent Dragons."

"Well, yes. But you never had the training they did." She squeezed his arm slightly. "Don't give up."

"He doesn't really have a choice," Karolus called.

Drystan and Callispa looked up to see Qeb and Eirin walking toward them. Qeb looked somewhat amused, but the look Eirin was giving Callispa was...

Pure unadulterated fury. Huh. He'd have to ponder that look more later. She hadn't glared like that at anyone since Nuru had tried to permanently maim her.

Callispa gave Drystan's arm one more squeeze before turning away and gathering her fallen arrows. A glowering Eirin sidled up next to Drystan on his left, and Qeb came to stand on his right.

"Are you done?" Eirin snapped.

Drystan threw Qeb a look of surprise, but Qeb's amused smile only grew. It seemed he found Eirin's fury humorous. Of course, Drystan knew better than to ask with Eirin beside them. She might have been the Citadel's weakest student, but she could throw a mean right hook.

Qeb chuckled again as Eirin marched on ahead of them, her head held high and her stride purposeful.

"It's like watching an indignant kitten," Qeb murmured, and Drystan had to cover his laugh with a cough.

Since taking his new form, Qeb had seemed...more himself. Which was strange, considering Drystan had never known any other behavior from his friend. But Qeb seemed more comfortable with who he was. Almost as if all the pieces were fitting together. Drystan enjoyed seeing the change in his friend. He'd feared that Qeb's shift might make him pull away and focus on those of his own race, much like what Thane was doing. Instead, he felt as though he was getting to know Qeb better than he ever had before.

If only Drystan could settle into his new station so well.

Not that he had much to complain about. With the many guards constantly encircling the city, on the ground and in the air, Drystan slept better than he had since boyhood. They were well-fed, they were being paid to train, and their sleeping quarters allowed their little group to stay connected even as they went their separate ways, something everyone but Thane seemed to enjoy. He couldn't object to his training either. Callispa was an excellent teacher. She was kind and encouraging, and he liked training with her far more than Karolus.

Then, of course, there was Eirin. Watching her in Mhaedin was like watching a rose bloom. She complained that she couldn't read fast enough for her liking, but her ability to connect pieces of information and remember history amazed even Mannish, who was no poor student himself. Often, an elder member of one of the other races would join them in their studies to share what he knew of his people and his history. Sometimes, Lady Phaidra or Hector would join them as well. But most of the time, it was just Eirin and Mannish together, reading or discussing things they'd read.

And Drystan was more than glad he was there to witness it all.

Because while Eirin generally remained lost in her studies, Mannish was often far too occupied with studying her.

As if hearing Drystan think his name, the insufferable boy appeared on the other side of the street, waving and calling Eirin's name.

"You can't blame him," Qeb said quietly as Mannish took his place at Eirin's elbow as they walked.

"He buzzes around her like a fly."

Qeb shrugged. "She's probably the only female he's ever seen or will see who can't easily kill or paralyze him."

"The irony is that she actually could," Drystan muttered. "Eirin might have been weak compared to us, but she learned just as much lethality as every other student at the Citadel."

"You know what I mean," Qeb said patiently. "As far as he knows, besides her mother, she's possibly the only other Human in the world. I'd wonder at his sanity if he didn't think to pursue her. Besides, it's not as if she's ugly."

Drystan knew all too well that Eirin wasn't ugly. She was far too attractive for her own good. Not the way Callispa or Eirin's best friend, Alys, was. They were the kinds of women to turn men's heads at a single glance. Many a stupid boy had pined after Alys at the Citadel without having the faintest idea of who she was. But Eirin…

Eirin had a sparkle, an inner light that seemed to connect her eyes to her heart. Seeing that light was like catching a glimpse of the brilliant star hidden within her small person. To see Eirin was to see her soul. And, unfortunately, Drystan knew he wasn't the only one to notice. Most of the young men in Mhaedin were wise enough to keep their distance. Neither had Eirin seemed greatly desirous of getting to know many of them. But Mannish…

Mannish was insufferable.

"All I'm saying," Qeb continued with a shoulder bump, "is that you'll need to make a decision sooner than later. She's not going to wait forever. Especially with someone raining attention on her like he does."

Drystan scowled. "I'm going to get breakfast," he mumbled. "Eirin, do you want something?"

"Oh, I already got her something," Mannish said, holding up a roll of sweet bread. "I'm sorry, I probably should have gotten extra."

Eirin accepted the bread from Mannish but stopped at a nearby stall with Qeb and Drystan.

"Two hunks of bacon," Drystan told the young man running the stall. The young man hurried to fill Drystan's order, but he paused to give Eirin a shy smile. He was so blond his hair was nearly white, and Drystan was sure he was one of Thane's Centaur friends. He gave Eirin a sweet, calf-like half-grin as he handed her the bacon, which was wrapped in grape leaves.

Drystan stared at the young man as Qeb sent him a pointed look over Eirin's head.

Only then did the young man seem to realize his mistake. His skin went even paler than usual as the woman standing behind him directed a glare at Drystan over her son's shoulder.

"Will you be needing anything else?" she snapped.

Drystan wanted to stare the young man down for good measure. But he knew better than to start fights with angry mothers. So he bowed his head slightly and took a step back. "Thank you, ma'am." He paid her, and then he, Qeb, and Eirin turned in the direction of their rooms.

"I...um, better get back to what I was doing too," Mannish said, backing up a few steps. "Will I see you this evening?" he asked Eirin.

She nodded, but as soon as he was gone, she turned to Drystan.

"That was rude of that woman."

Drystan chuckled. "You seem to forget that this is a daily occurrence." It was. And he had found it best that he pretend he didn't even notice the locals' animosity. Better to pretend it didn't burn like salt in a wound every time someone made a snide comment. At least, he told himself, it was better than back in Torbaine. Many people had hated him there as well. At least here, they didn't hide that hatred behind smiles and simpering. He'd prefer to look his enemy in the eye than worry about someone in his own ranks turning on him.

Eirin, however, generally had indignation enough for them both whenever others were rude to him. And she wasn't hesitant about expressing it. So now, he prepared himself for her usual sarcastic return, but when she said nothing, he glanced down.

He expected her to be glaring at her food or the road or something, anything to turn her frustration upon. Instead, she was simply staring ahead, holding her food as if she'd forgotten it was there.

"Eirin?" Drystan pitched his voice lower so the passersby wouldn't hear. They'd already learned that Mhaedin, for all its size, was full of gossips. "Is everything well?"

She just shrugged and took a small bite of food. Drystan looked at Qeb over her head, but Qeb just shrugged. Drystan shot him an annoyed look. Qeb was exceptionally good at reading others. But he was next to useless when it came to fixing whatever was wrong.

Eirin's mood settled over the group like a storm, and by the time they reached their rooms, Drystan was feeling discomfited himself. What he needed was a hard sleep to wipe away the day so he could be ready for that afternoon, when he and Eirin would start all over again.

Drystan eventually made it to his room. But when he lay down, sleep wouldn't come. Unwanted thoughts and questions circled in Drystan's head instead. And while the walls didn't seem unusually thin, Drystan's senses had sharpened significantly since his first shift, even in Human form. All of his senses had. Unlike Thane, however, and even Qeb to a point, he couldn't turn them off as he wished. They were always there, assaulting him with sounds from the street below or the smell of rotting food someone had forgotten to dispose of properly. Today, he could hear Eirin in her room.

She lay down at first. But less than ten minutes later, she got up and began to pace barefoot across the stone floor. Then she tried to lie down again. This time, however, she tossed and turned.

Drystan had the odd desire to go to her. Something was really bothering her. That never a good sign, as Eirin seemed to have a knack for finding trouble. But then again, he was reminded of what Qeb had said earlier.

Could she be...waiting for him?

Even more, did he want her to?

Drystan might have mulled over these questions the whole day except that he heard her put on her shoes and open the door. By the time she raised her hand to knock on his door, he was already standing on the other side.

"Oh!" she squeaked as he opened the door, her hand still in the air. "You surprised me." Then she tilted her head. "How did you know I was here?"

Drystan gave her a grin. She was just a little too fun to tease. "I can't tell you all my secrets now, can I?"

Eirin mumbled something under her breath about arrogant Dragons, which only made Drystan smile more. But remembering her apparent angst, he closed his door carefully and leaned on the railing facing their doors.

"What's wrong?" he asked.

She lifted her chin slightly. "How do you know something's wrong?"

"You've been a thundercloud since you left the scholars' room last night."

Eirin's shoulders slumped a little, and she leaned against the railing. And yet, for a long time, she didn't talk.

A lock of hair had escaped her braid, and the wind blew it in her face. Without thinking, Drystan reached out and tucked it behind her ear. Her big brown eyes followed his fingers even as he pulled them away, and he was suddenly tempted to run those fingers down her cheek. He just wanted to feel it.

"What were you thinking about?" Eirin whispered. "Before I came?"

Drystan paused and sighed. "I was *trying* not to think about my parents." He grimaced. "I wasn't that successful, though, it seems."

"You miss them," Eirin said.

"Yes...and no. It's hard to miss what was never yours to begin with." He rubbed a sore spot on his shoulder where Karolus had slammed into him during practice. "I think it's more that there's so much I wish I could ask them now. I wish I could ask them to explain..." He let the thought die.

But Eirin's sharp eyes were on him, and he could see her mind working out what he'd left unsaid.

"I can't say I feel exactly the same." She turned to gaze at the valley, which was gray with pre-dawn light. "I miss my family so much it hurts." She hugged herself tightly. "But I understand. Because I would give the world for one more hour to talk with my mother."

She laughed a little. "Though we'd probably spend most of it crying and hugging, to be honest."

Drystan watched her carefully. What would it be like to have a family like that? One that gave freely of their love and affection. Now that he could look back on his life, he could see that his parents had loved him as much as they were able. His father, though Drystan hadn't known the king was his father at the time, had spent countless hours training him in mortal combat, politics, and discernment. His mother, though she had never been his instructor, had always been hovering nearby under the guise of some other duty. She'd talked to him when it wouldn't draw attention to their meeting, and she had given her last breath to save him.

But in the end, their family had been broken and torn apart. As much as he might wish for it now, he would never have what Eirin had.

When had he started to want that?

"You still didn't answer my question, though." He tousled her hair, which made her protest and swat his hand away. "What's been bothering you? Because I'm sure you haven't been contemplating the loss of my parents since yesterday."

Eirin sobered immediately and looked down again as the yellow light of dawn began painting the distant valley golden. The bell rang out, and the sound of canvases unrolling filled the air.

"Eirin?" Drystan leaned forward to see her face better. "You're not–"

"I've been having more visions." Her brown eyes were even larger than usual, and her typical veneer of confidence and disdain was gone. Instead, a new fear filled her face. And it chilled Drystan to the bone.

He was about to answer when a nearby door opened, and one of their neighbors stepped out and leaned against his balcony as well. He held a piece of fruit in his hand and chewed on it slowly as he looked down upon the valley.

"Come on," Drystan said, putting his arm around her shoulder and drawing her toward the stairs. "Talk as we go get something for you to drink." He expected her to pull away, but to his surprise, she nestled closer against his side. The close contact nearly set the right side of his body on fire, and he had to keep himself from automatically pulling her more tightly against him. Unless...

Is that what she wanted? Drat Qeb for asking all those questions.

He didn't crush her against him the way he wanted to, but he kept her firmly under his arm as they made their way down the steps. Because of the somewhat nocturnal hours of the city, the streets were never completely deserted, and there were vendors open at all times of day. The streets were quietest this time of morning, however, as the canvas covers were lowered. It was getting warmer, now that summer was here, and many people preferred to wait until the covers were rolled out to leave the shelter of their homes. Perfect for strolling and talking without being overheard by nosy neighbors.

"So what about these visions?" Drystan asked as they walked casually down the street.

"They frighten me," she whispered.

Drystan stopped walking and looked down at her. "How so?"

She nodded at the street, and he started walking again. Best not to look conspicuous.

"I've touched the urn again. Several times. As well as other artifacts in the scholars' room."

"What did you see?"

"Nothing new." She shook her head. "But then I started touching other things...things that have been brought more recently from other parts of Solevar." She tucked a little deeper into his side, and despite the panic that should have been rising in his chest, Drystan found himself very distracted. She was just so...soft. And small. But no. He needed to focus.

"How does that work?" he forced himself to ask. "Seeing when you touch?"

She pursed her lips for a moment. "I'm beginning to find that I can control it somewhat. If I mean to See an object's history, I am more likely to do so when I touch it. But there are still some times when a vision takes me by surprise."

"And to be clear," Drystan said, "you can't See the future, correct?"

"That's right. I can only See the history of that object. Almost as if I'm watching the world from its point of view." She shivered. "So when some Brownies came in from the west yesterday, I decided to touch some of their farm tools." She shivered again, almost violently.

Drystan stopped walking and turned to face her. Whenever Eirin was scared, it generally meant the rest of them should already be running.

"They all show the same thing," she said. "The world is dying, Drystan."

He frowned. "But we know that."

"No." She shook her head. "Not like this. I see…thorns coming up from the ground and choking out the food. There's death and rotting and decay." She swallowed. "And I'm afraid if we wait until after the harvest, the way Hector was telling us we might, there won't be anything left to save."

Drystan felt a shiver of his own ripple down his body. If he'd learned anything in the last year, it was that Eirin's instincts shouldn't be taken lightly. "Have you told Lady Phaidra?"

She nodded. "I did. Yesterday afternoon she stopped in when you had stepped out to get something to eat." Her frown deepened. "She said they've known all about this for a long time, and not to worry. They'll get us out when it's time. But… I'm afraid we're going to be too late."

"Is it possible that this really is what they've known all along?" Drystan asked. "Maybe we're just the ones seeing it now that we're here?"

"No." Eirin shook her head adamantly. "The end is coming. Fast. And if we don't act–"

"Oy!"

Drystan and Eirin turned to look at the man who had yelled at them from his stall nearby. He was a large man. And though his rotund stomach implied a life without much physical exertion, he had wider shoulders than Drystan and was nearly as tall.

"You're blocking the way to my stall!" he called. "Buy something or get out of the way." But as his angry glare moved over Drystan and landed on Eirin, his countenance softened. "My apologies, Miss," he said to Eirin, tipping his hat. "Didn't notice the Seer there."

Eirin straightened, and an all-too-familiar indignation filled her dark eyes. "And if I *wasn't* here? If it was only my friend?"

Drystan tried to take her hand. "Come on, Eirin. Let it be," he said quietly. But Eirin yanked her hand out of his and stuck both her fists on her hips.

The man looked at Drystan again, and for a moment, seemed to war with himself. Eventually, however, he stood taller and sent a look of pure loathing Drystan's way.

"He's the spawn of the traitor who doomed us all to death." The man spat on the ground. "I'll not have it said that an Innaturalum was allowed to stand before my shop."

Drystan did not know what an Innaturalum was. But Eirin must have because before Drystan knew what she was doing, she'd walked over to the man and slapped him across the face.

Hard.

The man's body immediately began to ripple. Instinct took over, and Drystan's body did the same. His breath suddenly tasted of metal and smoke, and his vision was blood red as he stared down a Hibagon.

Hibagons were larger than what the Citadel had described. Drystan had been told that they were about his own Human height, but this one was at least two handspans taller than Drystan's Human form, and probably weighed three times as much. With thick, dark brown fur all around his body, except for his feet, chest, face, and hands, which had the tell-tale stark white bare skin of the Hibagon. Beating on his chest, he let out a deafening roar.

Which would have been terrifying, had Drystan still been a Human. But he was a Dragon, and in a moment, he'd grabbed the man with his teeth. The small remnant of his Human mind suggested he not purposefully puncture the vile creature's skin or organs. Eirin, the voice insisted, would probably dislike that.

Drystan shook his head to clear it of the Dragon's base thoughts. No, he couldn't kill the Hibagon. But he could teach him a lesson. After shaking his head again, which meant the Hibagon was also shaken, he spit the creature out. He tasted worse than he smelled.

Only when he'd dropped the Hibagon did Drystan become aware of screaming and crying around him. He turned his head to look. Had he frightened the onlookers? It would serve them right if he had.

But after a moment, he realized they weren't looking at him. They were all looking in horror at Eirin.

Drystan shifted back into his Human form as Eirin cradled her hand against her chest. Her face was screwed up in pain, and he could tell she was trying not to cry.

"Eirin, what happened?" He fell to his knees beside her. But even as he asked, he spotted the bright red of her hand, and he knew immediately what had happened. And it was all his fault.

As much as he wanted to blame the Hibagon for her injury, he could see that her hand had been badly burned. Hibagons were strong, but they didn't have fire.

He ran the scene back through his head once more. As soon as the Hibagon had shifted, Drystan had shifted in response. And he'd thrown himself between Eirin and the Hibagon as he did. Karolus's greatest fear had come to pass. Drystan had burned Eirin with his shift.

"Eirin!" a deep voice called.

Drystan's heart fell into his stomach as the sound of running feet came toward them. He knew that voice all too well.

Karolus knelt at Eirin's other side and immediately scooped her up in his arms. The Dragon inside of Drystan hissed, but he shoved it back down and followed obediently as Karolus made his way through the growing crowd.

21

$\mathcal{D}$rystan knew there were healing rooms in the city, but he hadn't known where they were until Karolus bought them there. Entering through the cavern that led to the throne room, Karolus walked past several connected tunnels before turning right and making his way down a smaller hall Drystan hadn't noticed the first time. They passed two doors cut into the flat, polished stone wall before Karolus kicked the third one open.

If Drystan hadn't been so worried about Eirin, he would have noted how ridiculous it was to have a healing room that was so difficult to access.

Only after they'd entered, however, did he realize why the room was located where it was.

Nymphs walked around the room, which had roots of all colors hanging down from the dirt ceiling. The ceiling was supported by large crisscrossing wooden beams. Beds made of soft, green grass seemed to have grown directly out of the walls. Mushrooms, herbs, and flowers grew out of the waters and ceiling as well. There were even some on the floor. A few other people lay in beds around the large room, but most of them seemed to be asleep, and for that, Drystan was grateful. The fewer people to observe his disgrace, the better.

Not that he deserved such a mercy.

One of the Nymphs approached them. She was slim and willowy,

199

and nearly as tall as Drystan. Her skin was a pale, waxy green, and she wore a tunic made of thin, silky material that was almost the same color as the leaves surrounding her. Her large, peridot eyes settled on Eirin. "The Seer!" She looked at Karolus. "What happened?"

"Dragon's fire," Karolus shot Drystan a look before turning back to the Nymph. "She was too close when he shifted."

"May I see?" The Nymph asked Eirin with a smile.

Eirin held out her hand, and Drystan's stomach turned when he saw the severity of the burn. Even worse was the knowledge that he had done that to her. The Nymph, however, showed no signs of revulsion. Instead, she scrutinized it, running her fingers up and down the burn. Drystan expected Eirin to wince or cry when the Nymph's thin, green fingers grazed the red, swollen skin, but instead, Eirin closed her eyes and sighed, leaning her head limply against Karolus's shoulder.

Drystan frowned. It should be his shoulder she was leaning her head against. But, no. He didn't deserve that now. Not after what he'd done.

"This isn't so bad at all," the Nymph said with a gentle smile. "It should only take a few minutes to heal. Of course, we'll wish to keep her here a while longer to make sure the poultice takes."

"Where shall I put her?" Karolus asked.

"Over there in that bed." The Nymph pointed to the nearest empty bed. Karolus carefully laid Eirin down and the Nymph covered her with a blanket of wide, flat leaves. Eirin closed her eyes and seemed to rest back into the strange plant bed completely.

"You."

Drystan looked up to see Karolus motioning to him. "Out in the hall. Now."

Drystan wanted to stay with Eirin. But he would be in the way if he did.

He also deserved whatever his uncle was about to throw at him. In fact, he deserved far worse.

"What were you thinking?" Karolus hissed before the door was even completely shut. "Shifting in a crowd like that? Around Eirin in particular? What do you think we have you training with a Phoenix for?"

"I wasn't trying to shift," Drystan said quietly. "He shifted first. Eirin had made him angry. I just…reacted."

Karolus's eyebrows went up. "What in the world did she do?"

Despite the severity of their circumstance, Drystan felt the corner of his mouth turn up. "She slapped him. In the face."

Karolus blinked. "What for?"

Drystan's smile disappeared. "He called me something. I don't know what it meant, but apparently, she did."

"What did he call you?"

Drystan looked at him in surprise. He hadn't expected Karolus to be interested in his side of the story. Or to even listen that far, to be honest.

"He called me a…an Innaturalum."

Karolus ran a hand over his eyes and muttered to himself for a long moment before shaking his head. "That was wrong of him. And I'm sorry he called you that."

He shook his head for a moment before turning back to Drystan, who was still stunned into silence. "But did she really strike a Hibagon?"

Drystan gave him a dry smile. "Apparently, you don't know Eirin very well. My mother used to worry she'd get herself killed with that mouth of hers. Unfortunately, or fortunately, whichever way you look at it, her fist isn't far behind." He paused. "But what does it mean? Innaturalum, I mean."

Karolus shook his head. "Don't say that aloud if you value your already precarious place in this world." He huffed. "It's an insult of the greatest kind. It means an unnatural creature. As base as the animals. It's an ancient insult, nearly as bad as a curse. Akin to Krakens and Windigos, creatures so twisted and mutated by dark magic that they're no longer Atharrachs but monsters."

Leave it to Eirin to know about some ancient malediction. And to attack a creature over Drystan's honor.

Karolus whistled. "That girl really doesn't have any fear, does she?"

Drystan smiled. "She does. But not about the things she should."

"Apparently. She attacked a creature that weighs at least four times what she does."

"Will she be well?" Drystan asked, all humor gone.

"I believe so. The Nymphs are skilled in healing and elixirs. Of course, the Unicorns were better, but that was before they died out." He frowned slightly. "But yes, to answer your question, I believe she will be just fine."

"I know it doesn't change anything," Drystan said, "but I didn't mean to hurt her. He shifted, and it was all I could do to throw myself between them." Drystan shrugged. "I was shifting before I even knew what I'd chosen to do."

"I know." Karolus sighed and closed his eyes. "Your heart was in the right place. And your instincts were as well. I wish you'd rely on them like that during practice." He opened his eyes. "But there's a reason we've been telling you you're not ready."

"Do you now?" Drystan asked, annoyance sparking as the Dragon within poked his steaming nostrils into the conversation. "Because you've been determined to think the worst of me since we arrived."

Karolus didn't immediately answer. Instead, he used a finger to trace the swirls in one of the flourishes carved into the flat, polished walls.

"It's not easy being a son of Oreck. Every move you make is under scrutiny. Every motive questioned, every judgment judged wrong." He shook his head. "I can only guess it's harder to be the son of Kamon."

Drystan folded his arms. "So you've noticed."

"Which is why I believe you speak the truth," Karolus said firmly. "You truly do care for her. Which is going to make your training all the more difficult. She's not going to make it easy on you. You're going to have to ask her to take care for her own sake." He gave Drystan a half-smirk. "I know better than to ask you two to stay away from one another. But...just try. For her." He turned and took a few steps toward the main entrance before pausing once more. "I'm glad you're here, for what it matters." And then he was gone.

Drystan stood staring after Karolus for several minutes after he disappeared. Had he heard right? Was Karolus no longer wishing him gone every hour of the day?

Unfortunately, he couldn't just stand gaping in the hall, trying to decipher his uncle's cryptic words. The more pressing matter was the conversation he would need to have next.

When Drystan made it back into the healing room, Eirin's hand was nearly back to normal. There were few signs of the angry, red welts that had covered the back of it. Eirin was laughing at something one of the Nymphs was saying. But as soon as the Nymph walked away, Eirin lay back in the bed and sighed as though she were the weariest person in the world. As she seemed ready to close her eyes, however, she saw Drystan and gestured for him to come near.

Drystan made his way over to her bedside, but even as she smiled sleepily up at him, he couldn't get himself to smile back.

"Before you start apologizing," Eirin said, holding up her injured hand, "don't. As you can see, I'm going to be perfectly fine."

Drystan lowered himself onto the bed beside hers. He leaned his elbows on his knees and took her good hand in his. Had it always seemed so small and thin?

Eirin scoffed. "I knew it. You're going to blame yourself. Even though I was the one who started everything." She eyed the door Karolus had exited through. "And if my guess is correct, Karolus has already done a thorough *'I told you so'* lecture about shifting around me."

"Eirin," Drystan sighed as he ran his fingers lightly over her knuckles, "we're going to have to be careful."

Eirin yanked her hand back and crossed her arms across her chest. "I *knew* this would happen."

"That I would hurt you?"

"No." She turned to glower at him. "That you'd blame yourself the first time things went wrong. Just a reminder, Drystan, but we live in a cursed world. Things will go wrong."

"That doesn't mean I have to put you in danger."

Eirin pushed herself up in bed and crossed her legs as she faced him. "And just how do you plan to fulfill your promise to protect me? Because up until about an hour ago, you were all about that."

"An hour ago, I didn't know how fast things could go wrong." Drystan stared at his own hands, scarred and calloused from his years of training. A small hand took his right hand and pulled it into her lap. His heart caught strangely in his chest as she held his hand in both of hers.

"Drystan." When she spoke, her voice was small, almost a whisper. "I need you."

He stared at her, unable to blink.

"I don't know how to...to say it," she continued, "but it's about more than protection." She glanced up at him, and her eyes narrowed. "Although I fully intend to hold you to that promise as well."

"If keeping my distance from you keeps you safer, I'd be holding up my side of the bargain."

"Shut up and listen." She huffed. "I...I can't really tell you why yet. I just...I need you near." When she looked up at him again, her brown eyes burned. "Because I think you're going to play a bigger part in breaking this curse than any of us thought before."

Drystan frowned. "But why me?" He jerked his chin at the door, still trying to ignore how it felt to have his hand in hers. "If you're referring to my bloodline, there are two other sons of Oreck in existence as well."

She let go of his hand and rubbed her eyes with the palms of her hands. "I knew you were going to be stubborn about this."

"Eirin," Drystan smiled, tugging playfully on an escaped lock of her hair. "Have you been reading again? That always gets you into trouble if you haven't noticed." He expected her to give him a feisty retort, something to lighten the suddenly heavy mood. But to his surprise, she gave him a slightly startled look, followed by a frown.

Drystan leaned closer. "What are you not telling me?"

"It's nothing. I just..." She sighed. "I know you. You...you lose yourself. I want you near me so I can make sure that doesn't happen. Because you're far more important than you think."

Drystan opened his mouth to tell her that she was sweet, but mristaken. His role here was to make sure his great-grandfather's wrong was righted. And if that was by protecting their last hope from harm—including himself—then that's what he was going to do. But arguing with Eirin was like talking to a wall. So instead, he gave her a wry grin.

"Fine. I'll keep my promise. But if you could just...try to stay safe, it would be a tremendous help." Then he ruffled her hair. "Maybe start by not picking fights with creatures bigger than yourself. For my sake?" Even as he spoke, the enormity of what Eirin had done by slapping the Hibagon hit him like a boulder. Eirin cared for him. What kind of care she had, he couldn't exactly say. But if there was anything he knew about Eirin, it was that she was loyal. And it filled him with a new kind of warmth to know how much she cared.

Eirin, unaware of his internal revelations, glared at him, then huffed." Fine. But only if you promise to stay."

"I'll be there. Just…a little farther away."

22

The Nymphs insisted Eirin eat and sleep before releasing her. Healing from Dragon's fire took a toll on the body, according to Melia, Eirin's attending Nymph. Eirin wasn't a large being to begin with, Melia said, so it was of the utmost importance that Eirin rest and be nourished before leaving the healing room.

Eirin loved the healing room. Plants grew out of the ceiling, the walls, and even the floors, and crystals were peeking up from between the plants as well. Varying colors for varying cures according to the Nymph.

"Red for burns," Melia recited while carefully chiseling a small red crystal from the wall. She put it into a mortar and ground it with the pestle, pausing every few seconds to throw in other herbs and ingredients. "Green for stomach illness. Blue for bone injuries. Purple for pain from unknown discomforts, and white for troubles with magic." She dropped her voice and winked. "Yellow for trouble of the bowels."

Eirin laughed and looked around eagerly. "What about black?" she asked, pointing to a small black crystal poking out of the wall.

Melia's face sobered, and she looked back down at her work. "Black is for the drawing out of bad Magic. Very dangerous work that."

Eirin knew better than to pry into something that made her healer so obviously uncomfortable. But she wouldn't miss the opportunity to find out everything else she could concerning Nymphs and healing. It was even better than finding the information in a book.

But Melia didn't allow her to ask questions forever. After several forced naps—which Eirin had been more grateful for than she was willing to admit—and a few meals, the Nymphs deemed Eirin fit to leave. In their kindness, they had allowed Drystan to sleep on the bed next to hers as well, as few other patients were present. And not even a single dour glance was sent his way, which made Eirin like the Nymphs all the better. By the time evening came and they were allowed to leave, she felt rested and ready for her time in the scholar's room.

"Did you know that there are no male Nymphs?" Eirin asked as they walked.

Drystan raised an eyebrow. "Then how do they make babies?"

Eirin's face flushed, but she tried to ignore it. "They live to be about eighty years of age. Three times during adulthood, which for Nymphs is twenty-five years old, a Nymph woman chooses an acorn that's still on a tree branch, and then she plants part of her own essence inside of it. The acorn grows and grows until it falls from the tree. Then the acorn cracks open, and the Nymph scoops up her baby girl." Eirin grinned. "I wish I could see that."

"The world would be far less complicated without all those fathers getting in the way, wouldn't it?" Drystan smirked.

Eirin bumped him with her shoulder. "You *know* that's not what I'm saying. I just think it's fascinating. All these people, and we didn't have a clue they existed, let alone that they were people just like us." She'd memorized her fair share of facts about Atharrachs back in the Citadel. But that had been back when she'd believed everyone in Torbaine was Human, and everything non-Human had been considered a monster.

Drystan's smile faded. "I know." He glanced down at her hand. "You're sure you'll be all right?"

Eirin huffed and rolled her eyes for what felt like the millionth time that day. Her hand was stinging fiercely even as they spoke, but she wasn't going to let on if it killed her. Drystan was the kind of man that if he felt something was the right thing to do, he would act. That was the problem with him. There was no waffling. In the hours since they'd had their tense conversation in the healing room, he hadn't touched her once. No hand-holding. No guiding palm on the small of her back, nor was there an arm on her shoulder, pulling her close to him.

Her worries about her visions seemed like they'd taken place eons ago instead of just a day. But maybe that was better. She would talk to Lady Phaidra later. Right now, she would focus on what she *could* change. Or at least learn about it.

By the time they arrived at the scholars' room, Mannish had already taken over the tables with his usual pile of books and papers, so Eirin made her way over to the neat little stack of books she'd left in the corner two nights before.

"There you are! I heard you'd been hurt!" Mannish exclaimed, then he paused. "What happened to your hand?"

Eirin tried to press it against her side, but he was already out of his seat and following her.

"It's fine," Eirin assured him. "The Nymphs said it should feel back to normal by tomorrow."

Mannish crossed his arms and narrowed his eyes at her. And then at Drystan. "But what happened?"

Clearly, he wasn't going to take no for an answer. And while it was sweet that he was worried about her, Drystan felt bad enough already. Eirin wasn't about to drag him through any more drama than she had to. So she sighed and rolled her eyes. "I did something stupid and slapped a Hibagon."

Mannish stared at her blankly, and his mouth fell open. "When Lady Phaidra said...I thought she was joking. You did...what?"

"I slapped a Hibagon. Though, in my defense, he didn't look like a Hibagon when I hit him. He shifted, and pandemonium ensued." Eirin waved Mannish away with her good hand. "Now, I've had quite enough excitement for one day, and I'd like to get back to our studies, if you don't mind." She edged past him and headed for her stack of books.

After a moment, Mannish followed her, but she saw his eyes dart back to Drystan several times. And for once, his expression wasn't friendly.

If he'd pressed more, she wouldn't have been able to deny Drystan's involvement. Hibagons were powerfully built, and their abilities to lift and crush large objects were extraordinary. But Hibagons didn't make fire. And her hand had definitely been burned.

"Oh, I meant to ask you," Eirin said before Mannish could ask another question. "Do you know if there are any other books or scrolls on Dragons?" She held up the small pile of books she'd gathered two days before. "I could only find these."

At the word Dragon, Drystan raised one eyebrow, but Eirin ignored him. She had been telling the truth when she said she believed he was a part of breaking the curse. There were…pieces of a picture that she was starting to put together. A picture that just might help them save Solevar. But he didn't need to know that much just yet. Because if she told him what she suspected, he would demand proof, and she didn't have it. Not yet.

"Hm," Mannish frowned thoughtfully, though Eirin couldn't help noticing that he wasn't as enthusiastic as usual. He walked slowly over to one of the large wall shelves and studied it. "What are you looking to find specifically?"

"I need to know about how King Oreck's throne is passed from one generation to the next. Lady Seren said something about a Blood Throne, but I don't remember everything, to be honest." Eirin paused. "And I'd like to read more stories about the royal family's involvement in Solevar. The princes, specifically."

Drystan, she could feel, was now staring at the back of her head so hard it was liable to catch fire. But he was stubborn and had a terrible sense of self-worth. He could handle a mystery for a little while longer. Even if it drove him a little crazy.

That thought made her smirk.

"There are lots of stories in here about Dragons," Mannish said, holding a scroll up. "Not King Oreck's line, specifically, but Dragons in general."

Eirin shook her head. "No, I need to know about the royal line. There's a reason."

Mannish hopped down from the stool he'd stood on to reach the scroll and walked back over to Eirin. "Do you want to tell me?" His smile was playful, but he was suddenly standing closer to her than usual. "We are both Seers, you know."

Eirin shrugged. "We are. But I don't exactly know what I'm looking for yet." She took the scroll he was holding and tapped him on the head with it. "But I'll be sure to let you know when I know."

"Before you start reading," Mannish said, suddenly standing taller, "I wanted to ask you something."

"Ask away." Eirin began perusing the bookshelves again.

Mannish took a deep breath, but when he spoke, his voice was nearly inaudible. "What do you know about Wizards?"

Eirin paused and turned to face him. "Wizards? Next to nothing."

Mannish looked surprised. "Really? I thought you had lessons on Atharrachs back in your city."

"Most of the dangerous ones, yes. But they wouldn't even talk about Wizards. All I know is that they were born Seers, but they traded their ability to See for magic." She paused. "Is that correct?"

"It is." His eyes lit up. "But there's so much more. Come here."

Eirin followed him to the table, where he held up a small, ancient book bound in leather that had probably once been blue.

"Wizards were first born when the son of the royal Seer Themba got lost and found a cave in the barren mountains on the south-western side of the kingdom." Mannish opened the book and pointed to words so faded they were barely legible. "In that cave were the Hidden Waters of Domhier."

"What are the Hidden Waters?" a deep voice asked.

Eirin and Mannish looked up to see Drystan leaning against the wall. His position was nonchalant, but as he hardly ever interrupted her study time, he must truly have wanted to know.

Mannish looked slightly peeved, but he did answer. "The Hidden Waters of Domhier is an underground river full of magic somewhere in the western mountains. Legend has it that the Time Keeper Himself drank from the pool, and when he did, he imparted a magic so potent nothing but the royal Dragon's power could rival it."

Mannish looked back down at the book and turned a page. "When the son of Themba...Jember was his name. When he got lost, he was little more than a boy. Which means his Seer abilities hadn't yet blossomed."

"What did he do?" Eirin asked, curiosity getting the best of her.

"He was thirsty and tired, so when he found the cave, he stumbled in and immediately knelt to drink."

"Did the magic hurt him?" Eirin asked.

"No. But it did put him into a ten-year trance."

Eirin nearly dropped the scroll she was holding. "Ten *years?*"

Mannish nodded, his eyes bright. "During those ten years, he was shown all the light and dark that such waters could produce, should he use them the way his heart desired. Mysteries of the ancient magic, magic that existed before The Time Keeper created Solevar. He was shown the depths of power and the secrets such power held."

Secrets. Eirin wasn't sure she would even wish to know such secrets. "That sounds…burdensome," she said quietly.

Mannish nodded. "It was. When he emerged from the trance, he was no longer a boy, but a man. It didn't take long for him to realize, however, that he had never gained the ability to See."

"How sad," Eirin whispered.

"But it wasn't so bad," Mannish hurried to explain. "Instead, he received something even better!"

"Better than Seeing?" Drystan looked unconvinced.

"Yes, better," Mannish snapped. Then he turned his attention back to Eirin. "He might have lost his ability to See, but unlike any Human before, he could harness magic!"

Eirin gaped. "But how?" In her long years of physical training at the combat academy in Torbaine, she'd been painfully aware of her lack of…something. She hadn't realized until recently that it was a lack of magic. And while she was perfectly happy with her ability to See both magic and visions of the past, she was very familiar with the wish to be *more*.

Mannish looked as though he felt that lack right now.

"Using the instructions he'd received in his trance, he built a staff using one of the unique stones he found deeper in the cave. And using his staff, he was able to manipulate magic in the world around him!" Mannish beamed.

"How?" Eirin asked.

"So you know how the world is filled with raw magic, yes?"

Eirin nodded.

"Most Atharrachs can't use that raw magic," Mannish said, his eyes bright. "They use the magic that was placed within them at conception. Their magic is a definitive part of who they are."

Eirin thought of Alys. "But can't the Fae manipulate magic? And the Elves?"

"To a point, yes. The Elves can manipulate the magic of others and meld it with the raw magic of certain materials. And Fae can do even more, selectively using the magic in the world around them. But most of them are gifted in one particular area. The water for some or flowers for another. Not to mention, they're mostly dead." He nodded at the door. "There's a Fae working for Lady Phaidra who can somewhat harness the power of the sun to heat things like clay and stoves. Not that she can actually touch it." He chuckled. "Watching her work was a little nerve-racking. Even for me."

"So what more could the Wizard do?" Eirin asked.

"He could command it *all*." Mannish was nearly glowing with excitement. "He was able to gather the magic from the world around him and use it all on his own." He paused. "Of course, the Wizards tend to each have a specialty as well. But they can do far more than most Fae."

Eirin studied Mannish. He was more excited than she'd seen him since her arrival. Perhaps a little too excited. "How many Wizards are there now?" Eirin asked. "Are they still all alive?" If so, they'd done a terrible job fighting back the curse.

Mannish's joy faded slightly. "Most of them died when the curse fell or soon after. Their magic does seem to be limited, and most of the Wizards who were alive at the time gave all their magic to save others." He frowned and ran a hand through his curly hair. "It seems that when the Hidden Waters bond the magic to their essences, they essentially became like Atharrachs, in that when the magic dies, the Wizards die as well."

"How many Wizards have there been?" Drystan asked from his corner of the room.

"Oh, many!" Mannish nodded enthusiastically, seeming to momentarily forget his annoyance with Drystan. "We have record of at least twelve. There were many who wanted to become Wizards, but the Time Keeper seems to keep the Hidden Waters hidden from most. He only shows it to Humans and never more than once. None of the Wizards has ever been able to go back." He paused. "Though none of the other Wizards ever seemed to have the strength of the first one."

"So they're all dead then?" Eirin asked.

"All but one that we know of. He lives on the other side of this mountain, and he wants nothing to do with us." Mannish scowled. It was a strange expression on his usually sunny face. "Mhaedin has asked for help countless times. He used to help, but in recent years, he's not only refused us, but he's pushed us away."

Eirin studied her friend. Where was he going with this interest in Wizards? It would make sense for him to wish for the last Wizard to help them, especially with the losses they'd recently incurred. But she'd never seen Mannish so excited about anything. He wasn't a Wizard, nor was she. And, it seemed, he had no idea where the cave of Hidden Waters was. So what did he want?

"Have you ever heard of the Stones of Kadar?"

Eirin glanced at Drystan, who shrugged. "I'm guessing this is more ancient magic?"

"Oh, yes! They're the stones the Wizards use to create their staffs. Each Wizard chooses one and builds his staff around it. They reside in the cave as well." Mannish's voice became reverent. "Those stones are the most powerful magic Solevar has ever seen. After the Time Stones, of course."

Eirin frowned. "What would one do with such powerful stones?"

Mannish's eyes grew wide. "Anything. Vanquish one's enemies. Create a safe path to Iilaedin." His voice dropped to a whisper. "Even bend time."

"Mannish," Eirin said slowly, "that sounds like forbidden magic." Not that she knew much of forbidden magic. But she had read enough to know that reaching too far beyond the scope of one's magic was...dangerous. The Time Keeper had expressly forbidden it.

But Mannish wasn't looking at her anymore. He was staring down at the little worn book in his hands.

"Just think about it. Something like that would allow us...an infinite amount of time to unlock the Time Stones. We wouldn't spend weeks or months getting to the Time Stones, arriving sick or half-dead." He looked at Eirin again, though his eyes were still distant. "We could break the curse."

Eirin glanced at Drystan again, whose face was drawn into a deep frown.

"That is exciting," Eirin said cautiously. "And very interesting. But…"

"But what?" Mannish laughed. "If we found something like that, we could save the world!"

"If the Wizard on the mountain hasn't used his stone that way already," Eirin said, "wouldn't there seem to be a reason not to?" She looked back down at the book in Mannish's hands. "After all, he knows the secrets of that magic more than any of us. It would seem…unlikely that he would refuse to use such magic to save the world. Unless…" She sighed.

"Unless what?" Mannish asked, his smile now gone.

"Unless the cost was too high."

Mannish stared at her for a long moment then looked back down at the book. "If there was any time to try something risky, this would be it." He gave her a sad smile. "The entire kingdom is on the brink of death." He ran his fingertips over the page. "And this is different from the forbidden magic from the stories."

"Perhaps," Eirin tried again. "But playing with time…that seems almost akin to what brought down the curse in the first place." She gave him her own sad smile. "Destiny and time are quite linked, you know."

Mannish stared at her for a moment before sighing. "I know." When he looked back up at her, the feverish light in his eyes was gone. He closed the book with a wistful look. Then shaking his head, he gave her a tired smile. "I just…I want it to end."

Eirin thought back to the brooding man behind her. "I know," she said softly. Then she forced a smile. "I need to speak with Lady Phaidra. Perhaps they've made more plans for our trip to Iilaedin."

Mannish looked unconvinced, but he smiled politely and bowed his head. "I can't wait to hear what you discuss."

Eirin went back to her Dragon books, but she struggled to focus. While she'd always wanted to know more about Wizards, the conversation had taken an uncomfortable turn. And she couldn't put into words exactly why.

But no. She was here to learn about Dragons now. Specifically, Oreck's line.

Drystan's line.

Because no matter where she turned...even in Mannish's tale of the origin of Wizards, the line of Oreck was there.

Everything always came back to him.

23

As they loitered outside the antechamber's outer room, Qeb sliced off a piece of apple and held it out for Drystan, who pulled it off the knife and took a bite, closing his eyes as he relished the explosion of juicy sweetness on his tongue. The Mhaedin residents could say what they wanted about their fruits' decline in taste. But even as Torbaine's Heir, where Drystan had tasted the most succulent delicacies the city had to offer, he'd never imagined food could taste so good.

"Want some?" Qeb asked Nuru.

"I do!" Mannish held out his hand eagerly. Nuru just rolled her eyes and shook her head as she went back to reading a scroll on Phoenixes that Eirin had given her on their way to meet with Lady Phaidra.

"I'm confused," Callispa said. "Why do we all have to be here again?"

"No one said you had to be here," Nuru said, her eyes still on the parchment. "You decided to follow us."

A blush spread across Callispa's freckled cheeks, and she glanced at Drystan before looking down at the ground. Drystan sighed. Nuru had many strengths, but tact was not one of them.

"You're welcome to stay," he said, giving Nuru a look, which she completely ignored. He turned to Callispa to explain. "We came together because Eirin needed to talk to Lady Phaidra, and we

219

thought it would be good to discuss Lady Phaidra's response afterward."

"That makes sense." Callispa flashed him a forced smile and turned to make conversation with Mannish, but Drystan wasn't fooled. He and his friends' behavior was confusing to more people than just the Phoenix.

The little group from Torbaine hadn't assimilated. Well, no one except Thane. Thane still slept in their shared room, but only just. He was gone nearly every waking minute, hardly having time for more than greetings and goodbyes as he ran to join his Centaur brothers every day. But everyone else...

Drystan's constant attachment to Eirin made sense. At least, the people of Mhaedin didn't question it. He'd sworn to protect Eirin, given her heritage as a Seer. And while he, much to her annoyance, was maintaining more of a physical distance these days, he was still fulfilling that vow by coming with her nearly every time she left her room. And Qeb's attachment to both of them made sense as well. He was a Griffin, and, apparently, Griffins attached them-selves to an individual until one of them died, and by extension, that person's loved ones. Nuru didn't have to come with any of them. But she did.

Then there was Mannish. Drystan just couldn't shake him, no matter how hard he tried. And now Callispa had joined them as well, though Drystan had the feeling that had more to do with his pres-ence than the camaraderie offered by their little group.

The door opened, and Eirin marched out before shutting the door slightly harder than necessary. Callispa and Mannish both jumped at the sound, but the others simply waited. Eirin wasn't particularly known for her patience.

"I take it that didn't go as you'd hoped," Drystan said.

Eirin glared at him. "Whatever gave you that idea?"

"She thinks you're overreacting, doesn't she?" Nuru asked.

"You've *been sheltered*," Eirin said, mimicking Lady Phaidra's smooth tones. "You're *only seeing what the rest of us have known for years*." She snorted and set off toward the training platforms. "It doesn't matter how many times I tell her I've been touching the arti-facts of our newcomers, too, she just won't *listen*."

"I'm confused," Callispa said, glancing from Eirin to Drystan. "What are we talking about?"

"Eirin's been having visions," Mannish piped up. His eyes were only for Eirin, but for once, there was no stupid smile on his face. "She's been touching the belongings of those who have recently arrived at Mhaedin."

"Why?" Callispa asked.

"She can See the pieces of history from the objects she touches," Mannish answered. His brow puckered. "And she thinks the curse's final destruction is coming sooner than we thought."

"Meaning…" Callispa said.

"Everyone is going to die if we don't leave *soon!*" Eirin snapped. "We can't wait until after harvest. The journey alone will take weeks or even months. We might not even get there until next spring." She glared at the evening sky. "Summer has already begun."

Callispa stopped walking, and her mouth fell open. "Why…why in the world would you think that?"

Eirin whirled around to face her. "Because the rot is spreading faster and faster. Thorns infest the ground and choke every good plant they can find." She shook her head. "We don't have time to wait."

The sound of thundering footsteps made everyone stop and turn. A group of Centaurs ran past them, laughing and talking loudly. A familiar face among the group brightened as he neared them.

"What a pleasant surprise!" Thane called out with a wave. Drystan couldn't help but notice that Thane was surrounded by four females who nearly walled him off from everyone else. The females giggled and smiled up at him longingly as he waved.

Mannish smiled uncertainly and waved back, but when Drystan glanced back, no one else waved or smiled. They just watched him run by. A look of slight confusion crossed Thane's face, but it was quickly replaced by a grin when one of the Centaur girls called his attention away. Then they were gone, and Drystan's group was able to continue their trek down the city street. This time, however, no one spoke.

The uncomfortable silence was unfortunately familiar by now and had been for the last two weeks, ever since Drystan had begun keeping his distance from Eirin following the incident with her hand. He stayed close but not close enough to touch her and far enough that he wouldn't injure her if he had to shift. And while it was the right thing to do, it felt...wrong.

Drystan hadn't realized until he'd backed off just how much he'd been touching Eirin as of late. Nothing long or intimate. Just little things. Guiding her at the small of her back, or standing near enough to feel her body heat when he felt danger might be at hand. Putting his arm across her shoulders and keeping her close. It had all felt so right. By bringing her close, he felt as though he was keeping her safe. He hadn't realized just how close to danger she had come by simply being near him.

Even worse, Eirin was taking it badly, and it was putting a strain on the group. He'd tried to give her that same feeling of safety by making sure that even if he wasn't close, Qeb was. And if not Qeb, Nuru. He'd even talked with Qeb and Nuru about coordinating their training times and sleeping hours so that she was never without one of them. Having Thane nearby, too, would have made it easier, but short of plucking him out of the Centaur group and dragging him back, there wasn't much to be done about that.

Only Mannish and Callispa seemed untouched by the frustration that seemed to be constantly bubbling beneath the surface these days.

"Up top again?" Qeb asked, breaking through Drystan's thoughts.

Drystan, coming out of his reverie, realized that they'd reached the training platforms.

Eirin nodded, and without a glance back at Drystan, followed Qeb up the stone steps to the next platform where she and Qeb had resumed their training during Drystan's sessions. A week ago, Qeb had suggested she begin her combat practice again, considering the likelihood that someone might try abducting her again, and Eirin had readily agreed. Now as she went, Nuru and Mannish followed them.

"I need your focus today, Drystan."

Drystan turned to see Callispa pulling her red ringlets into a thick knot at the back of her head.

"Aren't I always focused?"

"About as focused as a kitten in a basket of butterflies," she laughed. Then she sighed. "If you're really intent on keeping the Seers safe, you *must* know how to shift with perfect control. Especially," the corner of her mouth turned up, "if we're going to fly."

Drystan's attention was hers. "We're going to fly?" There were many things about being a Dragon that Drystan did not love. But flying? He desperately wanted to do that again.

Callispa beamed. "Karolus says you're ready! He was busy today, or he would have been here. Of course," she gave Drystan a knowing grin, "I didn't think you'd mind too much."

She was right about that.

"Nothing too hard or long tonight," she continued, "since it will be your first time."

"Third."

She rolled her eyes. "Fine, third. My point is that we're going to be traveling a long way, and you need to know not only how to fly, but how to fight simultaneously." She stepped back. "Shift and show me what you can do."

Drystan was so excited he trembled. It became quickly apparent, however, that the shaking wasn't from his nerves but from the Dragon within, inwardly screaming its good pleasure at being let loose once again. In fact, the shift hardly hurt this time, and in less than thirty seconds, he took a running leap and launched himself off the ground. And for one beautiful moment, he was flying over Mhaedin.

But he didn't soar for long. The wind did lift his body into the air. Higher than he expected, even. All too soon, though, he began to go down. Panic screamed in his head as he desperately flapped his wings.

The people below him looked up and shouted for him to watch out. The stalls below him rose up to meet him at an alarming speed.

Just when he was sure he would destroy the street he was hurtling toward, the breeze came up, and he was briefly lifted once more. Only to begin falling as soon as the wind deserted him again. Three times, the wind caught him just as he fell, but the fourth time, he sent people screaming in one of the lower streets as he tumbled down.

At the very last moment, he was hit by something hard. The impact forced him onto one of the small outcrops on the side of a street. The outcrop, covered in grass, was just below the training fields. Smashing into the ground hurt, but it was far less painful than it would have been landing on the cobbled street.

Drystan rolled over to see Qeb picking himself up, his wings already folding themselves neatly behind his large frame.

"Thanks," Drystan croaked. He lay on the ground and stretched his wings tentatively, grateful that nothing seemed to be broken. "And you can stop laughing at me."

Qeb shrugged. "I'm not laughing."

"You're laughing at me in your head."

Qeb's eagle face was incapable of smiling, but his dark eyes glittered. "I'm not sure what you were trying to do up there, but it was lovely."

Drystan turned around to snuff at him. "Shut up."

"Drystan!"

Callispa landed by his side as he pushed himself to his feet, her graceful wings of flame folding neatly behind her. "Are you hurt? I saw you go down, but I didn't see where you'd fallen."

"Qeb saved me from falling into the street. Or rather, he saved the street from me."

Callispa nodded, as though this were only to be expected. "I can tell you what you're doing wrong. I knew the moment you took off, but you couldn't hear me calling." Without waiting for him to respond, she pointed up to the practice platforms that were now a good deal higher up the mountain.

"You made the mistake a lot of young Dragons make by thinking you could lift off the ground directly."

Drystan frowned. "But I've done it before."

"You probably did. Taking off like that is hard, though. If you did it, you were probably under some sort of duress."

Drystan frowned. He'd flown before. The first time he'd shifted, when Eirin was being pursued by an angry Fae, and the time he'd followed Karolus to Mhaedin. He'd taken off those times... hadn't he? Or had it just been that first time?

"Taking flight by lifting oneself into the air is difficult, if not impossible for most Dragons," Callispa said, as if reading his thoughts. "Few can do it. In fact, only the most skilled, and usually those with the strongest magic can do it."

"Then what do the others do?" Qeb asked.

Callispa nodded back up to the cliffs. "They do what Drystan just did by accident when he fell. They glide."

Drystan scrunched his eyes shut. Now he remembered. When he'd followed Karolus to Mhaedin, they had been on the side of the mountain. Karolus had launched himself off the cliff, and only once they'd been in the air for a few seconds did he really begin to *fly*. Drystan had simply followed his example.

"I did fly back in the mountain when I saved Eirin from a Fae," he said, trying not to sound sullen.

"Oh, I believe you. You *are* a son of Oreck, so your magic is far stronger than most Dragons'. And if you were in fear for your life–"

"Eirin's," Qeb said casually.

A strange look flickered over Callispa's face, but she simply nodded. "Eirin's, then. Urgency can make you incredibly powerful." Callispa paused. "How about we try again. Would you mind if I ride you this time?"

The first thought in Drystan's head was that Eirin would not like that. Of course, it really wasn't up to her. After all, this entire venture out into Solevar was for her, so if this helped him get ready faster, she would have to learn to be content.

"If you think it will help..." Drystan said slowly.

Callispa beamed. "Oh, I know it will. Many Phoenixes were actually known as Dragon riders rather than trainers."

Drystan had seen the other Dragons-in-training heading out with their riders. Given, most of them were either married to their riders or fast on that path. But there was nothing intimate about letting his trainer ride him. How else would he learn?

Drystan shifted into his Human form to climb back up to the training pad and followed Callispa. Qeb walked behind him.

"Eirin's going to love this," Qeb whispered under his breath with a smirk. Drystan groaned.

"Is something wrong?" Callispa asked from the front.

Drystan sent Qeb a meaningful look. "I'm just sore." He might be more than that, though, when Eirin saw what was about to happen.

Drystan didn't know the depths of Eirin's feelings, or even really what they were. But even with his comparatively dull and impaired male senses, he *did* understand that there was *something* invisible between Eirin and Callispa, and that both women felt it. Unfortunately, he got the feeling that if he asked, he would find out that the invisible thing was him. Drystan wasn't really sure he wanted to do that. It felt very much like slapping a Hibagon.

When they got back to the top of the platform, Eirin, Nuru, and even Thane were watching anxiously. Eirin's face immediately relaxed when she saw him, and Thane said something that made Nuru scowl.

"Let's try that again." Callispa walked to the edge of the platform. "Go ahead and shift one more time. Then I'll climb up using your wing. When I tell you to go this time, run to the edge of the platform with your wings spread. You're going to catch the breeze."

"Are you sure this is safe?" Drystan asked before shifting. She waited to answer until he was done. "For you, I mean."

"You forget." She smirked as her wings of fire flamed up behind her. "I can also fly." Her eyes burned red along with her wings, and Drystan was pretty sure he'd seen a wisp of red flame at her fingertips as well. Fascinating.

Qeb cleared his throat as he walked behind them to rejoin the others on the ledge, and Drystan blinked several times. He needed to focus. He was about to leap off a cliff on purpose with another living being on his back. Yes, she might be able to fly, but that wasn't the point. If everything went as Eirin hoped, they would be doing this very soon. Only, in that instance, the one riding him wouldn't be able to fly. With Eirin, there would be no second chances.

Drystan squeezed his eyes shut, trying to visualize what Callispa had told him.

Spread his wings.

Leap off the ledge.

Ride the breeze.

Focusing was hard when a woman was climbing on one's back.

"Are you ready?" Callispa called down. Drystan grunted, which made her laugh. "You'll be fine. Just listen to me." She ran a hand down his shoulder blade, making him shudder. "Relax your muscles. You won't be flexible enough to ride the breeze if you're all bunched up."

Somehow, though Drystan tried to forget how hard it was after, he worked his back muscles to exactly the tautness that Callispa wanted. Then, in the middle of a sentence about how he needed to use his sensitive nose to sense changes in the wind, she interrupted herself.

"There it is! The wind! Go!"

Drystan sent up a half-crazed prayer to the Time Keeper as he ran toward the edge of the ledge.

And fell.

"Your wings!" Callispa shouted above the roar of the wind in their ears. "Tilt them up to catch the current!"

Drystan did so, and the abrupt change nearly knocked him out of the sky again. Several screams and shouts sounded from below, but Drystan was too focused on regaining his balance to pay heed.

"Another one's coming from the south!" Callispa called. "Can you feel it?"

Drystan sniffed the wind tentatively and was surprised to find that she was right. This current carried other scents than the one he'd been riding before.

"Tilt them just slightly higher!" she cried.

He obeyed, and this time, they were sent soaring high above the city, higher even than the other training pads. Drystan nearly let himself smile when he saw that they were almost two-thirds up the side of the mountain.

"Now!" Callispa called, her voice surprisingly near. She must have climbed closer to his neck. "There's another change coming from the north. It will try to send you into a spin, but don't let it do that."

"What should I do?" he called back.

He could almost feel the smile in her words. "Fly. Wherever you want, use it to fly."

As soon as the new smells hit Drystan's nostrils, he understood. The new current came crashing in, and he tightened his wings just enough to resist its force. Instead, he used it to slingshot himself forward toward the west.

Solevar spread wide below him, and for a moment, he forgot to breathe.

He'd flown over it the time he'd followed Karolus to Mhaedin. But that day, he'd simply been trying not to fall and die. This, though...

This made him almost wish he had a chance at being the crown prince of Solevar.

Some of the trees and fields had sparse patches. Patches that he was sure, during the day, would be dead and dry. Still, the blemishes couldn't steal from the beauty before him. There were countless kinds of topography, and he knew from Eirin's map that if he flew far enough, he would be able to glimpse the ocean. Iilaedin would be northwest in the corner of the kingdom, and Torbaine's mountain would be northeast, and another ocean to the right of it.

Would the ocean really shine green like Eirin's books liked to say?

"You're doing magnificently!" Callispa called down to him. They were soaring over a forest now with trees that would have dwarfed Giants. "But we don't want to go too far today," she continued. "It's only your second time. If you go too far down, it'll be hard to gain the momentum to get back up to the training platform without another cliff."

Drystan didn't want to go home. He wanted to fly forever. What she said made sense, however, so he was about to turn around when movement below caught his eye.

"What's that?" he called back.

Callispa was quiet for a moment. "That's not good," she finally said in a voice so low he nearly missed it.

"What do you mean?"

"It's a group of Fauns." She paused. "They're running from something."

A chill ran through Drystan, despite the flame in his chest. She was right. He'd gotten low enough that he could see dozens of Fauns sprinting through the brush.

Callispa spoke again, but this time, her voice shook. "They're heading for Mhaedin."

Drystan looked up to see the trees swaying in the distance. "Probably to escape from whatever that is."

"Don't get too close," Callispa warned him as he let himself get lower once again. "We don't know what—oh! Oh no."

'What is it?"

"It's a Windigo!"

Only then was Drystan able to see the creature clearly. And what he saw made his stomach turn.

The creature was the same height as a Giant, about three times that of a tall Human. But unlike a Giant, its body looked as if someone had taken a Human skin and stretched it thinly over its ridiculously long body. Yellow tangled hair stuck out in tufts from the creature's head, and pointed teeth jutted out of its jaw. Drystan couldn't make out its eyes well in the quick glance he took as he passed over it, but what he did see made them look like graves, sunken into the skull.

Just as he passed over the creature, it raised up one clawed hand and swatted at him. Drystan felt the disturbed air blow past his right side as he pivoted. It missed him, but the force of his turn nearly upset his balance, and he had to fight for it again as he turned, this time to fly back at the Windigo.

"No!" Callispa's voice was sharper than it had ever been before. "We have to go back!"

"But what about the Fauns?" he protested.

"We have to get Lady Phaidra."

He opened his mouth again, but she cut him off.

"Windigos bring the cold with them. One touch, and my fire could be extinguished."

Drystan had been building fire in the back of his throat already, but this made him pause. Like Dragons, Phoenixes had a fire spark. Theirs weren't as strong as Dragon sparks, however, and Drystan was familiar enough with his own shortcomings that he knew better than to hazard overconfidence with Callispa's safety.

"They eat anything in its Human state," she continued, "and their touch can freeze shifters so that they're unable to change forms."

"Well then," he said, pivoting so the current lifted them away from the forest tops, "I guess we're going back to Mhaedin." And he pushed his wings faster and harder than he'd ever dared before.

————

Lady Phaidra and Karolus were mercifully easy to find. They were standing together on one of the training ledges, and even from a distance and in the dark, Drystan could tell when they saw him. Another benefit of being a Dragon, it seemed, was sharpened eyesight.

His feet had hardly touched the ledge when Callispa started shouting over the wind.

"A Windigo! Coming this way from the west!"

Drystan expected them to ask questions, but both of them simply shifted. They went to the edge of the platform and prepared to jump off, so Drystan followed.

"No," Karolus said, hardly turning his head. "Not this time."

Drystan stared at him. "No?"

"You're not ready," Karolus said, his Dragon voice deep. "It's too dangerous."

"It was chasing a group of Fauns," Callispa broke in. "From the northwest, near the hills!"

"Let me come!" Drystan argued. "I won't interfere. Just let me see how it's done."

"He has a point," Lady Phaidra looked at Karolus. "He hasn't seen what the others grew up watching."

"Fine!" barked Karolus. "Just don't get in the way."

"Drystan!"

Drystan turned to see a Griffin and a Sphinx land on the other side of the ledge, Eirin astride the Griffin's back. And though Drystan knew his friend harbored no romantic feelings for Eirin whatsoever, he couldn't help feeling a prick of jealousy. Qeb could not only touch her in his Atharrach form without hurting her, but she could ride him.

Not that he had imagined such a thing for himself.

Eirin jumped off of Qeb's back and ran to Drystan. Karolus let out a warning growl, most likely telling her to stay back, but Eirin ignored him. Instead, she put her hands on his wing. And despite his armored exterior, her fingers left a tingling sensation that radiated around the place where they rested.

"I need you to get something for me," she said.

"This isn't a treasure hunting expedition," Karolus grunted. "We need to get going."

"*Please!*" She looked straight into Drystan's eyes. "I need to See!" She leaned so close she was leaning against him. "The more I See, the more I'll understand."

"We have to go now!" Lady Phaidra said, and she and Karolus leaped off the platform's edge.

"We need to stay close to them," Callispa said sharply as she climbed his wing again. "We have to go."

"What do you need?" Drystan asked. He could feel Callispa's legs tense with stress, but he kept his eyes on Eirin.

"If you kill it," Eirin said quickly, "I need something from its person. A scrap of clothing or lace or a ribbon or *something*."

"Drystan!" Callispa hissed, but Eirin ignored her. Instead, she neared until she was standing at the side of Drystan's head. So close to the fire. So unafraid.

"Mannish is considering…something," she whispered. "I don't fully understand it yet. But it makes me nervous." She glanced back at the city. "I need to See more so I can try to make sense of it all."

Drystan very much doubted at this point that he would be able to catch up with Lady Phaidra or Karolus, much less that he would be able to bring her what she was asking for. But when he turned to tell her so, her brown eyes were so large and hopeful…so trusting that all he could do was to promise to try.

"Thank you!" She placed her hand on the side of his face for a moment before running back to Nuru and Qeb. And terrified that he had promised the impossible, Drystan launched himself after the other Dragons, hoping he hadn't agreed to something incredibly foolish.

24

Drystan caught up with Karolus and Lady Phaidra faster than he thought. This was good, as the early morning hours were the darkest of the night. His Dragon eyes, he found, were nearly as good now as they were during the day, able to make out quite a bit of detail, even some colors, but he still wasn't familiar with the area.

"You're already catching on," Callispa called over the wind. Drystan could hear the smile in her words. "Hang back enough that they can maneuver without us getting in the way."

Drystan didn't have to be told twice. He did his best to tail them from a distance, watching from above as Karolus and Lady Phaidra slowly wound left and right over the forest.

But there was no sign of the running Fauns, no rustling of the trees. No matted yellow hair sticking out above the treetops.

"Where is it?" Callispa hissed, echoing Drystan's frustration.

"Could one of our guards have taken it out?" Drystan asked.

"It's not likely. We were farther out than most of the guards go, and even if we weren't, they probably couldn't kill a Windigo. Not by themselves."

Drystan watched as Lady Phaidra skimmed the top of the forest, lower than Callispa had let him go. "What are they exactly?"

"The Windigos?" He felt Callispa shudder. "They were Elves once."

Drystan nearly forgot to move his wings. "What?"

"There was a group of Elves ages ago who decided they weren't satisfied with channeling power into objects. So they chose to channel it into themselves."

"Can they do that?" Drystan asked, remembering his beautiful mother, shivering a little himself as he considered that the ghastly creature could ever have been anything like her.

"They did. And that's the result." Callispa's grip on his spines tightened. "Twisted, stretched shadows of what they once were, ruined by their stolen power. They have no speech that we can understand, and they spend their time hunting and eating anything that moves. In fact–"

She yanked hard on the spines she was holding, sending Drystan's whole body careening to the right. And none too soon. Where they'd been half of a second before, a rough wooden spear, at least half as long as Drystan's serpentine form, shot up through the sky.

"We need to take more care!" she called as he moved them higher. "One of those could go right through your heart!"

Drystan had already figured that out. Now he searched the forest below to find where it had come from. Karolus and Lady Phaidra seemed to have the same idea as well. They were diving down toward the place where the treetops were shaking.

The monster seemed to expect them because the treetops split to reveal its gaunt face as they dove down. Only, there wasn't one monster. There were three. No, five. There might have been more, but he couldn't see how many. It was too dark, and they were still moving, making their numbers difficult to count. Their yellow tangled hair looked absurdly like the treetops, which made the unnatural angles of their pointed teeth even more unnerving.

"Is this normal?" Drystan called back, watching as Lady Phaidra and Karolus climbed higher in the sky again. "Do they usually travel in groups this large?"

"Never. There are at least six here!" If Drystan hadn't known better, he would have believed her voice was shaking. "Those that live in a colony only send out one or two scouts at a time!" She paused. "And never...*never* this close to the mountain."

Drystan watched as Karolus and Lady Phaidra flamed at the

monsters. Lady Phaidra's fire made them stop and fight, but Karolus...

His flame was the stuff of legends. Tinted blue like Drystan's own fire, it tore down the Windigos' bodies, disintegrating them in mere seconds. If Drystan could fight like that–with precision and skill...

He might begin to feel a little more like himself. Like he had something to offer.

They had nearly demolished the entire group when Drystan spotted a slight movement behind Lady Phaidra. This Windigo was smaller than the others, and its wild tufts of yellow hair were nearly hidden.

"Callispa! Fly!" Drystan shouted over his shoulder.

"Why?" She paused for a second. "Oh, no. You're not doing that yourself."

"They're out of hearing range! I can't get their attention!" Drystan turned to look back as best as he could. "Stay here where you'll be safe!"

Callispa's blue eyes met his for a moment before moving down to the ground. "Then we're doing it together."

"Callispa–"

"Go! Or you'll be too late!"

She was right. The Windigo would reach Lady Phaidra within seconds. So Drystan dove down just as the shorter Windigo back-handed Lady Phaidra's head with one of its long, branch-like arms. The hit must have been violent because it knocked her down into the thick trees.

Drystan didn't stop to look for her. Instead, he circled the Windigo the way he'd learned to fight as a boy. Except now, he was flying instead of crouching, and his weapons were far more deadly.

Doing his best to remember everything Karolus had taught him about his flame, he sought to emulate Karolus's attacks with his own special fire. And while it wasn't as precise as the older Dragon's, it did make the Windigo scream before bursting into a cloud of sparks.

Drystan was still staring at the place where the Windigo had been when he heard a deep voice behind him.

"Perhaps he is Oreck's seed after all."

Drystan whirled around to see Karolus and Lady Phaidra, back in the sky, watching him with bright eyes.

Lady Phaidra was smiling, and Karolus looked somewhat mollified.

"You did well," Lady Phaidra said, her Dragon voice nearly at a purr. "And I am so grateful." She looked at Karolus and then down at the bodies, and her smile faded. Drystan followed her gaze and took in the devastating sight of the still forms of the dead Fauns. There so many.

"We couldn't save them," Callispa whispered.

Lady Phaidra nodded. Surely she was thinking of her husband.

After a moment, she swallowed and drew in a shaky breath. "This was a tragedy, but can't linger. We have much to discuss. Come, Drystan." She beat heavily against the sky, regaining the altitude she'd lost, and began to rise. Karolus did the same thing.

Drystan was about to thank them when he remembered something. When they were finally out of earshot, he looked back at his rider. "Could you fly me home?"

Her eyes widened. "You mean in Human form?"

He nodded. "There's something I need to get."

"Um…I suppose. But Drystan, if the Seer needs–"

"The Seer needs visions." He glanced down at the ground. "But I can't get them to her on my own."

Callispa was quiet for a moment. But eventually, she sighed. "Very well. Let yourself down. But we have to hurry, or more might come looking this way."

Drystan had to circle a few times before finding a place to land. Then he paused only to shift into his Human form before running toward the dead bodies that littered the forest floor. There were nine of them–fauns they'd been too late to save, and the charred remains of the Windigo he'd brought down.

Flies were already starting to buzz around the corpses. Or had they been there the whole time, feeding on the over-stretched flesh? Leaning down, he held his breath so as not to inhale the stench that hovered around the creatures.

What did one take from a Windigo? They hardly had any remaining clothes to begin with, just the remnants of ancient cloth.

He squinted in the dark, but just as he was about to try cutting the corner of the Windigo's clothes with his claw, he caught sight of something bright. He created a tiny flame just large enough to see several colorful beads threaded onto one of the Windigos' untidy locks of hair. The hair broke like rotted straw as soon as he tugged on the beads. Resisting the urge to gag, he shook the hair off and put it in his pocket.

Though his arms were in pain the entire flight back, Drystan couldn't suppress the feeling of success. After months of feeling like a useless failure, victory was intoxicating. He'd gotten what Eirin had needed. The Windigos had been defeated. And for the first time since arriving, he'd felt needed.

Really needed.

Back in the Walled City, Drystan had always expected to be the best and the strongest, and was given deference for occupying the role he'd merely been chosen for because of his strength. But here, he knew who he was–the great-grandson of the depraved prince. And yet... he'd done something right.

25

Eirin sighed as she watched the dark horizon. Nearly an hour had passed since Drystan had flown off with Callispa, and with each passing moment, her apprehension grew. Nuru had fallen asleep to her left. To her right, Qeb sighed too. She glanced up at him.

"Letting him fly off like that nearly killed you, didn't it?" she asked.

"No more than it did you." He quirked an eyebrow.

Eirin rolled her eyes, but she couldn't help smiling. It was nice having someone else concerned about Drystan. The people of Mhaedin seemed as though they couldn't care less what happened to Drystan. Nuru cared more than the people around them, but her devotion to Drystan was as strong as her devotion to anyone else in their little group. Thane...well, Thane hardly ever joined them these days. He'd deigned to make an appearance tonight, but as soon as his Centaur brothers had called him back, he'd given everyone an apologetic look and went bounding off again. Eirin wasn't even sure he was sleeping in Qeb and Drystan's room anymore. But right by her side was Qeb. Always Qeb.

When they'd first set out on their journey, Eirin had wondered if all of their bonds might dissolve as Thane's had seemed to do. But now that she knew Qeb was a Griffin, his undying loyalty to Drystan made sense. And it made her feel better too.

239

"I've heard that most Griffins wait until after they're married to choose recipients of their protection," Eirin said in a low voice. "Did you ever regret pledging your loyalty so young?"

"Not for an instant."

Eirin glanced up at him to see that he was in earnest. But of course he was. Once Qeb made a decision, he never looked back.

"You're curious." He was giving her a smug smile now.

She blinked. "About what?"

"What it's like–binding myself."

"What if he marries someone awful?" She raised her eyebrows. "Then you'll be stuck with her too." She leaned forward to whisper. "They might get him into trouble."

"Then whoever she is will need nannying even more than he does." He rumpled her hair, making her cry out in protest. Then he took a deep breath in and let it out slowly. "I suppose to others the extent of a Griffin's loyalty doesn't make sense."

"Not really." She sniffed.

He nodded. "You see it as an unequal relationship, one getting protection and companionship while the other gives it without question." He paused. "From what I understand of Humans, you need to *know* things. You don't feel complete without your Sight."

"That sounds about right." Eirin said slowly. Though she'd been *Seeing* for less than a year, she seemed to crave it more by the day.

"It was what you were made to do," he continued. "Just as Dragons were made to protect. Brownies need to provide." He glanced at Nuru's sleeping form. "Sphinxes need to rebel."

Eirin had to choke back a laugh.

"Griffins…we don't feel fulfilled unless we have someone to protect. But unlike many think, it's not a subservient relationship. It's one of honor, and no Griffin pledges himself to someone he cannot respect. I chose Drystan because even as children, I could see that he was good. I could be to him a brother, and he one to me."

"But you didn't know you were a Griffin back then," Eirin pointed out.

"No, but I did know that I wanted to fight at his side. And now, knowing what I do about myself and him, the knowledge that I'm his keeper fulfills me."

Eirin smiled up at him. "Well, I'm glad you chose him." She glanced around. "It's nice to have someone else around here who doesn't want to throttle him."

Qeb let out a deep, reverberating laugh. And as she laughed with him, Eirin realized that Qeb had moved beyond merely being Drystan's friend and her comrade. For the first time, she felt as though Qeb was her friend as well.

However, her smile disappeared quickly when two figures appeared on the dark horizon. One was flying with wings of fire, and she held the other figure in her arms.

The warning bells began to peal, and Eirin's heart beat unevenly as she scrambled to her feet.

"Is she…*carrying* Drystan?" she breathed.

As she and Qeb strained to see, they were quickly surrounded by those who had run to the ledge to see why the bells were tolling.

"I believe she is." Qeb's frown deepened as Callispa and Drystan grew close enough for them to see that Drystan was truly in Human form.

They came to rest on the platform in front of Eirin and Qeb. But before they could talk, Qeb had to yank Eirin to the side to protect her from being crushed by curious onlookers. At that moment, Lady Phaidra walked up the path in Human form.

"There you are!" she cried joyfully. "Karolus and I wondered what took so long. I want everyone to know," she said proudly, as if he were her own son, "that Drystan is the one who saved my life this night. There were not one but *seven* Windigos."

The crowd around them gasped. Eirin had never seen a Windigo, but what she'd heard about them sounded horrifying.

"Eirin."

Despite the chaos and chatter surrounding them, Eirin looked up to see Drystan calling her name. Drystan was motioning to her, but Callispa was hanging on his left arm, smiling in a way that made Eirin wish to snatch the joy off the girl's beautiful, blushing face.

"Here," Drystan said, seemingly unaware of Eirin's annoyance. He held out one hand and used his other, Callispa still attached, to grasp Eirin's, turning it palm up. Then he dropped a string of beads into her hand.

Eirin could immediately feel the vision inside, pulsing and throbbing. But the magic didn't come to her just with a touch. Just as with the Time Stone piece, this one was holding secrets. She would have to work on them. But oh, what a strength they had!

"Thank you," she said to Drystan, trying to smile despite the monster of jealousy that now raged inside her.

Callispa gave Eirin a polite smile, then tugged Drystan gently in another direction, murmuring about how another clan head would like to meet with him.

Eirin stared at the backs of their heads. Had she just been dismissed?

Nuru, who was now wide awake, sent her a sympathetic look. But Eirin couldn't stand it. Slipping away from Qeb in the press of the crowd, she walked in the opposite direction as fast as she could. People were still moving toward Drystan to see what all the fuss had been about, no doubt, but that simply allowed Eirin to walk faster.

She eventually found a garden and wandered inside. It was small and belonged to Lady Phaidra, who owned several all around the city, and it was open to the public. Eirin rarely saw the commoners enter it, though, which meant it was usually empty. Exactly what she needed today.

Sure enough, the garden contained only vines of vanilla orchids climbing the walls and trellises on every side. Eirin took a deep breath and seated herself on one of the small stone walls. Pulling out the beads Drystan had given her, she turned them over a few times in her hand.

"What are you trying to hide?" she murmured to the beads. There were five of them. Two blue, one yellow, one red, and one violet. She wasn't exactly sure what she was looking for. It might have belonged to the Windigo. Or might have been from one of the Fauns. If she'd been allowed to talk to Drystan, she would have asked. No matter the owner, there was power inside them, power that was just out of reach.

"What are those?"

Eirin looked up to see Mannish coming down the path. Had he followed her? Not that it really mattered.

"Drystan got them for me. They're from the dead Windigo. Or something out in the forest."

"Have you Seen something?" Mannish asked excitedly.

She shook her head and grimaced. "No. I can feel the vision from within, kind of like holding a stuffed bun. You can feel the heat from the outside, but you can't touch it. I can't seem to open it, though" *Just like the Time Stone* she nearly added, but she stopped herself just in time.

When he didn't respond, she looked up. "What is it?"

His grin only widened. "Only that you're so good at this."

She shook her head. "It's just–"

"No, I mean it. I don't think you understand..." He stopped and rubbed the back of his head and took a deep breath. "My parents were always supportive of me. I grew up knowing I was destined for great things." He laughed a little. "At least, that's what I was told." He gave her another look of admiration. "But you didn't know who or what you were. And you still thrive."

Eirin felt her cheeks redden slightly. "I spent my whole life fighting-literally-to survive. I suppose that enhanced my desire for success. Who knows what I would have been like without that kind of motivation." She looked back down at the beads. "I just wish I knew how..." She had an idea. "Tell me about Windigos."

"Well," Mannish scrunched up his face in thought, "I don't know a lot about them, but I do know that they were Elves at one time."

Eirin shivered as she remembered Alanna, her old mentor and Drystan's mother. Before this, if someone had told her that the monsters she'd glimpsed pictures of in some of the old books were of the same origins as Drystan's mother, Eirin might have thrown something at them for lying.

"They became addicted to the power they were channeling into objects," Mannish continued. "So instead of transferring it between other individuals and their tools, they became greedy and took the power of others into themselves."

Eirin shivered, and Mannish nodded.

"They weren't satisfied with a small amount, though. Unable to sate the raw desire for more, their addiction grew until they began to search for others they might drain of their gifts directly. And that raw stolen power mutated them into the beasts they are today. In fact, if those are what I think they are, those beads probably hold little bits of power that they used at one point to try and keep some of their stolen power near, back before they went mad." Mannish shivered too. Then he looked at her. "Why do you ask?"

Eirin frowned down at the beads, then closed her eyes and began rolling them between her fingers. "If the Elves became vessels of power, it only makes sense that..." There. She'd found it. A crack in one of the blue beads. As soon as she pressed on it, the bead exploded. And along with it, a vision that burst into life before her closed eyes.

The world the vision gave her was a strange color at first, blueish gray. But eventually, she could see that there were great, towering forests surrounding her. They were far taller than any giant, and they had grown close together.

And they were rotting.

The Windigos didn't give notice to the trees, however. They were moving south, trying to snatch up everyone in their path. But it wasn't just the Windigos and the Fauns who were traveling. There were people of all sorts traveling as well, be it at slower speeds. Some flying, some crawling, others running or climbing. The Windigos were the fastest by far, with their long legs and great strides. But whether fast or slow, they were all moving south.

This was no ancient vision.

A slight pressure on her left hand made her open her eyes, and she found Mannish holding her hand.

"Sorry," he said, dropping it quickly. "You looked frightened, and you weren't responding to my calls. I–"

"We don't have time for that now!" Eirin jumped to her feet. "We need to find Lady Phaidra."

26

Nuru, still in her Sphinx form, casually joined them as they left the garden. Qeb had probably sent her after them, as he would predictably want to see to Drystan's safety himself. He might not be able to control everything Drystan did, but he was rather mother-hennish about Drystan after his Dragon exploits.

The sky was quickly growing light, which meant the canvas covers were about to be rolled out. It was usually the quietest time of the morning, but today, there were people everywhere Eirin looked. Still, locating Lady Phaidra didn't take long. She was still outside on one of the lower platforms, relating what she had seen of the Windigos to the small crowd that had gathered around her. Her smile when she spotted Eirin was happy, but as soon as she met Eirin's eyes, her expression changed to one of alarm. Was Eirin really that easy to read?

"We must go sooner," Eirin blurted before Lady Phaidra had finished sending the others away. She held up the beads, and Lady Phaidra frowned at them.

"Where did you get those?"

"I asked Drystan to get them for me."

Lady Phaidra pursed her lips. "That would explain his odd return. Very well, come with me."

Eirin, Mannish, and Nuru followed her back into the mountainside, through several stone halls, up several flights of stairs, and into what looked like a small residence with one main living space and several rooms that branched off to the sides. The walls on the west side of the rooms had windows and let in a fair amount of light. The home was surprisingly humble for the great lady's station, but she relaxed visibly as soon as they were inside.

"Now," she said, collapsing on a couch. "Tell me what those cursed beads have shown you. But first, please sit. I know we've all had a–"

"The forests to the north have rotted," Eirin burst out, unable to wait any longer.

Lady Phaidra froze.

"And the Windigos are only just the beginning. Those Fauns must have just happened to be in the same place by chance." Eirin leaned toward Lady Phaidra. "The Windigo only got here faster than most because they have longer legs. But the rest are coming as well."

"The rest?" Lady Phaidra repeated.

"Atharrachs of all sorts. Thousands. They're coming too. They're just not as fast as the Windigos."

Lady Phaidra waved a hand. "People are always coming here."

Eirin shivered. "I don't mean a steady trickle. I mean, hundreds. Maybe thousands. They'll be here within a month, maybe two at the most. And if we don't make it to the Time Stones before they come, we'll be in a bad place. Because we *will* be overrun."

Phaidra studied her for a long moment, and Eirin was sure she was going to say it was impossible, or at the very least, brush her concerns off as unnecessary worries. But after a moment, the lady swallowed and looked around the room as though it held answers. "All right," she finally said. "We'll do it." Her face grew more determined. "We *will* do it. I'll call the others now."

Eirin and Mannish shared a relieved grin. Things were finally moving forward.

———

They were on the training platform an hour later. All Drystan's new followers and well-wishers had been shooed away, and now, besides Eirin, Mannish, Nuru, and Lady Phaidra stood Karolus, Hector,

Drystan, Callispa, Callispa's father, and representatives of every other major race in the city. Callispa and Lady Phaidra were talking quietly at the edge of the crowd. Qeb placed himself, arms clasped behind his back, near Drystan. Nuru, still in her Sphinx form, curled up near Eirin. Lady Phaidra gave both Nuru and Qeb a look but wisely said nothing. Qeb was very obviously staying put, and ordering Nuru around was like telling a cat to perform tricks.

She didn't.

Eirin put a hand on Nuru's shoulder, and to her surprise, Nuru didn't shake it off. Taking comfort in the familiar warmth of her friend's fur, Eirin tried to focus on Lady Phaidra as she moved to the head of the group to speak. She also tried to ignore the way it felt to see Callispa with her arm still in Drystan's. She whispered something to him, and it made him laugh. If her head got any closer to his shoulder–

"Thank you for coming so quickly." Lady Phaidra motioned up at the canvas covers, which had been erected over the training yards. "Especially in this heat. I don't usually call you like this, but I have something important that we learned this morning, thanks to our Seer."

All eyes turned to Eirin.

"It seems the northern forests have died," Lady Phaidra continued. A hushed murmur sprang up, but the lady raised her hand for silence. "They've rotted, through and through. And thousands of its inhabitants are heading our way."

"How many?" a man called out.

"How do you know?" a woman cried.

"When will they get here?"

"What will we do?"

The interruptions weren't whispers this time. Which made it more impressive when Lady Phaidra somehow managed to silence them once more.

"I will let you know when I know more. But for now, we must trust our Seers. They're our only window to the outside world."

"What are you suggesting we do?" the head Centaur asked.

"We're barely producing enough to keep our current population fed!" cried out one of the Brownies, a little woman about two feet tall. "We can't feed hundreds more! We just can't! Not now, and most definitely not through the winter!"

"Which is why we're not waiting until winter," Lady Phaidra said calmly. "Or even the autumn. Instead, we're going to the Time Stones in a fortnight."

There was a brief silence before someone, a young Fae from within the crowd, raised his hand. "Two weeks?" she asked incredulously.

Lady Phaidra nodded. "You heard correctly."

"But…" someone else called. "How?"

"We have more food now than we're going to in a month. Or in two months. Or in three. Am I correct, Mr. Gladstone?"

A second Brownie frowned. "Unfortunately, I believe you are correct. Our harvest this year will be smaller than anything we've brought in before."

Karolus sent Lady Phaidra a look of displeasure. Probably, Eirin guessed, for being left out of such an important decision. Lady Phaidra paid him no heed, however, looking at Eirin instead. "Will you be ready by then, Lady Seer?"

Eirin took a deep breath and nodded. "I'm ready now." However, even as she spoke the words, she wondered if she really was ready. For the stone that hung from her neck, still concealed beneath her shirt, had not yet shared its secrets. Its power ebbed stronger every day, but nothing Eirin did could loosen its truths. And she had the niggling feeling that whatever stories it held were precisely what they needed.

Drystan was painfully aware of the way Callispa's arm was wound through his the entire time Lady Phaidra was talking. He should have been paying attention to everything she was saying, but the feel of Callispa's bare skin on his own was more than a little distracting. Especially with Eirin watching them from the other side of the platform with narrowed eyes.

Callispa, on the other hand, looked blissfully happy. Though he didn't hear everything she said, Lady Phaidra did mention death and starvation several times, and not once did Callispa's blissful smile waver.

Her full, red lips and fiery hair seemed to shine, even beneath the canvas covers that had been rolled out over them to keep out the sun. Her freckled cheeks were a pretty pink, and her blue eyes reminded him of the sky. Getting lost in such eyes would have been easy for any man…had a pair of deep brown eyes not been watching him from afar.

The way Callispa had immediately paraded him around after they'd returned with the beads hadn't been lost on Drystan either. Anyone could see that Callispa wanted what the lower Dragons and their riders had. She wanted to be part of a whole, a couple that lived and loved and soared through the sky together. And if Drystan's heart wasn't already being tugged in another direction…

"Let's go get something to eat." Callispa beamed up at him. "I'm starving."

"I think," Drystan gently pulled his arm free, "that I need to get to bed." He glanced up at the place where Eirin had been standing. It was empty, of course. "I also think," he continued in a lower voice, "that it might be better if we were slightly less...familiar in the future."

Callispa's face fell.

"All things considered," Drystan hurried on, "I think it best if I simply focus on the task at hand. It's hard enough learning to be a Dragon."

At this, Callispa's expression smoothed. "I see. That's understandable enough. But if you change your mind..." She stopped and watched as Eirin walked past them. Eirin ignored them completely, but when Drystan looked back at Callispa, her brow was furrowed once more. "You'll know where to find me," she finished quietly. Then she turned and hurried off toward her father.

Drystan shook his head, wishing very much for a glass of wine and his bed. But instead of heading home, he jogged to catch up with the brown-haired girl marching in the opposite direction.

He would keep his distance. As long as he got to talk to her, everything would be fine. He wouldn't think about how much he wanted to touch her braid, or put his hand on the small of her back...

He caught up easily, keeping a safe distance between them, of course. But she stared straight ahead even when he was within her peripheral vision. "Eirin?" he asked softly.

She continued walking.

"It seems the beads were helpful."

She stopped walking and pivoted to face him. "Are you talking to me? In case you haven't noticed, my hair is brown. The one with red went that way."

"Eirin," he rubbed his eyes, "please don't do this."

She whirled around and began to walk again. "I have no idea what you mean."

Something inside Drystan seemed to catch fire from the flame inside his heart. Whether it was anger or hurt or frustration or helplessness, he really couldn't say, but when he shouted after her, he did so in his Dragon voice. "I'm just trying to keep you safe!"

The thunderous words echoed down the mountainside, and everyone in the street around them scattered. Eirin froze as well. Slowly, she turned to face him. He expected to see anger reflected in her own eyes. But for the first time, she simply looked…tired.

"I know," she finally said after a moment. Her hand went to her chest and lingered there before she moved it back down to her side. "I know. And I'm sorry. But…" she shook her head.

So that was what troubled her. Drystan stared at her from across the street, wanting so much to join her, to rub her hair gently and pull her against him so he could press his lips to her forehead as he had once done. But even now, he didn't yet trust himself to be so near. Only after he mastered his magic would he feel safe near her once more.

"I believe you can do it," he said softly instead.

Eirin gave a humorless laugh and looked up at the bright canvases spread above them. "That only makes it worse."

It felt strange to be having their conversation from across the road, but anyone else who might have heard their words had fled the small street when he'd let his Dragon voice out. That he'd accidentally used it at all made it more evident than ever that he still wasn't ready to be near her. Not yet, at least. "While we were waiting for the meeting to assemble, Lady Phaidra told me how you broke the beads to reveal a vision. She was really impressed."

Eirin simply nodded, but he'd seen the shadow of a smile on her lips before she'd pushed it back down. She was gratified by his praise whether she wanted to be or not. Encouraged, Drystan continued.

"I know things haven't been…straightforward lately."

Eirin scoffed, but Drystan continued. If he was going to make a fool of himself in the street, he might as well do so for her sake.

"Life has been…" he faltered. "I feel like I don't know who I am anymore." The words were out of his mouth before he was aware of it, but he knew they were true the moment he uttered them. He couldn't embrace his Dragon, and he was unable to give up the Man. "But I'm trying," he continued. "I'm trying to protect you. Only now,

I feel like I have to protect you not only from others, but from myself as well."

The hardness in Eirin's eyes melted as he spoke. Even from a distance, Drystan could see their warm brown soften. The way she looked at him made Drystan feel as though she could see through him.

She probably could.

"I know who you are," she called softly. "You're my friend. The Dragon...and the Man."

Drystan suddenly felt as though he could breathe again. Of course, he was vaguely aware, *friend* seemed the wrong word for... whatever they were. But for now, Eirin's friendship was exactly what he needed. He thought she was done, but as he began to turn away, she spoke again.

"And as my friend," Eirin continued slowly, "I need you. You are the one who followed me out of Torbaine. And you were the one who believed before anyone else did. You're the only one who under- stands the...the—"

"The burden?" he asked gently.

"Yes. The burden." She fixed her eyes on him, and he couldn't have moved if he'd wanted to. "Don't leave me alone in this."

As she spoke, Eirin suddenly looked very small and vulnerable, standing there alone. Never had Drystan wanted so badly to pull her into his chest and wrap his arms around her. He wanted to kiss the furrow of her brow and smooth its worry away. And that, perhaps, frightened him nearly as much as the monster he had become.

"I'll try," he promised. "I can't guarantee anything. But I'll try."

28

In the week that passed after Eirin broke the bead, the entire city was in an uproar. The Brownies combed the fields looking for any food that had ripened early that might be hidden in safe places for when the hoards arrived, or that might be packed away with those going to Iilaedin. The ones who were guarding or traveling trained even harder.

Eirin and Mannish searched the scholars' room more carefully than they ever had before, not even stopping to laugh or joke. The air was a mixture of excitement and discomfort. Part of Eirin yearned to enter the valley and make their way toward the great emerald palace. And yet, a part of her wanted to cower away in the mountain, clinging tightly to everyone she held dear. The even more cowardly part of her wanted to race straight back to her family and Alys, hang the consequences, and clutch them tightly as the world went down in flames.

And, of course, there was Drystan. True to his word, he returned to protecting her himself more often than not. Qeb and Nuru no longer had to bear the brunt of the duty. But following their conversation, enlightening as it had been, Eirin found herself watching him more closely than ever.

Unfortunately, that meant watching Callispa as well. For even though she no longer hung on his arm or stood as close as she had

259

the week before, she was always there in his shadow…the shadow which had once, briefly, been Eirin's.

"That's it," Nuru said as Eirin stormed into their room. "I can't take any more."

"Any more what?" Eirin flopped down on her bed. She and Mannish were now beginning their studies earlier in the day so she could train with Qeb at night. So she, like everyone else, was getting less sleep than ever.

"Your moping." Nuru swung her legs over the side of the bed so she was in a sitting position. "You were bad enough when you were determined to offend everyone back at the Citadel. But this is inexplicably worse."

"I don't know what you're talking about."

"You're like a thunderstorm everywhere you go. Especially after Drystan walks you home." Nuru tilted her head. "I thought you *wanted* him to walk you everywhere again."

"I did. Until that Phoenix decided she's his most adoring follower."

Nuru snorted. "Eirin, you are one of the most bull-headed, stubborn people I know. But when this girl steps in, all you do is pout. It's like you're not even trying."

"I–"

"You just sit there glaring at him the way you're looking at me right now."

Eirin huffed. Her day had not been wonderful, and arguing with Nuru was not on the list of things she really wanted to do right now. "I've tried to talk to him. And when I do, he says he's trying. But he stays as far away from me as possible without actually breaking his promise. Emotionally and physically."

Eirin didn't add that she'd thought they'd really connected for a moment the week before. The morning Lady Phaidra had announced their journey to Iilaedin, he'd opened up to her again. But almost as quickly as the day was over, so was his vulnerability. Now he was all polite smiles and quiet, vague conversation again.

And that was only whenever he was even close enough to engage in conversation.

"Look." Nuru rubbed her temples. "I know you believe that he would never hurt you. And now, I don't think he ever would. Not on purpose, at least. But if Drystan's anything, it's annoyingly self-righteous, and if he thinks there's a chance that he might hurt you, it only makes sense that he'd stay away."

Eirin didn't answer. She did not need to hear this right now. Even if it was logical.

"You should be grateful," Nuru said, lying down and rolling over to face the wall. "At least you've got Mannish." She paused. "At least someone is paying attention to you."

Eirin sat up and huffed. "Well, maybe I don't *want* someone else paying attention to me."

"Well, we don't always get what we want, do we?" Nuru snapped back. "You think we're special? Just because we came from the Walled City? Because you were born with special blood? All of that means nothing when it comes to choosing our own destinies. Because you might be the coveted Human. And Drystan might be a Dragon prince. But if you die by fire or in someone's teeth before this all ends, everything will have been for naught." And with that, she flipped over and pulled the covers up to her chin.

"You know what?" Eirin snapped as she got to her feet. "I don't think I'm tired anymore." She threw her shoes back on and stomped outside once more. Her common sense screamed for her to wait until Drystan or Qeb appeared to escort her, which would be in about ten minutes, as Drystan's training now took place during the day. Her anger, however, drove her forth, and before she realized it, she was outside and walking once again.

And finally, blessedly alone.

Because what she didn't want Nuru to see was how close to the mark her words had been.

The truth was that their little group was indeed starting to unravel. Qeb were as loyal as ever, of course, and Nuru seemed disinclined to put up with anyone else. But Thane was little more than an acquaintance at this point. And as much as Drystan did his best to be there for her, he was never near without Callispa. Even Mannish, as kind and helpful as he was, was a stark, nearly constant reminder that their camaraderie had changed. Which was strange. Because up until this year, none of them had been special to her. In fact, she had avoided them all, with the exception of Thane, who hadn't noticed her above the fact that she was the lovely Alys's best friend. But now, Thane was gone more than any of them.

When she'd arrived in Mhaedin, Eirin had thought she knew who she was. She was a Seer, and she was one of the few who had escaped the Walled City. For better or worse, she was a part of her ragtag band's core. Unlikely traveling companions as they'd been, they had a shared history, and that had bound them together. Especially Drystan. He was every bit as faithful as Qeb.

Or at least, he had been. But what was there to bind them together now besides time? They all had new purposes and new duties. What did they even need one another for now? Drystan was trying to hold to his promise, she knew, but that was different from wanting to be together.

And still there, even worse than her worry about her friends, was the burden of the Time Stone. Every day, every hour, every minute it lay there against her breast, cold, unmoving, and pulsing with a power…with a *vision* she couldn't See.

And her instinct told her she desperately needed to See that vision.

Eirin had been wandering, not really paying attention to where she was going, as she pondered. But now she realized she was standing in front of a stone tower that seemed to pierce the sky. Built at the outermost edge of the city, it was one of the lookout towers, she realized, created to see miles and miles of land from the south side of the canyon.

Dark was falling, but still too annoyed to return, Eirin opened the door and went into the tower, where she began to climb to the top. Four stories later, she arrived. She was slightly out of breath, so she remained on the inside and stared out the windows at the valley below.

"It's all unraveling," she whispered. There was no response except the wind that whipped around outside the tower. So she tried again. "I'm told that You're the one who wove it all together. So why does it feel like everything's falling apart?"

"It does often feel that way, doesn't it?"

Eirin hadn't really expected the Time Keeper to answer. So when the man's voice came from behind her, she nearly fell over. No less was her shock when she realized that voice belonged to none other than Rangvald.

He was sitting on one of the ancient stools in the back of the little round room, and his eyes were trained on the outside world as well. His robes draped against the ground, but he either didn't notice or didn't care.

Eirin stood frozen. Did she dare try sliding past him? Or did she continue talking? He obviously knew she was there, even if he looked as though he were in a trance.

"I used to come up here when I was weary," he continued, his eyes still trained on the window.

"It seems as though you still do," Eirin said cautiously, placing her right hand into her robes, searching for her knife.

He laughed softly and finally turned his gaze upon her. It was strange to see Drystan's blue eyes in the older man's face. "You have no need to fear, love. I'm not here for you. Phaidra called me to discuss your upcoming plans."

"I thought you didn't work together anymore," Eirin said cautiously.

He sighed. "We had an unfortunate misunderstanding, yes. But we share the same goal." His eyes went back to the window. "I fear we have little time left to squabble before there's nothing left to squabble about."

He looked directly at her once more. "And how are you faring?"

She stood straighter. "As...well as can be expected, I suppose."

The corner of his mouth quirked up. "And that pause wouldn't have been caused by your young Dragon, would it?"

Eirin stared at him, not knowing what to say.

His smile grew when she didn't respond. "From what I hear, he's been trying to keep his distance."

Eirin looked back out the window and took a deep, steadying breath. But inside, she was anything but steady. What interest did he have in their relationship? And how did he know how about it? Even more important, why did he care?

He stood and came to stand beside her. She thought about stepping a little back but decided against it. She didn't want him to think her rude. Or afraid.

"In Drystan's defense," he said gently, "being a young Dragon is unbelievably difficult. The early shifts are excruciatingly painful. And the constant, nagging fear that you'll hurt someone you love is even worse." He leaned forward and squinted at something outside in the twilight. "Of course, there's also the fact that there are only, to our knowledge, two remaining Humans left to save the entire world. Risking your safety for his own satisfaction would be rather selfish, don't you think?"

His words were kind, and the way he posed them reminded Eirin painfully of her father. They also, however, pooled a nauseating shame in the pit of her stomach. She looked down at her arm, where bandages had been not that long ago.

"Be gentle with the boy," he said with a warm smile. "I've seen the way he looks at you. He really does care."

"I'm not sure how much he cares," Eirin mumbled. It was childish, but she was feeling rather childish at the moment. "I'm not sure if he knows how much he cares."

To her surprise, Rangvald let out a roaring laugh. "I may be a hundred and fifty-two years old, but I hope I'm not so old as not to recognize that depth of affection when I see it." He quirked an eyebrow at her. "Or love, for that matter."

Eirin's face heated. "He has an affection, of course, but it's only–"

Rangvald was already shaking his head. "I can assure you, my dear. That boy has more than a mere friendly affection for you."

It was strange. Rangvald reminded her so much of her father. Gentle-spoken and kind. Not at all the way she'd imagined him the first time she'd heard his name uttered. Every time she'd met him in person, he'd defied all expectations. But then again, he'd sent people to kidnap them when they were in the mountain, and he'd waged war against her people.

Who was this man? Really?

"Why *did* you leave Mhaedin alone in the battle?" she asked.

He sighed and ran a hand down his long, graying hair, which was pulled back neatly at the nape of his neck. "That's a long story for another day. Suffice it to say now that I was too late to arrive at a critical point in the battle. Then I was delayed further by a freak blizzard." He made a face. "My guess is that we can thank the Ymir for that. Spiteful beasts."

Eirin frowned, trying to recall that particular group from her Citadel training, but Rangvald shook his head and went on.

"Unfortunately, but understandably, my intentions were suspect after that. I thought it would be better to retreat to my fortress with my people so there wouldn't be any more fighting." He stretched his arms and neck. "But that doesn't mean we don't still confer with one another now and then."

"Karolus–"

"My nephew lost his son." Rangvald stared darkly out the window. "That's enough to harden any man. Especially when I was the one who might have saved him…had I made it to the battle on time." He turned his familiar, sad eyes on Eirin. "As I said before, however, we're running out of time. I make my own plans, and Karolus and Phaidra make their own. But that doesn't mean we don't talk. It's not as though we can afford to be petty when we're all awaiting death's final call."

Eirin wondered if it might be too bold to ask about his plans, but before she could decide, he took a deep breath.

"I'm afraid I must go," he said, turning away from the window, his mouth set in a grim line.

"Before you go," Eirin blurted out. "Why did you attack Torbaine?"

He blinked at her, then understanding lit his eyes. "I am sorry about that. I didn't mean to frighten you. I have no excuse but that I'm a desperate man." His face hardened slightly. "And I'm aware of how they treat their people. I've had several contacts over the years who describe a world such as I would never treat my people."

"If…if you had gotten me," she asked slowly, "would you have taken me by force?"

"I had hoped you would be interested enough in learning the truth to listen. My informant in the city had reported to me that there was probably a Seer. And I've known enough Humans in my day to know that you all have an insatiable appetite for knowledge." His blue eyes gleamed slightly. "I had hoped that once you saw the truth, you'd be willing to stay to make things right. But I knew you wouldn't listen any other way."

Eirin frowned. His informant had been Alys's father, no doubt. Hardly a trustworthy source. "How did you meet Elder Gerard?" she asked.

He glanced back at the door once, but then settled back down on the stool. "He came to me about two years ago. Being as he was one of the city's Elders, or so he told me, he was one of the few who knew how the world really was."

"And that didn't seem suspicious to you?" Eirin asked.

He shrugged. "I'm always suspicious. But what he said matched what little we knew of my younger brother's betrayal."

"What did he want?" Eirin had heard the story before from her friend, Alys, but she wanted to hear Rangvald's side as well. According to the journals Alys had found, Elder Gerard had contacted Rangvald to offer him Drystan to satisfy a personal vendetta. And when he'd realized Eirin was a Seer, Gerard had offered her up as well for personal gain. The deal had led to a deadly attack on Torbaine, and it had set in motion Eirin's journey out of the Walled City, deeper into the mountain and then out into Solevar. But Elder Gerard was far from honest, and while Eirin trusted Alys through and through, the journals Alys had found had been written by Elder Gerard himself. Perhaps Rangvald would shed light on some details she hadn't heard before.

"He wanted a trade, he said. "It was a personal grudge, but one I could profit from."

"He wanted to give you Drystan," Eirin said.

Rangvald raised his thick, dark brows. "You've heard this story before."

"Yes, but I wanted to hear your side of it."

"It seems," he chuckled, "that you're as suspicious as I am. And that is wise, little one. It will serve you well. Yes, he wanted to give me Drystan. Too long had my brother's line been ruling, he decided, and he claimed that he was now powerful enough among the Elders that he might betray Drystan safely. And I decided I would accept. His requirement of money was paltry. Gold isn't much good now that food is running as short as the days. And though it shames me now to say it, I was eager to give my people some answers. I would have another Dragon. One from my father's line at that. Drystan owed me his life, I reasoned, and I would perhaps get some good yet from the blood of my dead little brother."

"Why did you choose to attack Torbaine when you did?" she asked.

"To put it simply, Gerard got greedy and tried to extort us. So I let him think he was wielding the power until I had convinced him to give us the maps to the city." He gave her a wry smile. "Truthfully, my people made a mess of things. I was unable to attend the attack myself. Something here had gone dreadfully wrong, thanks to the curse, and my generals mucked everything up without me. We underestimated what it would take to penetrate the city. And by the time I was able to organize another search party, a very unhappy Gerard admitted that you were already gone."

"And do you feel that way now?" Eirin asked coldly. "That Drystan is merely a pawn to serve you?"

Even in the falling darkness, she could see his eyes soften. "I'm afraid it's easy to see your enemy as a beast from afar. But seeing the light in his eyes brings the painful reminder that he, too, has a soul." He stood with a slight groan. "So to answer your question, no. Drystan is very different from his great-grandfather." He let out a gusty sigh. "Unfortunately, desperation pushes me to do things I never dreamed would be an option."

Eirin raised her chin. "Then why do them?"

He gave her a sad smile. "That's easy enough to say in the quiet of a moonlit tower. When you watch mothers sobbing because they're afraid their children will starve, such decisions are suddenly less black and white." Standing, he turned to the stairs. "I am sorry, but I really must go now. But– Oh! Before I forget."

He reached into the folds of his robe and pulled something out that was small and white. "This is called a Lechlien," he said as he pressed it into her hand.

Eirin held it up to examine it. It fit in the palm of her hand and looked to be made of parchment. Or was it flower petals? Eirin couldn't tell, even in the moonlight coming through the window. Whatever it was, it was folded so it looked much like a small bird.

"It's an Elven messenger. Made by the Elves to communicate with those far off. If you ever need help, you have only to speak your message into it, and it will find whoever you send it to." He paused. "You may send it to whomever you choose. But know that if you ever send it to me, I will answer."

And with that, he turned and was gone.

29

After Rangvald left, Eirin stayed in the tower until her conscience got the better of her. She had grown used to seeing everyone's magic within them and was no longer completely overwhelmed by the lights and flashes around her, but tonight she wanted to stay in the quiet tower with only the moonlight. She knew, however, that as one of the two remaining Humans on earth, someone would notice that she was gone soon if they hadn't already. Once Drystan's study had been moved to the daytime, she and Mannish had moved their study sessions to the early part of the evening. Which meant she should have been in the scholars' room with Mannish ages ago.

By the time she reached the bottom of the steps, she half expected to find an anxious mob out searching for her. But instead of a mob, there was only Qeb.

Of course it was Qeb.

Eirin gave him a dry smile. "Do I want to know how you found me?"

But Qeb didn't return her smile. "Drystan would go half-mad if he knew you were alone with that man."

Eirin straightened her shoulders. "I appreciate your concern, but if Drystan doesn't like something, he can tell me himself." She started to walk by him, but he put out a hand and gently grabbed her elbow.

"Have you noticed he no longer smiles?" Qeb asked softly. "There's a reason for that."

"He smiled enough the other day when she had his attention," Eirin spat out. Even as the words came out of her mouth, she was ashamed of them, especially after what Rangvald had told her. But the pain was still too fresh. She'd seen Drystan and Callispa laughing about something from across the street just that afternoon. And as much as her head told her that he'd been telling the truth the week before, her heart was having a hard time believing him.

Qeb just frowned more deeply. "Eirin."

Eirin hung her head and sighed. "I'm sorry."

"Give him time." Qeb let go of her arm and started walking. Eirin followed him, the fight suddenly leaving her like the flame of a candle being snuffed out.

"We don't have much time," she murmured.

He turned and gave her a sad smile. "I know."

They arrived at the scholars' room only to find Mannish gone. He often left in the middle of their study sessions, however, to get something to eat, so Eirin went to the table to pick up the book she'd left off with the day before. Sure enough, there was a note.

"Supper didn't agree with my stomach, so I'm going to see the Nymphs. I'll be back soon, though."

Supper not agreeing with Mannish wasn't an uncommon occurrence, Eirin had learned early on. Mannish had a rather sensitive stomach but not the sense or self-control to avoid the foods that made him ill. He would probably return in a few hours and then stay late to make up the lost time.

As Eirin lifted her book and prepared to retire with it to one of the plush carpets, she realized that the table itself was a mess. Or rather, messier than usual. She leaned over and read the titles of the books nearest her. To her surprise, they were familiar.

There was the one Mannish had shown her on the history of Wizards. Another was on Wizards' staffs. A book on spells. Another on use of the natural elements. The one book, however, that was most battered and had obviously been read more than all of the others, was lying on top of the pile. It was titled, *The Stones of Kadar*.

Eirin was sure she'd never seen this book before. Leaning in to see it better, she realized that it not only looked as though it had been read the most, but that it was ancient, far older than the books the first Humans in Mhaedin had tried to recreate from their memories, as many of the books in the scholars' room were. Its cover looked newer, but the pages were tinged black and yellow with age.

She reached out to pick the book up, but the moment her fingers brushed the leather cover, the scholars' room disappeared.

She was outside, and once again, it was the middle of the day. The sun did not burn her skin, and the field she stood in smelled sweet like freshly cut wheat. Most interesting, however, was the man standing before her.

Or rather, she was standing behind him. He was facing away from her, and by the gem-tipped staff in his hands and the pointed hat upon his head, she knew immediately that he was a Wizard. That, and his entire body glowed with magic, something she'd read only Wizards could do.

Wind rushed over the field, making the green grasses bend and sway. The Wizard paid the wind no heed, though. Instead, he was staring intently at the dark rolling evil that was consuming the sky to the north.

Eirin wondered in the moment how she knew it was evil. This she couldn't really say. Only, she knew that it was. The frigid winds the storm sent made her shiver as the gales raced past them toward the south, and its shadow made her heart flutter as it reared up in the sky until it nearly blocked out the sun.

The Wizard didn't so much as glance back, however. Instead, he raised his staff to the sky and began calling out incantations in a language Eirin didn't understand.

As the words left his lips, the wind began to glow and grew even stronger, this time swirling around her until Eirin feared it might lift her from the ground. But then it shot off to the north, and for one beautiful moment, Eirin thought it might chase the tempest away.

He might just win.

But then the dark cloud seemed to double before their eyes, and his words were lost to the wind as they raced into the cloud...the cloud that was suddenly charging toward them.

As the roiling black cloud, which smelled of smoke and sulfur and soil, met the Wizard's light, the Wizard screamed. And yet, even as he screamed, the light held the dark. Then there was an explosion that seemed to sear Eirin's entire body. Her eyes. Her skin. Her heart even faltered.

But the pain wasn't even comparable to the horrible violence of the raw power that surrounded her, sparking in the air, creating small bursts of lightning everywhere. The dark power surrounded them, devouring her from without.

The Wizard was barely visible in the smoke. She could only see him because he had burst into an orange pillar of flame. Then, after one brief moment in which he shouted up one more incantation, he dissolved into nothing.

Eirin screamed as the heat and the power then enfolded her completely within its darkness.

As her skin crawled with pain, though, she felt yet a new sort of pressure. First on her arms. Then her legs. This, too, hurt, and she shrieked again until she heard what sounded like a voice in the distance. She pleaded for the voice to come to her, to save her, but even as she did, she knew she couldn't escape the pain. The fire was too intense. Whoever it was had surely run if he was able.

And yet, the voice returned. And then another. And then more. Until there were many. Still, one voice drowned the others out, and Eirin realized slowly that she was now aware of two distinct sensations.

The pain was still there, but it had dulled slightly, enough that she could detect motes of strangely colored magic drifting through the air around her. Second, she wasn't standing or even sitting. She was being rocked.

As the burning continued to recede, she realized that she was holding onto someone's wrist. Then she could smell him, the recognizable smell of smoke and earth. Not the scents that had floated in the wind, but the pleasant ones.

Then the vision was over. There was no more burning and no more magic floating through the air. Instead, Eirin was in Drystan's arms, sobbing as her friends, Mannish, Lady Phaidra, Karolus, Callispa, and Hector all looked on in terror. Even the unshakable Qeb looked disconcerted.

"Don't leave me," Eirin sobbed into Drystan's shirt, bunching it in her hand in a pathetic attempt to keep him close. The pure, strong magic within his heart flowed as brilliantly as ever, and Eirin pulled herself as near to it as she could. After experiencing the darkness, his light was like air to a man buried alive.

"Please don't leave me!" she cried again, still gripping his shirt.

"I won't," he said softly into her hair, his strong arms pulling her tightly against him. "I'm right here."

30

$\mathcal{E}$irin trembled for hours after the vision. She'd never experienced such a potent magic, and if she was honest with herself, she never wanted to again. Even when she went to bed in the Nymphs' healing room, where she was rushed after opening her eyes, she was too terrified to close them again, and it was finally decided that Drystan should sleep on the healing bed beside hers.

The Nymphs worried and fussed, but Eirin heard the head Nymph tell Lady Phaidra that, unfortunately, there was nothing they could really do beyond giving her a calming tea.

"It is a sacrifice none of us can truly understand," she said quietly, giving Eirin a pitying look.

"Why haven't we seen this before?" Lady Phaidra hissed. "We've had countless Humans come through our gates in the last hundred years, and none have ever experienced this."

The Nymph pursed her lips. "I have only two guesses, though they could both be incorrect. First is the possibility that the book held enough of a remnant of the Wizard's magic that it nearly killed her."

"Humans can't be cursed!"

"No, but the magic in its raw form might have been nearly more than her mind was able to sift. Wizards bend unimaginable amounts of magic from innumerable sources, including dark, tainted sources

277

such as Windigos. They have the protection of their staffs, though. But Eirin–"

"I'm still not understanding how that's any different from a curse!" Lady Phaidra protested.

The Nymph took a deep breath. "Seers can see raw magic, unlike the rest of us. But when they See...when they See events from the past, they're not reading raw magic. They're reading the imprints of the magic of the past. Often on those imprints, the dust of past magic remains."

"So..." Lady Phaidra said slowly, "you think she might have been overwhelmed?"

"Eirin wasn't attacked by a curse. She was Seeing. We can't know what magic that book experienced before this. Or *how* many kinds of magic the book experienced, especially if it belonged to a Wizard. There's no saying what a mix of potent magics might do to a Human mind if experienced all at once."

They were silent for a moment before Lady Phaidra asked in a low voice, "You said you had two guesses."

"My second guess," said the Nymph, "is that Eirin is the most gifted Human we've ever seen."

"Which would mean?" Lady Phaidra asked.

"It would mean that Eirin was overwhelmed because of her sensitivity to the magic. It would be like taking someone with more sensitive eyes than the rest of us and exposing him to the sun."

A movement caught Eirin's eye, and she glanced up. Drystan was staring at her, his brows furrowed. Unlike Lady Phaidra, he didn't seem to be fooled by her sleeping act, and Eirin was sure he was listening to the conversation as well.

Personally, she hoped the Nymph's first guess was correct. Because she could choose not to touch that book again. But if the experience were an indication of the kind of life she was destined for...

Eirin shivered, and the Nymph let the conversation die as she hurried over quickly to drape another blanket over Eirin's bed.

"I wish we had a Unicorn," she sighed as she turned back to Lady Phaidra. "From what I can tell, Eirin's in perfect health. But a Unicorn would have been able to tell..." She let the thought trail off as she and Lady Phaidra looked up at the shelf where the Nymphs kept their salves and remedies.

"What exactly happened to the Unicorns?" Drystan asked, sitting up.

The Nymph looked surprised to see him awake, but she answered anyway.

"Unicorns were the most skilled healers in the world. Many worked themselves to death, trying to heal the pain and suffering after the curse. Others were hunted for their horns." The Nymph shuddered, her waxy, pale green skin seeming to pale even more. "The fools didn't realize that a horn is useless once you sever it. Anyhow, we had several for decades after the curse fell. But they generally only live up to eighty years at most. And our last one died of old age about thirteen years ago. Before she died, she made as many bottles of horn elixir as she could, but we only have one bottle left." The Nymph looked back at Eirin and frowned. "I'm tempted to use it now, but as she's lucid, I'm not sure what good it would do other than to calm her nerves."

It was decided soon after that Eirin would recover more fully in her own bed. She was still too shaky to stand, so Qeb carried her while Drystan changed into his Dragon form. Eirin understood this precaution, but as Qeb carried her, she mourned the lack of warmth she felt ebbing from within Drystan's chest. Qeb's magic was strong, but it wasn't the same.

Neither was his chest.

Once they were back in her room, Drystan changed back into his Human form and pulled up a stool to sit beside her bed. After Eirin had tossed and turned several times, he reached out and took her hand in his. And as his magic slowly seeped from his hand into hers, his heart pumping it rhythmically through his blood, Eirin was finally able to relax. Its warmth was comforting, similar to the memory of the safe sun in her visions.

The vision of the Wizard was still before her whenever she closed her eyes, but slowly, so slowly, the magic from his hand chased it away.

And the way his power overcame the dark vision only solidified the suspicions she'd been forming in recent days.

But he wasn't ready to hear those yet. And she didn't have the strength to argue with him now. So instead, she closed her eyes and fell asleep.

She didn't have the energy to ask about what happened until the following day, when hunger finally overcame her exhaustion and forced her to get up.

Drystan was still sitting beside her, staring out at the window. From what she could tell through the canvas covers, it was late morning. She could hear familiar voices coming from outside the door, and she was relatively certain that they belonged to Karolus and Lady Phaidra. And possibly Mannish. For once, Callispa was nowhere to be seen or heard.

"What…" Her voice was scratchy, so she cleared it and tried again. "What happened?"

Drystan looked at her, and she could see him exhale heavily. He cupped her chin in his large hand, studying her intently before standing and going to the door to tell those outside that she was awake. When he came back in, he refused to tell her anything until she started eating. Only when she was holding a plate piled high with food did he begin.

According to Qeb, Eirin had been reading a book when she passed out. When Mannish had returned from his errand, he'd found Qeb leaning over her on the floor, where she was thrashing, sobbing, and pleading incoherently. Qeb had ordered him to get help.

"I should have been there," Drystan said darkly, glaring at the ground. "But I've been having difficulty training these last few days, and I thought Qeb could…" He closed his eyes and shook his head.

"You and Qeb have hardly been getting any sleep," Eirin said after swallowing her bite. "I don't blame you, you know."

Well, she did somewhat. But that wasn't going to help either of them right now.

"I don't want to stay away from you." Drystan met her eyes, his own burning with something she couldn't name. "I was just so afraid

I would hurt you again." He swallowed. "I still am. But seeing you like that last night..." He shuddered.

Eirin shifted uncomfortably. "What happened after that?"

"By the time word had spread and I arrived, Qeb hadn't been able to wake you, so Mannish had insisted on trying." Drystan's eyes flashed somewhat. "The annoying little fop was still trying when I got there. The Nymph finally convinced Mannish to move, but she couldn't pull you from the vision either."

Eirin shivered slightly as she remembered how long the vision had seemed to last. Apparently, she wasn't the only one who had thought it long.

"I tried to hang back when it first happened," Drystan whispered.

"What made you change your mind?" Eirin asked.

He gave her a funny look. "When you started screaming my name."

Eirin sat taller and blinked at him. "I don't remember that."

Drystan smiled wryly. "Well, you did. And we have a room full of witnesses if you doubt me."

The door opened, and Lady Phaidra peeked her head inside.

"I'm glad to see that you're awake and eating." She stepped closer. "Do you think you could tell us what the vision was about? I don't wish to rush you, of course, but–"

"But you need to know the vision." Eirin nodded and dusted off her hands. "Of course." She drew in a shaky breath. "I can tell you. It just...it was frightening."

Drystan reached out and took Eirin's hand again, and she squeezed it gratefully as Karolus entered behind Lady Phaidra. Karolus frowned at Eirin and Drystan's clasped hands but said nothing as he sat on a stool beside Lady Phaidra. Drystan frowned as Mannish let himself in behind them.

"What happened?" Lady Phaidra asked gently.

"Yes," Mannish said, looking at Eirin and Drystan's hands as well. "Tell us everything!" As he spoke, Drystan's hand tightened around hers.

So Eirin told them about the field and the Wizard and the roiling darkness. "The air tasted metallic. And sour." She shuddered again.

"But watching the Wizard die... That felt like the death of hope itself. And I don't even know why."

Lady Phaidra glanced at Karolus.

"Aed, most likely," he said grimly. "He was protecting the plains at that time."

"He was especially gifted with using the wind!" Mannish leaned forward on his stool. "From what we know, he died in the–"

"The falling of the curse," Lady Phaidra finished with a sigh. "At least we know for sure now."

"If he died, how did she see his death by touching the book?" Drystan asked, his brows furrowed. "I thought objects only retained memories they were present for."

"Another Wizard, Isayas, went looking for him and found his belongings in the field," Mannish said. "His staff had been destroyed, but he must have removed his belongings before trying to fight the curse. The book must have been among them."

"What book was it?" Karolus asked.

"*The Stones of Kadar*," Eirin answered.

Karolus turned to look at Mannish. "I thought you were seeking information about the curse itself."

Mannish colored slightly. "I am. I mean, I was. I just wanted to find a particular answer to something." He looked at the ground.

Karolus pursed his lips, but Lady Phaidra spoke again. "I'm afraid we don't have all of the answers. But what I learned from prior Seers is that conventional wisdom states the stronger the vision, the stronger the source of power. Which would only make sense if you witnessed not only the falling of the curse but Aed's attempt at stopping it."

Eirin nodded slowly. "That would make sense. Because most of my visions aren't nearly that real. Most are murky and blurry at best. It's like trying to look through muddy water."

"Did you touch anything else with the intention of Seeing that day?" Karolus asked. "It's most likely from the book, but perhaps the vision was latent."

Eirin started to shake her head, then paused. "Wait, I did touch something else that...I think it's rather old." Her neck felt hot as she gently pulled the little Elven messenger from her pocket. She hadn't planned on telling anyone about it. Not yet, at least. But she was also determined to avoid another vision like that at any cost.

Karolus sucked in a fast breath, and Lady Phaidra gasped.

"What is it?" Drystan asked as he and Mannish watched with wide eyes.

"I haven't seen one of these in years," Lady Phaidra breathed. "It's an Elven messenger!" She squinted at it. "I didn't know any more existed."

"Where did you get it?" Karolus asked.

Eirin glanced at Drystan. Suddenly remembering Qeb's words of warning, she could only cringe now as she avoided looking at Drystan.

"Rangvald gave it to me."

Drystan, who had been rubbing her knuckles with his thumb, went perfectly still, and the others gaped again.

"Rangvald?" Lady Phaidra echoed.

"I was in one of the lookout towers last night. He joined me and said he'd once used the same tower to find peace and quiet." She shrugged. "We weren't there together for long. He gave this to me and said to send it out if I ever needed help."

"What exactly is it?" Drystan asked in a strained voice.

"An enchanted messenger," Lady Phaidra said, taking the little folded paper in her hands. In the light now, Eirin could see that it indeed looked like a bird. "These were expensive and difficult to create, from what I understand. I haven't met an Elf who makes them...for decades."

"How does it work?" Eirin asked.

"The magic awaits within," Lady Phaidra continued. "When the owner needs to send a message to someone far off, he needs only whisper the message into the bird and then tell the bird which person the message is directed to. Then the messenger will fly it to them." She handed it back to Eirin. "They take a heavy amount of magic to make, hence the shortage."

"You don't think the vision came from the bird, do you?" Mannish asked, doubt in his voice.

"No. I'm convinced the vision was from the book, as that's what she was touching when she had it," Lady Phaidra said. "Besides, I don't know how Rangvald would have gotten a bird that was Aed's possession."

"Is it safe?" Drystan asked, leaning forward in his seat.

"I believe so." Lady Phaidra glanced at Karolus. "Once the messenger is made, it can be used by anyone. Its magic is not loyal or disloyal. Simply a tool as much as a hammer or a saw. And I think," she continued, "that it's actually a wise little trinket for Eirin to carry. I wish we had one for Mannish as well."

Eirin felt relief as she put the little paper bird back in her cloak. Still avoiding Drystan's gaze, which she could feel on her face, she looked back up at Lady Phaidra. "About the vision, though. Where were the other Wizards? Surely Aed wasn't the only one to try and stop the curse."

"There were six wizards alive at the time the curse fell," Mannish said quickly, his pale eyes brightening as he spoke. "Aed, the one you saw, Isayas, Kanan, Tafari, Marek, and Dal. All but Isayas died fighting the curse when it fell, and Isayas only survived because he was in the mountains with his wife when it happened. He went in search of his brothers afterward but could only conclude that they had all died. He was the one who brought us Aed's belongings for safekeeping."

"Is he still nearby?" Eirin asked. She doubted it, as it seemed as though having a Wizard might have made life much easier for Mhaedin, but she couldn't help asking.

Lady Phaidra was already shaking her head. "We've begged him to stay with us. But his wife lived and died in a village deep in the mountains, and now he refuses to leave her grave."

"I feel terrible about that book," Mannish said, scratching the back of his neck. "I've never had an inkling of a vision while touching it." He gave her a sheepish grin. "But then again, I think it's clear who the more sensitive Seer is by far." There was no jealousy or resentment in his smile. Just more of the awe that was always so pure it made Eirin somewhat uncomfortable.

"All the same," Karolus said, still frowning, "I think it would be wise to put such books away. We're leaving in a week, and we won't be encountering any Wizards on our journey. It would be best to avoid such incidents as we continue to prepare."

"Of course," Mannish said, looking at the ground.

"And I think," Drystan said in a firm voice, "that Eirin needs some more sleep."

Lady Phaidra gave him a smile. "Right you are. I'll be back later to see how you're doing, and the Nymphs have promised to send someone to examine you every hour. Which means they should be here soon." She stood, and the others followed. "If anything," she said, looking back at Eirin with one hand on the door, "I think this episode has proved that we need you now more than ever."

31

The final week before they began their journey passed ridiculously fast. Eirin felt like she'd scarcely laid her head down in the early hours of the morning before she was raising it up again in the afternoon.

Wake up.

Eat.

Search for answers in the scholars' room.

Train with Nuru and Qeb.

Eat.

Sleep.

Do it all over again.

Unfortunately, her vision of the thousands of refugees from the rotting forests proved true. The day after her vision of the Wizard, they began to arrive. And as she'd suggested, the Windigos had only arrived so early because they could travel faster and farther than the others without rest. The flying creatures came next, followed by the faster land creatures. And while most were simply tired, hungry, and desperate to keep their families alive, there were a number of groups, such as packs of Cerebus and Tokoloshe, that seemed determined to take what they wanted without respect for boundaries.

Drystan and Qeb got even less sleep than Eirin did, taking turns guarding her, training with their mentors, and even leaving the city for short increments to quell the skirmishes that were now popping up in the valleys below as hordes flocked to Mhaedin. Eirin couldn't fathom how her friends continued on unflinchingly as they did. But, as Drystan said, they really had no other choice.

But they weren't the only ones. Phaidra and Karolus led even larger bands of their warriors out to meet the attackers. Even Rangvald sent out a number of his own soldiers to create hastily erected outposts to clear the way for Eirin's looming venture.

"I still don't trust him," Nuru announced one evening when they were all together, eating and discussing their defense plans. "It seems suspect to me that he would help now."

"We may not see eye-to-eye," Lady Phaidra said grimly, "but we're all realizing now that we have no time to be at odds with one another. Eirin was right. The end is coming sooner than we believed, and if we don't work together, we'll soon have nothing to work toward."

"She was right about the trees too," Mannish added from the other side of the table. They were eating in Lady Phaidra's home, where they often gathered now to speak of secret topics. "I spoke to a woman who fled their village in the forest. She says the entire forest to the north—at least, the part she was from—is now unlivable. One night, they went to sleep with everything as it always was. The next morning, they awoke to the sound of trees collapsing in on themselves. Everything had rotted overnight, and they had no warning."

Eirin doubted there was no warning. But maybe that was only because her ability gave her such an advantage over everyone else.

"How are the harvests coming along?" Karolus asked Hector. The Faun wiped his mouth on a napkin and sighed. "We're nearly ready with the journey preparations. It's the city stores, unfortunately, that I'm afraid are terribly short of what they need to be. We're halfway through the summer, and the crops aren't promising."

"How so?" Callispa asked.

Hector shrugged. "Many of the seeds never came up this year. And of the plants that did come up, many are sickly and brown." He leaned back in his chair. "I'm glad we moved everything up. Because if this doesn't work..." He let the words die, but everyone knew what he meant to say.

Callispa looked around the table, which was now quite solemn. "Well, I for one, can't wait for the feast!"

Mannish's face lit up. "Yes! Tell us how preparations are going for that!"

As Lady Phaidra launched into a lively description of everything they had planned, Eirin let her mind wander.

Much to Eirin's chagrin, Callispa returned to traipsing around after Drystan once Eirin had been healed. The only improvement was that Drystan was physically with Eirin more often now, rather than watching from afar. And even more telling, he no longer turned away whenever she glanced in his direction. Instead, his blue eyes burned unabashedly whenever she met them, holding her gaze for as long as she held his. Eirin's breathing hitched slightly whenever this happened, and from the way Drystan's mouth would turn up at the corners, she knew he was aware of it too.

So what did it all mean?

Unfortunately, Drystan's close proximity to Eirin meant Callispa was always nearby as well.

In truth, Callispa wasn't an awful person. Eirin would probably have disliked her less…or possibly have even liked her outright if she hadn't continued watching Drystan like he was a prize to be won. But she did. So Eirin gritted her teeth, and for Drystan's peace of mind, forced her own mouth to keep shut.

Still, hope flitted around the city like an early autumn breeze on a hot late summer's day, even amidst the worry and angst. It was nearly palpable. A celebration had been planned for two days prior to their journey.

"There will be dancing and toasts and a feast!" Callispa was still gushing the morning of the celebration. As she spoke, she gave a graceful little spin in the street as they walked back to their rooms from the night's training. "I'm so excited I don't even want to sleep!"

"Celebrating two nights before we leave seems more than a little foolhardy." Nuru scowled as she walked.

Hector, who had been carrying on a quiet discussion with Qeb, looked up. "Perhaps it would seem so. But hundreds of young people and hardened warriors will be leaving their families, possibly forever. This provides them a chance to wish their loved ones off with passion and confidence. Besides," he added softly, "if we don't succeed this time, it soon won't matter how much food we have left in our stores."

They arrived at their rooms, where Eirin was more than glad that Callispa had to say goodbye, and laid down to sleep before the celebration. As she laid in her bed, however, she was heavily conscious of the sleeping girl in the bed across from hers. And the silence that had settled between them in the last few days.

She regretted her harsh words to Nuru, flushing whenever she remembered them. And though Nuru hadn't cried or stomped around or gotten angry, she'd been noticeably absent. Eirin had hardly seen her over the last week, and she was convinced that Nuru's absence was of her own doing. When Lady Phaidra had assigned Hector to teach Eirin about all the dangers they would encounter on the way to Iilaedin, Nuru had requested to go out with Karolus's bands. It seemed patrolling for marauding gangs was suddenly preferable to helping Qeb train Eirin at night. And now that Nuru was gone so often, Eirin couldn't apologize even when she wanted to.

She finally got her chance later that day, however, when they had awakened from their sleep and began to prepare for the celebration.

The gowns being provided for them would be made of silk and crafted by one of the Tsuchigumos who lived within the city walls, they were told. Gifts from Lady Phaidra for all they were doing.

Eirin's prior experience with that particular race of Atharrach had been anything but pleasant, so she had been more than a little apprehensive about meeting another giant spider shifter. When they'd finally arrived at her shop for their fitting, however, Madame Mayumi was everything Eirin's first Tsuchigumo was not. Short and somewhat stout, she kept up a string of chatter so fast Eirin had a hard time keeping up. Eirin did understand, however, when the woman shoved a sweet biscuit in her hand and then began to take her measurements. That had been two weeks ago, and now, for the first time, Eirin was to see the fruits of the little woman's labors.

"I wonder what colors she'll have chosen," Eirin said, seizing the opportunity to speak as they got dressed.

"Guess we'll see," Nuru mumbled as she lifted the parcel off the table where it had been left.

Eirin took and unwrapped her own parcel. Then she gasped.

Her gown was a rich blue, but swirled in varying shades of deep violet. Little gemstones had been sewn into the skirts to look like stars in the night sky. Eirin inhaled sharply again as she stood and shook the dress out.

The gown was simple with short sleeves that rested on the shoulders and a skirt that flared out slightly at the hips. The ruffles were subtle, but flowed down like a graceful waterfall, where the skirt stopped just a few finger widths from the ground. Over the short sleeves lay a small shawl that was so thin it was see-through.

"Oh!" Eirin breathed.

Nuru seemed no less enchanted with her dress. But instead of oohing and ahhing as Eirin was doing, she simply stared. So Eirin squealed for her. Like Eirin's, the gown had thin straps that rested on the shoulders. Nuru's dress, however, was a layered set of colors that looked much like a sunrise with red, orange, yellow, and what looked like little ribbons of gold woven in and out.

"There's a note," Eirin said when she was finally able to tear her gaze from the gowns. Picking it up, she read it aloud.

I've been saving these materials for years. Might as well use them if the world is going to end.

    -M. M.

"Someone has a lot of confidence in this little excursion." Nuru shook her head and went back to staring at her dress.

Suddenly, Eirin couldn't take it anymore.

"I'm sorry!" she burst out.

Nuru turned slowly and raised a single brow. "I'm sorry?"

"For the way I spoke to you. When you were trying to tell me about Drystan staying away from me." Eirin felt like she was tripping over herself, but if she didn't get the entire apology all out at once, it would probably evaporate, and she'd simply be left standing there like an idiot. "I was upset," she continued, "and–"

"It's fine." Nuru waved an arm.

"But I–"

"Look." Nuru finally looked directly at her and gave her a wry smile. "I always knew you were a little prude. It's good to see that you're fallible sometimes." She gave Eirin another wistful smile.

"I never meant to be," Eirin mumbled.

"I know. Actually, when I wasn't insanely jealous of you and your perfect family, it was kind of nice in a weird way."

Eirin paused mid-stroke as she brushed her hair. "What was?"

"I may not have liked you," Nuru said slowly as she began to coil her own hair, "but you were constant. And that was something I didn't have much of in my life." She gave Eirin a knowing look. "Even if you are annoyingly good like Drystan, I knew what to expect from you."

"You were right, though." Eirin shrugged. "And I was wrong. About Drystan, I mean."

"Don't grovel. It doesn't become you." Nuru rolled her eyes, but her smile was genuine, even if it was small.

Eirin paused slightly before daring another question. Nuru probably wouldn't like it. She didn't generally like questions that were too personal. But if she was opening up to Eirin now, Eirin would take every little insight she could get into her mysterious friend's life.

"I was wondering…you don't seem to spend much time with the other Sphinxes." She gave Nuru a hesitant grin. "Does that mean we're that much more fun? Or are they–"

"A bore? Excessively." Nuru snorted. "Most of them have been paired off for marriage since they were children. They don't like outsiders or newcomers. Which is perfectly fine with me." She sniffed. "I don't like them either."

Eirin stared as it finally dawned on her. Nuru was lonely.

No wonder Nuru had reminded Eirin that not only was Drystan there for her, but Mannish was as well. Especially after Nuru's most faithful companion seemed to have abandoned her as well.

"Have you heard from Thane? About tonight, I mean?" Eirin asked softly.

"No. Why?" Nuru sniffed again.

Eirin paused for a moment before tossing her gown on the bed and marching over to Nuru's side.

"Because we're going to make him wish that he had asked." She gave Nuru a fierce smile.

And though she could tell Nuru was trying not to, Nuru smiled back.

———

By the time Eirin and Nuru stepped outside their room, the sun had gone down, and the canvas shades were rolled back. And Drystan, Qeb, and even Thane were waiting for them.

Drystan was handsome in a dark silk vest that crossed his chest over a white shirt, then wrapped around his waist in a thick band. His trousers were only slightly flared before being tucked neatly into his boots at the bottom. Eirin had to put extra effort into not staring at the way his trim waist moved up and out into his wide chest and shoulders.

Looking at the dumbstruck expression on his face helped.

While Eirin considered herself generally unspoiled by excessive vanity, she felt slightly smug when all three men stopped talking and stared. Qeb was the first to come to himself and nudged Drystan, who closed his mouth and cleared his throat. But it took several sharp nudges to Thane's arm before he gathered his wits as well.

Eirin turned and gave Nuru a subtle wink, but Nuru just rolled her eyes. Now that she was getting to know Nuru a little better, however, Eirin was convinced she could see satisfaction in the taller girl's dark eyes.

What Eirin was happiest of all about, however, was the absence of Callispa.

"Are we going or not?" Nuru snapped.

"I'm actually not attending tonight," Qeb said, sharing a measured look with Drystan. Drystan nodded slightly in acknowledgement as Qeb continued. "I told my mentor that I would share duty with him tonight."

"You're going to miss it?" Eirin cried.

Qeb smiled. "I'm not sure what the dancing here involves, and I have no desire to learn." He looked at Drystan again. "You'll be well?"

Drystan punched him playfully on the shoulder. "I do survive now and then on my own."

"I'll be nearby if you need me." Qeb ignored the jab and nodded at the others. "Have fun."

"I'm not sure he would know how to have fun if he tried," Eirin murmured to Drystan as Qeb changed form mid-stride and took to the twilight sky.

But Drystan didn't smile. "I think he's relieved to miss tonight, actually."

They began to walk, Nuru leading the way, Thane trailing her, and Eirin and Drystan behind.

"Why?" Eirin asked.

Drystan sighed. "He chose to tie himself to me at a young age. From what I've gathered, real Griffin communities don't allow their children to tie their loyalties so young. But Qeb didn't have Griffin guidance, and he's been with me so long now that unless I died, it would cause him excruciating physical pain to break his bond." Drystan paused to watch his friend's winged form disappear into the night. "Some say the bond can't be broken by anything except death, though that's debated."

"I asked him once if he was sad he'd given his loyalty away so young," Eirin said, frowning up at Qeb's shrinking figure. "He said he doesn't regret it at all."

"Oh, he doesn't regret it," Drystan replied quickly, then he paused. "I think, though...I think he's lonely."

Understanding dawned on Eirin, and she sighed. "He doesn't think he'll find a wife who will be willing to follow him."

Drystan nodded. "Griffins generally don't find someone to give their loyalty to until after they're married, and that's usually done by arrangement through their parents. It keeps allegiances from being so... messy."

Eirin pursed her lips. "I can see how that would be difficult. If someone doesn't want to join the family the Griffin has already created..." She let the thought die.

"Speaking of not wanting something..." Drystan nodded up at

Thane, who was still trying to get Nuru's attention. "I don't think I've ever seen any man fail so hard as that one is doing right now."

Eirin laughed. "Serves him right."

"She's driving him crazy."

"Funny how that works." Eirin snorted. "Ignore a girl for weeks, and there's a possibility she'll want nothing to do with you down the way."

But again, Drystan didn't laugh. Instead, he gave Eirin a long look. Eirin returned his gaze, but before either of them could speak, a familiar voice came from behind.

"Eirin, don't you look lovely?" Lady Phaidra came to walk on Eirin's other side. The streets were getting busier the closer they came to the city square that had been set aside for the feast. "And you, too, Drystan." She nodded at him. "That jittok is what your ancestors wore. Thankfully, Madame M. has a long memory and knows how to make them still."

Lady Phaidra was lovely with her hair pulled into a complicated knot at the back of her head. She wore a silk dress that was tied in a way similar to Drystan's vest, though instead of stopping at trousers, hers extended into a full skirt. Her ears and neck sparkled with jewels.

"Everyone seems so excited," Eirin said, looking around. Sure enough, there were colored ribbons hung from every shop and window. Laughter and lively chatter was everywhere, and Eirin couldn't find a single sour or frightened face in the crowd that pressed in on them.

"They have you." Lady Phaidra smiled down at her. "And you, my dear, are a powerful Seer." Then she looked past Eirin and smiled at Drystan. "And another son of Oreck."

Eirin couldn't help but smile slightly as she realized just how long it had been since anyone had called Drystan a son of Oreck.

"You and your friends have brought hope, Eirin. The most hope we've ever had. Now, I need to see to some details, but you all have fun tonight. That's an order." And with that, Lady Phaidra was gone.

"Here," Drystan said, weaving Eirin's arm through the crook of his elbow. He winked at her. "So we don't get separated."

Eirin laughed and allowed herself to walk much closer to him than they had in recent days. But as they spilled into the street, which had been closed off and decorated for the celebration, a familiar figure bounded toward them, and Eirin's laughter quickly died.

Callispa was breathtaking. Her fiery curls were gathered at the nape of her neck, and she wore a dark green dress of velvet with a red sash draped across her chest. Her figure was long and graceful, much as Alys's was, and her blue eyes sparkled.

Suddenly, even in her beautiful midnight gown, with her dark brown hair braided and pinned in delicate coils on her head and borrowed pearls in her ears, Eirin felt short and frumpy in comparison.

"Drystan! Eirin!" Callispa had the decency to include Eirin in her greeting, but only just. Her eyes were all for Drystan. Where were Nuru and Thane?

"Isn't this wonderful?" Callispa asked, reaching out and grabbing Drystan's free hand as she bounced up and down. "Are you excited to dance?"

Drystan gently extracted his hand from hers and put his left hand on Eirin's, which rested on his forearm. Eirin suddenly felt as though she could breathe again.

"Everything is absolutely wonderful," he said with a gentle smile. "Though, I'm afraid, Eirin and I hear that your dancing is different from ours. I'm not sure we'll know how to jump in."

Callispa, who had blushed when Drystan had withdrawn his hands, now cocked her head to the side. "You don't dance where you come from?"

"We dance," Eirin said, determined not to be left out of the conversation, "but only jigs and large group dances. Nothing…individual." At least, that was the way Mannish had described the kind of dances that would happen here tonight. Couples would partner off and dance exclusively with one another. Torbaine had nothing like that, and Eirin wasn't sure how that made her feel.

As if conjured by her thoughts, Mannish appeared as well. He was wearing a vest similar to Drystan's, but it wasn't made of silk and looked far less complicated. Still, its shade of brown made his pale eyes seem bluer than usual. The cut of the vest also made him look taller.

"Oh, um, hello, Mannish," Callispa said, looking slightly flustered. Then she beamed. "We're going to have to teach Drystan and Eirin how to dance. They've never danced before. At least, not the way we do."

Eirin stared at Callispa. She wasn't even trying to be subtle. Eirin tightened her grip on Drystan's arm.

"Oh! Oh, yes." Mannish blushed profusely as he bobbed his head up and down a few times. "Dancing. My...my mum taught me a few dances."

"I still think," Drystan said gently, "that Eirin and I are going to sit back and watch a little before we try anything." He gave Eirin another wink. "Want something to eat?"

"I'm starving." Eirin beamed up at him as they left a dazed Callispa and still blushing Mannish behind them.

The food was good, but honestly, Eirin tasted little of it. All she knew was that he had chosen her. Callispa...radiant, fiery, capable Callispa had been standing right in front of him.

And he had chosen Eirin instead.

They stood at the edge of the crowd in companionable silence for a while, nibbling at the finger foods they'd gathered from the countless trays set out on tables. People laughed and shouted, and children scampered about underfoot. A few tried playing pranks that involved what looked like paint at one point, but they were thwarted. Still, no one scolded them too harshly.

"These people are so good at celebrating," Eirin said.

Drystan looked down at her. "As opposed to?"

She shrugged. "Back at home. Even when we had weddings or parties, there was always a sense of fear. It's as if we were too afraid to really live."

"Not everyone's having fun." Drystan looked up, and Eirin followed his gaze. Her eyes took a moment to adjust, but eventually, she spotted Karolus in Dragon form, flying slowly over the celebration.

"He's not the only one," Drystan said, returning his gaze to the part of the street where dancing had begun. "Many didn't think it appropriate to celebrate this close to setting out."

"I understand now what Lady Phaidra meant," Eirin said. "Giving everyone the chance to spend one more happy night before the journey begins."

A roar sounded above the din, and Eirin took a moment to locate Lady Phaidra, who was standing on a wall near the center of the throng.

"I'm sorry," she said laughing. "I just couldn't get your attention any other way." Laughter went up from the people, and she waited until it was quiet again.

"In two days," she finally said, her voice quieter this time, "we leave for the most important journey we've ever made. And I want you to know that we're not unaware of the hardships you've suffered." She paused, her throat seeming to catch. "Because we've suffered them too."

Eirin half expected the crowd to scoff at this, but instead, they simply listened.

"But just when all seemed lost," Lady Phaidra's eyes brightened, "the Time Keeper sent us the ones we'd been waiting for."

Eirin's face heated as she felt hundreds of eyes turn to her.

"Not one but two Seers!" Lady Phaidra wiped a tear from her face. "More warriors. Even a long-lost son of Faradoon." She smiled at Drystan then turned back to the crowd. "I know some question our decision to celebrate tonight. But I'm going to say this now, and I'm going to say this loud." She stood taller, and her eyes briefly flashed amber. "We cannot forget how to live, even when...*especially* when death approaches. We all know our time may be short. It is short. Embrace your children. Dance with your husband. Kiss your wife. And don't mourn." Tears were streaming down her face, now, and Eirin gritted her teeth to keep her own tears at bay. Lady Phaidra was surely thinking of the child she'd lost.

"Defy the curse," the great lady said through suddenly gritted teeth, her voice closer to that of a Dragon again than a woman. "Live and love."

Eirin wasn't the only one fighting tears as she watched. Many people wiped their eyes.

"Music!" shouted Lady Phaidra. "Now I want you all to dance!"

The musicians—a few Fauns, a Mermaid, and two Nymphs—began to play and sing.

Eirin had thought the crowd had been dancing earlier, but now she could see that they'd simply been going through the motions. Now, the music began, and as couples paired off, her breath caught in her throat.

"What is it?" Drystan asked.

"I can see why we didn't dance like this in Torbaine," she breathed.

Drystan looked back at the dancers and raised his eyebrows. "You can?"

Eirin nodded, mesmerized. "They don't just move their bodies. Their magic is a part of it." She studied them a moment longer. "Their…magic moves out of their bodies and meets in the middle."

Drystan stared at her. "You can see that?"

"It's beautiful." Even as she uttered the words, though, Eirin's heart fell. Even if she and Drystan knew how to dance, she had no magic to entwine with his. "I think," she said, shrugging her disappointment off as much as she could, "I think it's something in the music. Their magic is moving with it, ebbing and flowing with the song."

As she spoke, a head of red curls caught her eye. Callispa was dancing with a tall male Phoenix, but even as Eirin watched, the girl sent a glance back at Drystan. Thane must have succeeded in getting Nuru's attention somehow because they were dancing together too. Not nearly as gracefully as everyone else, but they were beginning to fall into the melody as well, their magic reaching tentatively out of their bodies toward one another.

"I never realized dancing with a partner required so much…proximity," Drystan said. When Eirin glanced up at him, he was looking at her with a new glint in his eyes. "Would you like to try?"

"I don't have any magic," Eirin said, trying to keep the warble of disappointment out of her voice. "I can sway with the song, but–"

Drystan picked her up and plopped her at the edge of the dancing crowd. He took her right hand in his left and wrapped his own right hand around her waist, the way the people around them were doing.

She sucked in a deep breath as he pulled her body against his. His chest was warm and made her knees wobble slightly.

Determined not to let her ridiculous hopes ruin her chance, Eirin did her best to watch the others around her. There weren't any particular steps they took, but they did more than wobble in a circle the way she was doing. She couldn't quite–"

"Eirin."

She snapped her attention back to Drystan. His face was shockingly close to hers, and the corner of his mouth was still turned up.

"Stop trying so hard," he said softly.

Eirin's heart beat so fast that she was sure he could feel it. His lips were just inches from hers now, and she was suddenly struggling to concentrate on what he was saying.

"I have to try. I don't have any magic," she whispered.

"Then you can have some of mine," he whispered back. As he spoke, Eirin's chest grew warm. She looked down to see her own body alight with his gold and blue flame. She gasped and looked back up at him. "Are you doing that on purpose?"

He grinned this time. "I may not be the most talented Dragon in the history of Solevar, but I'm not completely inept."

"But Drystan! You're not just..." She glanced around at the couples dancing around them. The other people had their magic touching in the middle, but theirs was nothing compared to Drystan's. His golden and blue flames of magic engulfed her entire body. And she knew it wasn't her imagination because Mannish, who was dancing with a Nymph several couples away, was staring at them, gaping.

"Do you remember when we were up on the Elven castle top?" Drystan asked, reclaiming her attention once more.

She nodded, not quite trusting herself to speak. That had been a night of dreams and nightmares. And not just because the SgaethOir had come from Torbaine to hunt them down.

"You said you would never get married," she said breathlessly.

He nodded. "I was confused. I'd buried what I wanted for so long that I'd given up hope of ever finding it." His next smile was sad. "And now, life is still confusing. I don't really... it's hard to understand what I am or what my place in this world is. My blood is too tainted to ever even consider kingship."

Eirin opened her mouth to object, her recent research just on her lips, but he put a finger over her mouth. "This is hard enough," he said with a gentle smile. Then he took a deep breath, and his brow furrowed slightly. "I just wanted to say thank you."

"For what?" she asked.

"I know it's hard. The burden you carry–not being your own but belonging to Solevar."

Eirin felt as though her heart might burst. This was why she had missed him so much. He *knew*. Drystan knew what it meant to have an entire civilization depending on him for survival. He'd been raised to be a king. And even now, when no one else saw...he did.

"I can't do it on my own," she whispered. She suddenly felt like she was in one of the dark tunnels she'd used to escape the mountain, and he was her tether. If he let her go...

She didn't want to know what would happen if he let go.

"You don't have to." He released her hand and waist and placed his hands on her lower jaw, instead. Gently, gently, he brushed his lips over hers.

Eirin forgot how to breathe.

Then he lifted his mouth from hers and brushed it against her forehead before leaning his own head against hers.

"Is the boy watching you?" he asked.

Eirin glanced at Mannish out of the corner of her eye. Sure enough, he'd given up even pretending to look at his partner.

"Yes."

"In that case..." Drystan cupped the back of her neck in his hand and bent his head once more. This time, he met her lips with his, and there, enveloped in the warmth of his heart's flames, Eirin was first kissed as she spun endlessly into the night.

32

They set out just after sunset two evenings later.

The city was hauntingly quiet after the loud celebration that had lasted long into the morning, and Drystan wasn't sure he liked it. But now, on the evening of their departure, there were more things to think about than the quiet.

Mhaedin's forces were divided into three groups. The first group was made up of the ground forces, which consisted of Centaurs, Giants, Will-o'-the-Wisps, Fauns, Fenris, their lone Elf, and any other lone Atharrachs who couldn't fly. The Dragons, Fae, Phoenixes, Sphinxes, Griffins, Pegasi, Rocs, and other flying creatures were to travel overhead. And the few who couldn't fly but were pertinent to their mission, such as the Seers and the Nymphs, were to ride on the backs of appointed creatures, sometimes flying, other times riding along the ground, depending on the wind.

"Has anyone seen Eirin?" Drystan asked as he made his way through the crowd of flyers. The travelers were standing on one of the cliffs overlooking the ground forces, who were organizing themselves in the foothills.

"Why aren't you in Dragon form?" Callispa asked as she landed beside him. Her eyes and wings were alight with flame, and her cheeks were pink with excitement.

"I'm trying to find Eirin."

Callispa blinked at him. "Why?"

"She's riding with me."

Callispa shook her head. "I'm riding with you. Eirin's riding with Karolus."

When had that been decided? "Where is he?" Drystan asked.

Callispa pointed, but her lips stayed pursed. "Over there. He's in a mood, though, just so you know."

Drystan stomped over to where Karolus stood, barking orders. "Why isn't Eirin with me?"

Karolus didn't even look up from the parchment he was scrolling. "I wasn't aware that you'd perfectly mastered your Dragon abilities yet," he said in a flat voice. "Forgive me for overlooking such a thing to celebrate."

Eirin was standing beside him, looking none too pleased herself.

Drystan tried again. "But I–"

"You still struggle with your powers during practice." Karolus finally looked at him, his eyes an icy blue. "What makes you think you'll be able to protect her during outright battle?"

Drystan glared at him but couldn't find an immediate reply. As much as he hated to admit it, Karolus was right. He still hadn't mastered his abilities completely. Not even close. While his shifts were faster and less painful these days, and his flying had greatly improved, he still felt as though his two natures were at war within him more often than not, the monster fighting with the man.

He also was all too familiar with the threats Eirin would face once they left the safety of the mountain city. Hector had made that quite clear to them several days before.

"Aside from every miscreant and desperate soul wishing to claim you as his own, you'll face the dangers of the elements," Hector had said. "When the original curse fell, in addition to what it did to the sun, it released an ash that literally fell over everyone and everything in the world. The water, the soil, the trees, the food, even the roots are toxic. And while it's not pleasant or safe for Atharrachs, our magic protects us somewhat." He'd leveled a hard look at Eirin. *"Not so for you. So eat nothing but what we give you, and touch as little of the environment as possible. Understood?"*

"Remind me why can't we just fly directly there?" Eirin had asked. *"Why must we take so many such a long way around?"*

"Because a strong southern wind picks up residue from the southern

dunes, which are more toxic than any other place in Solevar. We're protected from it in most places on the mountain. Exposure to the high winds on a Dragon's back would kill you faster than any poisoned food on the ground. You'll have to go back and forth, depending wholly on the weather. And, of course, any predators who might be lying about."

"Is there an outright battle planned?" Drystan asked now in a low voice.

Karolus shook his head. "No. But there are always skirmishes. Usually within the first week."

"With whom?" Eirin asked.

"Marauders. People driven to desperation." Karolus jerked his head at Callispa. "Are you really ready to fight without her? Much less protect our most precious cargo?"

Drystan wanted to argue, but he couldn't. "No," he growled instead.

Karolus studied him a moment longer before his face softened slightly. "You've only begun your transformation," he said in a quiet voice. "Dragon training takes years. If not decades." Then he tilted his head slightly. "I'm not saying this to discourage you. I wish you to succeed. But right now, we have no place for ego, nor do we have room for pride."

Drystan wanted to snap that neither of those were what drove him now. He'd hardly seen Eirin since the party two nights ago. At least, not in a situation where they could talk. She'd gone off to fittings for her travel gear with Nuru, and Lady Phaidra had bade her sleep as much as she could to prepare her for the difficulty of the journey. And after their kiss during the dance, he found himself desperate to remain near her. A strange worry...some unnamed sense niggled at him, heightening his anxiety about her safety.

"Do you trust me?"

Drystan looked up to see Karolus studying him still. Drystan's initial response was that no, he didn't trust his temperamental uncle. But one glance at Eirin told him that she trusted him. And Drystan trusted Eirin. So with great reluctance, he nodded.

"Yes. I trust you."

"Then go prepare yourself. I will keep her safe."

Eirin gave him a small smile and a nod, leaving Drystan nothing else to do but nod back and begin trudging his way back up to the ledge from where he would be leaping.

Before he got five steps, though, Lady Phaidra landed in front of him, looking grim.

"Rangvald won't be joining us," she said in a low tone, her eyes going from Drystan to Karolus.

Drystan froze.

"What?" Karolus snarled. "But he said–"

She drew in a deep breath and let it out slowly, smoke shooting from her nostrils. "There was an incursion on his western border. More Windigos and a pack of feral Fenris." She shook her head. "I can't say I blame him for quelling that first, but the timing is disastrous. He says he'll join us when he's finished, but who knows when that will be?" With a huff, she straightened. "But at least he's still giving us use of his scouts. They're already in position. And will be up until we hit the far edge of the forest."

While Lady Phaidra and Karolus talked, Eirin waved Drystan over.

"You're taking this surprisingly well," he said, pulling her in for a hug. She wrapped her arms around him, and he briefly wished the world would end like this.

"Oh, believe me. I wasn't thrilled." She gave him a wry smile. Then she pulled back and looked him up and down, and his heart sped slightly. Did she like what she saw? Did he measure up?

"But I think he's right," she finally finished with a nod.

His heart gave a clunk. "That I'm not ready."

"No. I mean I think you're more of an asset when you're free to fight." She gave him a knowing look. "You may be a Dragon now, but you were raised as a warrior. You fight best when you're free to do what you need to." She took his hands and held them tightly in her small ones, sending ripples of pleasure up his arms. "You'll be able to better protect me if you're not worried that I'll fall off your back the entire time."

He scowled at her, but she just grinned.

"I don't like it when you do that," he groaned.

"Do what?"

"Make sense."

She threw her arms around him again. He pulled her in close and pressed his face into her hair. Closing his eyes, he pressed his lips against her head, and a prayer popped into his thoughts.

Don't let this be the last time I hold her.

Drystan accepted now that there was a Time Keeper. He'd seen too much to believe otherwise. But the idea that the Time Keeper was deeply involved with the people of Solevar? Drystan found that hard to believe, especially when he looked around at the ravages of the curse.

Except...

Except that in moments like these, Drystan felt that maybe the Time Keeper cared something more.

The moment couldn't last forever, though. All too soon, Callispa was gently pulling at his elbow, telling him that they needed to take their places. Eirin threw the girl a dirty look, then surprised Drystan with a soft kiss on the cheek. Drystan stared down at her as Thane came sauntering up with Nuru at his side.

"Isn't this fantastic?" Thane beamed.

Qeb, who had come to stand behind him, gave him a look of disgust. "You do know that we're trying to keep the world from complete destruction, do you not?"

"Obviously." Thane made a face before grinning again. "But we're actually doing something!"

"Eirin," Karolus called. "Lady Phaidra needs to speak with you and Mannish."

Eirin gave Drystan's hand a squeeze before following Karolus. Drystan opened his mouth as she walked away, but Nuru held her hand up before he could speak.

"Yes, I'll keep an eye on her." She pursed her lips and glared at him. "Take care of yourself too."

Thane threw his hand over his heart. "Nuru," he announced dramatically. "That's so thoughtful–"

"Because if you get hurt," Nuru said, still glaring at Drystan, "Eirin's going to kill you."

The corner of Qeb's mouth turned up, and Thane burst out laughing, but Drystan cringed. "I know."

Still wiping his eyes, Thane gave a dramatic bow. "I must go as well. But first..." He turned to face Nuru. "Beautiful lady, would you honor me with a kiss for luck?"

"I will not." Nuru scoffed. "But take this as you will. If you do something stupid, I'll nurse you back to health so I can strangle you myself."

Thane's eyes grew wide. "I didn't hear you threaten anyone else. I'll take that as a token of your affection."

"No one else has a head as big as yours." She bumped him with her shoulder as she walked away.

Thane watched her walk away then scowled at Drystan. "You got a kiss. It's not fair."

"For Nuru, kisses and threats are basically the same thing," Qeb said. "Consider yourself blessed."

"Drystan," Callispa tugged at his arm again, looking slightly annoyed this time. "We really do need to go."

Drystan sighed and nodded to the others. "I suppose we do." So he said goodbye to his friends and followed Callispa back up the hill.

A few minutes later, Drystan was on his assigned ledge again, this time in Dragon form. Callispa was on his back, and they, like everyone around them, were silent, awaiting the signal.

Callispa, as always, looked unflappable. Strong and sure, she moved as though she hadn't a worry in the world. Drystan wished he could exude such confidence.

Her confidence, however, seemed somewhat forced when she leaned down to tell him quietly that there had been a change in plans.

"Lady Phaidra's announcing it in a minute," she said in a low voice, "but we're going to head west then hug the barren western mountains and follow those north instead of cutting northwest through the forest."

Drystan frowned. "Won't that take longer?"

"It's more ground to cover, but we'll be less vulnerable near the mountains. We've got a large group of foot soldiers, and Lady Phaidra thinks we're more likely to be successful with adequate places to hide, such as the caves in the mountains." She looked around and lowered her voice again. "Besides, Rangvald has been sending out his scouts for the last two weeks. And the scouts know the new path better because of its proximity to his fortress." Then she shrugged. "Either way, we'll get to miss the center of the forest. Who knows what's festering there?"

"How long will it take with the change?" Drystan asked, looking back in the direction Eirin had gone once more.

Callispa's eyes followed his. "It would be faster if we had fewer people traveling with us. Our sheer numbers are going to slow us down. We've got at least four dozen on the ground and half of that in the sky, plus a number that will be going back and forth in between. So…" she scrunched up her nose, "a month at the very best if nothing goes wrong. But probably five weeks or more, if we're being realistic."

Drystan frowned. Though it felt like another lifetime, he remembered the last time Eirin had gone into Solevar. At the time, he hadn't known what the cause was, but she'd suffered from headaches and exhaustion, and most likely other symptoms she was too proud to share. It was, he had learned afterward, the effects of the curse. They were felt more acutely by Humans than Atharrachs because Humans had no magic to shield them. Eirin had made it safely in and out, but the effort had been great on her part, and she'd spent less than three days in Solevar before returning to the mountain.

How would she last five weeks?

Drystan had brought it up with Lady Phaidra the first time they'd discussed their plans, and Lady Phaidra's response had been optimistic.

"We've found that flying above the land helps on days that aren't too windy," she'd said. "Of course, we'll have to land every day and take cover. And the Humans are also less affected when we set up tents made of thick canvas–including canvas to cover the floors and keep out the flora and fauna. There are also a number of herbal teas and mixtures the Nymphs have discovered over the years to help fight the discomfort." She'd smiled brightly and told him he was good to care so much.

But Drystan's fears weren't allayed. Fighting the discomfort and preventing the curse from settling into her body were two different things. And while he believed they meant the best, he was also fast losing confidence that they understood Humans as well as Lady Seren had claimed they did.

Still, there wasn't much he could do about it now.

"Have a little faith in her."

"What?" Drystan asked.

Callispa leaned down so he could see her. "You're worried about Eirin." She gave him a knowing smile." She's stronger than you give her credit for."

"I don't doubt her strength. I rely on it." Drystan returned to his ledge. "It's her reaction to the curse I'm worried about."

"I understand." Callispa put her hand on his shoulder. "But you're not going to do her any good by worrying. The faster we end the curse, the sooner she'll be safe. Now what you can do is focus on flying. Because we're going to be leaving soon, and you're not going to help her by being distracted."

Drystan nodded and shook his head to clear it. "You're right. Let's get ready."

"That's what I want to hear." And as much as Drystan wished he could have been the one to carry Eirin, he was suddenly glad Karolus had that responsibility. Karolus was right. Drystan wasn't ready to defend her on his own yet. But with the freedom of the air...

The beast inside purred with pleasure.

Drystan was assigned to fly with the front forces. A few of the smaller Dragons were flying on the wings and the rear. The other flyers were to be interspersed around and between so their strength would be evenly spread. Karolus and Lady Phaidra would carry Eirin and Mannish in the center.

The first signal was given, and silently, the ground forces began to move. They were distant from the cliff where Drystan stood, and he knew to wait until his own signal was given. There were no horns or shouts, nothing to alert the world to their movement. Not that the small army would be easy to miss. But, as Karolus said, there was no reason to make the desperate creatures of Solevar even more aware of their movement sooner than they had to.

Soon enough, Drystan saw his signal to go, and excitement rippled through his veins as he pushed off and glided through the air.

The most challenging part of planning had been keeping the

ground and air forces at a similar pace. The ground forces were fast—far faster than Drystan and his friends had been when they'd trained Human form. But the air forces were still faster. So Drystan had to take special care to glide, rather than to cut through the air the way he'd learned to do when he wanted to pick up speed. Even wing beats had to be measured.

And every so often, he was warned, he would need to move up, over, and back down so he didn't move too far ahead. The smaller Atharrachs didn't have such troubles, so whenever he needed more lift, Drystan was to motion to Qeb, who would give the sign to the other front forces to close the gap as he swooped up and over and then back again. Lady Phaidra and Karolus would need to do this far less than he did, as they were in better control of their Dragon forms, but even they would have to raise their altitudes every so often, and the whole group would shift again.

But they weren't that far along yet, and before long, Drystan was soaring over the trees, the wind rushing against his face. Unlike his Human eyes, his Dragon eyes didn't water or sting. Instead, the wind only made him want to go faster.

"Hold steady," Callispa called. "Karolus and Phaidra aren't even in the air yet."

Drystan slowed down, and soon he was surrounded by Qeb and the other Atharrachs assigned to fly with him.

As much as the Dragon within wanted to fly faster, slowing down was helpful. It gave Drystan the chance to really see. Not as Eirin would, of course, but to get a fuller view of the land that had once been ruled by his fathers. Trees stretched out west and north as far as even his Dragon eyes could see. And beyond that...the ocean. He couldn't see it, of course, but he *knew* the ocean was somewhere to the west.

The moonlight was nearly as bright as day. That wasn't a surprise, though, as they had planned to begin their venture in the full light of the moon. Drystan could easily see the ground forces running beneath them, nearly frightening in their speed. It made Drystan want to press harder and faster, to see how high and fast he could go too. But the slight pressure of Callispa's legs against his sides kept him obediently in line.

While his worries about Eirin and all that was to come still whispered in the back of his mind, a strange sort of peace filled him as they soared forward. This was it. Thane had been right. It felt good to finally take the first step. Drystan and his friends had escaped Torbaine and left all their loved ones behind so they could find Iilaedin and break the curse. And Drystan could think of no better way to go.

After they'd flown a good distance from the city, Callispa tapped his left side and pointed.

"See that silver reflecting at the foot of the mountain?"

Drystan looked to his left and saw the metallic gleam of a structure at the mountain's base where it stretched out to the southwest. He could only see the corner of a tower, but it looked large and well-set.

"That's Rangvald's fortress. It was once a military lookout point, but he moved there and had it built up as soon as the curse fell. And because he was the eldest of the three princes, many of the people followed him."

"It seems large," Drystan called back.

"It's nearly impregnable. At least, that's what Karolus says. Not that I've ever tried to break its doors down." She laughed then paused. "Drystan, you're going to break your neck if you keep trying to look at her."

Drystan snapped his gaze back to the wild forest beneath him. "I'm only checking," he grumbled.

"Well, you nearly knock me off every time you do. Look, Eirin has a lot of common sense. I can guarantee you that she's not about to go leaping off of Karolus's back."

Drystan huffed, but he knew Callispa was right. Everything was going well. He should simply be thankful. Who knew how long it would last?

The sky was just beginning to lighten when one of the younger Phoenixes who had been assigned to flit back and forth with messages between the ground and the sky forces announced that it was time to make camp. The sun would appear within the hour.

"We've met with Rangvald's scouts," he called. "And they say the vicinity is clear! There are a few smaller hills with caverns we can rest in for protection. There's even drinkable water near the surface."

As they'd agreed, Drystan led the way down with his assigned escorts in tow. By the time he would reach the forest floor, which was more difficult to see now, thanks to the thicker foliage, the ground forces should already be setting up the sleeping tents. But when he broke through the branches and alighted on the ground, that wasn't what he saw.

33

A stranger holding a torch stood before Drystan. He was in his Human form, so Drystan couldn't tell what kind of Atharrach he was. Whatever he was, it wasn't friendly. Rangvald's scouts, identifiable by their purple uniforms, were being held hostage by several men Drystan didn't recognize. Drystan's own people had formed an arc around them, glancing back at Drystan, well-trained enough to wait for their orders. Many snarled and hissed, but to Drystan's relief, they didn't attack. Callispa's legs were taut against Drystan's sides. He considered sending her up to tell the others, but hesitated. There was no telling what these men might do.

The man kept his eyes on Drystan.

"And who might you be?" Drystan asked coldly. "And why do you take our allies captive?"

But the man was silent, lifting the torch higher and examining Drystan slowly.

"You can now bring us the girl," he finally said without emotion. "Let us finish her journey, and you'll be allowed to go free."

Girl. That meant they didn't yet know that there were two Seers.

"If you give–" the man continued, but Drystan had heard enough. He nodded at the Griffin beside Qeb and raised his eyes up toward the sky. The Griffin nodded and shot up into the air. As the Griffin flew up into the sky, Callispa jumped off Drystan's back and began to pull an arrow from her quiver, but the man put up a hand.

315

"They won't be able to wait for long," the man said with a sour smile. "The sun will be rising soon."

"Under whose orders are you acting?" Drystan asked, hoping to stall long enough for Lady Phaidra and Karolus to decide what they wanted to do. He let a little of his flame puff out as he spoke. A few of the other men who were holding Rangvald's men captive moved nervously.

"We act on our own accord." He spat at Drystan's feet. "Of course, that should be obvious." He shifted before Drystan's eyes, revealing the body of a Wyvern. "What doesn't seem obvious," he continued with a sneer, "is why you seem to think we should care or be impressed that you're a son of Oreck."

Drystan actually had been hoping that his blue-tinted fire would impress them. As little as he was keen on throwing his bloodline around, he knew from his time in the Citadel that sometimes a fight could be stopped before it started if his opponent felt grossly over-powered.

Unfortunately, it seemed Wyverns had yet to learn that sort of fear. The beast within Drystan growled with pleasure. He would just have to teach them.

"You've had a hundred years to fix what your ancestor broke," the Wyvern scoffed. "Now we're here to do better before it's too late. None of this foolish fanfare." He waved his hand at Drystan's forces. "Just us."

As he spoke, Wyverns seemed to materialize behind him, appearing in the forest shadows. Far more than had been in the small party Drystan and his friends had faced on the side of the mountain. There were at least four dozen here. Maybe more.

The sound of wind stirred behind Drystan. The leaves rustled and the trees swayed, and the ground shook slightly as Lady Phaidra landed beside him. Mannish was not on her back.

She had gotten the message.

Eirin was safe yet.

"There's a reason the Time Keeper took away your flame!" Lady Phaidra snapped. "And it seems you still don't know your place. Carry on with your work, and let us get on with ours."

"We're tired of letting the Dragons lead!" the Wyvern hissed.

"People are starving. You may not see it in your ivory mountain, but the food is inedible here." He held his arms out. "People are dying. The rivers, one by one, are going bad. You've made a mess of it all, and we don't mean to let you ruin this final chance." He stood taller and lifted his chin. "The age of Dragons has come to an end."

"If you wish to join us," Lady Phaidra began, but the Wyvern hissed again. "Enough!"

The dozens of Wyverns behind him emerged from the shadows, each snarling or screeching as they shot forward out of the darkness.

Drystan began to flame, but Callispa grabbed his neck.

"No! You'll hurt them!"

At Lady Phaidra's silent signal, Drystan's own ground forces had rushed forward to meet the enemy, and he could see that she was right. A normal Dragon would have been able to hit his targets, but Drystan's fire was far too hot, and he wasn't yet well enough trained. Targeting enemies would be too difficult amidst the chaos. So instead, Drystan began bounding, along with Phaidra, from one fight to the next, bringing his jaws down on the Wyverns' bodies and squeezing until he heard their bones crunch between his teeth. The Human part of him wanted to vomit, but the Dragon inside reveled.

Because the Wyverns had no flame, they were fairly easy to bring down when they were fighting individual opponents, and their attention was on the fight. Callispa's flaming arrows were sure and straight, and Qeb's war hammer and sword flashed silver even in the dull early morning light.

Unfortunately, Callispa's arrows eventually ran out, and the enemy seemed to multiply even as they fell. Lady Phaidra, though more graceful in her attacks than Drystan, seemed to be having the same problem. Then Drystan had an idea.

He turned to face Callispa, who was now fighting at his side. Qeb, who was on the other side, didn't seem to notice Drystan had paused.

"The sun is going to rise soon," Drystan told her. "I need you to fly up to Karolus. Keep watch for my signal so they know exactly when they can make their way down to the caves."

"Drystan—"

"I'm going to do something dangerous," he said.

"No!" she cried. "You're not ready!"

"Callispa, go!" Drystan shouted.

She glared at him but raised her fiery wings and shot back up into the sky.

Once she was gone, Drystan closed his eyes just long enough to focus. His Dragon instinct screamed at him to remain as he was, but he fought against it.

As soon as the shift was complete, Drystan grabbed his sword from where it had been strapped to his side. Recalling his years of training in the Citadel, he ran to a rise in the land on the northern side of the gully where the battle was taking place.

Qeb still hadn't noticed what Drystan was doing. He was too busy with a clump of Wyverns on the side. Good. Drystan's plan would work better without him.

"You want revenge?" Drystan shouted, his Human voice aided by the Dragon. "Come get it!" Then he raised his sword and ran deeper into the wood.

There was a slight pause before he heard the pursuit. Throwing up prayers that were half nonsense, half desperation, Drystan ran until he found a slight opening in the trees, a dry, bowl-shaped pond bed. He could see through the break in the trees that the sky was decidedly lighter, and if they couldn't get Eirin and the others down soon, everyone in the sky would perish.

He didn't have much time to prepare himself. Sure enough, dozens of greedy Wyvern faces appeared over the ridge. Drystan closed his eyes.

"Shift," he half-whispered, half-shouted to himself. "Shift!"

"Is the Dragon having a hard time?" one of them called, and the others laughed. Drystan opened one eye to see them slowly, cautiously coming down the hill toward him.

"Shift!" he hissed at himself.

They continued to creep closer, laughing as his sides shivered with the effort.

Just a little closer.

Then, just as they bent their legs to spring, Drystan let the beast loose.

For once, he relished the way the flames felt as they ate their way down his body. The Wyverns let out a cry as they consumed them, and those who weren't thrown to the ground by his change were destroyed in the fountain of flame that he let loose over the crowd as they scrambled to fly out of the clearing. They didn't get very far. Those who tried to flee were easy targets. Trees were set aflame, and bodies littered the forest floor, but his pursuers were gone. He made sure he got every single one.

But even as he studied them, he realized something. Not all of the enemy were Wyverns. There were several others mixed in with the Wyverns. A few Fenris, several Centaurs, and even a Faun.

There wasn't time to dwell on this, though. One Wyvern had somehow escaped his flames. It had used one of its friends' bodies as a shield and had begun scrambling up the hill when Drystan was looking the other way. He had just inhaled deeply to let forth another flame when a familiar form appeared at the top of the ridge. With one swipe of Qeb's war hammer, the Wyvern went down. Then Qeb turned his dark gaze on Drystan.

"Don't you ever do that to me again!" he snarled. It was probably the first time he had ever raised his voice at Drystan, and despite the ferocity, it almost made Drystan smile.

"We may not have had a choice!" Drystan nodded at the sky. "Look!"

Without another word, they darted back through the trees. Unfortunately, though many Wyverns had followed Drystan, it hadn't been enough. There was still much fighting, and too many familiar bodies lay still on the ground. Callispa was shooting flaming arrows at the Wyverns who tried to climb into the sky to find the missing Human, and Lady Phaidra was taking the enemy down several at a time with powerful sweeps of her tail. Thane and the other Centaurs were pushing through, and Nuru and the other Sphinxes were leaping out of the shadows to attack the enemy unseen from above. But there were still too many. Drystan hadn't realized there were so many Wyverns in all of Solevar, and he nearly froze as he looked up again to see the pink that was now bleeding into the sky.

"Drystan!" Nuru called from across the battle. Drystan ran to her side. She indicated for him to look up. From where they were standing, he could now see their sky forces in a tight circle. Eirin and

Mannish were both on Karolus's back, and the smaller Dragons and other sky forces were fighting off the Wyverns who had taken to the sky.

"There's a cave to the west!" Qeb called over the sound of the weapons, snarls, hisses, and shouts. "We just have to get them there!"

Drystan nodded. "Tell the Sphinxes to head west!"

"Callispa!" he shouted as Nuru darted off. "Tell Karolus to come to me!"

She nodded and flew up in the sky, running a Wyvern through with one of her arrows before she'd even cleared the trees. Then Drystan turned to look for Phaidra. But she found him first.

"Drystan! The sun!" she cried.

"Everyone!" Drystan shouted. "To the caves in the hill! Make way for the Humans!"

A brief pause sounded in the battle. Then everyone, enemy and ally alike, started streaming toward the caves. Hopefully, they would have sense enough to shift into their smaller Human forms, and hopefully, they would have the sense to clear enough space for Eirin and Mannish first.

A line of dark silhouettes appeared in the sky as all the fliers began to descend.

"The caves are that way!" Drystan shouted to Karolus as the larger Dragon hit the ground. But before he'd even finished, screams erupted as brilliant sunlight burst over the forest floor.

The trees provided some cover, but not enough. Drystan felt the searing pain on his back scales as he raised his wings to create a cover for the people making their way into the caves.

Qeb grabbed Eirin from Karolus's back and held her as he ran, shielding her with his smaller wings, and Drystan tried to shield them both. People fell on every side, all those unable to stand the sun's burning. Only the Dragons seemed able to stand the pain. But even then, when it was finally time for Drystan to join the others, who were standing in the shadows of the cave as the sun rose higher and cast long shafts of light from the east, he no longer had the strength to shift back into his Human form. Qeb had to drag him inside, where he fell on the floor, and everything went black.

———

Drystan slept most of the day, though he awakened several times as someone rubbed his back with a pungent ointment. Only when the night came could he fully rouse himself from a sleep that felt much like death.

"I'm sorry," the Nymph said with an apologetic smile. "You wouldn't lie still for me to treat your burns, so I had to help you sleep. But it should be out of your blood soon."

Drystan shook himself. His head still felt extraordinarily fuzzy. "Did…did Eirin and the others…"

"We're all here," someone said softly. Drystan reached out to find Eirin's hand already in his own.

"What…" He cleared his throat. "What now?"

Silence answered him. A few people whimpered from where they lay at the edges of the cave. His stomach growled, reminding him that he hadn't eaten all day.

"Most of our supplies were destroyed in the battle," Eirin finally said. "Lady Phaidra and Karolus are outside talking to one of Rangvald's scouts, but I don't think–"

"You're awake," came Lady Phaidra's voice. Drystan started to look up, but she put her hand on his head. "Rest. We'll be on the move soon enough."

"When?" Eirin asked, sounding relieved. "Once everyone's well?"

"Yes," Lady Phaidra said softly. "But we won't be going to Iilaedin."

Eirin had been rubbing Drystan's dry, cracked fingers, but upon hearing this, she froze.

"I'm afraid," Lady Phaidra said quietly, "that our supplies have been destroyed. More than we first thought. Over half of our forces have fallen. And the road would only get more difficult than this."

"Which means?" Mannish's voice sounded from the darkness.

Lady Phaidra was silent for a long time.

"I'm afraid," she finally said, "that we're done. We must go home."

34

$\mathscr{E}$irin's head hurt, but her frustration pushed the awareness of the pain to the back of her mind.

They were going back.

She could see the disappointment in a few faces, but none so acutely as what she felt. Even Mannish seemed nearly relieved to be going back. And perhaps, from their perspective, it would be best. They could return to kin and comfort rather than dying out here alone from starvation and sun.

But Eirin saw what they didn't. She felt it. In every tree and rock...even the soil told her that the world was broken.

And now, they were going to leave it that way. Unless she did something about it. Pushing herself up off the boulder she was seated on, Eirin walked over to where Lady Phaidra, Karolus, Callispa's father, and the other race heads had gathered.

"Eirin," Nuru called in a warning tone. Still in her Sphinx form, she'd been lounging several boulders away from Eirin, where Qeb had made her promise to stay when the Nymphs had sent her away from Drystan.

Eirin looked back at her. "I have to try."

"They're not going to listen." Nuru yawned and stretched. "I can hear them from here."

"I have to try," Eirin repeated and picked her way over to the meeting. Torches lit the way, but as nearly all Atharrachs had better eyesight than Humans, they hardly provided enough to see by. Still, Eirin made her way carefully over the rocks and holes to her destination.

Rangvald had arrived several hours after the battle with a wave of reinforcements after several of his scouts had escaped to tell him of the attack. Unfortunately, they had been too late. Now, he conferred with the others in low, serious tones.

Unsure of how to begin, she cleared her throat.

"We have to go on," she called. But none of them heard her. They kept talking in their little group. So Eirin tried again, louder this time. "We have to keep going!"

This time, they turned and looked at her. Instead of waiting for their reply, she pushed on.

"Maybe not everyone," she said quickly. "But a small contingent. We'd move faster and be less conspicuous. My friends–"

"Your *friend*, Drystan, is nearly dead!" Callispa exploded. Eirin hadn't seen her within the group, but now she was impossible to miss, her fiery hair matching the fire in her eyes. "Dozens of our own are *dead*! And while that may mean nothing to you–"

Something inside of Eirin was set aflame. Closing the distance between them in two long strides, she glared up into Callispa's face. "You think they mean nothing to me?" She was now screaming as well. "You're too blind to perceive it, but I have seen and tasted death tenfold what you can possibly conceive."

Callispa's eyes widened. "I–"

"Every stone I touch and every blade of grass I stand on exhales death! And I've seen it again and again and again, just in this last hour! And if you'd rather sacrifice the future for a moment's peace, that's your myopia to wrestle with. But I would like them to live! And we can't do that if we go back!"

Her words rang out through the suddenly silent cave. She felt all eyes on her, but she didn't care now, her breath coming too fast as she and Callispa stared one another down.

The fire had gone out of Callispa's eyes as she stared at Eirin.

"Come, dear," Lady Phaidra was suddenly at Callispa's side. "Let Eirin rest. She needs to sleep."

Eirin didn't move until the Nymph was gently tugging at her to sit down again.

"You must take care with your health," she was murmuring. "You're in Solevar now."

Suddenly feeling somewhat lightheaded, Eirin let her. When she was seated once again with a mug of rather potent tea in her hand, she glanced over at Drystan. He was lying on his side now, watching her but saying nothing, his mouth turned down unhappily. He'd shifted back to his Human form in his unconsciousness, and though he'd survived, unlike two of the smaller Dragons, his back was already blistering, so dark red that it was nearly violet. The Nymph had administered a few drops of Unicorn elixir in a salve but said it would be a few hours yet before he was able to get up or walk again.

Now she and Drystan stared at one another, though for once, Eirin couldn't read his face.

This bothered her more than she wanted to admit.

"I suppose this is where you say, 'I told you so,'" Lady Phaidra admitted quietly to Rangvald. Eirin could hear her now from where she sat, as her new boulder was closer to the group than her first one. Nuru came and curled up at her feet, and Eirin absently ran her fingers along Nuru's strong shoulders, just below the wings. Nuru purred slightly.

Rangvald didn't smile. "I don't wish to say that," he said quietly. "I only wish you would have waited for me. We've been preparing our own plans for years. We could have worked together, if you would have been willing to listen."

Karolus raised an eyebrow. "Without a Human?"

Rangvald shrugged. "Would you have me tell my people there was no hope?"

They all glanced back at Eirin, who stared them all down.

"I only wish this hadn't been so reminiscent of the last time we were to join forces." Rangvald ran a hand across his face and tugged at his short beard. "I sent the scouts out, hoping they would be able to guide you until we could meet. The Wyverns came so fast..."

"I would call it an excuse," Karolus said in a hard voice, "if we hadn't been dealing with such ourselves."

Eirin felt a sudden queasiness in her stomach as her headache began to throb harder.

"Eirin?" Mannish had been lying on a cloak in a corner, but now he appeared at her side. "Are you well?"

Eirin vomited, which caused another uproar as the cave came to life. Callispa was suddenly moving Mannish out of the way as several women made way for the Nymph, who held the tea to Eirin's sour lips once again.

"You *must* drink the tea." She frowned as Eirin swallowed. "It will help rid your body of the poison."

Callispa handed Eirin a cool, moist handkerchief to wipe her face with, and Eirin accepted it grudgingly. Nuru rubbed against Eirin's legs and sent Callispa a warning glare, but Callispa either didn't notice or ignored her.

"We need to get Eirin back to Mhaedin before we make any more decisions," Karolus said grimly to Lady Phaidra.

Lady Phaidra nodded. "Get her and Mannish more blankets, and put them as far to the back of the cave as you can. We'll organize tonight, and then we'll leave tomorrow evening."

"Are you sure?" Rangvald asked gently. "You're already a day into your trek."

Eirin shook her head, silently pleading for them to remain.

But Lady Phaidra sighed. "And our speed will decrease significantly the deeper we go into the forest. No, I'm afraid we have no choice. We must go home."

"To do what, though?" Eirin whispered.

But no one answered.

35

$\mathcal{E}$irin never wanted to sleep again. Neither did she want to be awake. Upon returning to Mhaedin, she and Mannish had promptly been put to bed in the Nymphs' healing room and were each given a sleeping draught. They spent days coming in and out of dreams, waking just enough to exchange a few sleepy words before the Nymphs put them unconscious again.

"The drink is to speed healing," a Nymph explained during one of Eirin's few lucid moments. "Unicorn elixir would be better, of course. But as neither of you are in immediate danger, natural healing will do. Now, drink it all. You're not free of the poison yet."

There were times when Eirin sensed Drystan beside her. Those were her favorite moments, though there was an underlying fear as well. Did he blame her for the damage done to his body? The look they'd shared in the cave hadn't been one of affection. His face had looked…empty. Eirin shivered as she fell unconscious once more.

But one day, Eirin awoke, and for once, no one held a steaming mug under her nose or gave her tea that tasted like dirt and grass. Instead, Drystan was sitting on the empty bed beside hers.

"Good morning," he said in a low voice. "Or should I say, good midday?"

Eirin rubbed her eyes and groaned. "How long have I been here?"

"Four days."

Eirin stretched, feeling like every bone in her body might crack

329

from disuse. "Where's Mannish? I thought he was a prisoner here too."

Drysatn's mouth turned down, but he controlled his expression quickly. "He woke up about an hour ago."

Eirin pushed herself up onto her elbows and blinked at Drystan, only then realizing that he was wearing full black. "Why are you dressed like that?"

Drystan's eyes went to the floor. "There's to be a vigil soon. I thought you'd want to go."

Eirin froze as the memories of the last week returned. "Our friends–"

"All alive," Drystan said gently. "But Mhaedin lost many. At least two thirds of those we set out with."

Eirin let her head fall back against the pillow. Maybe she did want to go back to sleep.

And yet, an hour later, she was standing in line with Drystan wearing her own black cloak. The line moved slowly as the people of Mhaedin made their way into the Bastion where the singers were gathered with the bodies.

Eirin closed her eyes. "This is too familiar," she whispered. And yet, somehow it was worse. These people weren't just mourning those they had lost. They were mourning the death of their future as well.

Drystan reached out and took her hand in his. She knew that, like her, he was thinking of the vigil they had passed through together last spring.

"So what happens next?" she whispered as they slowly made their way toward the singers.

Drystan's mouth tightened. "I don't know. Callispa says we should wait to resume our training until a final decision is made."

Eirin swallowed. "A decision about what?"

He looked down at her for a long measured moment. "Whether we ever try again."

Eirin stared back at him until someone behind them cleared his throat. They moved up again, and she tried to fight back the panic that was threatening to choke her.

"But if we don't go–"

"I know." He squeezed her hand, and she nodded, forcing herself to take deep breaths.

She ground her jaw. "We shouldn't have listened to Lady Seren." We should have gone straight to Iilaedin from her castle. We were closer there, and–"

"Eirin, you wouldn't have lasted a week."

Eirin bit back a scream of rage. He was right, of course. She was only in Solevar's forest for one night, and she'd had to spend four days recovering. And that was with the Nymphs and their herbal remedies. If she and Drystan had tried to make it to Iilaedin alone...

She shook her head to clear it. Something else. She had to think of something else.

"I'm... I'm sorry if I embarrassed you in the cave." She swallowed. "I was just so frustrated, and Callispa–"

"You could never embarrass me." He gave her a long look, and she felt a faint smile trying to lift her mouth.

"You just seemed so quiet, I thought maybe I'd gone too far with Callispa."

He gave her a strange look. "You certainly made your opinions known. But they weren't invalid. And Callispa is sorry for raising her voice with you as well. She's afraid the excitement might have set off the attack you suffered after."

Of course Callispa was sorry. Because Callispa was perfect.

"But I wasn't angry with you. I was in immense pain...nearly as much as the first time I shifted, so that was part of my silence. But mostly, I was thinking of you." He touched her face, and her skin tingled as his finger traced it. "You looked fainter every moment. And it was hard for me to imagine trying to cross through Solevar with you on death's doorstep every moment of the way."

Eirin shrugged. "I'll also die if I sit here and let the curse have its way. I'd much prefer one death to the other."

Drystan frowned, but they were nearing the singers and candles, so they said no more. Instead, Eirin tried to focus on mourning the dead as the singers trilled the songs of pain their survivors felt in their hearts.

Just as she and Drystan made their way through the exit, Callispa ran up, breathless.

"Drystan! Eirin." She gave Eirin an awkward nod. "I'm glad to see you well again."

"Thank you." Eirin forced a smile that was just as awkward, but Callispa had already turned back to Drystan.

"Now that Mannish and Eirin are awake, they're going to have the meeting in just a few minutes. Karolus wants you both to join us in the annex as soon as you can."

"Karolus?" Eirin looked at Drystan. "What about Lady Phaidra?"

"She'll be there." Drystan grimaced. "But I doubt she'll be running much of anything."

"Why?"

Drystan took a deep breath and stopped walking. "Because Hector was injured badly during the battle. They pronounced him dead about five hours ago."

Eirin gaped. "Dead?" Hector couldn't be dead. He was too...

Too what?

Too important? Too kind? Too helpful? Too much of what Lady Phaidra was not?

Eirin and Drystan resumed walking, but a great deal of new dread pooled in Eirin's chest, and she suddenly did not want to go to this meeting at all.

———

The room was silent as people filed inside. Eirin had begun to hate this room, as she'd never felt anything but anxiety within its doors. Karolus was already there, as were Qeb, Thane, Nuru, and a few others. And to her surprise, Lady Phaidra. Eirin recognized the head of the Griffins, the head Centaur, who was sitting beside Thane, Callispa's father, and several of the Nymphs. They had but one Elf, and he was looking bored in the corner, and there were a few other creatures she hadn't yet learned to recognize by power when they weren't in their Atharrach forms. Eirin and Drystan sat down quietly as Callispa entered and closed the door behind her. Then she came and sat on Drystan's other side.

For several minutes, no one spoke. Lady Phaidra was staring off into the distance. She looked as though she'd aged at least ten years, which, Eirin guessed, meant she'd probably given away many of her scales, and her magic had gone with them.

And she'd lost her husband. What did that kind of pain do to someone? Eirin glanced at Drystan and decided she didn't want to know.

Karolus looked even grimmer than usual, and everyone else stared either down at their hands or glared up at the wall.

The spread of food was also different, the portions less than two-thirds of what they'd been a week ago. They'd fallen so far so fast.

"Lady Phaidra?" the head Griffin finally spoke. "Do you wish to begin?"

Lady Phaidra didn't answer. She simply stared, unseeing, at the wall.

"Lady Phaidra?" Callispa's father called.

"Phaidra," Karolus said in a gentle voice. "Would you like to begin?"

"Oh. Um, yes." Lady Phaidra blinked a few times and took a deep breath. "Uh, I'd like to ask..." Her voice trailed off, and she fell back into a distant silence as she stared at the wall behind the head Griffin.

"I think," Karolus said quietly, "that Lady Phaidra wishes to discuss what our next step will be. It seems we're unfit to make our way to Iilaedin. We've lost more than half of our able forces, and we've depleted our food stores so that we won't be able to make it through the winter." He opened and closed his hands. "We need answers."

Eirin cleared her throat. "If we took a smaller number...when could we possibly leave again?"

"We are not leaving!"

Lady Phaidra's shout made Eirin jump as it filled the small room. She had lost the faraway look, and now her eyes were on Eirin, blue but flecked with ember. Drystan's eyes immediately glowed as well, and he leaned closer to Eirin.

"Phaidra," Karolus said softly, putting his hand on her arm. "She's only asking–"

"Because she was asleep during the aftermath and has no idea how much blood was shed!" Lady Phaidra shook his arm off. Then she turned and glowered at Eirin again.

But Eirin wasn't cowered. She'd faced too many warriors and been beaten nearly senseless too many times in the Citadel's practice rings to be cowed by anger.

"There is a way!" she snapped. "I know it! There's always a way!"

"You–" Lady Phaidra sputtered, but Eirin stood and lifted her chin.

"I've read the ancient texts, the laws and rituals. And I believe I know what happened."

Karolus frowned. "We know what happened. Someone interfered with the Time Stones."

"But it goes much deeper than that!" Eirin banged her fist on the table. "It's not just that someone tampered with the Time Stones. It's that the original order...the relationship with the Time Keeper was broken. He'd made the world with a particular...agreement between himself and the creatures He made." She huffed. The words were difficult to find because the ideas were still new and only infantile in her head, and she'd spent many long, frustrating hours even coming up with what little she had.

Yet...she was convinced she was right. She knew she was right. So she tried again, more slowly this time.

"From what I understand of the ancient texts," she said slowly, "The Time Keeper created each race with a purpose. Each race covenanted upon its creation to fulfill its purpose. All were important, yet some had more weight than others. Seers, for instance. And Dragons." She looked at Drystan, whose brows were now deeply furrowed.

"So when Seer and Dragon together broke that covenant, all created order was thrown into darkness."

One of the Sphinxes sniffed. "So what you're saying," she smirked, "is that you've learned what we've known all along. The Dragon and the Seer broke the Time Stones, and we shall all die unless we fix them."

"Not exactly." Eirin frowned. "What I...believe to be the answer is that the most powerful representatives of our world broke what was given to us. Better yet, they broke the bonds that were given to us.

Therefore, such a break can only be mended by those same representatives of our peoples. Someone must fulfill what has been left undone. I also believe," she said, daring a glance at the incredulous faces around her, "that the Time Keeper has a spirit of mercy. And it's only because of His mercy that the curse hasn't fully fallen yet. Because..." She took a deep breath. "Because I believe He plans for those bonds to be healed."

Lady Phaidra snorted, but Eirin went on.

"Over and over again, I've read stories of his mercy. How He intervened often in ages past when His creatures acted the fool. And I believe we can depend upon His mercy now to provide a way to bridge the gap in what has been broken between us."

She took another deep breath and looked at Lady Phaidra. "I'll admit I don't understand it all. There is still so much I don't know. But I am confident that we can be successful with only a select few. All we need," she turned her eyes to Drystan, "would be a Seer and a son of Oreck."

As she spoke, the stone that still rested above her heart seemed to burn against her skin. And yet, as it always did, it seemed determined to elude her attempts to draw out its secrets that only swelled with importance by the day.

"These are difficult things you say, Seer."

Everyone turned to look at Karolus, and Eirin's mouth nearly dropped open. She'd expected Karolus to scoff as he did with most suggestions by his trusted circle. Instead, however, he simply frowned at the table before him.

"These are difficult things," he repeated, "but not entirely implausible. Only... I'm not sure they're something you can expect us to understand or trust just yet in one sitting."

He said they were difficult. He had no idea. If he could see inside her head, he would realize just how much she felt as though she were drowning in all the possibilities the ancient texts had revealed. Nevertheless, she was confident that she was on the right path. And the more she mulled over all the options, the more she was led back to this.

Even deeper, the more she was led back to Drystan.

Not that everyone here needed to know that. Not yet, at least.

"You have no idea what you're asking!" Lady Phaidra sat up, her jaw taut. "You fill our ears with these conjectures, but you bring not a shred of proof as you ask us to sacrifice more of our lives in pursuit to fulfill an end that will bring you glory!"

"I'm not–" Eirin began, but Karolus interjected.

"That's not what she's saying."

"You!" Lady Phaidra pointed at her, seeming ignorant to her companion's gentle admonition. "You who were raised in your privileged protection of the mountain! You who have never known hunger or watched your family and friends die with every failure to fix what his ancestor destroyed!" She pointed at Drystan this time.

"Now, that's not fair–" the head of the Griffins began, but Lady Phaidra whirled around and bore down upon him, her eyes flashing again. As she spoke, she seemed to grow in height, and her fair skin began to turn a shade of purple.

"I am still mistress here!" she roared. "And I will judge what is right and just!" Then she whirled and glared at everyone else sitting at the table. For a long moment, no one moved, though Eirin realized Drystan was now so close they were nearly touching. Karolus, too, seemed larger than he had been the last time she'd looked at him, and he was sitting in a manner that was more crouch than reclining. Lady Phaidra breathed deeply for a minute more before her natural color returned, and she shrank back down to her usual height.

"We will…give our people the dignity of the best lives they can keep with their loved ones for as long as we possibly can," she said breathlessly.

"But–" Eirin tried again, but Lady Phaidra was louder.

"The Time Keeper seems determined to punish us forever for the sins of a few!" She threw a nasty glare at Drystan. "And I'm not about to play yet another of His games, Creator of this world or not!" Then she turned back to the others and sat again.

"As to Eirin's request, she has no idea what resources and power we would need for something of the magnitude she's asking for. No small contingent could protect her as she suggests!" Lady Phaidra's eyes still glowed ember, and she gripped the edges of her chair until her knuckles turned white. "An entire army hardly kept her safe. She might not think she needs an army, but to truly protect her, we would need...we would need..." Lady Phaidra's breath was coming fast, and she suddenly seemed to shrink back from her rage. Wrapping her arms around herself, she shook her head as though to clear it and left the room, closing the door behind her.

For a long time, the room was silent.

"We'd need a wizard," a small voice finally said.

Everyone turned to look at Mannish.

"A wizard," he repeated, looking from face to face. "A Human imbued with magic."

"We know what a Wizard is," the Sphinx scoffed.

"We tried that," Callispa's father said softly. "He told us not to ask him again, and he swore to punish us if we did."

"Besides," Karolus said, leaning back. "We weren't successful even when he was with us back then."

"Oh, I know!" Mannish nodded quickly. "But...we have Eirin now. You didn't have her back then. And I don't even mean to venture into Solevar with us. Perhaps if we could simply ask him to help us learn about these gifts–"

"What kind of gifts?" their lone Elf asked warily.

Mannish blushed slightly. "There are several I've been reading about. But if we had someone to help us, perhaps we could...I don't know. Try something new. In my books–."

"As Evens said," Karolus frowned, "we've asked Isayas multiple times. He's made it clear he's not going to help us again."

"If Eirin's right, though," Mannish said, sending Eirin a shy glance, "we have less than a year left. Barely half a year. What could it hurt to try one more time?"

Karolus let out a gusty sigh and looked at Callispa's father, then the other race heads. "We'll talk to Phaidra." Then he looked back at Drystan. "For the moment, keep up your training." A sardonic smile lifted the corners of his mouth. "Who's to say we won't have any more visitors here like those we ran into in the forest?"

The others stayed to talk over Lady Phaidra's outburst, as well as the implications of what was being suggested. But Eirin was suddenly exhausted. She'd spent long enough in this stifling room tonight. Quietly opening the door, she slipped out into the evening.

Drystan followed.

The canvases had been rolled out by the time Drystan followed Eirin out of the annex. Silently, she turned north and hiked toward the training pads, which were now mostly empty. Knowing she needed some space, Drystan simply followed.

When they arrived, Eirin sat down on a patch of grass and looked out over Solevar, and Drystan sat beside her. The air smelled sweetly of clover and honeysuckle, and Drystan suddenly found himself wanting to doze off. The air was still warm, and the desire to sleep–to escape, rather–was strong.

"The flowers were blooming here a few weeks ago," Eirin said softly.

Drystan opened his eyes. "What?" he asked.

She picked something small and brown off the ground. Her eyes widened, and she sucked in a fast breath. Then tears began to fall, and suddenly, she was sobbing.

Drystan sat up quickly. "What's wrong?" he asked, taking her hand, which still held the small brown thing. It was a flower. And it was dead.

Drystan pulled her against him, where she shuddered in his arms. "No flower lives forever," he said gently, brushing her hair away from her face. But she shook her head and pressed her face into his chest, and Drystan felt tears running down his own face as well.

"They don't understand," she gasped into his shirt. "She thinks

I've never seen blood like that, dripping from the sky as our people fought them back. But I have!" She sat back, squeezing her eyes shut, her small hand holding onto his for dear life. "I've seen death a thousand times over, and I know it will only get worse!" She opened her eyes and looked up into his. Her eyes were searching and beautiful. They were vulnerable. And Drystan knew those eyes saw what no one else ever could.

"Everyone here is going to die," she whispered. "And it will be painful." She turned and looked down at one of the lower streets where a gaggle of children played.

"I thought you couldn't see the future." He frowned.

"I can't." She continued to watch the children. "But I've seen what has been. And how it's only getting worse." She reached back and untied the leather cord from her neck. The stone slipped out from where it was always hidden beneath her clothes. She fingered it, scowling at the small, broken rectangular stone.

"It's here," she whispered.

"What is?" Drystan looked at the stone, knowing better than to ask to touch it.

"Something important." She threw the stone down in her lap. "The vision is there, waiting for me. I can feel it. I know it will answer my questions. It might just have what we need to save us." She glared back down at the stone. "But I just can't See it!"

"You'll get there." He pushed a lock of hair that had escaped her braid back behind her ear. As he spoke, resolve hardened within him. "And I'll make sure you get the chance to put it back." Unable to help himself, he pressed his lips to her brow. She closed her eyes and leaned into him. But after a moment, she leaned back and looked up into his face, her eyes suddenly sharp.

"You do believe what I said about the Dragons… don't you?"

Drystan laughed uncomfortably, but her eyes stayed on him. "I think you're right about a Dragon." He sat back slightly. "I'm not so sure why you seem to think it has to be me."

Eirin pursed her lips. "How do I explain this?" She huffed and tied the leather cord around her neck once more. Drystan watched her warily as she tucked it back into her shirt. Eirin was generally right. Her instinct, even when missing details, was usually pointing in the correct direction. But as to involving him? He wasn't sure he was ready for that. Or that he wanted to be.

When she was finished putting the stone away, she faced him once more, but now her face was determined. "I always had the feeling that there was something different about you. But the night you brought me out of the vision was the night I finally knew I was right. At least..." She paused. "I began to understand."

"And?" he asked apprehensively.

"Do you remember how I told you that during the dance, the people...shared their magic?"

"Something like that. What about it?"

She took a deep breath. "You do that with me."

Drystan stared at her. "I do?"

She nodded. "But I don't think you even know you're doing it. I can see it, though. The magic from your heart...you often project it over me. Especially when you think I need protecting or I'm scared or sad." She paused. "You're doing it now."

Drystan blinked. "I am?"

She nodded.

"But surely Karolus or Rangvald could do it if I can." Drystan couldn't imagine himself doing anything his mentors could not.

But she shook her head. "I've been in their proximity or directly protected by them more than enough times to realize that they've never tried to protect me with their magic. Not, I think, out of spite. But more because they don't even think to try. I would hazard that they don't even know it's possible. I've never heard anyone speak about it, at least. The closest thing would be the way the Elves can move magic out of a person and into an object. But you..." She tilted her head and fixed him with a scrutinizing gaze. "You don't even mean to do it, I don't think. You just do. And I..." She held up her empty hands. "I have no magic. And doing what I do–every time I'm subjected to watching death or suffering, I leave feeling empty. But you...you give me what I didn't even realize I needed until you pulled away, and I didn't have it anymore." Her voice hitched, and Drystan could only stare at her before pulling her into his arms again. He rested his chin on her head and closed his eyes.

As always, Eirin made him feel as though he was sinking in flood waters. But the higher the water, the deeper he felt compelled to dive.

Would this be the time he paid the price? Would *she* pay the price?

"Why did you agree to protect me?" came her voice, muffled against his shirt.

"You mean besides the very large, very scary Dragon lady standing over me and telling me to swear?"

She elbowed him, and he laughed. Pulling her against him more tightly, he thought for a moment.

"You were always different."

She leaned back to give him an unimpressed look. He smiled and ruffled her hair. "You complicated *everything*. And as much as I tried to ignore it, that included my life as well." Then he sighed as the smile left his face. "I couldn't understand my father's determination to keep you in the Citadel. Moreover, his unsubtle attempts to foist you on me. Then Rangvald's forces attacked, and I knew your presence at the Citadel was no longer a poorly executed attempt at charity. But when we left the walled city...you began to make sense."

He looked down at Solevar. "Everything began to make sense. The Time Stones. The sun's poison. The Time Keeper..." He frowned. "I could see a pattern trying to emerge, even when I was ignorant of most of what we know now. But when it all began to fall into place, I couldn't feign ignorance anymore."

Eirin spoke slowly. "Could it have been because *you* wanted something more? Did it make you more willing to see what everyone else ignored?"

"Oh, I wanted something more for sure. I wanted to know there was something...someone strong enough to fix everything."

And here he was, gambling what was left of the world on that hope. Was it courage? Or utter foolishness?

"You're still fighting it."

She was gazing steadily up at him, her brown hair waving slightly in the breeze.

"I can see you vacillating between what you believe and what you want to believe." She paused. "What is it that keeps pushing you toward what you hope for rather than what you've seen?"

That answer was simple. "The truth," he said, tapping her nose.

"Recognizing the truth for what is was like…it was literally seeing the world for the first time. And the trouble is that no matter how much I should like to wish the truth were another way, going blind wouldn't take away what I've already seen." He studied her. "And you were a part of that. You were like the key that unlocked everything else."

She gave him a small smile, but it was strained.

"That's what frightens me a little," she said. "I was always next to invisible back at home. But now…I wonder if I'll always be the means to an end." She gave him a wry smile. "They treat me so kindly now, but if this doesn't go well—"

"You," he said, interrupting her, "have never been merely a means to an end. Not now, and not ever." He smoothed her hair behind her ear. "You, my little one, are the reason I can hope."

As he spoke the words, Drystan felt as though light were pouring into his soul. He could hope. Yes, he was still angry. And no, he wasn't fully convinced he agreed with everything the Time Keeper was doing. But the more he learned, the more he realized there had to be a Time Keeper. And there had to be something better than what they had now. There was too much beauty around him. He traced Eirin's face with his finger. "So much beauty," he whispered.

Carefully, he leaned forward, her lips pink and perfect, begging to be caressed by his. He could see their shape, but he needed to *feel* them. And when he reached out, she allowed him to take her face in his hands and guide her gently toward him.

A shadow to their left caught his attention, and he had just enough time to throw himself in front of her as three Wyverns appeared at the edge of the ledge on which they sat. Drystan immediately recognized the oldest one on the left. It was the same Wyvern he'd addressed in the forest.

"I would have made the same offer I did in the forest," the Wyvern growled, "if you hadn't killed so many of our brothers and sisters."

Drystan needed to shift. Immediately. But Eirin was too close. Silently he cursed himself as he drew his sword. This was exactly why Karolus had fought so hard to pull them apart.

"Drystan!" Eirin cried, her sword already unsheathed as well. Four more Wyverns appeared behind them. Their guard had been depleted during the battle, and the Wyverns must have known this. They hadn't wasted any time.

Drystan thanked the Time Keeper for his father's insistence on practicing swordplay day in and day out when he was at the Citadel. If he'd had any less training now, he would have been killed immediately, and Eirin would have been taken. As it was, as soon as he killed one Wyvern, it seemed another took its place. His sword bit flesh again and again as he struck out at the ones that came closest. But for all his strength, he was only a man in this form, Oreck's blood or no.

And Eirin was only Human. She did marvelously for her size and strength, but those were small in comparison with the Wyverns. Though they lacked the fire of their Dragon cousins, they were nimble and tricky, and finally succeeded in dragging her halfway across the training pad before a much larger shadow descended upon them. Qeb sliced through the Wyvern that had Eirin. She grabbed her sword where it had fallen and jumped up again.

"It's about time!" Drystan shouted as he sliced through another.

"I thought you wanted some privacy," Qeb called back. "I didn't realize you wanted to have all the fun to yourself."

"I need to get her away so I can shift!" Drystan shouted. More and more Wyverns were descending from the skies. They had, it seemed, been waiting to see if their leader could pull the Seer out without trouble. Shouts and cries of the guards and their allies reached Drystan's ears, but they were all too far off. This fight would be over in seconds. And at the moment, he, Qeb, and Eirin weren't winning.

"There's a crevice over there!" Drystan cut his way through the hoard of the enemy and jerked his head over to the mountain wall. "Get her in it so I can shift!"

Qeb tucked Eirin beneath one of his thick arms and began to run. Drystan stayed at his side, doing his best to fight off Qeb's attackers. Flaming arrows joined his sword, picking off the attackers that hovered around Qeb and Eirin. Callispa's father was flying toward them, already in Phoenix form, as were several other Atharrachs.

But just when Drystan felt they might be gaining the upper hand, Qeb let out a grunt and stumbled, and one of the Wyverns managed to snatch Eirin from his arm. The beast in Drystan roared, and before he was aware of what he was doing, he'd shifted faster than he ever had before.

The power of his transformation knocked the surrounding Wyverns out of the air, including the one holding Eirin. Drystan tried to catch her, but the transformation was still finishing when she hit the ground along with the Wyverns. And though their allies made short work of their attackers, Drystan stood frozen where he was as he watched Callispa's father lean over Eirin and speak to her softly. Still, she did not get up.

37

<p>rystan could feel Nuru and Qeb exchanging glances over him as they waited anxiously outside the Nymph's healing room. Qeb's arm was already stitched up from where a Wyvern had bit him, and as soon as it was finished, he had insisted on staying outside with Drystan. Drystan almost wished he hadn't.

"It wasn't your–" Callispa began.

"Don't say it!" Drystan snapped.

She shrank back and bit her lip. Drystan should feel bad for that, just as he should have felt guilty about the way he was ignoring his friends' attempts to help. But his disgust for himself overrode his desire to be gentle. This was the third time he had waited outside this room, praying she would heal. And for the second time, she was here because of him.

The door at the far end of the hall banged open, and Thane ran in in his Human form, sweating and breathless.

"How is she?" he gasped. "I came as soon as I heard!"

Nuru opened her mouth to answer, but Drystan spoke first.

"If you really cared, you would have been there to know, wouldn't you?" Drystan glared up at him. "But just like always, you were gone."

"That's not fair!" Thane protested. "The Centaurs are–"

"Exclusive at best and unashamedly arrogant at worst." Drystan stood and leaned against the wall. The beast was roaring inside of him as he spoke, demanding that he break through the door and insist they let him sit at her side.

But he would ignore the beast, just as he had for the last hour. If he hadn't been with her in the first place, she wouldn't need healing again.

"I'm not sure what you want me to do." Thane raised his empty hands helplessly. "I came here with you, just as I said I would. I shifted, just as I said I would. And now you're angry because I've joined my people in an attempt to get *her* where she needs to go?"

Before Drystan was fully aware of what he'd done, he had grabbed Thane's shirt in his left hand and had his right arm against Thane's throat, pressing him into the wall.

"Don't be the victim here," he spat, hating the way Thane's pale eyes widened in shock. "You stay with the Centaurs because they make you feel good about yourself. If you really cared, you would have wasted just a little of that precious trotting time helping Nuru watch over Eirin. Or keeping watch with Qeb!"

"Drystan!" Nuru hissed. "Stop!"

But Drystan ignored her, pressing slightly harder until he saw Thane's face turn slightly red.

A strong hand clamped down on his shoulder. "Drystan," Qeb's deep voice yanked back on the beast that was on the cusp of taking over from the inside. The pressure of Qeb's firm grip slowly called Drystan back to himself. Not that he forgave Thane. But he let go enough for Thane to breathe.

"Just leave," Drystan said as he turned, "like you do so well." Then he let himself fall back onto the bench where he could adequately glare at the wall.

Thane's mouth was still hanging open, his pale eyes still wide, and Nuru looked like she wanted to cry when a deeper voice came from down the hall.

"I would like a moment with the young prince."

Karolus strode down the hall toward them. Thane left even faster than he had come, and Nuru paused to throw a look of disgust at Drystan before heading for the door as well. Qeb seemed hesitant to go until Drystan eventually gave him the tiniest of nods. He'd been dreading this moment for the last hour. They might as well get it over with.

Karolus came to a stop beside him. But instead of scowling down at Drystan and beginning the lecture that would most decidedly end in his exile, Karolus simply sat down beside Drystan and put his elbows on his knees.

They were silent for a long time. Finally, Karolus rubbed his eyes, leaned back, and cursed. "Drystan, you look like death."

Drystan didn't answer.

"I'm not here to say 'I told you so,'" Karolus said quietly. "I'm not blind. It's obvious Eirin chooses to be with you of her own volition." He laughed softly, then sighed. "She reminds me of my own daughter when she was young."

In spite of himself, Drystan looked up. "You have a daughter?"

But Karolus only let out a gusty sigh and shook his head. "I was able to get some information out of one of the Wyverns." He turned and looked directly at Drystan. "Enough to know that they were there to kill you. The fact that Eirin was with you was simply a happy convenience for them. They changed their plan as soon as they saw her."

"I should have seen them coming."

Karolus shrugged. "Perhaps. But if it makes you feel better, we've never had an attack that deep in the city. Our shortage of watchmen is heavy after the deaths of the battle. Reaching you there should have been impossible." He frowned. "But then again, our defenses have never been spread so thin."

Drystan stared at the door. Where were the Nymphs?

"I heard you fought with a sword at first," Karolus spoke again. "Impressive, considering most Dragons wouldn't know what to do with a sword. And it would have worked well had Eirin been just a little further away."

"But she wasn't." Drystan swallowed. "Because she trusted me."

"I was young when my fire first came," Karolus said. "So my father secluded me from all of our family and friends. Minus, of course, the Phoenixes and himself. I hated it. I tried to escape again and again, not understanding that my mother would likely die if I were set free."

"How long did you have to stay away?" Drystan asked.

"Two years. But then again, I shifted much younger than most Dragons. My father says it was most likely the blood of Oreck in my veins, as our magic flows stronger than most." He sat back and studied Drystan with a frown. "I promise, the control will come. But first," his brows furrowed, "you're going to have to embrace the Dragon within."

Drystan scoffed. "The Dragon loves bloodshed and violence. Unleashing him would be deadly. Besides," he made a face, "he never seems to come fast enough when I want him. He seems to appear randomly and unpredictably." The Dragon, it seemed, was to blame for many of Drystan's woes.

Karolus stood. "That may be, but you're going to have to make some hard decisions before either your Human form or your Dragon form takes charge. Because one of them will take charge, and not knowing which one will rule can be worse than choosing the wrong one yourself."

Before Drystan could tell Karolus that unleashing the Dragon would create more danger than either of them could imagine, the door to the healing room opened, and the head Nymph came out. She gave Drystan a frosty look but addressed them both.

"The burns were bad," she said. "Thankfully, faster to heal than the poisoning from Solevar, but we had to use up our remaining Unicorn elixir."

"Which means?" Drystan asked.

The Nymph hesitated, her green eyes going back and forth between the men. "She shouldn't be exposed to another burn like that again. It will most likely kill her."

"Can I see her?" Drystan asked.

The Nymph pursed her lips, but Karolus nodded. With an annoyed look at the older prince, she sighed and led the way.

Eirin was lying in the same bed she'd been in during the two previous visits. She looked many times better than she had when they'd fetched her from the training pad, bright red with burns all over, her deep brown eyes closed and her body limp. Still, she looked exhausted, as though a small breeze might blow her over.

"You know," she said in a low, conspiratorial voice as Drystan knelt beside her bed, "it really is rather inconvenient to be a weak Human. I'm getting rather tired of this place. But," she said, her eyes dancing, "they say I can leave tomorrow. Which means we can start planning our journey as soon as I get back to the scholar's room where I left my map. And I think I know exactly how–"

As she prattled on, Drystan knew what he had to do, and he hated himself for it. But it would be best to get on with it rather than letting her dreams run away with her and break her heart more.

It was going to break enough as it was.

"Eirin…I won't–I won't be taking you to Solevar."

Eirin froze. "What?"

He grimaced. "I can't. Not after this."

"But…But you promised!" Eirin's face flushed red, and she sat upright.

"And I meant it when I said it," he went on. "But I can't endanger you like this. Not again. Twice is too many times already."

Eirin made a face. "The first one doesn't count. It doesn't count as a real burn if it's my fault."

Drystan ground his teeth. She wasn't making this easy. "Eirin, I'm deadly serious. I'm not going to put you in danger again."

"I'm already in danger!" she protested. "Everyone is in danger! All the time! Everywhere!"

"Exactly! And you can't help anyone if I kill you!"

Eirin swallowed hard. When she spoke again, her voice shook slightly. "Drystan, I haven't told anyone else what I told you about your magic, but you know. I need you. You're the only person who ever understood my desire…my need to fix this. Your magic…" She closed her eyes, licked her lips, and tried again. "We were born into power whether we wanted it or not. And yes, the others went along too. But you understand. You know why I need *you*. And you know why we have to finish this. And if you leave, I can…I can promise you that we're not going to." Tears were running down her face now, and Drystan had to resist the desire to wipe them away.

"I promised to get you to Iilaedin. And I'm going to keep that promise. I'll talk to Karolus and Qeb. Or someone else. But not me." He turned and strode toward the door, his eyes stinging at the corners as she uttered his name in broken, tearful cries.

As he expected, his faithful friend was standing once again outside the door. Drystan went over to Qeb and closed his eyes, leaning heavily against the wall.

"Drystan–" Qeb began, but Drystan spoke before his nerve fled him and her wails, sharpened and tinged with fear, changed his mind.

"I'm going to ask you to do something you're going to hate," he said, his eyes still closed.

"Why?" Qeb asked.

Drystan finally opened his eyes. "Because I need you to help me break her heart." As he spoke the words, a pain rent his chest inside as if a bolt of lightning had struck him from within. It was all he could do not to let his knees hit the floor. The agony filled his head with fog, and he had to search before he even remembered how to stand up straight.

"Drystan?" Qeb's voice was distant and full of worry. But Drystan did his best to wave him off and stand tall again.

"I'm fine."

He wasn't. But Eirin had to be kept safe.

He'd tried to distance himself before. He'd even been somewhat successful. But in that success, he'd lacked the ability to stray too far. He might not have walked beside her, but he had stayed close, close enough to hear her whenever she called.

This would be different. No longer would he allow himself the luxury of proximity. That proximity was what had put her in danger. No, this time, his absence would be different. It would be real.

Even the thought of that made him nearly groan as he stumbled out toward the street. But as much as leaving her hurt–and it hurt like he hadn't known he could hurt before–it was the best he could do.

38

$\mathcal{E}$irin let out a huge breath when she and Nuru walked back through their bedroom door once again. Flopping down on the bed, she groaned.

"We shouldn't even be here now. We should be out in Solevar making our way to Iilaedin."

"That's a lot of complaining for someone who just escaped death twice." Nuru lay back on her bed as well. She'd been the one to escort Eirin back to their room when the Nymphs had finally released her...again.

"I hadn't been planning on spending yet another night in the healing room," Eirin retorted. Or another night crying her eyes out because of Drystan's pigheadedness.

Stupid, stupid man.

Nuru sat up on her elbows and scrutinized Eirin.

"What?" Eirin looked back at her.

"I just have to ask. If there is a Time Keeper, why would he do this?"

"Do what?"

"I don't know. Everything." Nuru swept her hand at the window. "All the failed trips into Solevar. The famines. The sickness. The curse." She let her hand fall. "We were so close." There was a wistfulness in Nuru's voice Eirin hadn't heard before.

355

"I...I can't say for sure, of course," Eirin said. "I mean, I've certainly wondered about it, though."

"What? No answer in your books?" Nuru gave Eirin a dry smile.

"In all the records I've read," Eirin said slowly, "the Seers trusted the Time Keeper without question. They recorded that everything had a purpose, even the bad things. From the smallest theft to the greatest calamities." She paused. "Even more importantly, though, my mother thinks so too."

Nuru snorted. "Sounds like optimistic nonsense."

Eirin thought about explaining what she meant but decided against it. When Nuru was determined not to like something, the only way to change her mind was to prove it. And Eirin was too tired for that right now. Her chest had ached since yesterday, and words felt difficult to conjure.

"What about you?"

Eirin looked up at her. "Me?"

"Why do *you* think He's kept us from succeeding?"

Eirin frowned down at the blanket she was sitting on, tracing the seams with her fingers. "I... I'm not sure." She paused. "But I want to believe He has a reason."

Nuru stood up, and to Eirin's surprise, she came to sit beside Eirin on the bed. Eirin's breath caught in her throat as she was reminded of how Alys used to do this exact thing. Did that mean Nuru thought of her as...a friend?

"How is Thane?" Eirin asked. After Drystan had left her in tears, begging him to come back, Qeb had come in and told her a little about what had unfolded outside the healing room. He hadn't wanted to, but Eirin had made him explain the shouting she'd heard in the hall earlier.

"He's fine," Nuru answered flatly.

Eirin knew better than to press, but she was saved from needing to respond by a knock on the door.

"I've... I've brought your dinner," came Mannish's muffled voice. After a pause, he added, "if you wish, I can bring it in."

Eirin had no wish to see anyone right now, but she didn't want to hurt Mannish's feelings. Before she could respond, however, Nuru was shaking her head.

"Leave it on the step. I'll get it."

"Oh, very well. I, um… I'll see you later then," came his confused reply.

Eirin opened her mouth to gently chastise her friend for her sharp tone, but Nuru sent her a challenging look.

"Don't even go there. We're having an important talk, and in case you didn't notice, I don't particularly enjoy those. Which means no lovesick puppy is going to interrupt us and delay its end."

Eirin blinked at Nuru in shock and was still too surprised to object when Nuru got up and fetched Eirin her plate. Its contents were noticeably less than she would have received a few weeks ago, but Eirin didn't mind. She wasn't really hungry anyway.

Nuru returned to sit beside her on the bed. "So the question is," she said, stabbing a piece of mutton on her plate, "what are you going to do?"

Eirin shrugged. "I'm not really sure. I need to get to Iilaedin, but that's about all I know." She thought of the messenger in her pocket that she'd nearly sent out during the battle. Only the reminder that Rangvald was fighting elsewhere had kept it there. But now…

"Before you make any decisions then, you should know that plans have been made to fetch the Wizard." Nuru raised one delicate brow. "Lady Phaidra agreed to what Mannish asked. Karolus, Drystan, Callispa, and a few of the others are going over the mountain to try and convince him to return and help."

Eirin froze. "When?"

"Six weeks. They would go sooner, but Drystan has to acclimate to the cold weather. They say a Dragon's fire can go out if he moves through the cold too fast unprepared."

Eirin suddenly found it somewhat difficult to breathe. Drystan was embarking on another dangerous quest…and Callispa was going with him. She wanted to have a good cry and scream. Maybe throw a few things. But Nuru was still watching her with that overly interested glint in her eye, so Eirin cleared her throat and put her plate down.

"Well, I…suppose I'll do what I've always done. I'm going to continue reading and learning about the Time Stones. I'll wait to see if the Wizard will come, but only until then." She frowned, trying to force her mind to focus on what was really important. "Six weeks is a long time, though. By then, we'll be getting close to the end of summer."

"Not so close. I'm told summer has been lasting longer each year." Nuru paused. "But you think the Wizard might really change his mind? They say he's always refused before."

"True," Eirin said slowly, "but then again, we have two Seers now. Perhaps he'll be feeling as desperate as we are, and…maybe Mannish and I will bring some hope?" She looked at Nuru, who only continued to stare back. Eirin shrugged her shoulders and picked up her food again. "Either way, I'm not about to let Drystan off as easily as he might think. We've come too far to give up without a fight."

"And if the Wizard refuses help?"

Eirin squared her shoulders. "Either way, I'm going to convince Drystan that he has to come with me. The more I think about it, the more I'm convinced he has a larger part to play in this. One that goes beyond sacrificing himself continually for minor things."

Nuru snorted. "I'd hardly call you minor."

"You know what I mean. He's always running off at the first call. In fact…sometimes, I think he hopes he'll die some heroic death. So then he'll have brought some honor back to his family's name." Eirin scoffed. "Not that that will do anyone good unless he actually does what he was made to do."

"I know what you're hiding, you know," Nuru said, nodding to Eirin's shirt. Eirin had unconsciously moved her hand to touch the stone through the fabric of her shirt. She yanked her hand back, but Nuru was smirking. "Who do you think helped bathe you when the Nymphs were too busy?"

Nuru had…what? Eirin blushed crimson, which made Nuru laugh.

"I've known you since we were six, Eirin. It's not like a complete stranger scrubbed you clean."

That might have honestly made it worse. But Eirin knew better than to speak such thoughts aloud. That Nuru had taken such care of her without her knowledge was touching in an…embarrassing way.

"You didn't touch it, did you?" Eirin asked.

"No. I'm not that stupid. If you've been hiding something from everyone, there's a reason. And I like being alive, thank you very much. I might be daft compared to you Seers, but I know danger when I see it."

Eirin exhaled slowly and nodded. "Thank you." And in spite of herself, she smiled. "I mean it."

"Eirin," Nuru said, hesitant this time. "I know my mother was...is an awful person. But that doesn't mean I want her to die. And for some reason, you seem the only person willing to do what needs to get done to keep that from happening."

"I—" Eirin began, but Nuru cut her off, her voice hardening again until it was nearly a growl.

"So I mean it when I say that you need to decide what it is that you want. If you could have everything the way you wanted right now. As in, if everyone yielded to your demands, what would they be?"

Eirin stared at her for a moment before giving a nod and a huff. "For one, the stone is keeping secrets from me. I wish it would just reveal them the way everything else does when I touch it." She paused. "And I'm also confident that Drystan is far more important than he thinks he is. The more I read of the past kings..." She shook her head. "Something is missing there too. I just don't know what yet. I feel like the manuscripts are incomplete. Which they would be, as the majority were left behind."

"So if you could have those two things, do you think we could fix this then?"

Eirin nodded. "If we included a way to get to Iilaedin, then yes. I think we could."

"Then here's my next question." Nuru was smirking again. "What are you going to do about it?"

Eirin snorted. "Well, for one, I'm not about to just let Drystan be, if that's what you mean."

Nuru gave her a sardonic grin. "I would expect nothing less."

39

Nuru wouldn't let Eirin venture out even under the canopies for another three days. If she went out, it had to be at night, and even then, it was only for the barest of exercise and to get meals. By the fourth day, Eirin was ready to lose her mind.

"You don't need to glare at me like that." Nuru gave Eirin a dry smile. "It was the Nymphs who made the rules, not me. Besides, the four days are up, so you're free now. Go annoy Drystan to your heart's content."

"I'm not sure why they bother with my health if we're not going to Iilaedin," Eirin grumbled, pulling her boots on. "I'm no use to anyone here."

Nuru shrugged as she examined the piece of dried beef she was eating. "Who knows? Maybe the Wizard will change his mind."

Eirin gave her a look. "Do you *really* believe that?"

"No. But it's better than giving up."

Eirin sighed as she paused at the door. "I suppose," she said quietly. And then she slipped out.

Mannish had come to check on her daily, and Nuru had grudgingly let him in on the third day. Eirin knew he meant well, but in the wake of Drystan's stubborn, misguided responsibility, she didn't really want to see Mannish. The hope in his eyes was a little more than she could bear.

The only man she didn't feel annoyed with at the moment was

Qeb, who now followed her quietly as she walked. And that was because he looked just as annoyed as she was. She slowed until he was by her side.

"Would it be of any use asking where he is?" she asked over her shoulder.

He let out a huff. "I'm not supposed to tell you. But I can say that the group making the expedition should have returned from the cliffs about an hour ago."

"Which means they'll be eating now." Eirin nodded. "Thank you for your lack of information. If Drystan asks, tell him I was very angry with you."

Qeb gave her a sympathetic smile. "He's determined to keep you safe, you know."

"And you don't agree with him, do you?" Eirin studied his face. "In fact, I think you're a rather unwilling participant in this scheme."

Qeb's smile faded. "What I want doesn't really matter. If he's determined to keep you safe from a distance, I shall do what I can to assist him."

She studied him. "And what would you do if he asked you to do something terrible? Would you follow along then?"

Qeb's brows drew together, and he looked out over the city, which was currently bright despite the canvases being rolled out everywhere. The morning was already hot and growing hotter. "He cares for you, Eirin," he finally spoke again. "When he burned you, it was the closest to madness I've ever seen him." He paused. "As much as I'd like to deny it, Drystan truly hasn't mastered his Dragon form. And until he does, he *is* a danger to you. I may not like it…and I may not agree with how he's going about trying to protect you. But…." He trailed off with a frown.

"That doesn't answer my question. Would you be compelled to obey even if he gave you an order that went against your conscience?"

"I'm not a slave. I don't have to obey him. My job is to protect him and those he claims as his own. I do what he asks often because he is my friend. But I'm doing this," he gestured to Eirin, "of my own volition."

Eirin nodded and sighed before turning back to the road. She was fully healed from her brush with death, according to the Nymphs, but she still tired easily, and was quickly out of breath. It was tempting to turn right around and make her way to the comfortable scholars' room or to retrace her steps and sleep again. But Eirin was determined to find Drystan, and fifteen minutes later, she did.

He was sitting on a little wall with Callispa and a few other individuals Eirin only vaguely recognized. She paused to watch him. But there wasn't much to see. He mostly stared down at his bread, looking up to respond when asked something, but not volunteering any words of his own without being asked.

"He looks sad," Eirin said softly.

"He is," Qeb murmured.

At that moment, Drystan looked up, and from across the road their eyes met. Then a large cart was pulled down the road between them. When it had passed, he was gone, as were his friends.

Finding him was no easier over the coming weeks.

What began as wistful looks on Eirin's part and a haunted look on Drystan's quickly became a game of cat and mouse. Every day, on her way to the scholars room, Eirin sought Drystan out. She would talk with him if it killed her. The last time they'd spoken, she'd been exhausted and sick. But now, she was in control of her faculties, and she was determined to talk with him as such.

Unfortunately, Drystan seemed no less determined. He was maddeningly good at getting away. She only ever glimpsed him from afar. Still, she saw him enough to notice over the weeks that his melancholy mood began to lift. Each time she saw him, he was laughing and talking with the others a little more.

It wasn't fair.

Eirin's only outlet for revenge was in her studies. She threw herself into studying Oreck's line even more than she had before. She hadn't been exaggerating when she told Nuru and Drystan that she believed him to be an integral part of fixing the Time Stones. And she meant to prove her hunch.

First and foremost to learn about was the Rite of the Blood Fire Throne.

"Mannish," she said one day. Five weeks had passed since her accident, and Drystan was nearly impossible to find. Eirin was sure he'd enlisted help in disappearing because no one ever seemed to know where he was. Mannish, however, was always ready to be found.

"Yes?" Mannish asked, smiling pleasantly from his seat at the table.

"Tell me about the Rite of the Blood Fire Throne."

His eyes widened. "What for?"

Eirin pointed down to the parchment she'd been scribbling notes on. "I've been reading about the succession of the throne from king to prince. I know that the eldest son doesn't always inherit the throne. But I can't find any specific record on *how* an heir was chosen."

Mannish scratched his head. "Now that you mention it, I'm not exactly sure. I know the vast majority of the manuscripts were left in Solevar, and many of the ones we do have are incomplete. The prior Seers added what they knew, but I suppose that's..." He snapped his fingers. "You should ask Karolus! He'd know better than anyone!"

Eirin slumped in her seat. "He's been on a three-day visit to the lower cliffs with the group who will be going to find the Wizard. They're acclimating Drystan to the cold, apparently." She hoped it was extremely uncomfortable. "They're supposed to be back later today to hold a briefing on how their preparations are progressing, but I doubt Karolus will have time to speak with me individually."

"Then ask Lady Phaidra." Mannish shrugged. "She's a Dragon. She would know."

"I'm afraid she's not terribly fond of me at the moment." Eirin cringed. "Still, I suppose I need to know."

"I'll go with you," Mannish said. "If you want, of course."

Eirin smiled at the eagerness in his voice. He couldn't help but be endearing. "Thank you. That would be nice."

"Then we can go to Karolus's meeting together after." Mannish's smile seemed to somehow brighten.

For once, Mannish seemed to realize that Eirin didn't want to talk, which meant she was able to walk in peace. So instead of imagining that Drystan was following them to Lady Phaidra's home, rather than Qeb, she tried to focus on what she needed to say.

She hadn't spoken to Lady Phaidra since their clash at the meeting, and Eirin was in no hurry to see her again. It wouldn't have been as awkward, she reflected, if Hector hadn't died. No matter how angry Lady Phaidra might have been, it only made sense for her to lash out. Her child had died. And now her husband.

Eirin didn't blame her a bit for being angry and hurt. She just hoped Lady Phaidra wouldn't blame her either.

Her anxiety was forced to wait, however, for when they arrived at the lady's door, there was no answer to their knock. After knocking several times, Eirin left Mannish at the front door in case someone came back or appeared, and Eirin began to search on her own. With Qeb in tow, of course.

But she didn't have to search long. Around the corner, Eirin discovered Lady Phaidra sitting on a little bench overlooking much of the city. Tears were running silently down her face. Eirin sat slowly beside her, and for several moments tried to think of something to say. In the end, however, she simply wrapped her arms around the great lady's shoulders. It was probably incredibly impudent to touch someone of import in such a familiar manner, but just as Eirin was beginning to regret it, Lady Phaidra leaned her head on Eirin's, and a sob escaped her.

"I miss him," she whispered.

"I know," Eirin whispered back, tightening her embrace.

"He used to play his whistle harp to me here." She smiled even as the tears continued to fall. "When she was little, our daughter would only fall asleep if he played it for her while he held her in his lap. 'Play, Daddy. Play,' she would urge him. And he'd smile and–" Lady Phaidra's breath caught, and for a moment, she closed her eyes and didn't breathe. Finally, she opened her eyes again and gave Eirin a watery smile. "I'm sure you didn't come here to hear me reminisce."

"I don't mind," Eirin said. "They're good memories."

"I just keep asking myself why," Lady Phaidra whispered, looking back out at the canvases that stretched down the mountain. "They sacrificed their lives, and we still failed. What was the point?" Lady Phaidra's jaw grew tight, and her eyes glowed ember for several long seconds as she glared in the direction of Solevar, which was currently blocked by the canvases. But then she shook her head again and looked down at Eirin, all signs of anger gone. "Why are you here?" The question was not unkind. Just confused.

"I can't find a record of how the Rite of the Blood Fire Throne worked," Eirin said cautiously. "I know the crown didn't always pass from the father to the eldest son, but I can't make out any more than that. Mannish said you would know."

She nodded. "I remember some of the Seers complaining about how few records were left behind. They tried to recreate what they lost, but it's impossible to replace thousands of years of written history." She gave Eirin a sad smile. "I suppose it was something so well-known no one thought to write it down. And yet," she sighed, "here we are. I'm not sure how it will help, but I'll tell you."

She stood and went to the little gate that separated the sitting area from the street below. "The Time Keeper created a way to pass the crown on to the most deserving of the heirs. Of course, if there was only one heir, this rite was considered rather simple. But if there was more than one Dragon born to the royal family, it was the greatest event of the generation."

"So every royal Dragon was involved then?"

"Yes. Of course, there was a way for a Dragon to withdraw his bid for the throne. But it was considered dishonorable, and no Dragon has ever done it."

Eirin shifted. "How…how exactly did it work?"

"I never got to see one for myself." Lady Phaidra's voice grew quiet. "We had traveled to the Glittering City—another name for Iilaedin. If you could see it, you'd know why." She smiled to herself, her eyes distant. "Anyway, my family had traveled to Iilaedin to see the event. King Faradoon was dying, and his three sons were ready to take part in the rite." She stopped, and her smile faded.

"Lady Seren said something about…" Eirin paused, trying to remember the exact wording. "A rift between the brothers."

Lady Phaidra nodded. "Yes. Rangvald is the only brother alive now, of course. But there was a disagreement between all three. I asked Rangvald once what happened, but he refuses to speak of it. Even to Karolus, his brother's son. All we know is that Kamon, in his anger, convinced a Seer to do the unthinkable to try and alter fate.

The curse fell before the rite could happen, and Solevar has been without a king ever since."

She sighed and went to sit beside Eirin again. "I've asked countless people what separated the brothers, but Rangvald's supporters won't utter a word. My guess is that he's ordered their silence." She rolled her eyes. "Karolus's father, Dimitrius, came here. Kamon's supporters went with him to the mountain. You know more about that than I would." She gave Eirin a wry smile. "Then there were the rest who were confused and scared. Few knew what had happened, and then so many people died in the days after that…" She shook her head. "I never did find out. And Karolus's father never told him. Something about how he didn't want to worsen what was delicately balanced."

Eirin frowned. "Do you think he was protecting Rangvald then?"

"Possibly. From what I've gathered, the main consternation was between Kamon and Rangvald, and Karolus's father was trying to keep the peace. My guess is that he didn't want the argument resurfacing when everyone was trying to simply survive. And in spite of our disagreements, we would have all died long ago had our city and Rangvald's fortress not been there to protect one another." She turned and studied Eirin. Eirin tried to straighten under the scrutiny of the great lady's eyes.

"You're still hoping, aren't you?" Lady Phaidra asked softly. "I can see it in your face." Eirin didn't answer, but Lady Phaidra shook her head and smiled indulgently. "You're a remarkable girl, Eirin." Her smile fell. "I hope you get all you've ever dreamed of." Then, seeming attacked by a sudden burst of sniffles, she got up and swiftly went back into her home.

So much for learning more about the rite.

Eirin wandered back into the city in a daze, only vaguely aware of Qeb and Mannish's presences nearby. She was too occupied by what she'd just learned to pay much attention to her surroundings.

But then, she had learned something. The Rite of the Blood Fire Throne was meant to involve all possible heirs to the throne. Which now meant Rangvald, Karolus, and Drystan were alive to take part.

But why was it so important to her that she learn this? The princes had nothing to do with the Time Stones. Only a Seer could fix them. So what was this burning need in her chest to see the throne of Oreck restored? Eirin felt as though she had the pieces of her little brothers' stone puzzle all jumbled in her mind, and their placements didn't make sense. She *knew* the throne had something to do with restoring Solevar.

She just couldn't say why.

As she mulled over this, a flash of color caught her eye. She looked up to see Callispa, Drystan, and their friends walking by. Callispa was in her Phoenix form, and the flame on her wings had been what had caught Eirin's attention. They spread gracefully behind her, extending out from her shoulderblades, and stretching from just above her head to down to her knees. And though the rest of her body remained like it was in her Human form, the flame that lit her wings matched the orange and red flames that had sprung up in her eyes. But that wasn't what made her stare.

What made her stare was that Callispa had reached out and grabbed Drystan's hand. And he let her. And as Eirin's mouth fell open, Drystan turned and looked right at her. And yet, he didn't let go of Callispa's hand.

The air was suddenly too thick to breathe.

40

*D*rystan forced himself to keep Callispa's hand in his until they'd rounded the corner and were safely hidden behind a small copse of trees.

"She's gone," he said, letting Callispa's hand drop. Then he leaned back against a tree and rubbed his eyes.

"I know that was hard," Callispa said gently. "But it's what she needs."

"I feel dirty." He groaned and stood again. It was one thing to tell a girl he was leaving her for her own good. It was another to pretend to find love with another in front of her.

"She didn't try to follow us this time," Callispa said. "Which is the whole reason we decided to do this."

Drystan rubbed his aching chest absentmindedly and nodded up the path to where their companions were already heading. "Let's catch up with them before she does come looking."

Callispa nodded and turned to follow the path. Drystan brought up the rear, feeling very much like a villain.

Pretending to fall in love had been Callispa's idea after Eirin refused to leave Drystan alone. For five weeks, Eirin had done her best to follow them. Which, of course, defeated Drystan's purpose of leaving her alone. He couldn't keep her safe if she wouldn't let him. When Drystan had brought it up to Qeb once, Qeb's cool response had been that Drystan had asked him to keep her safe.

371

"You said nothing about telling her where to go." He'd snorted. "Not that she'd listen."

"I don't want you to tell her where to go," Drystan huffed. "I just want her to stay out of danger!"

To his chagrin, Callispa had been right, however, in that for the first time since the incident, Eirin had stopped trying to follow him. But for some reason, this only made Drystan feel worse.

Much to Drystan's relief, their quest to find the Wizard was in one week, which meant they were nearly always training, and there was very little time to think. The crops at the foot of the mountain continued to dwindle, and Eirin's predictions about the death of Solevar seemed to be coming true before their eyes.

"Thank you for coming in a timely fashion," Karolus said, giving Drystan and Callispa a look of annoyance as they entered the little clearing after everyone else. "Lady Phaidra doesn't have much time, so we're going to try to make this as quick as we can."

"Who else besides Lady Phaidra is coming?" Alexei, Callispa's father's Griffin, asked.

"Zozan," Karolus said, referring to one of the head Brownies, "and the Seers. Speaking of which, here they are. Along with their entourage." He frowned at the other side of the clearing as Mannish, Eirin, Qeb, and Nuru arrived.

Drystan's face burned as he watched Eirin join the circle. Her head was held high, but her eyes were red and puffy. Qeb gave him a pointed glare. He knew, of course, what Drystan was doing. That didn't mean he approved.

Drystan didn't approve either.

He would have preferred to bury himself in the dirt.

"Ah, Lady Phaidra, there you are." Karolus nodded as the lady entered and seated herself beside him. The spot on her other side remained empty, as it had since Hector had died. She stared at it as Karolus stood.

"After discussing this at length, the plan is still the same. Drystan, Abrax, Callispa, Vadik, Bahiti, and I will leave in one week. It will take us two nights to make it to the crevice where we can safely camp. We'll have three nights to convince him to join us, then we'll have to head back, or we'll run out of food."

Qeb, who had been leaning against a tree, straightened. "How will your food stores run so low so fast?"

"It wouldn't if we were in Human form the whole time," Bahiti, the Sphinx head, said. "But the cold will force us into our Atharrach forms most of the time. And in those forms, we'll consume far more food than usual."

Qeb frowned at Drystan again, but Drystan could see that this frustration was born of worry. It had taken a good deal of time to convince Qeb to stay behind with Eirin. Not that he wanted to abandon her in any way. But allowing Drystan to go off and face a threat without him had been difficult for Qeb to accept. Only Drystan's insistence that Eirin was his key to survival had convinced Qeb to–very grudgingly–stay behind.

"Mannish, Eirin, have either of you Seen anything that might make this difficult?" Karolus asked.

Mannish glanced at Eirin, who was staring blankly at the grass. Then he turned back to Karolus. "I'm afraid our visions haven't been of the sort to relate to this expedition," he said slowly. "Not mine, anyway. Eirin?" This time, his voice was gentle, and to Drystan's great annoyance, she responded by turning her eyes to him. "Have you seen anything regarding this venture?"

Eirin shrugged half-heartedly, then shook her head. As she did, Nuru moved closer to her.

It was funny. The two girls that had once been mortal enemies had somehow come to seem like two halves of the same person. Whenever Eirin sat, Nuru stood. When Eirin pulled back, Nuru moved forward. It was as if they had been created to bring about balance. Often opposites but always in sync.

"What happens if you can't convince the Wizard?" Nuru spoke up as Eirin drew back. "Then what?"

Eirin may not have realized it, but in Drystan's absence, Nuru had become nearly aggressively protective of her. This was a good thing, of course. Drystan just wished they both didn't resent him for it.

"I was asking Bahiti the same thing," the head Griffin, Abrax, said, gesturing across the circle to the high-ranking Sphinx. "This will be our last chance."

Lady Phaidra spoke up this time, her voice so quiet it was nearly inaudible. "If you have to? Abduct him." She raised her eyes, the amber fire within them burning. "There's a reason we've chosen our finest for this mission. I don't care what you have to do to get him here. Get him back with his staff, and I will handle the rest." Her eyes turned a molten yellow.

Karolus cleared his throat. "What about your visions?" he asked Eirin, his voice noticeably gentler this time. "Has there been any change we should be aware of?"

"I've been monitoring the new arrivals," Eirin said in a flat tone. "Just more death. More rot." She gave Drystan a sharp look, and he quickly looked away.

"What in the name of Oreck do you think you're doing?"

Everyone looked up to see a bristling Rangvald enter the circle.

"I'm sorry!" a young man came puffing in behind him. "I tried to stop him, but–"

Karolus waved his hand, and the young man nodded and bowed himself out. Drystan had never seen Rangvald so angry. His blue eyes burned with rivers of orange.

"Hello, Uncle," Karolus said dryly.

"Did I hear correctly?" Rangvald fumed. "I told you all that I have a plan. I've been preparing it for years. I invited you all to take part. I even agreed to make concessions to accommodate whatever you desired. And now I hear you're seeking the *Wizard?*"

"Your help wasn't requested." Lady Phaidra hissed.

"You know my plan will work!" He whirled to face Karolus, eyes still smoldering. "I gave you your chances. Even when you had your foolhardy schemes, I went along with them. But then you failed. And even now that you have nothing–"

"We have a plan," Vadid the Elf, retorted. "We're finding the Wizard."

"The Wizard who's rebuffed you more times than I can count." Rangvald snorted and turned his back on the Elf. "Now I'm offering you a real chance at success, and you're turning it down for what? Delusional wisps of smoke?"

Drystan watched Eirin as they spoke, and he could see her interest sparking the more Rangvald spoke. He glanced at Qeb and saw his friend studying her as well.

"It's because you don't trust me, isn't it?" Rangvald straightened his shoulders. "That's why you're determined to take these insane risks."

No one spoke for a moment. The air felt heavy, as though it might spark at any time.

"You've admitted it yourself. The events that have taken place every time we asked your help before have been...suspect," Karolus said slowly. "From what we–"

"Do you know how many scouts I lost during that battle?" Rangvald hissed. "How many good men and women gave their lives helping you escape the Wyverns? How many suffered death by sun as they tried to help yours live? And let's not forget that before all of this, you treated me as a traitor and sent me out. Then you came crawling back, asking for help. But no." He straightened, looking even taller than usual. "You only trust me when you need something. Well, I'm sorry. I can't sacrifice my people for your stupidity any longer." He turned to Drystan. "If you want to tramp about the mountains chasing these fools, then by all means, remain with them. But," his voice suddenly lost some of its cutting edge, "if you wish to give her a chance, you're always welcome to come to me. We'll be ready the moment you decide you are." And with that, he stomped out.

The circle was silent for a long moment. Eirin and Nuru were having a long, tense, silent exchange, and Qeb was sending Drystan a similar meaningful look. Drystan frowned. Were Lady Phaidra and Karolus playing the fool? Lady Seren had sworn Lady Phaidra would have answers. She could show them the way. But so far, they had nothing for their pains but the jagged scars that now plunged down his back and Eirin's near-death several times over. And yet, Karolus had a point. Drystan wasn't sure he believed Rangvald's excuses for his not one but two failures to come to their aid as they set out toward Iilaedin.

Who did he believe?

"Forget him." Lady Phaidra broke the silence. "He's covering for his own disappointments. We have a plan to get the Wizard. We're going to carry it out. Then we will go to Iilaedin." She narrowed her eyes at Eirin and Mannish. "I promise."

Karolus spent a few more minutes going over the details of their journey before letting everyone go. After he dismissed them, Drystan allowed Callispa to pull him into a circle with Vadik, Bahiti, and Abrax, but his mind refused to be tethered. Instead, it followed Eirin as she, Qeb, Mannish, and Nuru made their way in the opposite direction. What was she thinking? He was dying to know. Eirin rarely allowed the tides of life to carry her along. She was thinking of the stone. He was sure of that. But how desperate to get to Iilaedin was she? Would she do something foolish without him?

Suddenly, he felt somewhat squeamish about leaving her behind.

"Come," Callispa said, taking his hand and pulling him along behind the others, who were making their way up another path. "We're going to practice making fires in the snow."

With a sigh, Drystan followed along.

41

$\mathcal{D}$rystan watched the edge of the training platform from which they were taking off, but the path that led up to the platform remained empty. The final canvases were being rolled back as evening chased away the remnants of the day.

Callispa came over and followed his gaze, a sympathetic smile coming to her face. "It's what you wanted," she said softly. "She'll be safer this way." She patted his shoulder and walked back to where their bags were stacked with the others'. "Speaking of which, it's time to shift. We leave in five minutes."

The others, with the exception of Callispa, for whom flying in snow or rain in her Atharrach form was dangerous, had already shifted, and helpers were strapping their bags to their shifter forms, something they would have to do themselves when the helpers were gone. But after the first meal, Karolus had pointed out, there wouldn't be nearly as much to carry. The plan was to eat heavily for the first few days, so they were ready and full of energy. Also, so they would have less to carry upon their return.

Lady Phaidra had wanted to send them off with a big goodbye. "The people will be encouraged," she'd said. "They *need* to see that we're fighting for them." But Karolus had refused outright.

"We need to keep this quiet. The Wyverns might not have known about our plans if we hadn't made them so obvious." He'd scowled.

"That we'll be missing will be rather obvious within a day or so. People will talk enough on their own without our help."

"Are you ready?"

Drystan startled when Callispa's voice brought him back to the present.

"I am," he said without thinking.

"Good. We're going to head out after Bahiti. The wind is coming from the north today. We'll be going southeast, so it should make flying a lot easier once we get into the current. Takeoff might be a bit bumpy, though." She climbed up and sat astride him, then pointed to the direction from which the wind was coming. It howled like an angry child, but Drystan gritted his teeth and stretched his long neck out. The wind could scream all it wanted. He wasn't in the mood for tantrums.

Despite the worries that weighed on him like boulders, and the hollow ache in his chest, his heart lifted the moment his feet left the ground. Awareness of his power surged through him as he tilted his right wing up to the sky and allowed the wind to sweep him away.

He had needed this—a change. Drystan could handle a great number of burdens. His father had taught him to do such when he'd been Heir in Torbaine. But stagnating was something he couldn't abide.

Now, though, he was free, relishing the night chill as it pushed him up and forward over the cliffs below.

"Carefully," Callispa called, squeezing his sides slightly to get his attention. "Not too high. The wind shear is dangerous near the higher cliffs."

Drystan still hadn't mastered his Dragon form fully, but he was getting better. And though he was the least experienced of the group, he was far from the slowest. He had to focus on holding his speed steady as he flew between Bahiti the Sphinx, who was carrying Vadik, and the Griffin, Abrax, who brought up the rear. Drystan had already been warned that they would need to stop often to switch who was carrying Vadik. Both Bahiti and Abrax had strong wings, but neither was strong enough to carry the Elf for long distances, and Karolus needed to be free to scout out the front.

Twilight's gray eventually disappeared from the night sky,

followed by night's velvety black. Drystan did his best to focus on Bahiti, but he couldn't help looking up at the sky, which twinkled like diamonds above them.

"It's breathtaking, isn't it?" Callispa called.

"It is," Drystan rumbled. Eirin would have loved it. His heart twisted when he realized how much he wished he could take her out like this. What would it be like if it were Eirin on his back rather than Callispa?

They landed just before dawn. Because they'd made this trek before, Karolus had a number of safe crevices and caves memorized from which they could choose to make camp.

"So what did you think?" Callispa asked as they made their way into Karolus's chosen cave. Drystan shook off the snow that had begun to fall shortly before landing.

"It seems like a lot of flying for such a short distance," he answered.

Callispa laughed. "It really does. Navigating the peaks is dreadful. But you're doing well. More than one Dragon has fallen when trying to navigate those currents for the first time. My father nearly lost one of his young Dragons once when the boy refused to stop climbing."

"I remember that," Bahiti said. She had shifted into Human form to untie the wood from her pack. "They both nearly died."

Callispa nodded and shivered, though it didn't seem to be from the cold. "It took Karolus's father three days to find them."

"The back of the cave is clear," Abrax said, returning from the deeper part of the cave.

"Good," Karolus said, "we can eat and sleep. Don't take too long. It's too cold to stay in our Human forms for long. And we'll want to head out tonight the moment the sun is down."

As soon as the food was cooked, they all shifted to their Human forms to eat, all except Callispa, whose Phoenix form was conveniently fiery enough to help warm them all from the boulder on which she sat.

"How many of your people actually get to train Dragons now?" Drystan asked Callispa as they ate. "I can't imagine there are many of us."

Callispa sighed and pushed a lock of red hair out of her face. "There aren't. I was incredibly honored to be assigned as your trainer. More than a few older Phoenixes were offended that I was paired with you, especially as you're a son of Oreck."

"She's not exaggerating," Bahiti laughed. "You should have heard the uproar from the Phoenix tent the night Lady Phaidra made the assignment."

Drystan paused. "Out of curiosity, why did they pair us together?"

Bahiti laughed even louder this time, joined by Abrax. Even Vadik smiled, and Callispa blushed.

"If you can't figure that out, I'm not going to tell you," Karolus said.

Drystan looked down at his food and felt his face warm. He had a feeling he knew, but he didn't really want to explore that line of thought, and especially not with all the others there to witness.

Callispa kindly turned the topic of conversation to the training of Phoenixes and away from Drystan's blunder.

Phoenixes, it seemed, learned to fly before they even walked. One of the few Atharrach races who could shift from birth, they were raised in seclusion for the first few years of life, or until their tantruming was ended, as they were prone to set things on fire. Once they had more self-control, usually around the age of six or seven, they began to study flight and all forms of flying.

"We also study teaching techniques," Callispa said, examining her mostly eaten hunk of dried meat. "So that by the time we reach adolescence, we're ready to begin training. Not that many of us have had the opportunity since so many of the Dragons died." She sighed.

Abrax, who appeared not to be paying them any attention at all, was looking at Karolus. "What do you propose to do if he hides again?"

"Again?" Drystan asked. "You mean the Wizard?"

Karolus nodded and frowned. "Vadik has come up with a few tracking devices. And he says he can make more if needed."

Vadik inclined his head and pulled something from his pocket. "It's not as well-made as some of my ancestors'," he said with a delicate snort. "I would need to have touched the Wizard to create an individualized tracker. But this," he held up a little bottle with red sand inside of it, "can help us follow the direction of his magic in general."

"Finish up," Karolus said, going to the edge of the cave and rubbing his bowl with snow. "The winds have shifted, and they'll be bringing in more poison from the southern dunes. We'll be safer in Atharrach form."

Drystan turned to Callispa. "I thought the mountains were safer because they shield us from the wind."

"They do," Callispa said, standing and gathering her bowl and waterskin. "But when we're this high up, we're no longer protected by the mountain itself. For some reason, the southern dunes seem to have collected more poison than the rest of Solevar. And with a southern wind, we'll be flying right into it."

"What will you do?" Drystan asked. "It'll be snowing tomorrow, won't it?"

"If it does, I've come prepared." Callispa held up a very large cloak with a smile. Even though she lifted it above her head, it still dragged on the ground. "Made specifically for Phoenixes by the Tsuchigumos. It's fire-proof, water-proof, and very comfortable." She pulled her fiery wings in until they were nearly curled around her. Then she wrapped herself in the cloak and slowly let her wings unfurl beneath it. The back of the voluminous cloak lifted off the ground as her wings filled it, but to Drystan's amazement, it didn't catch fire. Instead, she just pulled it tighter and nestled herself in a cozy corner of the cave.

But a moment after laying down, she smiled and opened one eye. "Is something wrong?"

Drystan realized he was staring and shook his head. "No. Sorry, just tired." And it was true. He'd never flown so hard in his life, and all of his muscles had a pleasant ache to them. After shifting himself back into a Dragon, he found a place to curl up and nestle down, just as the others had.

The first day was done, and everything had gone according to plan, including Eirin staying away from their training pad rather than trying to sneak along with them to say goodbye.

And he wasn't sure how he felt about that.

42

$\mathcal{E}$irin felt Drystan's absence the moment she opened her eyes. Sitting up, she rubbed them, trying to chase the bleariness away. What time was it?

As if hearing her question, the door opened, and Mannish walked in. His fair hair was combed, and he looked as though he hadn't fallen asleep on the floor, nodding over a book.

"I brought you some tea," he said, holding out a teacup and saucer.

She forced a smile and accepted the tea gratefully, sipping it slowly as though she enjoyed it. She should have. It was her favorite flavor, and Mannish had gone out of his way to procure it for her. But she hadn't enjoyed the taste of anything recently. Then again, she'd felt less and less like herself since Drystan had pulled away.

She knew why he'd done it. He'd told her why he was doing it. She'd nearly expected as much the moment she'd awakened in the Nymph's healing room.

While it wasn't surprising, it was still enraging because it was such a...*Drystan* reaction, and then his holding hands with Callispa...

That had hit her like an elbow to the stomach.

"I don't think it's real," Nuru had snorted as soon as they'd left Drystan and Callispa behind. "It's too fast." Qeb had grunted, but Qeb's grunts could mean anything. Eirin wanted to believe Nuru–

needed to believe Nuru. And yet, if only Callispa holding his hand hadn't looked so…perfect.

It made perfect sense, really. Eirin had seen how close the other trainers were with their Dragons. Even worse had been the royal genealogies she'd been forced to read through in her research, where the princes' Phoenix trainers eventually became their queens over and over and over again.

And what wasn't to love about Callispa? She was everything Eirin wasn't. Strong. Tall. Stunningly beautiful.

Eirin and Alys had once overheard two of the boys at the Citadel discussing the girls of their year. It was a conversation Eirin would have preferred not to be privy to, but as they'd been doing exercises, she couldn't exactly get away.

"I'd really like to get Alys to look at me," one of them had said.

"Alys doesn't look at anyone," the other had snorted. Then he'd glanced at Eirin, who had been pretending she couldn't hear. "What about her little friend?"

The other boy had shrugged. "She's cute. In a hapless puppy sort of way."

Alys, unable to endure anymore, had sat up.

"Oh, I'm looking at you," she'd snapped at the two boys. "And I think you're both idiots. Now shut up and get to work." Then she'd looked down at Eirin, who had been doing push-ups. "Don't listen to them," she'd said soothingly. "You wouldn't want them to look at you like that anyway."

And Eirin really hadn't. Only one boy at the Citadel had ever caught her eye. Unfortunately, it seemed now like he was of the same sentiment as the boys who had imprinted their thoughts on her mind ages ago.

Her chest ached as she wished again that Alys had come with them.

"Eirin?"

Eirin looked up to see Mannish still standing over her, his eyes wide.

"I'm sorry." She gave him a tired smile. "I'm a little distracted."

"I can tell." He gave her a sad smile as he sat down beside her. "I'm… I'm sorry you had to see that today."

She looked up at him.

"Drystan…and Callispa, I mean." He frowned. "I certainly wasn't expecting that."

"I'm tired of Seeing things!" she blurted. "All things."

He blinked at her.

"At first, I was excited," she continued, setting her teacup down. "I thought I could help people. But now, it's just a constant succession of different forms of doom. Everyone who comes has suffered, and we have to watch it again and again and again until I almost wish the end would come just so I could stop watching."

"You're hurt," Mannish said quietly. "And angry."

"And what if I am?" Eirin stood and went to stare out the window. Her voice shook but did not break. "I've just lost my best friend. But really, I didn't lose him. Someone else has him. And now they're off to save the world again, and we're stuck here seeing death in everything we touch."

Probably a stupid thing to say to someone she knew had hopes of his own. But Eirin was tired of holding it all in. Even more, she was angry with herself. When had she started to rely on Drystan this way? She'd been vulnerable with him, and it had made her weak.

Eirin hated feeling weak.

Not just weak, though. Brittle, in a sense that she'd never felt in Torbaine. There, she'd never been a warrior like the others, but she'd lived with a shield around herself, and it had served her well. She hadn't needed anyone. Not like this. Now, here, without his warm, golden magic to support her, to fill and surround her, she felt as though she just might break.

"I know what it's like to be angry." Mannish had stood and was standing beside her again. Eirin wanted to scoff and stomp off to be by herself, but something in his pale eyes made her stop. She'd never seen that look in them before.

"My parents broke my leg when I was a baby."

Eirin blinked at him. "They…what?"

He nodded but kept his eyes on the window. "They were convinced it would keep me safe. People would wonder about an Atharrach who never shifted, but they wouldn't give a second thought to a sickly cripple whose parents hid him away."

"But your father—"

"My father was a Human, yes. But my mother had managed to convince everyone that he was an oversized Dwarf. One look at me upon birth, however, and they knew I would never pass for a Dwarf. So they decided I would be safer as a cripple than as a normal Human boy."

He was no longer smiling, and the muscles in his neck and jaw were taut. "I found out just before my father died. They told me when we were safely on our way out of the mountain." His voice hitched, and it was a moment before he could go on. Eirin could only stare at him in amazement.

"The things I said…" He closed his eyes, then opened them again to look at Eirin, his pale face haunted. "I wouldn't dare repeat them to you. I hardly dare to remember them myself."

"Mannish, I'm sorry," she whispered.

He drew in a deep breath through his nose, then let it out slowly before giving her a small smile again. "Unfortunately, I found out too late that they might have been right."

Eirin frowned. "What do you mean?"

"The Wyverns. When I saw the way they tried to take my father after they found out he was Human…" He shuddered and grimaced. "I know they say we're safer because we're Human, and no one would dare hurt us. But the Wyverns were so desperate to have him, they didn't…" Mannish let the words die.

As Eirin stood beside him, looking up, it occurred to her just how tall he was. Nearly as tall as Drystan, though not nearly as heavily muscled. Still, without the others nearby, he looked much more like a man than the boy Drystan liked to call him.

He gave a shaky laugh and looked down at her again. "All that to say, I know what it's like to feel betrayed by those who love you the most. So I have a proposition for you."

"What is it?" Eirin asked, honored by his vulnerability but unsure of where he was heading.

He took her hand and held it in both of his own. His fingers were long and thin and warm. "How about," he said, "we ignore our books today. Instead, let's go out and get something to eat. Then we'll find a quiet place and sit and not talk about Drystan or parents or anything." His voice softened. "And we'll sit that way as long as we need."

Despite the tears that wanted to fall, Eirin felt herself smiling. "I'd like that very much."

43

$\mathcal{D}$rystan had never been so sore in his life as when he woke up the next morning. He groaned as he pushed himself to his feet.

"Get up, Drystan." Karolus nudged him hard with his heavy Dragon shoulder, knocking Drystan back down again, despite being in his own Dragon form. "We've got to eat and take off in less than half an hour."

Drystan glared at him through dry eyes, but as he did, he realized everyone else was already awake and eating in Human–or Phoenix–form at the fire.

Callispa laughed and made room for him as he shifted and hobbled over to join them. "You'll get used to it, I promise." She used the palm of her hand to rub the shoulder Karolus had knocked into, then she handed him a bowl of food. "Now comes the fun part."

Drystan paused, his food halfway to his mouth. "The *fun* part?"

"The part we've failed at three times before." Bahiti grinned at him from across the fire. "Where we try to get the Wizard to talk to us, and he causes an avalanche or makes the wind so strong it knocks us over or melts the snow until it becomes a muddy slush pile we get stuck in."

Drystan looked at Karolus. "Did he really do all those things?"

"And more." Karolus grimaced. "I'm not really sure how we're going to change his mind this time." He sat and studied Drystan. "But

391

having your little friend back at Mhaedin can't hurt our chances." He glanced at Bahiti. "Especially as his wife was a Seer."

"And having Drystan here with us might be helpful as well," Callispa chimed in.

"On the contrary, it could endanger our chances greatly," Karolus murmured.

Abrax and Bahiti exchanged a look, and Callispa looked somewhat deflated, but Drystan focused on eating. Being the pariah wasn't new anymore. He just hoped Karolus wasn't right.

They left not long after that, just as the sun set. Drystan and Callispa had to climb somewhat higher than the others to find a good ledge from which to jump, but in a short time, they were back in their set order once again and heading south.

The wind howled and lashed out as it had done the night before, but they reached their destination in less time than Drystan had expected. They still had several good hours of night left, and the clouds had cleared so that the moon was shining brightly on the snow-laden ground. They shifted into their Human forms and stood at the edge of what looked like a little bowl-shaped valley in the mountain itself.

"How will we get his attention?" Drystan asked Callispa, but it was Karolus who made a move.

He shifted just enough that his eyes were blue pools filled with liquid amber, and he changed his hand into a claw. One of the benefits of being a Dragon, he had once told Drystan, was that they were one of the few races who could change forms to whatever degree they wished. Because their magic came from the heart, it was pumped all over the body through the blood. This allowed them to change any parts of their bodies into Dragon form without changing the rest. If Drystan hadn't been terrified of ruining Eirin's chances, and deadly tired as well, he would have quietly done the same just to see if he could do it as fast as Karolus.

Breathing into his hand, Karolus formed a ball of fire in the palm. This he held up and threw into the sky. It hung in the air for several seconds before raining down in drops that made the snow sizzle when they hit the ground.

For a long time, no one came. Drystan began to feel uncomfortable from the cold, and was beginning to wish Karolus would tell them to change back into their Atharrach forms when a small light appeared down in the bowl-shaped valley.

Drystan allowed his Dragon vision to overtake his Human vision, and after a moment, he could see that the light was attached to a long stick. An ornately carved staff, it seemed. And the staff was held by a small figure with a pointed hat.

"I told you not to come back, Karolus!" a man's voice called up to them. His words echoed in the snow.

"Circumstances have changed," Karolus called back.

There was a pause. Then the voice called out again. "And what stupid new soul have you convinced to challenge a wizard? The rest of these I know for you have brought them before. But that one is a stranger to me." The staff pointed in Drystan's direction. At least, Drystan assumed it pointed at him.

"This is Drystan, son of Egen, son of Maskal, son of Kamon, son of High King Faradoon."

Drystan looked at Karolus out of the corner of his eye. Was he mad? Bringing Drystan seemed like enough of a gamble. But to announce his presence before even telling the Wizard they had two new Seers?

"He hates being lied to," Callispa murmured. "He would have punished us more severely if he'd found out who you were after."

The Wizard stopped moving, and with his Dragon eyes, Drystan could see a strange look come over his face. Was it fear? Or hate?

"We also," Karolus continued, "have two new Seers. And one is unlike any Human I've ever seen. At least come talk with us. Hear what we propose!"

The Wizard shook himself slightly and straightened. Drystan's hopes fell as a look of resolve hardened his face.

"I will not speak with you. And you will not come near sacred ground." He lifted his staff in the air, and the light at its tip flashed as he brought it smashing down onto the ground.

"Oh, dear." Callispa grimaced as the wind began to pick up and swirl frantically about them. "That's not good."

"Head back to camp!" Karolus called. "Now!"

Drystan didn't have to be told twice. Except for Callispa, they all shifted mid-run, but it almost wasn't fast enough. The snow, which was being tossed about by the wind, began to take shapes of its own, growing until those shapes were as tall as Giants. But unlike the Giants Drystan had gotten to know in Mhaedin, these Giants were stocky and fierce.

"Ymir!" Bahiti screamed. "He made Ymir out of wind!"

Drystan didn't know what Ymir were, but he didn't want to find out. He slowed his run just long enough to scoop Callispa up on his back. The cave was within sight when one of the wind Ymir hit him head on with a face full of snow and rocks. Drystan was knocked sideways and barely kept his feet.

"Callispa!" he shouted. "Are you all right?"

"I am!" she called, but her voice was faint. She was still in her Human form, so the cold and exertion had to be affecting her.

"Hold on!" he called back.

Drystan braced himself as another wind giant hit him from the other side. Then two more.

"Use your fire!" Callispa screamed.

Drystan immediately felt like a fool. He flamed into the storm, and immediately, the air cleared enough for him to see the cave. They'd been running too far to the left, but Drystan was able to correct enough to reach the cave just before he was hit by three more attacks.

By the time they had all reached the cave, they were breathing hard. To Drystan's great relief, the monsters, though one gave Drystan a menacing glare, began to blow away with the wind.

"What now?" Bahiti asked.

Karolus charged back out into the snow. Everyone followed him to the edge of the cave, and they waited in silence until he returned a few minutes later, cursing.

The Wizard was gone.

44

True to her word, Eirin did not think about Drystan. She did not spend the four days after his departure thinking about all the places they'd wandered together. She didn't think about his absence every time she noticed Qeb trailing her, nor did she think about him when the other Dragons took flight in the night.

She had also moved back to sleeping during the day and working at night. The difficult schedule they'd kept before and after the battle was wearing on everyone, so Eirin, Qeb, Nuru, and Mannish all agreed to return to a nocturnal shift. And while Eirin missed the sun, she found the stars were far more rewarding if she wasn't dead on her feet when she looked at them.

Tonight, however, the stars were far from Eirin's mind. Sweat ran down her temples and neck as she warily circled the training pad with Nuru. Nuru was in Sphinx form, and her tail twitched with anticipation as she and Eirin each waited for the other to make her move.

Eirin lunged forward. The attack was false, and Nuru seemed to sense it. She feinted to the side and resumed circling.

"You're fighting differently tonight," she said as Eirin backed off.

"How so?" Eirin asked, breathing deeply, swinging her wooden training sword around a few times.

"You're more aggressive." Nuru dodged another attack, her wings lifting her easily up out of reach.

"You never fought me at the Citadel." Eirin said. She sprang forward and brought her sword down hard. Nuru neatly dodged, of course, but this time, she brought her other paw up and swatted Eirin's sword away as though it were a toy.

Eirin flicked her wrist and followed up with a series of attacks that forced Nuru backward to the circle's edge.

Nuru was playing with her, of course. Eirin could never dream of beating her. But going on the attack, even if it was only an illusion, was freeing. Eirin could pour her anger into the sword that stood no chance of hurting her friend.

Nuru allowed her to push on for a few more minutes before lithely leaping over Eirin's head and knocking her to the ground, pinning her neatly with one large paw. Eirin's first response was to press her training sword against Nuru's leg, but Nuru swatted it away again.

"Whoa, there," Nuru said. "Let's take a break." She backed up slowly and sat down on her haunches. Eirin sat up and stretched her neck and right arm. Nuru watched her as she did.

"I mean it, Eirin. I've never seen you fight like that. Well, except the time you fought Drystan." Nuru raised her furry brows. "Is there something you want to tell me?"

Eirin huffed and shook her head. "I'm sorry. I just..." She took another deep breath and tried again. "Everything felt like it was coming together. All the puzzle pieces were fitting properly into place. And now everything..." She ran a hand through her sweaty hair. "It's all wrong. Drystan's gone–"

"He's coming back."

"But even when he does, he's still going to be gone." She picked up the wooden training sword and tossed it into the nearby pile of training weapons. "And now Mannish is doing everything he can to confuse me, and–"

Nuru snorted. "How in the world is Mannish confusing you?"

Eirin shook her head. "He has these moments where he's so sweet and empathetic, and I really think he's a wonderful friend. Maybe even..." She shook her head again.

"You know," Nuru muscles rippled across her furry shoulders as she shrugged. "It wouldn't be a crime to let the boy try."

Eirin rolled her eyes. "I'm not a game, Nuru. There's no prize for saying all the right things."

Nuru smirked. "That's not what the men think." She opened and closed her claws. "Look, all I'm saying is that if Drystan is being a goon, it wouldn't kill you to look in another direction." She shrugged her furry shoulders again. "It'll drive him crazy if nothing else."

Before Eirin could answer, Mannish appeared coming up the path.

"Eirin!" he called, a bright smile on his face. "I brought food!"

"Finally!" Nuru muttered as she nearly pounced on the basket of food Mannish had produced.

"Thank you." Eirin grinned at him. "I've not been a very good friend when it comes to making sure everyone gets regular mealtimes."

"Well, it's not your fault." Mannish laughed as Nuru shifted back into Human form to dig through the basket. "The Atharrachs burn through far more food than we do. They need it for their magic." He paused. "I was wondering, actually, if you'd like to celebrate."

Eirin looked at him in surprise. "Celebrate what?"

"Well, we've been working hard for days, and I think we deserve to eat something nicer than Atharrach training food."

Eirin turned to Nuru, who had chosen an assortment of flatbread cakes with different flavors. "Nuru, do you mind if–"

"Go." Nuru waved her on. "I'm going to sit here and eat."

With Nuru's blessing, Eirin set off with Mannish. Maybe it wouldn't be a crime to enjoy herself in Mannish's company. She might even be tempted to enjoy it as such if Qeb hadn't been trailing her like a ghost. Drystan might as well have been walking behind her.

Still, she did her best to pretend he wasn't. And before long, she did forget his presence briefly, but not for the reason she'd hoped.

"The markets are so bare," she said, frowning as they made it to one of the main streets. The food Mannish had brought for Nuru was from Lady Phaidra's personal stash, something she set aside for the Atharrach guards and those who were training as guards. But for the general public... "It seems even sparser than yesterday," she added with a sigh.

"It is." He winced. "It's a good thing I found these on the way up." He pulled an apple from his pocket and handed it to her, then pulled a second apple from his other pocket and took a bite.

She accepted the apple gratefully. "What do you think your parents would have thought of Mhaedin? If everything had turned out the way it should have, I mean." Then she added quickly, "You don't have to talk about them if you don't want to, though."

"No, I don't mind." He smiled at her. "Actually, it's rather nice to talk about them. No one here knew them, and people are so afraid of offending me that they pretend my parents didn't exist sometimes." He shrugged. "I actually like to imagine what they would have thought of this place. My father would have loved it. Getting to walk around as a Human and not having to hide?" Mannish laughed. "His head would have probably grown about three sizes. He always wanted to be someone important. And my mom would have been down in the fields telling the Brownies how to grow the vegetables, but she would have felt like a queen getting to pick through so many different stalls. At least, when it was all plentiful, she would have." He looked at her as they turned onto another street. "What about you? Sometimes, I feel like you just materialized here. Tell me about your family."

Eirin smiled. "My father is a Will-o'-the-Wisp, which would explain his family's work as cartographers. He could walk backward around the mountain blindfolded and know where he was. My brothers, of course, are Will-o'-the-Wisps too. And they're the orneriest little monsters to ever walk the planet, but I wouldn't have them any other way. My mom..." She sighed. "She was worried about me. And I know she always felt guilty that she didn't go on the journey herself. But she and my father got married so young she never had time. I came along almost immediately, and now she has my brothers to care for, and..."

Eirin caught herself just in time. She had nearly mentioned her mother's condition but then thought better of it. They were in a public place, and the fewer people that knew of her unborn sister's existence, the better. Drystan knew, of course, but–

No. He was not allowed to take up space in Eirin's thoughts. That was the rule.

"I understand," Mannish said. "I wouldn't wish this on anyone else. I mean, it's exciting." He chuckled. "Maybe a little more exciting than I would have preferred."

"Do you think they'll be successful?" Eirin asked as they sat down on a wall. Below them lay the streets that zig-zagged down the mountain. "With finding the Wizard?"

He took a deep breath and blew it out slowly. "If I'm honest with myself? Probably not."

"But that doesn't seem to bother you much," she said, studying him. Indeed, he looked rather calm as they discussed their hopes being dashed. "You seem...strangely optimistic about it."

"Not optimistic." He studied her back for a moment, then leaned forward, his eyes gleaming suddenly in the moonlight. When he spoke, his voice was pitched low, and his words came fast. "I have an idea, but I don't want to discuss it with too many people until I know if it will work. Or at least, I'm decently sure."

"An idea to change the Wizard's mind?"

"To do what the Wizard should have done decades ago."

Eirin frowned. "How can we do what a Wizard can't? We don't even have magic."

"Wizards were Seers once." He sat back, smiling smugly. "The only difference is that they drank the Hidden Waters of Domhier."

"And they each spent ten years being instructed by the Time Keeper Himself. And they have staffs," Eirin added.

"True," he said slowly, "but what I've learned of Wizards since coming here is that...even they don't understand exactly how the magic works. Not just their own magic, but that of their staffs."

Eirin fingered the hilt of the knife she kept in her boot. "I haven't seen that in any of the books. Where did you find it?"

"I haven't had the chance to show you all of the books on Wizards." Mannish looked down at the streets below. "After your episode with the first book, I thought maybe it would be best to put them away."

"Like Karolus said," Eirin added. "But you've continued studying them, haven't you?"

He gave her a one-shouldered shrug. "I'm not as sensitive to magic as you are, so it doesn't seem to bother me." Then he shook his head. "I didn't mean to get in so deep. My idea isn't anywhere near ready. And probably wouldn't work, just like this expedition to get the Wizard probably won't." He gave her a sad smile. "But if we don't do something, the world's going to end anyway. So why not try?"

Eirin watched him carefully as he looked back out into the blackness. How deep in the world of Wizarding did Mannish mean to go?

45

Drystan and the others were huddled around their fire, shivering in their Human forms as they ate the little portions Callispa had doled out for their last meal on the mountain. The evening sun had set and made the snowy world outside the cave look ridiculously picturesque.

"We'll have to start back tomorrow night, Wizard or none," Callispa said. "We've only got enough left for one more meal. If we eat it tomorrow morning, we should be able to make it to Mhaedin without losing too much strength."

No one answered, probably because there was little to say. Two days had passed since their arrival, and after their first unsuccessful run-in with the Wizard, they hadn't seen him since. Not even a footprint left in the snow.

They'd been able to stay awake during the day and sleep at night, as the mountain pass was so hidden from the sun that they were in constant shade, but it didn't seem to matter. Neither their day searches nor their night watch, which they took turns keeping, had been able to find any sign that anyone even lived there now or ever had. The only evidence of any Human or Atharrach activity Drystan had seen was the stone floor of what had once been the town square, which was mostly covered in thick, powdery snow. And even that was covered up within minutes of discovery, thanks to the constant wind.

"Do you have any more of the trackers left?" Karolus asked Vadik. The Elf shook his head. "We used the last one last night. I…I think he lives somewhere on the northern side of the town, but unless you wish to melt all the snow with your fire, there's no way to find out."

"They tried," Bahiti said grimly. "Yesterday, while you were setting the trackers, both Drystan and Karolus did their best to melt the snow. But the Wizard has enchanted it."

"Then if the sons of Oreck can't melt it, there's little I can do." Vadik said. "I may be an Elf, but I do not have the Heart Fire of the royal line."

There was a long pause. Finally, as though she could bear it no longer, Bahiti broke the silence.

"How long do you and Lady Phaidra believe we have? If the curse isn't broken, I mean."

Karolus put his bowl on the ground slowly, as though he were a stiff, old man. Finally, he dragged his gaze up to Bahiti's. "Half a year at best. But that factors in which groups will die first."

There was a long pause again. Callispa, who was sitting next to Drystan, sighed and leaned her head against his shoulder. Drystan was surprised, but he let her be. They were all exhausted.

"Should we head back tonight?" Abrex asked in his gruff voice. "There seems little purpose in risking ourselves further for a hopeless cause."

Karolus shook his head. "No. The people will be waiting to hear. If they find out we gave up a day early, they'll despair."

"Many have despaired already," Bahiti said with a heavy sigh. "But I agree. We should finish out our time. Maybe something will come of our search tomorrow." She paused. "I suggest we wait to go out in the morning. Maybe, if he thinks we've gone, he'll come out."

"Searching for a Wizard when he doesn't want to be found is a fool's errand," Abrex said, stoking the fire.

"Then why are we doing it?" Vadik raised his luminescent eyes to meet the Griffin's.

"Because we can't just do nothing," Callispa said.

Karolus stood and cursed before stomping deeper into the cave.

Drystan had his own thoughts on the situation, but he divulged none of them. He was, after all, the newest member of their expedition, and there was a good chance, at best, that his scheme wouldn't work. At worst, it could get them all killed. But for Eirin's sake, he would try.

"What did you say earlier about the Wizard's wife?" he asked Callispa later that evening as they cleaned their bowls with snow. "That she was a Seer?"

Callispa nodded. "They met and were married when she lived in the plains. She was quite young then, from what I understand. Not long after, she was chosen as Seer of this particular village's Time Stone Circle. She died after the curse fell, but he's remained here ever since, even after the town was abandoned." She frowned thoughtfully. "No one knows why."

Drystan was somewhat confident that he knew why. But he stayed silent until it was his turn to be on watch that evening. Once he was sure everyone was asleep, he slipped out of the cave and into the blue-tinted snow.

The constant wind, which had become nearly a lulling sound in the cave, made it difficult to listen and hard to smell. Thankfully, he didn't need to listen or smell much. He just had to get back to the town square, and he had a feeling the rest of his scheme would take care of itself.

As he searched, he rubbed his chest, as he often did these days, hoping to relieve the aching sensation that now seemed permanent. It wasn't as sharp as it had been at first. But it was always there.

Just as Eirin was not.

He had to search for longer than he would have liked to find the old cobblestone square, as snow had blown in again. But just as he was about to give up, he stumbled upon it. Then there was nothing left to do but speak.

"I know you can hear me," he called softly. Too softly. He'd better add some Dragon…just not enough to wake his friends. "I'm here not on my own behalf, but on the behalf of the Seer."

Only the sound of the wind answered him.

"I know you once loved a Seer," Drystan continued. "I know you would have given anything to give her the chance to break the curse if you could have."

Something sharp was shoved into his back, and it took all of

Drystan's will to keep the hissing Dragon at bay inside of him. The Dragon didn't like being poked.

"And how would you know something like that?" a deep voice growled.

Drystan drew in a sharp breath. "Because I'm doing it for Eirin right now."

The sharp thing stayed pressed between his shoulder blades, but there was a pause. "And who is Eirin?"

Drystan swallowed. "She's my Seer. I...I mean a friend. My friend who's a Seer. I made her a promise." As he spoke, he slowly turned. The old man didn't impale him, thankfully, but he kept his gem-tipped staff raised. As Drystan turned, though, he saw some unnamed emotion flash across the Wizard's lined face.

"And?" the Wizard asked after seeming to recover himself. "Is that all you have to say in your defense?"

"I'm not sure I can keep that promise. If you don't help us, that is."

The old man grumbled to himself, but he lowered his staff slightly. Then he whirled around and started making his way toward one of the mountain's stone walls. After a few steps, he stopped and turned. "Well, do you want to tell me about Eirin or not?"

Drystan didn't have to be asked twice. He jogged after the man then walked beside him in silence until they reached the north mountain wall itself. Then, to Drystan's amazement, the wall, which they'd searched relentlessly the day before, melted away to reveal a snow-covered cottage, complete with a thatched roof and wooden door.

"Don't be getting too many ideas," the Wizard said with a sardonic smile. "It'll be gone again tomorrow when you tell your friends where to look."

"I hadn't planned on telling them."

The Wizard rolled his eyes, but then he touched the door with his staff, and it opened of its own accord. "Wipe your shoes," he grumbled as he made his way inside. "My wife never liked mud or snow tracked in on the floor."

Drystan did as he was told and was surprised to find himself in one of the coziest little houses he'd ever seen. It was small, with only one room in the front and one in the back. But there was definitely a woman's touch about the place, from the braided rug on the floor to the arrangement of the teacups on the mantle. Embroidery depicting flowers and sky and sun hung on the walls, and a faded quilt was folded neatly on the bed he could see through the open door in the back.

"Tea?"

Drystan gave a start. "I'm sorry?"

"Would you like tea?" The Wizard was pulling a kettle out from over the fire. When Drystan hesitated, he fixed Drystan with a mocking smile. "I'm not going to poison you, if that's what you're worried about."

"Yes," Drystan said slowly. "I will take tea. Thank you."

The Wizard nodded once and set to filling the teacups. A few minutes later, he handed Drystan a steaming cup of something that smelled like lavender.

"Sit." He waved his hand at a chair in the corner by the window. Drystan obeyed as the Wizard sat in the other chair, which was slightly closer to the fire. From there, he stared unabashedly at Drystan as he sipped his tea, so Drystan stared right back.

He was oddly like the Wizard Drystan had envisioned in his head. He had a thick gray and white beard that reached all the way down his chest, and his silver and gray hair was just as long. His lined face revealed sun and wind exposure, but there was something about his eyes...Drystan found he couldn't easily meet them for more than a second or two. They were too sharp, too keen for comfort. The only person he'd ever known with a gaze even comparable to that was...

Well, Eirin.

But he could gaze into Eirin's eyes all day. This man's eyes were like knives, exacting from Drystan what knowledge he wished never to reveal to anyone. At least, that's how it felt.

"So after two days of my intentional avoidance, why did you come seeking me now on your own?"

That was easy. "Desperation," Drystan answered.

The Wizard snorted. "Everyone is desperate." He leaned forward, those piercing blue eyes boring through Drystan. "Tell me why I should grant you the privilege I've denied everyone else." He gave Drystan a cold smile. "Change my mind."

Drystan leaned forward to match the Wizard's stance. "I told you. I'm here for Eirin."

"And what makes Eirin any different from the hundreds of other Humans who have been sent to their slaughter in Solevar? Why am I obligated to help her die as well?"

Hundreds of Humans? Drystan tried not to let this acknowledgment shake him. He'd known lots of Humans had been sacrificed in the race to break the curse. But not...not hundreds.

"Eirin is...different. She always has been."

"All Humans are different. You're speaking to one, you know." The Wizard snorted. "Well, one with Magic, albeit, but a Human nonetheless."

"Eirin didn't grow up like all those other Humans." Drystan frowned down at his cup. "She and I grew up in Torbaine."

The Wizard's bushy eyebrows rose. "The Walled City."

Drystan nodded. "Apparently, the one my great-grandfather escaped to after he set off the curse."

The Wizard's face darkened considerably, but Drystan kept talking.

"Eirin's line stayed well-hidden. It worked out conveniently for her family that the city Elders dosed the rest of the city with bruthsi root to suppress their Atharrach forms. All but the Elders—and Kamon's line—forgot. Eirin's family, of course, being the exception. My father discovered Eirin when she was small. And in what I fear was misguided hope, determined to have her raised in the Citadel where he could keep an eye on her. He believed she had the best chance of survival. There she would be taught how to defend herself, and he would be able to watch her as she grew."

If the Wizard had looked surprised earlier, his face seemed made of stone now. "You don't mean..." He sat back. "He raised that child with the Atharrach *warriors?*"

Drystan gave him a dry smile. "My former Elders would be dismayed to know so many of our secrets are public knowledge outside the mountain." He drew in a deep breath and let it out slowly. "Eirin grew up thinking she was weak and spent every day for thirteen years trying to prove that she was more than just a failure."

"So where do you come into all of this?" The Wizard asked. His frosty demeanor seemed to have thawed slightly as he listened.

"Someone–an Elder with a vendetta, we learned later–was carrying out his grandfather's will to kill off the line of Kamon." Drystan sipped his tea and marveled for a moment as it warmed not only his throat and stomach but all the way down to his toes. "So after my father's failed attempt at rebellion, I was brought forth in secret. Only my grandmother, who was an Elder as well, my mother, and my father knew who I really was. Instead, I was treated as an orphan child with extraordinary potential." He paused, his stomach curling slightly as he thought back to that other lifetime, even though that existence had been his less than a year ago. "I only learned most of this as my mother lay dying in my arms." He had to swallow several times before continuing.

"My father sent us out of Torbaine with a few friends–and my mother, though I didn't know she was my mother at the time–to find the Dragon Lady Seren."

"And did you find her?" the Wizard asked, his voice gentler this time.

"We did. She told us what this world really was and told us to go to Mhaedin." He paused. "She believed that Eirin might be the last Human in Solevar, and she made me swear to protect her as she made her way to Iilaedin."

The Wizard held his hand up, and Drystan went back to sipping his tea. After several minutes of silence as the Wizard stared into the flames with a thoughtful frown, he spoke again.

"As interesting as this all is, you still haven't convinced me why this girl is so special, besides being one of the few Humans left in Solevar." He sat taller. "Why would Lady Phaidra even consider that this child stands a chance when all others have failed?"

Drystan studied the Wizard carefully. Should he tell him about Eirin's secret? The stone wasn't really his secret to tell, especially after he had bade her keep it hidden herself. But then again, this might be their last chance. This man could help them survive. He could get Eirin to Iilaedin.

He could also make them all fall if he so chose.

"She's been having visions," Drystan said slowly.

The Wizard's eyebrows rose again. "Without the stones?" he asked.

"With everything," Drystan said. "She can touch nearly any object and experience a memory. That's what she calls them...the visions. Memories based on something that object witnessed."

"She's not wrong."

"There's a second Seer in Mhaedin now as well," Drystan continued, watching the Wizard's face for any sign of danger. "But he doesn't see the visions as she does. Sometimes, the visions are so strong they... They'll make her pass out. Or she'll forget where she is."

At this, the Wizard sat upright. "You mean," he said in a soft voice, "she's having visions like that...*without* the stones?"

"Not just visions." Drystan hesitated. "She has one of the stones as well."

The Wizard's mouth fell open. "Who...who is she?" he whispered. "From where did this child come?"

"It seems," Drystan continued with cautious hope, "that one of her ancestors attempted to take the false stone out of the circle after it had been forced in by my great-grandfather's Seer. Only part of the stone came out, and her family has passed it down for generations, hoping one day someone would be able to return to remove the rest."

The Wizard fell back in his chair and stared, unseeing, into the hearth. His breathing slightly hitched.

"She believes," Drystan said softly, "that the stone will be our path to survival. And I promised her I'd make sure she gets to try."

"Then why haven't you?" The Wizard was staring at him again with those piercing eyes. "You're a son of Oreck. You were closer to Iilaedin at Seren's fortress than you are here. Why haven't you put her on your back and flown to the Emerald Palace already?"

Drystan sighed. He would have preferred to skip over this part of the conversation. But he was here now and couldn't very well go running out.

"Aside from Eirin's extreme sensitivity to the curse, I'm afraid I won't be taking her anywhere on my own for a very long time."

"Oh?"

With great shame and chagrin, Drystan related the most recent accident to the Wizard, as well as the one where he'd scorched her hand. Even weeks later, it filled him with hot remorse as he recalled the way she had looked, trying not to cry while cradling her charred hand in the marketplace, and worse, how she had lain still on the charred grass of the mountainside. When he was finished, he stared into the bottom of his empty teacup. Surely now would be the time the Wizard would rake him over the coals for what he did. What he could have done. Instead, however, the Wizard stood and merely poured himself a second cup of tea.

"You must both be unusually strong," he simply said.

Drystan blinked at him. "Pardon me?"

"Given that you're a son of Oreck, *and* that you were kept on bruthsi until recently, it's not terribly surprising, I suppose, that your powers are somewhat bubbling up uncontrollably. But..." He looked out the black window, and his words tapered off into silence. Eventually, he shook his head and moved over to pour Drystan more tea. "You look as though you have a question."

Drystan frowned. "Eirin had a vision once in which one of the Wizards tried to stop the cloud that brought the curse. She watched him die." Even now, Drystan could recall the terror in her screams as he had tried to pull her from them. "Forgive me for my ignorance, but what exactly is it that Wizards can do? I've heard that your power is great after drinking the magical waters, but how does that power manifest?"

"It's not a bad question." The Wizard stood and went to the door, where he'd placed his staff. Picking it up in his hands, he handed it to Drystan.

The staff was smooth, though not the way it would be if it were rubbed by sand. More as though its rough exterior had been rounded off by heavy use. The staff was taller than the Wizard, who was about Drystan's height, and at its top was a gnarled knot of wood in which was caught a white gem nearly the size of a radish. After examining it for a moment, Drystan handed it back to the Wizard, who took it with a somewhat pained look on his face.

"I never meant to drink the Hidden Waters. As it is with all Wizards, I found myself there quite by accident. I'd gone off to search for a lost pony for my father." He paused. "Tradition says that the Time Keeper calls Seer boys away for the purpose of making them Wizards. Raising up helpers for times of trouble."

"So you have the power to help?"

The Wizard nodded. "You Dragons were given the role of protectors and leaders. Wizards are more of a…stopgap, if you will. We all manipulate magic to a certain extent, much the way the Fae do, but we're stronger than the Fae. And while we can manipulate all raw magic to a point, we each have particular gifts of our own." The Wizard rubbed the staff with his fingers as he spoke, seeming unaware of what he was doing.

"My elder brother, Kanan, for example, was gifted with sunbeams. He could channel their power to gently burn away the ills of an infection or clean out the darkness of rot. Aed—the one your Seer most likely saw—was gifted in wind. He could use it to coax rain over a parched land, which isn't easy to do without ruining someone else's weather. Dal was particularly deft in the workings of sound. Music was his favorite, but he always thought it extremely funny to make quiet animals roar."

The Wizard shook his head and smiled indulgently. "Amrit was gifted in stone. Which was unfortunate, as he chose to ally himself with some rather unsavory Dwarves." He paused. "Shedding the blood of one of our own was the darkest day the Wizards had ever lived. Not that we had a choice." He shook his head and murmured something incoherent.

"What's your gift?" Drystan asked.

"Mine is…somewhat unusual." The Wizard studied Drystan. "In fact, I'm sure you won't understand. So to answer as simplistically as possible, I can combine magics. Elf with Faerie. Dragon with Fenris, not that anyone would want such an untoward combination." He shuddered.

He sounded powerful. Drystan wanted to ask him more about his unusual ability, but he sensed that the Wizard wouldn't give away much, so he asked another question instead.

"How many Wizards were there?" Drystan asked.

"Since the birth of Solevar? Twelve of us. When I gained my staff, I was the tenth." He sighed. "When I first received this staff, I thought I would go out and do great things in the world. But as the ages went by, everyone I knew died…with the exception, of course, of my Wizard brothers. But even they began to pass. We're not immune to evil, you know. Neither its outpouring nor its influence."

He shook his head and absently rubbed the end of his beard. "Every time we thought we'd saved Solevar from some great evil, another evil would rear its head. Again. And again. And again. And I grew tired. So, so tired."

Suddenly, the lines of his face eased, and he relaxed. "Then I met my wife. Say what you want about this Eirin, but Sarah was an unrivaled beauty."

"I was crossing through a wheat field, plucking the heads of grain to eat as I walked. She wasn't from a prestigious Human family. Her father was a Brownie with a small farm, and she was out gathering in his fields." He smiled distantly. "I was younger then as well. Looked a lot younger too. Not as ancient and decrepit as this curse has made me seem." He chuckled quietly to himself. "Ah, but she was like a sunbeam incarnate. Golden hair with sky blue eyes. Her skin was sunkissed, and when she smiled…" He sighed. "It was as though she had cast a spell on me."

"I'm not sure why she fell in love with me. But she did, and we were married less than a month later. Not long after that, she was given oversight of the Time Stone circle here in the mountains." He paused. "You *do* know why there is a circle of Time Stones here, do you not?"

Drystan thought for a moment. "Is it because of the great separation between this village and the others?"

The Wizard nodded. "There are other towns up on this mountain as well, and all were created for mining. As this was the largest, though, the Time Keeper saw fit to add a Time Stone circle here after the original circle in Iilaedin had been created with the forming of Solevar."

"Did you have children?" Drystan asked.

"No, and that was always a great sorrow to us. Especially to Sarah." He lifted the cup to his lips, then lowered it again without drinking. "But she was of a hardy constitution, and when she was deprived of the chance to love babes, she loved me and everyone around us that much more."

"Did the curse affect her?" Drystan asked, shuddering as he remembered Eirin's pale face every time they ventured off the mountain.

"It did. She fought for years, but in that fighting, she suffered. Slowly, I had to watch her fade. She wanted so desperately to go to Iilaedin to see how the Stones might be fixed." He looked at Drystan. "All of the power came from there, you know. All of the other circles, including this one, were mere extensions of the original. But she was too sickly after the curse fell. To take her would have been to kill her. I would have called a Unicorn, but they can't survive in this brutal climate. Too cold. I would have gone to fetch the elixir myself, but she begged me not to leave her. So we came to an impasse." His blue eyes glistened in the firelight. He sighed heavily and leaned on his staff. "Which means she never went. But before she died, she asked me to keep watch over the stones here to make sure they weren't used improperly or desecrated."

"That's why you've stayed here, isn't it?" Drystan whispered. "Because she asked."

The Wizard raised his bushy white eyebrows high. "You're here, aren't you? Risking the anger of a Wizard for the sake of your Seer?" He gave Drystan a smug smile.

Drystan flushed. "She's not *my* Seer–"

"That's hogwash, and you know it." The Wizard snorted. "I've not lived four hundred and twenty-nine years to be unaware of the desire of man."

"You said you promised to prevent the Stones from being desecrated," Drystan said, desperate to change topics. "Who would do that?"

The Wizard rolled his eyes. "Usually, people who think they're special enough to change the world by taking someone else's role. Even those who weren't Seers got it into their heads that they could fix the Stones. Some tried to destroy them. Others have been attempting to change or add to them." He raised his staff. "After Sarah asked me to watch over this circle, I began watching the others as well. From afar, of course. And I've brought a sandstorm or rockslide down on more than one fool who tried getting too close. And all the better for him it was than if he had touched what is sacred, even in the stones' state of sleep." He huffed. "But I've kept my promise, and they all lay untouched by any but Seers."

He sat there for a long moment before turning to Drystan once more. "For the girl's sake, I'll come and see her. And if I think that you have a chance of making it, I'll consider helping you." His eyes grew stormy. "But only if. For I refuse to escort another group of youth to the Blood Fire Throne only to watch them die painful deaths yet again."

"They're all going to die anyway," Drystan answered quietly. "And so will the elderly. The babes. The young people. Everyone else we leave behind."

But the Wizard simply shook his head. "Not by my hand. Not again."

Drystan, feeling his welcome worn thin, stood. "I shall let you sleep." He paused. "What time should I expect you? We set out tomorrow evening just after dark."

The Wizard, without standing, waved him off. "I'll find you. Don't tell the others, though. Let me have a bit of fun first. Pack up as usual." Then he turned and leaned toward Drystan, still in his chair. "What about your Phoenix friend there? She seems to think Eirin isn't so special after all."

Drystan stared. "How did you know Callispa–"

The Wizard only gave him a devious smile. "Do you think snow drifts can keep me in ignorance?" He fixed that sharp gaze on Drystan again. "So what does she think about you and Eirin?"

"It's only a facade," Drystan mumbled at his feet.

"Perhaps for you," the Wizard said with a sad smile. "But I doubt your Phoenix thinks so."

Drystan made his way back to the cave, not seeing the world around him as he stumbled back. He'd learned many things this night that should have discomfited him. But for some reason, the Wizard's warning about Callispa bothered him most of all.

46

To Drystan's relief, no one seemed to have noticed his absence from camp. He might have accomplished their near impossible task, but he doubted either Rangvald or any of the others would have approved of the way he'd done it—alone.

He also couldn't shake what the Wizard had said about Callispa.

Yes, she was attracted to him. He knew that. But she hadn't really gotten her hopes up, had she? She, of all people, was aware of the feelings that had passed between Drystan and Eirin, and though she'd been the one to suggest this charade when nothing else had kept Eirin at a safe distance, she'd nodded when he'd made it clear that the hand-holding would only be a ruse.

And yet, was it possible that she still had something more in mind?

As soon as he thought it, Drystan knew it was true. Eirin was no longer with them here in the mountains, and yet, Callispa acted as if she were. Though they didn't hold hands, now that he thought about it, she seemed always in his shadow. And the way she'd leaned into his shoulder as they'd sat by the fire...

He looked now at the silhouette of her form, lit only by what remained of their fire. She was beautiful. There was no question about it. Not to mention intelligent, witty, and fun as well. Whoever married her would be a happy man if she gave her whole heart to him as she gave it to everything else she was passionate about.

419

He had made it clear, though, that that man couldn't be him. After all, he was simply putting Eirin off until he had full control of his Dragon form.

But what if you never gain control of your Dragon form? a cruel voice whispered in his head. *Or what if it takes years? Will you put Eirin off indefinitely?*

Would Eirin wait indefinitely?

Against his will, a vision flashed in his mind, Eirin in ten years' time. And though he was no Seer, he could only see this future far too well. Her dark eyes were sparkling as she laughed. In this vision, she wore no defensive clothes, but the white robes that belonged to Seers in the books Eirin had shown him. Two small children clustered around her legs, and she leaned forward to kiss a man whose face Drystan could not see. The man's pale hair and skin gave him away, however, and Drystan had to bite his tongue to keep the Dragon inside from roaring as Mannish, older and broader, wrapped his arm around her waist and pulled her close.

His vision was suddenly stained red, and several moments passed before Drystan could calm the Dragon within enough to continue with his thoughts. When he finally did, though, one single question shut the Dragon up completely.

Could he be the one to take that future away? Was it fair to make her wait on his lack of self-control? Or would it be kinder to let her go forever so that she would be happy? She had made it clear she loathed his abandonment now, and Qeb had said as much. But surely she wouldn't always. Eventually, she would find happiness somewhere else.

She was too good not to.

He was reminded of that night on the roof of the Elven fortress when he and Eirin had discussed their deepest desires. It seemed like another life, but in truth, only months had passed.

What about you? Eirin had asked him. *What if it weren't for all the future Heir nonsense?*

Drystan had spent all but the last few months of his life sure that he couldn't have a family. For years, he'd been haunted by stories of the dead wives of his fathers.

Why wish for something I can't have? he had responded.

That was the problem, though. For a brief moment, he had let himself believe he could have it, and that he could have it all. Dancing in the moonlight with Eirin in his arms, he had opened a door that had always been closed.

He had let himself love.

It wasn't the silly, boyish pining of Mannish, nor was it the kind of passing fancy Thane had harbored for dozens of girls over the years. Drystan didn't even really understand it himself. All he knew was that he had fallen for Eirin irrevocably. The door he'd allowed to open had been yanked off its hinges and would never close again.

Drystan rubbed his chest for the hundredth time that night, but it did nothing to ease the aching inside.

Callispa, this beautiful, vibrant woman, had made it clear she wanted happiness with him. And not only was she a wonderful person, but she was also one of the few Drystan couldn't injure with his mishaps. She could continue training with him, as he slowly became the Dragon Solevar needed him to be.

Perhaps she could have been that person in another life, one without Eirin.

But Eirin was very much real and alive, and Drystan was too aware of her with every fiber of his being to fix his eyes...or his heart on anyone else.

———

Drystan must have fallen into a light doze because the next thing he knew, Callispa was shaking him gently awake.

"Karolus wants us to search the town one more time," she said, an apologetic smile on her face. "But we get to leave first thing after sundown."

The others might have found the errand a waste of time, but Drystan was thankful for an excuse to put his mulling aside. Karolus was determined to search every inch of the town one more time. And though Drystan knew they wouldn't be finding anyone, he also remembered the Wizard's warning and kept his mouth shut.

Sure enough, just as they prepared to begin their journey back after sunset that evening, a seventh figure appeared beside them. The others let out a burst of small hisses and growls at his sudden materialization, leaping back as the Wizard shook the snow from his robes. Callispa, who was not in her Phoenix form because of the snow, gave Drystan a look of amazement.

"Well, are we leaving, or aren't we?" the Wizard asked Karolus.

Karolus blinked at him a few times before stuttering that they were. Then he seemed to come to himself and bowed his head slightly. "We're honored you've chosen to–" he rumbled in his deep, Dragon voice, but the Wizard interrupted him.

"It wasn't for you. It was for him." He jerked his head at Drystan. "Now, let's go before I change my mind."

Karolus stared at Drystan for a moment before nodding slowly. "Very well. Let's be on our way."

"What did you do?" Callispa whispered as she climbed on Drystan's back. But Drystan just smiled. He was still torn over the future. But even if he couldn't be everything to Eirin that she wanted him to be, he was bringing help.

47

$\mathscr{E}$irin put her book down, stretched her back, and yawned. It was the second-to-last night before the Wizard-seeking expedition's return, and Eirin and Mannish had agreed to put in a few extra hours before daybreak, as it would probably be difficult to get any work done once the group was home. Eirin, having given up on getting any useful information out of the despondent Lady Phaidra about the Blood Fire Throne, was reading a rather tedious record of the lesser Dragon families. Mannish, on the other hand, looked riveted by his book. Which, from what Eirin could tell, was one of the Wizard texts.

"I assume those have something to do with your secret plan," she said, nodding at the books piled around Mannish.

Mannish put the book down, but instead of smiling, he simply looked thoughtful.

"They do," he said slowly.

"Then tell me about them." She climbed down from the stool she was sitting on to kneel beside him on the floor. "Because what I'm reading is dreadful." She'd dozed off while reading three times already.

"I did try to tell you," he tweaked her nose. "In fact, I tried to show you. But I trust you recall how that turned out."

Eirin held up her hands, which were covered in silky white

425

gloves. "But I'm prepared this time." She wiggled her fingers and her eyebrows.

He laughed but shook his head. "You know better than I do that those only work half the time. You still had a vision while wearing them yesterday."

Eirin stuck her tongue out, which made Mannish laugh again. Then he sobered and looked at her thoughtfully once again.

"What?" she asked. "Whatever the answer is, do it. I'm bored to tears."

Qeb harrumphed loudly from where he sat in the corner. But Eirin kept her eyes on Mannish. If Qeb couldn't handle a little light flirting, he could wait outside.

But instead of smiling, Mannish only took her hand and studied it. Then, slowly, he took the glove off and gently ran a finger down her palm. Eirin's breath hitched at the unexpected touch.

"I'm… I'm afraid I'm not very good at this." He huffed and sent an exasperated look at Qeb, who was glaring at him, before looking back at her, his pale brows furrowed.

"Good at what?" Eirin asked somewhat breathlessly, gently pulling her hand free. What was he doing?

"I can't…" He closed his eyes, took a deep breath, then opened them and tried again. "I can't make you a princess."

Eirin stared at him. "I…never aspired to be," she finally managed to say.

He let out his deep breath and gave her a small smile. "Well, that's good because…" His eyes locked onto hers, and suddenly, they steeled with resolve. "I love you, Eirin."

Eirin could only stare at him. That was not where she had planned for her flirting to go.

"And…while I know you still love him—and I should hate him for that—I can't help feeling grateful to him."

Eirin felt her mouth fall open slightly, but still, no words came.

"Because he truly cared enough about you to let go so you could stay alive. And I know you're not ready yet. Because it's too soon, and you've known him a long time…" He paused, then his words came out in a rush. "But maybe one day, you could…I hope." He suddenly leaned forward and pressed his lips against her cheek.

If Eirin had been shocked before, she was in a frozen stupor now.

"I think we could do great things together. I just…" Gesturing at his pile of Wizarding books, he continued. "I only ask that you trust me." He gave her a lopsided smile. "Because I really think we can save the world."

Someone cleared his throat so close to them that Eirin jumped and looked up. Qeb had somehow crossed the room without her noticing and was now standing over them.

"We have less than an hour until sunrise." He gave Mannish a baleful glare. "I think it's time you both got some sleep."

Mannish looked for a moment as though he might argue, but then he glanced at the window and nodded. "You're right. It is late. Or early. However you want to look at it." He chuckled to himself then looked at Eirin once more. "Are you tired?"

"I am," Eirin managed to say.

"Well, good day then." Mannish bowed and grinned. Eirin's senses returned just as he turned to go.

"Wait." She grabbed his sleeve, and he looked at her with wide eyes.

"Yes?"

She took a deep breath in and let it out before answering. Finally, she found her words. "I… I'm greatly honored that you consider me that way." This time, her smile didn't feel so unnatural. "You really are very sweet."

Mannish beamed, but she held up a hand.

"Before I give you an answer, though, I'm afraid I'll need…a little time."

Mannish's eyes, which had been blazing moments before, softened. "Of course," he said. "I wouldn't have it any other way."

———

For once, as they made their way out into the pre-dawn streets, it was Qeb who seemed bursting with questions and Eirin who was trying to ignore them. Not the other way around, as it usually was. But Eirin didn't slow down or give him a chance to talk until they had reached a small herb garden that looked down over the zigzagging mountain streets. Eirin let herself sink onto a large rock, and Qeb stood behind her, his arms crossed over his wide chest.

The canvases would be rolled out in less than an hour, and Solevar would be cut off from view. But for now, she could look out over the carpet of trees that covered the valley below the mountain. She knew from her brief time in the forest that many of the branches were withered and dying, but from here, they looked like a soft carpet of moss, and she wished she could stretch her hand out and touch them.

"Nuru will be awake soon," Eirin said as Qeb opened his mouth. "We can get her to switch places with you, so you can get some rest."

"Griffins don't need much rest," he growled. "Two hours is more than enough."

Surprised, she forgot her determination to keep her eyes glued to the valley, and she turned and looked at him. "Really?"

"Really." He glared down at her. "Now about what just happened in there."

"What happened in there is none of your business."

Qeb glowered at her, but she just glowered back.

"Drystan has made it perfectly clear that his loyalties lie elsewhere." She raised her chin defiantly.

But defiance wasn't needed. Qeb's glare softened. "Drystan cares deeply for you."

Eirin rolled her eyes. "Cares deeply. I cared deeply for my puppy when I was four. That didn't mean I was beholden to him for anything."

"I would know if it were otherwise." He leaned against the railing that separated the garden from the small drop below. "My pull to protect you is just as strong as it ever was."

Eirin wanted to scoff at that. Or better yet, to repudiate it. But for some reason, all she could do was stare down at the valley below in silence.

"So what was–" he began, but she cut him off.

"I know you said a Griffin forms his…bond with someone he respects. But what happens if the person the Griffin is tied to changes? What if he becomes a person the Griffin no longer respects?"

Qeb gave her a knowing look, but he finally answered her question anyway.

"Do you mean Drystan?"

She shook her head. "I was actually thinking of Rangvald." This was true. She had been wondering about Rangvald and his Griffins the day before. And now was the perfect chance to use it as an excuse not to talk about Drystan or Mannish.

Not that Qeb was fooled.

Qeb looked away from her out over the slowly brightening sky. "It is technically possible to break a tie. But it's excruciating. Not just for the mind and the heart, which have been connected to that of the person the Griffin is tied to, but physically. It's nearly impossible for a Griffin to kill the person he tied himself to, even if he manages to break the tie." Qeb stood and stretched. "It's why Griffin ties are sought so highly among the rich and powerful. A Griffin tie all but guarantees loyalty at all costs." He paused. "Or *were* sought out, at least, before the curse."

"Qeb," Eirin laughed, "when in Solevar do you have time to learn all of this? You follow me around so much you hardly have time to sleep."

He gave her a smug smile. "I told you, Griffins don't need more than two or three hours of sleep. And believe it or not, I've had training too." His smug smile disappeared then. "But you asked about Rangvald. Why?"

Eirin made a face. "In truth? I'm not sure what to think of him. After meeting his Griffins in the mountains, I was convinced he could only be a monster. But now..." She shrugged. "He seems just as well-intentioned and imperfect and frustrated as Lady Phaidra and Karolus."

Qeb nodded slowly, a thoughtful frown on his face.

"What about you?" Eirin nudged his leg with her shoulder. "What do *you* think of him?"

"I don't trust him, if that's what you mean. But that's simply because I don't know him well enough to trust. And he did have us chased down like animals." He scratched his chin. "Something that I find impressive, however, is the number of Griffins who are tied to him."

"Oh?" Eirin considered this. She'd always guessed that the loyalty of Rangvald's lackeys–the ones who had tracked them down during their run through the mountain–had simply been purchased by the highest bidder. She hadn't considered loyalty to be a possible cause for their obedience.

"Having one Griffin tied to you is impressive enough," Qeb continued. "A Griffin never ties himself to anyone he can't respect." He gave her a sideways grin. "No matter how much he's being paid."

"Well then, could the fact that he's a high prince have something to do with it?"

"It could. From what I hear, royals and aristocrats would often play the host and raise young Griffins alongside their own children in the hopes that ties would be created as naturally as possible as young as possible. And as we live a hundred and fifty years–"

"Hold on." Eirin turned and stared up at him. "You live *how* long?"

"Exactly a hundred and fifty years." He smirked at her again. "Unlike other races, we don't age or begin to weaken with time. For a hundred and fifty years, we're healthy and strong. Then, traditionally, the week before a Griffin's hundred and fiftieth birthday would be one of celebration and feasting with his loved ones. On the evening of his hundred and fiftieth birthday, he would simply...go to sleep and never wake up again." He smiled. "It sounds very peaceful, actually."

Eirin realized that, as much as she wanted a distraction, she also did not want to talk about Qeb's death. And it was getting late. Qeb might not need much sleep, but she soon would, and she still had unfinished business. So she stood and dusted off her clothes.

"Would you mind walking me back to the scholars' room?" She glanced in the direction of their rooms. "I have something I'm not finished with just yet."

He fell into step beside her, but as they walked, he looked down at her with a critical eye. "Would it have something to do with all that flirting?"

Eirin sniffed. "Perhaps." Poorly timed flirting, if she was honest with herself. Not that she cared to discuss it right now. "Again, not that it's any of your business, but I *was* actually hoping to get a little more information out of him. And I can flirt with whomever I want to. Since Drystan–"

"You can. That doesn't mean it's wise."

As Eirin had discovered so vividly less than an hour before.

They arrived back at the scholar's room. Qeb began to follow her in, but she stopped in the doorway. "If you don't mind, I'd like to study on my own for a bit. I really need to focus."

He gave her a look, and she huffed and held her gloves up. "I came prepared. And you can check on me anytime you want."

"And by *on your own*, I'm assuming you also want me to keep other parties out as well?"

Eirin sighed. "If you can without starting a war, yes, please."

Qeb stepped closer, and when he spoke, his voice was low. "You're worried about what he's planning. That's why you flirted earlier. You were trying to get him to tell you what he's doing."

Eirin hesitated before answering slowly. "I just...I need to see things without distractions. That's all."

Qeb's brows drew closer together. "That's not convincing."

"I think..." Eirin looked out over the now light gray sky. "Whatever he's planning, I think he means well. I just want to know what it is. That's all."

"I'm not convinced he means well, though. That boy–"

"Is only a year younger than you, Qeb. He's not a boy." Eirin wasn't sure why she felt so bristly. She was, however, about five seconds from swearing off talking to any male ever again. It might save her sanity.

"That makes it even more urgent, then, that you understand," Qeb said. "Whether or not you heed them, he's made his intentions toward you clear. And I'm not sure he's the kind of man who can graciously have those intentions rebuffed."

"Who says they'll be rebuffed?" Eirin asked archly.

"So you want to marry that boy-man?"

"I *want* to be left alone."

Qeb snorted and rolled his eyes before turning away. "Go inside before you fall asleep and drool on a book again."

"I'll drool on a book whenever I want to!" And with that, Eirin whirled around and stomped inside.

As she let the door swing shut behind her, she closed her eyes and did her best to let all her exhaustion-fueled pettiness melt away. Good intentions or not, it was time to find out what Mannish was up to. And for that, she really did need to focus.

48

$\mathcal{E}$irin tried to shake off the doubts and fears that whispered in her head as she went to where Mannish had left his books and scrolls on Wizards. She pulled her gloves on before touching them and began to sort through the pile to see if he had anything new.

The gloves, as both Qeb and Mannish had pointed out, didn't work perfectly. She still sometimes had a stray vision while wearing them, especially if she touched something particularly potent. But more often than not, all she felt were whispers of the past, similar to what she had felt before her abilities had fully manifested, the sensation that there was something more to the item than just the material itself.

She recognized most of the materials Mannish had left out. They were the ones he'd shown her back when he first tried to introduce her to the study of Wizards. But she realized quickly that one of his most commonly read books, one she'd seen him poring over multiple times, wasn't there. It was a small leather-bound book with various drawings of plants, rocks, minerals, and little scribbled notes as to their uses.

Eirin moved to the shelf where Mannish usually kept his favorite sources and looked for the missing book.

It wasn't hard to find. But as she pulled it out, something blue

435

caught her eye in the shadow behind it. She had to stand on her tip-toes to reach it, but when she put her hand into the space behind where the book had been, she felt parchment.

"Qeb!" she called.

Qeb burst in, looking from side-to-side, looking so worried that Eirin laughed.

"No villain. Just my lack of height." She pointed at the shelf. "There's something stuck in the back there, and I can't reach it."

Qeb took a deep breath and shook his head, but he did come over and pull the hidden object out. Sure enough, it was a blue leather-bound journal.

"What does it say?" he asked, handing it to Eirin.

The leather was so old that Eirin worried the binding might fall to pieces if she wasn't careful. So she took it over to the table and laid it down gently.

"I can't read the words on the front," she said. "But it looks like…"

She held her hand over the words, which had been engraved with gold. Hesitantly, she removed her glove and laid her fingers on the gold.

Immediately, the room around her disappeared, along with Qeb, and she was standing beside a woman seated at a desk. The woman was writing in the journal, which was now new and sturdy.

A man with a graying beard and deep-set brown eyes was pacing behind her chair. His robes swished softly as he walked.

"Ungthru ngahn thruck," he said. Then he paused and looked over the woman's shoulder. "Good. Now write that two more times."

"Do all spells repeat themselves this often?" the woman laughed as she bent to write.

"Only the stronger ones. The repetition draws more magic from the environment. Not to the extent that it multiplies the magic, but it gathers remnants that might have been left behind." He patted her on the shoulder and resumed pacing. "Let's see, where to… Oh, yes. After that phrase has been uttered three times, it changes. Ahventhen avength lothrohil tatinthan."

"Eirin?"

Eirin opened her eyes to realize that she must have opened the book during the vision. For now, rather than touching the cover, her fingers were resting on a page with the exact spell she'd just witnessed the woman inscribe.

"You were frowning. Is something wrong?" Qeb asked.

Eirin took a deep breath in and let it out. "No, nothing's wrong, I just..." She looked back down at the book. "I think I need to read a few more."

Qeb pursed his lips, but he nodded and stayed quiet as she moved a few pages to the right and rested her hand there.

The woman was writing in the book again, but this time, she wasn't at a desk in a cozy, fire-lit room. Instead, she was sitting outside on a low stone wall. The robed man was there again as well, uttering unfamiliar words once more. But this time, rather than simply saying them, he held firmly a staff with a purple gem, and he was raising his voice to the sky, eyes lifted up as he shouted the words at the heavens. Common stones, which must have been scattered across the field, rose into the air and then arranged themselves into a neat pile at the edge of the field.

Eirin opened her eyes, and the vision disappeared again. A few pages over, and she closed them again. Once again, the woman was transcribing. And once again, the man was holding his staff. This time, however, he was pointing it directly at a boulder in the center of the field before him. He shouted new words, but this time, instead of the boulder lifting into the air, it disappeared briefly before reappearing immediately beneath him, raising him into the air as he chanted.

Eirin dropped the book.

"What is it?" Qeb asked.

"I need to see something," she muttered as she ran to the side of the table where Mannish's books had been stacked. Qeb came to look over her shoulder as she rummaged through them.

"What do you need? Can I help?"

Eirin grabbed a book and flipped through it before putting it to the side and trying another. "We know that Wizards were all once Seers who were brought to the Hidden Waters of Domhier. They drink from the waters and spend ten years seeing visions of what their power can do and what will happen if they abuse them." She grabbed another book and yanked it open.

"Then they're released from the vision, and they find themselves in a cavern full of gems. They choose one and use it to build their staff." "What does the staff actually do?" Qeb asked, moving a stack of books to the side for her.

"Thank you. As for the staff, the Wizards can manipulate magic on their own, much in the way Fae and Elves do, but to a far greater extent. The staff, from what I understand, heavily magnifies their ability to draw power from the world around them."

As she was skimming the book, a small stack of folded parchments fell from the pages. Eirin bent to pick them up. As she put them on the table, she realized that the first parchment was a map.

This map was new. The ink was dark and still smelled fresh, and the parchment was white instead of yellow.

"It's Solevar," Eirin said, spreading the map out on the table.

The map was a poorly drawn replica of the map Eirin's father had given her before she'd left Torbaine the first time. But unlike her map, the mountain range to the west had several circles drawn over various places, some at the foot of the mountains and others at the top. Notes had been scribbled beside the circles.

"This is Mannish's handwriting," Eirin said, squinting at the messy hand. "But I can't read…"

"This might help." Qeb handed her another parchment. This one was also new.

"It's a list," Eirin said. "It looks like…a list of necessities."

"The kind of necessities one would take on a journey." Qeb frowned.

Eirin grabbed up the blue journal again. But this time, instead of flipping randomly through the pages, she turned to the first one. And instead of touching the words, she began to read.

THESE ARE THE RECORDS OF AMRIT, WIZARD OF STONE IN THE FOURTEENTH AGE.

She skimmed the lines written beneath the introduction, but nothing seemed of much import until she reached the third page.

THIS RECORD SHALL BE DEDICATED TO THE POWER OF THE STAFF AND ITS PRECIOUS STONE. MY BROTHERS DO NOT BELIEVE I SHOULD BE WRITING SUCH THINGS DOWN, BUT THE POWER OF THE WIZARD'S STONE IS FANTASTICAL ENOUGH TO MERIT ITS OWN WRITING ON THE SUBJECT.

MY BROTHERS DO NOT UNDERSTAND STONE AS I DO, BUT VALUE AS EQUAL WATER, WIND, TREES, SOIL, AND SUCH. IF THEY COULD SEE THE RAW POWER IN STONE, THEY, TOO, WOULD WISH TO SEEK FOR THEIR VERY OWN THE POWER THE TIME KEEPER HAS SEEN IT RIGHT TO DEVOTE TO ME. FOR IT IS MY BELIEF THAT SO MUCH POWER HAS BEEN PRESSED INTO THE STONES AT THEIR CREATION THAT EVEN A SIMPLE SEER WOULD BE ABLE TO DIRECT THEIR PATH.

Eirin looked up from the book. Her head felt as though it were spinning, and she wasn't sure if she could get it to stop.

"I don't think," she said slowly, "that Mannish meant to show this to me."

Qeb held out his hand, and Eirin handed him the little book. He read the page as well, then he looked over at the loose parchments that now lay unfolded on the table.

"It would seem so." He picked up the list again. "You did say he was making plans of his own."

Eirin shook her head. "It just…it doesn't feel right."

Qeb put the paper down. "While I'm hardly Mannish's closest friend, I don't really see anything wrong with it. What is it to us if he charges off to find some ancient cavern with magical stones?"

"Because," Eirin said, reaching for the map again, "Wizards have rules."

Qeb gave her a blank look.

Eirin pointed to the book. "The other Wizards had made it clear that they believed the author of this book–Amrit–shouldn't have made recordings of the magic as he was. There are…boundaries that even Wizards should stay within." She ran back to the shelf for another book. This one was larger with red binding. Snatching it off the shelf, she flipped it open and searched until she found the page she was looking for.

"What kind of boundaries?" Qeb asked.

"Well, the greatest is that they can't bend the raw magic of the world too much."

"And what happens if they do?"

She looked up at Qeb. "It breaks things." Then she looked back down at the red book. "Here. Amrit was put to death by the other Wizards because they said he had taken his magic too far after he began hoarding it. He was putting what they claimed was stolen magic into stones for his own use, rather than using it to help others as he'd been charged with doing." She looked up. "In a sense, Amrit was doing what Kamon's Seer did, abusing his gifts and resources." She frowned down at the mess of books and parchments before them. "When I was watching the visions of Amrit in the book, he was casting his spells. And while most of them seemed benign enough…" She paused, remembering the stone, how he had made it disappear and appear again in another place. "I think maybe he was beginning even then to change things too much. Over-bending the magic, so to speak."

She looked back down at the blue book. "I don't have a good feeling about this. If he's been hiding this book by Amrit–"

"He could be up to something worse," Qeb finished grimly.

Eirin nodded. "I think we need to tell someone. If Mannish attempts something dangerous the way Amrit was…" She shook her head. "We could end up with a much bigger mess than the one we have now." The stone around her neck, which constantly thrummed and hummed with unreadable power, was a constant reminder of how such dangerous gambles could turn out.

Qeb gestured to the door. "Then lead the way."

49

$\mathcal{E}$irin carefully placed the blue book and the loose sheets of parchment into the leather bag she and Mannish sometimes used to take reading materials back to their rooms for further study.

"Where do you think Lady Phaidra is right now?" Eirin asked, carefully fastening the bag shut.

"Probably in the annex," Qeb said. "She often called Drystan there before they left to hear of his progress."

Eirin nodded. "Good. Hopefully, she'll be there today. Next comes the problem of Mannish. I get the feeling we ought to do this without him."

"He usually sleeps for about five hours and then returns when we wake up," Qeb said as they turned a corner.

Eirin paused and looked at him incredulously. "And how do you know this?"

Qeb gave her a wry grin. "Do you think Drystan would let a stranger spend that much time around you without knowing what he did when he wasn't with us?"

Eirin shook her head. "Meddling again." Not that she really minded his meddling in general. But right now, everything Drystan did was irritating.

"Yes," Qeb said pleasantly as he strode beside her. "But with the best intentions."

Eirin bit back the reply she wanted to spit out. It wasn't Qeb's

443

fault Drystan was being stupid. No need to insult his best friend to Qeb's face.

She would insult Drystan to his own stupid face.

They didn't speak again until they reached the annex. Sure enough, they were told, Lady Phaidra was inside, and she would be happy to see them.

Eirin and Qeb made their way inside to find Lady Phaidra finishing off a small cake of bread as she stood to greet them.

"Excuse me," she said, gesturing to the empty plate. "I didn't sleep much, so I thought I would start the day here."

Eirin didn't dare reply that Lady Phaidra didn't seem to ever sleep much these days. Black circles always hung below her eyes, and she seemed to have aged decades since her husband had died. Of course, that might have also had something to do with the fact that Eirin knew Lady Phaidra had also been giving out a shocking number of her scales since the battle, despite forbidding Drystan from giving away any of his scales until he was older.

Was Lady Phaidra trying to dispose of her scales so she could join her husband and daughter in the afterlife?

But this wasn't the time for that now.

"What's the matter?" Lady Phaidra asked, her brows drawing together as she looked back and forth between them. "You look as though you've been visited by a Specter."

Eirin glanced at Qeb before speaking. "I... I'm not sure how to say it, but..." She frowned. "For the last few weeks, Mannish has been speaking of some sort of plans. But he won't tell me what they are. Only that they involve Wizards."

Lady Phaidra nodded, wide-eyed. "Yes, the Wizard search was his idea."

Eirin shook her head. "This...seems to be another sort of plan. One to implement in case the search doesn't work." She carefully opened and dug into her bag. "I was studying last night, and after he left, I came upon these."

She placed the blue book on the table in front of Lady Phaidra. "It was shoved back behind the other books."

"And you think he hid it?" Lady Phaidra asked. Eirin could tell that her interest at this point was polite. The lady seemed to have no misgivings as of yet.

"I think so. Largely because these fell out with it." Eirin pulled out the parchments as well. "Those are in Mannish's handwriting, and the ink is new. They were tucked into the book."

"I see." Lady Phaidra picked up the book and flipped through it. "I'm sorry, you'll have to explain to me what this is about. I can't decipher the words or the pictures."

"From what I understand," Eirin said, "this is a record of the Wizard Amrit's experiments." She took a deep breath. "The ones the other Wizards put him to death for."

Lady Phaidra jerked her head up and looked straight at Eirin. "And what," she asked in a low voice, "do you think he plans to do with this?"

"I think," Eirin said slowly, "that he wishes to find the cave with the Hidden Waters of Domhier."

Lady Phaidra stared at her for a moment before breaking into a laugh. "And what do you suppose he would do there? He's not a Wizard. And even if he became one, he would need ten years to mature."

"I don't think he wants to become a Wizard," Eirin said slowly. "I think–based on something I read in this book–that he wants a Wizard's stone."

Lady Phaidra exhaled sharply then began to walk back and forth in front of the fire. "But," she said slowly, "suppose he even found the cave. And the stone. What would he even do with it?"

"My concern is not so much that he could or could not use it," Eirin said, "but that he would try." She was suddenly very conscious of the stone that was pressed against her chest. "Kamon's Seer wasn't able to change fate by inserting a Time Stone of his own. But he tried. And look where we are now a hundred years later." She looked down at the map. "I'm afraid Mannish or anyone else trying to claim a Wizard's stone inappropriately would only bring us further pain."

Her heart clenched slightly as she said the words. Mannish wouldn't take kindly to her betrayal. She knew that in her heart. Qeb had been right when he'd said that Mannish wasn't the kind of man to take rejection lightly. What she was doing now was even worse.

"Thank you for telling me," Lady Phaidra said slowly, looking down at the papers again. "I'm afraid...Not that I don't believe you." She gave Eirin a sad smile. "You're rarely wrong. But this is a weighty matter, and I hope you'll forgive me if I wish to speak to Karolus about it before I make any further judgments?"

Eirin nodded. "Of course. I understand."

Lady Phaidra smiled. "Don't worry about it for now. If this is where he believes the cave to be," she pointed down at the map, "he won't be able to make it on anything slower than Dragon speed before the sickness begins to set in in earnest. And I'll make sure none of the other Dragons will take him anywhere without our permission." She gave Eirin another gentler smile. "Now, go get some rest. We'll figure this out later. Karolus and the others should be back tomorrow."

Eirin thanked her and wished her a good day. She didn't miss the worry returning to Lady Phaidra's face, however, as she turned to go.

———

"I'm afraid," Qeb said as they stepped out beneath the now unfurled canvases, "that she's not going to act quickly enough."

"I agree." Eirin squinted in the bright light.

"You agree with what?"

They turned to find Nuru slink out from behind a lower wall. She was in Sphinx form, as she was most of the time these days. "In the future, by the way, I would appreciate some sort of notification before you two go gallivanting about without me."

"Sorry," Eirin said with a smile. "We wanted to let you sleep. And this kind of took us by surprise."

"Well then, you can tell me now."

Eirin glanced around before leaning in and whispering in Nuru's long ear. It twitched a few times as Eirin raced through the facts, but when she was done, Nuru's eyes were bright with excitement. It was her hunting look.

"So he's been busy then." Nuru turned her bright eyes on Qeb. "Let's go to our room. We can talk there."

Qeb began to nod, then paused. "We should wait to make any

decisions, though, until Drystan gets back. They should return tomorrow."

Eirin rolled her eyes. "You can tell him whatever we discuss. He's not coming if I'm there, and you know it."

The frustration was evident in Qeb's eyes, but Eirin knew she had won when he gruffly nodded his assent.

"What about Thane?" Nuru suggested. "He should be there at least."

"Let's go get him," Eirin said.

Nuru shifted into her Human form, something which Eirin chose not to make a sly remark about, and then they made their way to the Centaurs' practice circle.

"I have no idea how they get this many Centaurs to fit in one small space," Nuru grumbled. "Nor do I want to."

"Nuru! Qeb! Eirin!" Thane called from across the circle, smiling as though he'd won a prize. His long hair was pulled at the nape of his neck, and the muscles in his legs rippled as he trotted up to them. "What brings you here?"

Eirin edged forward and pitched her voice low. "Something's come up, and–"

"We need you right now," Nuru interrupted her. "It's urgent." Her dark eyes were wide and pleading, and without seeming aware of it, she reached out and took his hand.

The smile fell from Thane's face as he looked at each of them in turn, then down at the hand Nuru held. "You mean it," he said softly. "It is something important then."

Nuru hissed and dropped his hand as though it burned her. "Do you think we're lying?"

Apprehension tightened Thane's features as he turned and glanced back at the other Centaurs behind him. At least a dozen were looking at their little group with intense curiosity.

"I'm sorry," Thane said in a low voice. "But I…I made a promise to my herd. Today—"

Nuru's voice was low and dangerous. "What kind of promise?"

Thane grimaced. "That my allegiance would be to my kin before my companions." He shrugged his broad shoulders. "I'm sorry, but I can't help without my captain's permission."

Qeb's face, which had so far remained impassive, darkened. "You swore first to help Eirin."

"You *swore*," Eirin said. Her voice quivered slightly. "You promised to be a part of this when we began, and–"

"I know." Thane gave Eirin a pained look. "I am truly sorry, Eirin." Then he huffed and rubbed his face. "Look, if I ask after this exercise, maybe my captain will let me–"

"Forget it." Nuru's words were as sharp as her teeth. "You can just stay away. You'd probably be a risk to us all anyway. Come on," she snapped at Eirin and Qeb as she turned away. But Eirin didn't miss the tears streaming down Nuru's face as she stalked down the road ahead of them. Eirin caught up and put her arms around Nuru's shoulders, but Nuru just shoved her off. Before Eirin could say anything, though, the sound of many voices erupted from behind them. They turned back to see a boy running down the path from an outpost higher up on the mountain.

"They've come back!" he shouted. "Karolus and the others have come back! And they've brought the Wizard as well!"

50

The return trip, which should have taken two nights, only took one, thanks to the Wizard.

"How far is it from here to the city?" he had asked as dawn began to approach.

"Four hours at most," Karolus had replied over the wind. "The currents are with us today, so once we take off after sunset tonight, we should be home soon."

"Which means we'll need to find somewhere to sleep soon," Bahiti called from behind.

The Wizard nodded and lifted his staff. Uttering strange words from his place on Karolus's back, he pointed his staff up. Wispy white clouds began to form in the perfectly blue sky. Before long, however, those wisps started to congregate, and within minutes, the thickest cloud Drystan had ever seen was traveling over them. Drystan gaped as he realized they now had protection from the sun.

"It wouldn't last for a whole day," the Wizard called out, "but it should get us to the city well enough. Do you think you can fly faster?"

"By all means." Karolus turned his head just long enough to give the others a nod before increasing his speed. And like that, the Wizard cut their trip home nearly in half.

"Thanks for the ride," Callispa said, tapping Drystan's shoulder when they finally landed. "With the wind he put at our tails, flying in that would have been…interesting."

"You mean he would have blown you out like a candle." Bahiti laughed. Callispa laughed along with her, but Drystan simply changed form and hoped the others would do likewise.

As soon as they were safely beneath the highest canopy, just below the highest lookout point on the mountain, the cloud which had covered them melted into pieces of nothing. Thankfully, no one seemed to be in the mood to watch the smaller pieces bleed back into the sky.

"Show me this Seer," the Wizard announced, already making his way down the path.

"Wouldn't you like some sort of rest or refreshments?" Karolus asked.

The Wizard scowled. "I can drink tea and eat bread any day I choose. I came here to visit the Seer."

Drystan had never liked the man more.

Word must have gotten around about their return, for by the time they made it down to the first main square, the streets were already packed with people. Drystan breathed a sigh of relief when he spotted Eirin standing between Qeb and Nuru in the far corner of the square. Thane, of course, was nowhere to be seen. Unfortunately, Mannish was there, and he was standing even closer to Eirin than Qeb.

It wasn't fair, of course, but Drystan wanted to punch him in the face for that.

"Isayas!" Lady Phaidra called as she came forward to meet them. "We're delighted to have you again." Her smile and words seemed earnest enough, but the Wizard just waved her off.

"You're not glad to see me. You're just hoping I'll do something to fix what you've broken. Now, I came here to see her. Dragon boy," he called, waving to Drystan. "You're the one infatuated with her. Where is she?"

Drystan's face blazed red as he pointed Eirin out. "She's there, sir."

"These," Lady Phaidra said proudly, as though Isayas hadn't just dismissed her, "are our Seers, Eirin and Mannish." She walked over to Eirin and put her arm around her shoulders. "You would have known them earlier had you wished."

Drystan didn't miss the gentle reprimand, and he doubted Isayas had either, but either the old man didn't notice or didn't care as he made his way over to Eirin. Then he stopped and looked between the two Seers. Mannish looked as though he might faint from sheer joy, but Eirin regarded the Wizard with the same distrust she had regarded Drystan with back in the Citadel.

He was sure her disdain was much worse for him now than it ever was then. That was, he might find out if she ever decided to look at him again. She still hadn't as of yet.

After a moment of studying the pair of Seers, Isayas pulled a ring from his right hand. It had a single blue stone in it and appeared to be made from silver. Holding it out to Mannish, he gave a strange smile.

"Touch it, boy," he said. "Tell me what you see."

Mannish brushed his fingertips over the ring's center and down the side, his breath audibly leaving him as he did. His eyes grew somehow brighter as they unfocused.

"What do you see?" Isayas demanded, but it was a moment before Mannish could answer.

"I saw...stones. And lightning. And magic." His eyes focused once more, and he looked up at the tall man in awe.

The Wizard looked down at him for a long moment before letting out a huff and turning to Eirin. "And what do you see?" he asked in a gentler voice.

Eirin's distrust seemed to have deepened during Mannish's turn with the ring. As she looked from the Wizard's bearded face down at the ring again, Drystan had the sudden urge to throw himself between her and the ring. But he restrained himself. This was why he'd brought the Wizard back, after all. Besides, Qeb was standing just behind her.

For the first time, Eirin looked at Drystan. He could see the questions in her wary eyes. He forced a small smile and a nod, to which she responded with a sigh. But never one to shy away out of fear, Eirin's small hand slowly reached out toward the ring. But instead of caressing it as Mannish had done, she rested it directly on the stone.

Immediately, she gasped and stumbled backward into Qeb's steadying arms. Drystan had never been so jealous of his friend nor so thankful for him. He felt a thin hand on his own arm, and he looked down to see Callispa with a small smile on her own lips.

"She'll be fine," she said softly. "This is why you brought him, isn't it?"

Drystan looked down at her for a moment before giving her a terse nod and looking back down at the scene before them. The crowd had never been so silent before.

"Why would you do that?" Eirin glared at Isayas accusingly. "You knew what I would see, didn't you?"

Rather than being offended by Eirin's sudden anger, however, Isayas only looked back at Drystan and grinned. "You were right. I like her. Thank you for convincing me to come."

Drystan could feel Callispa's gaze on his face, but he didn't return it. Instead, he met Qeb's eyes from across the square.

"Well," Isayas said, rubbing his hands together, "if I'm to stay here, I'll need quarters and food."

"Of course," Karolus said. "We will have them prepared immediately."

"And you," the Wizard said, turning back to Eirin, "will join me again after I've slept. When do you study? You people are always keeping the oddest schedules."

"At night," Eirin said carefully. "After sundown."

"Good. Then after we've all slept, we'll go to your study room or scholars' room or whatever you call it. I haven't been there in ages."

"You mean both of us?" Mannish asked eagerly.

Isayas gave him a cold look. "If you wish."

Drystan glanced at Eirin again. She was indeed looking at him this time, but it was with that enigmatic look he knew only too well. When he did his best to smile, she only stared at him in return.

Lady Phaidra announced that she would lead the Wizard to his quarters if he would like. So Isayas and, it seemed half the city, made their way to some of the smaller rooms on the southern side of the city, not far from where Drystan and Eirin's rooms were located. When Lady Phaidra handed Isayas the key, Drystan didn't wait for the Wizard to close the door behind him. Instead, he followed him inside.

Isayas, however, didn't seem surprised. Instead, he merely locked the door behind them both and turned to Drystan.

"Why didn't you include Mannish in your plans for later?" Drystan asked.

"Simple," Isayas said, lowering himself onto the bed. "Your little friend was strong. Strong enough to recognize danger when she perceived it." Something flashed through the Wizard's gray eyes. "The boy, however, was not."

"What did you show them?" Drystan asked.

"I allowed a hint of the ring's power to channel through it. Elven-made, you know. Incredibly dangerous in the wrong hands."

"And Eirin was wary," Drystan said.

Isayas nodded. "And the boy was not. Or at least, not enough to be properly alarmed." He suddenly leaned forward, his eyes flashing again. "Whatever happens, don't make the mistake of underestimating that one. He's not as strong as she is, but he's by no means weak."

Drystan did his best to keep his breathing even. And Mannish wanted to court Eirin. The Dragon inside both hissed and reveled. The future Drystan had imagined for Eirin couldn't happen. Mannish really was untrustworthy. His chest ached slightly less.

"What exactly concerns you about him?" Drystan asked. "I need to know for Eirin's sake."

Isayas stared grimly up at him. "The boy saw power," he finally said. "And he liked it far too well."

51

The Wizard sent for Eirin before she'd even finished eating her supper of dried, salted figs and bread.

"He couldn't wait until after we broke fast like a normal person?" Nuru grumbled as she shoved the rest of her bread into her mouth.

"Technically, we've only been fasting for four or five hours." Eirin smiled. "Sleeping during the day and all."

Nuru put her mug down with a clink. "I don't care. We only went to bed at noon. He said we could meet at night." She jerked her chin at the window, through which they could see the canvases still rolled out over the city, where they would remain for several more hours.

"My guess is that he wants to see me without Mannish," Eirin said in a low voice. "He made it very clear that he has no interest in him."

"Do you think he knows what Mannish is up to?" Nuru asked as they made their way toward the scholar's room.

"I doubt it," Eirin said. "From what I understand, when Seers gain their Wizard abilities, they lose their gift of Sight. My guess is that whatever test he gave us with the ring yesterday, Mannish failed."

They stopped talking for a moment as they passed a group of Fauns, behind which appeared a hulking, broody figure.

"Good evening, Qeb," Eirin said. "I thought you'd be with Drystan tonight."

"Yes," Nuru added. "If I'd known you'd be here, I would have eaten my supper in peace."

457

Eirin got the feeling that supper wasn't the only reason Nuru wanted to be left alone, but she knew better than to bring Thane up in public like this. Nuru might be ready to talk about it in a couple of weeks. Or years. But not yet.

"I looked for him after escorting you home," Qeb growled, his expression dark as he fell into step beside them. "But when I returned, I couldn't find him anywhere. Someone said he'd been assigned to guard the Wizard while he rested. And as of this evening, he's disappeared again."

"Do you think someone is trying to keep you two apart?" Eirin asked.

Nuru frowned. "Why would they do that?"

"I don't know. Lady Phaidra seemed to believe us yesterday, but..." Eirin sighed. "She said not to tell anyone. She probably also knows, though, that you would tell him. You're tied to him, after all."

"And Thane, though he seems to no longer be a concern," Nuru muttered.

"You're not wrong," Qeb said with a frown. "We'll need to be even more cautious now. Something has changed. I just don't know what."

Nuru looked as sullen as Qeb by the time they arrived at the scholars' room, but to Eirin's surprise, she came to a stop just outside the door and leaned against it to keep Eirin from entering.

"Are you going to tell the Wizard about what we discussed?" she asked Eirin.

Eirin hesitated. "I'm not sure," she finally said. "I guess I'll see what he has to say first." She took a deep breath. "Unfortunately, I'm not...I don't think I have complete confidence in Lady Phaidra's judgment anymore."

Nuru smirked as she opened the door. "You never did."

Eirin laughed at this as they made their way inside. The Wizard was standing at the table studying Eirin's map, which she'd forgotten to roll up the last time she'd consulted it.

"Excellent mapping this is," he said without looking up. "Though it lacks certain landmarks, and a few of the mountains are in the wrong place."

"My father made it," Eirin said as she came to stand a respectful distance from the Wizard. "He's never been to Solevar. His father taught him everything he knew."

The Wizard nodded slowly. "Excellent work, all things considered." He turned his sharp pale eyes on Eirin. "I suppose it would be asking too much to leave your entourage outside?"

Eirin gave Qeb and Nuru a smile, and they both nodded and went to stand outside the front door. When they were alone again, the Wizard sat on one of the stools and studied her. Eirin, in return, studied him.

He was as tall as Drystan, and though not built as powerfully as he probably once had been, his shoulders were noticeably wider than Mannish's. His beard, which reached down his chest, must have once been dark, but was now streaked with white and silver. He had thick, peppered brows and piercing blue eyes.

"Do you know how I can fix the Time Stones?" Eirin blurted. She was somewhat startled by her own abruptness, but she didn't take the question back either. She'd been waiting, she realized afterward, for this moment since she had known there was a Wizard still in existence. And from what she heard, he himself was no stranger to the Time Stones.

If anyone would know, it would be him.

"I'm afraid I don't have any new advice." He gave her a sad smile. "Above the common understanding that the foreign stone must be removed. But my wife," he said, his smile warming, "always believed she could do it if she could only travel to the stones themselves."

"She never went, did she?" Eirin asked softly.

His smile faded, and he took a small locket out of one of his robe pockets. Inside the locket was the carved silhouette of a woman. "No," he said. "She suffered greatly during the first wave of poison, and she was never strong enough to travel again."

"Even with magic?"

He gave her another sad smile. "It's dangerous for us to bend the magic of the natural world too much. Wizards were created to aid the people of Solevar, not to be gods unto ourselves." He picked up a book. "When you touch this book, you See the imprint that prior magic left on its surface, somewhat like an engraving. The magic has engraved its own form onto the object, and you can read its history because of it." He put the book down.

"Once we become Wizards, we can no longer see the imprints of magic as you can. Instead, we can manipulate the magic itself. Unfortunately, too much manipulation can break the very world we are meant to help."

"Like Amrit," Eirin breathed.

The Wizard gave her a solemn nod. Then sighed. "The Time Keeper forbade certain kinds of magic, as I'm sure you're aware."

Eirin nodded. "The texts I read weren't explicit, but from what I understood…anything that destroyed the natural ability of another to conduct life as it should flow."

"That's a good way of putting it. Unfortunately for us, not only did we have to be aware of the amount of power we were taking in and using, but once the curse fell, we also had to accept that the magic we were using was now tainted. Using it in that form took even more care than it had before. It was almost easier not to use any at all than to risk killing someone in the process."

Eirin paused for a moment, chewing her lip. The words were on her tongue, but she found that she was suddenly terrified to ask. Because the answer might break the will she'd been working so hard to protect.

Doubt was always knocking at her door.

"Do you…" She licked her lips and tried again. "Do you think I can even make it through Solevar?" The headaches that had pounded behind her eyes and ears every time she left the mountain suddenly felt as though they'd returned even as she thought of them.

"I can't say for sure." The Wizard looked down at his hands. They wore several rings of various metals and stones. "But I can say this," he lifted his head again, this time with a gentle smile, "you are young and strong. And my wife…" His eyes grew distant, and he swallowed. "Well, let's just say that recovering from a miscarriage is not something a woman of tender heart and health does easily."

"I'm sorry," Eirin breathed.

"I am too." He met her eyes. "What is it?"

Eirin shook her head. "You just… you're different than they told me you'd be."

At this, he threw his head back and laughed. "And that is because I've made sure my reputation precedes me!"

But Eirin didn't laugh. She understood all too well the need for armor against the demands that the world must place upon him. She'd seen the same expression in her mother's eyes.

Her heart suddenly ached as it hadn't in months.

The door burst open, and Mannish ran in, breathless. "I'm sorry," he gasped. "I didn't realize you'd already begun."

Eirin gave him the best smile she could manage. No reason to make him think she suspected anything yet. The Wizard, however, glowered openly at him.

"I have so many questions," Mannish continued as he dumped the contents of his bag on the table. "Your ring yesterday made me think about the magical properties of stones. I know the Dwarves are sensitive to their magic, as are Elves. But how do Wizards know which stones to use according to their needs?" Mannish fumbled for a stack of parchments, which were scattered all over the floor, and the stack of pens he also knocked over.

Eirin knelt to help him pick them up, for which he gave her a grateful smile.

"It depends on the need," the Wizard said stiffly. "What sort of need are you suggesting?"

The door opened again, and Lady Phaidra entered. She was once again in her stately dress, looking similar to the way she'd looked when Eirin had first met her. Only her eyes were far older than they had been at the beginning of summer.

"I see we're already busy," she said with a smile. "Were your provisions satisfactory, Isayas?"

"They were."

"I was wondering specifically about flint," Mannish said, staggering to his feet as he put the stack of parchments back on the table. "I've read that the sparks can be useful for expanding the merits of all sorts of spells."

And so Mannish continued to pepper the Wizard with all sorts of questions as the evening passed into the night. It was almost like a duel, Eirin quickly realized. Mannish would hurl questions at the Wizard, who would answer in the tersest, most ambiguous way possible. This, of course, never seemed to frustrate or irritate Mannish, who simply attacked with a new question. Finally, after an hour of this, Lady Phaidra rose from the chair she'd seated herself in near the window.

"I'm afraid," she told Mannish gently, "that I need to interject my own question here."

Mannish bowed his head and nodded. "Of course, my lady."

"Isayas," Lady Phaidra said as she turned to the Wizard, "I didn't want to overwhelm you when you arrived, but I'm afraid I must ask now so I can know what to tell the people." She drew in a deep breath and clasped her hands in front of her. "Will you accompany us to Iilaedin?" Then her voice dropped. "You know this will be our last chance."

The Wizard turned his gaze to Eirin. And then to Mannish. Then back to Lady Phaidra.

"On one condition," he finally said.

Eirin let out the breath she didn't know she was holding, then immediately sucked in another one.

"Anything," Lady Phaidra said with a smile. Then she paused. "But...what is it?"

"If I go," the Wizard said, drawing himself up to his full height, "the boy stays behind."

Eirin felt her mouth drop open as Mannish and Lady Phaidra let out cries of dismay.

"*Why?*" Mannish demanded to know.

"But...we have two Humans!" Lady Phaidra sputtered. "If something happens to one, we need to have the other one there as well!"

But the Wizard just gathered his robes and his staff and made his way to the door.

"You can take my offer as it is," he said, his hand on the door, "or you can leave it. I'll make no other."

52

Drystan looked down at his hand, which he had successfully turned into a claw. It was strangely fascinating how the skin blended into the scales in the place where he'd initiated the change.

"That was good!" Callispa beamed. "You did it!"

Drystan snorted. "It only took me seven tries." He looked down the path again that led to the training pad. "Are you sure you don't know where Qeb is? Usually, he would have been here by now." It wasn't like his friend not to check in with him after one of them had been gone for any length of time. Even on the days he'd practiced flying, Qeb would always come to see him. But then, maybe Qeb had tried. Drystan hadn't slept in his own bed the afternoon before, as Lady Phaidra had asked him to guard Isayas's door. And once one of the Centaurs had come to relieve him, the night was so spent that it was simply easier to curl up on one of the training pads just outside the meeting room and let sleep take him. He was exhausted.

"He and Nuru have been sticking to Eirin like sap, from what I've heard," Callispa said. "He's probably just taking extra care with Isayas here and all."

"Most likely," Drystan said, but his eyes lingered on the path for another moment, and unease played in his stomach. He wasn't used to being separated from his closest friend for so long a time.

To his surprise, a familiar figure did appear on the path, but it wasn't Qeb. Instead, Karolus approached them.

"Isayas has agreed to take us into Solevar," he announced. "Be ready to leave at any time."

Drystan suddenly felt like collapsing from relief. The Wizard was coming with them. Eirin was getting her chance.

"I did mean to ask you," Karolus said, studying him. "Eirin mentioned that you were refusing to go with us?" His eyes bore into Drystan. "You aren't serious about that. Are you?"

Drystan sighed. "I'm coming. I'd always planned to come. Just... not as her escort." He gave Karolus an unhappy grin. "More of a hidden figure."

Karolus studied him for a moment, then nodded. "Very well. But you'd better be ready either way. There's no way Phaidra will allow you to remain behind."

Relieved, Drystan nodded. He turned to Callispa with a relieved smile. But for some reason, Callispa wasn't smiling.

"What's wrong?" she asked Karolus. "I can see it in your eyes. Something's not right."

Karolus frowned down at his hands before shaking his head. "Something feels...off. I don't know." He glanced around before lowering his voice. "For one, the Wizard's ultimate stipulation was that if he accompanied us, Mannish would not be allowed to go."

Callispa gasped, but Drystan found himself unsurprised. And if he was honest, he felt relieved.

Karolus shook his head. "But let's not speak of it now. Lady Phaidra will tell the city when she has all the details worked out." He glanced at Drystan. "Just be ready to leave at any hour. This will be our last chance."

After Karolus parted, Callispa decided that it was time to practice again. But for some reason, either elation or nerves had ruined Drystan's focus. Only a few minutes passed before he attempted to shift only his hands but lit his entire self up instead.

The flame passed onto Callispa, who was standing close to him, and consumed her. Drystan let out a shout, but before he'd recovered, she had reappeared once more in full form.

"I'm sorry," he groaned, pinching the bridge of his nose. "That was not what I meant to do."

But Callispa only smiled and sat cross-legged on the ground. Then she patted the place beside her, and he sat down as well.

"I know you're worried about Eirin," she said softly. "And Qeb. And Nuru. And Thane. And all the others." She gave him a sad smile. "I'm worried about my family as well."

He looked up. "Tell me about them." Hopefully, he wasn't encouraging her. He just needed to think about something else and for someone else to do the talking. His chest was aching dreadfully again.

She shrugged. "There's not much to tell. You know my father is one of the head Phoenixes, and my mother's family is one of the most respected Phoenix lines in Solevar. Our family has trained royalty for generations. A number of us married into the lesser Dragon families as well." Her smile faded. "I don't want to see all of that end with me."

She let out a deep breath then shook her head. "The truth of it is that the Phoenixes are a dying people. Ironic, isn't it? The indomitable race is failing." She ran her hand through the grass. "We stayed strong when the curse first fell. Or so I'm told. But after a generation or so, we seemed to lose the will to live. We stopped getting married, having children..." She shook her head. "If this doesn't work..."

She didn't finish the sentence, but she didn't have to. Drystan understood perfectly.

They sat there for a long time. A slight breeze came up and cooled the hot summer day. The breeze tousled her red curls, and Drystan felt suddenly that it wasn't fair how they had assigned her as his trainer. The Phoenixes had known what they were doing, pairing a young, beautiful Phoenix trainer with the long-lost prince. But the hopes she'd harbored could never come to be.

"I know what's wrong with your shifting."

Drystan looked at her. "What?"

She stretched slightly then leaned back. "When we tell you to embrace the Dragon, it means you have to accept it for all it is. For all you are. You are powerful, more powerful than I think Karolus or Phaidra expected you to be. Especially being the descendent of the youngest prince. Often, the eldest son is the largest Dragon, and so on. But you're still fighting who you are. And no one can fight that battle for you."

"Now you're sounding like Eirin," he said, trying to keep his voice light.

She raised her eyebrows. "Well, Eirin's right."

"She usually is." With the admission came what felt like an arrow to the heart. How many times had Eirin told him he was running away from the man he was supposed to become? If anyone but Eirin had said it, he would have laughed them away. Now, as he usually did, he attempted to ignore it.

He stood up. "Shall I try again then?"

Callispa grinned. "Always."

53

$\mathcal{E}$irin watched Drystan and Callispa practice from a distance. How in Solevar were they able to fight, let alone stay awake?

Once again, she and her friends had moved back to sleeping during the night and taking lessons during the day, largely because the Wizard had refused to adopt a nocturnal schedule.

"I've been here two days," he'd announced that morning to Lady Phaidra. "And I'm not going to have my sensibilities knocked about by your infernal ever-changing schedule."

Eirin had silently groaned, as had her friends. Changing sleeping schedules was no easy task, and they had done it far too many times in the last few months to relish yet another one.

So here she was now, sitting on a low wall in the late afternoon, feeling half asleep but not being able to tear herself away. Qeb was leaning against a tree trunk nearby as Nuru dozed in one of its lower branches.

Eirin ought to announce that they were all returning to their rooms for the time being. Such a decision would be kinder to them. But they were both sleeping already, and Eirin was on a mission.

A mission that was thus far a miserable failure.

Eirin, though she hadn't told her friends, was here with the express purpose of numbing herself to seeing Drystan and Callispa together. But even after an hour of watching, it still felt like a knife to the heart each time they touched.

There was nothing intimate about the way they made contact. No more holding hands. Everything looked very much like a Dragon being trained by his rider. No hands lingered. No fingers caressed. At least, not on his side. Callispa could have hurried a few of her instructions up. But then again, it didn't really matter. No matter how long Eirin watched them, the pain grew no less. Whether or not he was counting himself as Callispa's, the fact was that he'd left Eirin behind.

Eirin had tried to get over this. She really had, taking Nuru's advice to consider life with someone besides Drystan.

"What if he takes years to control himself?" Nuru had asked. "Or what if he never does?"

"I think it's a little soon to be considering that," Eirin had said.

"Well, we don't always get what we want, though, do we?" Nuru retorted.

Eirin hadn't spoken to Nuru for the rest of the day.

Unfortunately, Nuru's words weren't something Eirin could ignore completely. As much as she hated to admit it, there was always the chance that Drystan would never be able to control himself around her. Which, if Eirin had been her own person, free to do as she wished, wouldn't have bothered her for a moment.

But Eirin didn't belong to herself. She was a Seer, possibly one of the last four in the world. And if Solevar was to continue using the Time Stones, should they ever get them back, they would need Seers. Whether she wanted to marry and become a mother really wasn't a choice she could make selfishly. If Humans were to survive, she would need to have children. Which meant that, at the moment, she had very few options.

Since his declaration of love, Mannish was only too glad to accept any notice she spared him. He'd been all attention and adoration since. And Eirin could find no fault in his courtship, except possibly his desire to please, which could be slightly overenthusiastic.

And yet, something was always...lacking. There was something Eirin couldn't name that lingered beneath his gentle, innocent smile. Something that Eirin's poor attempt at flirting had confirmed in her revelations about his plans. And the Wizard's declarations had only served to cement what concerns she'd come to own.

Of course, that didn't do anything to smother her longing for Drystan. Even as she attempted to move her affections away from him, her weeks of waiting afar had done nothing to dull the pain.

What was it about him that she wanted so much? She studied him from her hiding place beneath the tree. He was handsome, yes. One would have to be blind to deny that. And even if she were blind, the strong angles of his jaw and nose, and the curve of his mouth…

But no. It wasn't about his appearance. Nor was it the power he carried, neither in his heart nor in his line to the throne. It wasn't even the way he'd kissed her gently under the moonlight as they'd danced a lifetime ago.

No, Eirin decided. What left her feeling gutted and hollow was that they had chosen to make this journey together. It wasn't sparks or touches or flirtation. She had trusted that he would be by her side as they faced the perils of the world together. And she was determined to be there for him. They had agreed at Lady Seren's fortress to make the trek together. Their purpose had been one, and they had been a force of their own against the curse and its struggles.

Now the strong wall they had formed together was left with a gaping hole. And while Eirin treasured Nuru and Qeb beyond words, they couldn't fill the hole that he had made. Because it was shaped just like him.

Qeb snorted and rubbed his eyes. "How long have I been asleep?" he asked, his words slurred.

"About an hour," Eirin said.

"Why didn't you wake me?"

Eirin shrugged. "I didn't think we really needed to. Nuru's here. And Drystan's up there." She gave Qeb a dry smile. "Do you see anyone nearby with a death wish?"

"Disturbing my doze would require a death wish," Nuru growled as she stretched in the tree above. "Can we go back to the room? I'd like a few hours of decent sleep, if that's not too much to ask."

Eirin nodded, and they set out on their way back. But before they'd gone very far, Eirin glanced up at Qeb. "Are you sure you don't want to stay? You could talk to Drystan when he's finished. Or now, even. I'm sure Callispa wouldn't mind."

Callispa, for all her faults, had no problem sharing Drystan with

Qeb. Probably because she'd grown up around Griffins. For some reason, this annoyed Eirin more than it should.

Qeb's mouth set in a grim line. "I've tried six times to go and see him in the last two days. And each time I get within hearing distance, someone comes and fetches him away to see to some sudden emergency. Watch." He turned and raised his hand to his mouth.

"Drystan!" he shouted. His voice, even in Human form, echoed off the mountain, and Drystan heard and looked around. But before he could find the source, Abrax–the head Griffin and Qeb's mentor–was making his way up the hill and had already claimed Drystan's attention again.

"That's not an accident," Nuru hissed.

Eirin shook his head. "No, but they know enough of him now to play on his sense of duty. If they're presenting him with important questions or measures, he'll stop to discuss them."

Nuru gave her a sour look, but Eirin just shrugged.

"He was raised to do it."

"He could get away if he wanted to," Nuru sulked.

Qeb frowned as he watched his mentor lead Drystan away. "They could be telling him anything." His frown deepened. "But they won't be for long."

Eirin shook her head and turned. "I have a headache. Let's head back to…" Her words trailed off when she noticed Mannish sitting on a little stone wall. He had a book open in his hands, but instead of reading it, he was looking through a spyglass.

"Wait for me," Eirin told her friends in a low voice.

"Eirin–" Qeb began, but Eirin waved him off as she went to sit beside the other Seer. Lady Phaidra didn't want her talking to other people about her revelations involving Mannish? Well, that was fine. She would do her best to get the information out of him herself.

"What are you looking at?" Eirin asked casually as she seated herself beside him.

Mannish jumped slightly, then gave her an embarrassed grin. "Sorry, I didn't hear you." He pointed across the canyon to the other side where the chambers were.

"What are we looking at?" Eirin asked.

Mannish handed her the spyglass, but he continued to study whatever it was with naked eyes. Looking through the spyglass, Eirin could make out the tall figure of the Wizard standing out on his room's balcony.

"They gave him quite a room," Eirin mentioned, still looking through the glass. "It's far fancier than anything we have. But why are we watching him?"

Mannish chuckled. "They gave him the best room. But look." He pointed again. "See all those little jars on the ground?"

"Yes. What about them?"

Mannish held out the book so she could see the page he had it opened to. "I'm pretty sure he's going to cast a protection spell. He's been pouring them out in powder rings around his bed." He looked down at his book again, which had pictures similar to what Mannish had been describing. A lone figure surrounded by various circles of what looked like soil or clay or other forms of powder.

"I'm still trying to understand this one, but it's difficult without a teacher." He gave her a half-hearted grin. "At least I can learn from afar."

Eirin put the spyglass up to her eye again, and sure enough, as the Wizard was waving his hand around the jeweled top of his staff, a flame of green and purple began to flicker, just like in the picture.

Eirin kept the spyglass up to her eye, but she spoke to Mannish. "I'm sorry the Wizard wants to leave you behind." And she was. While she was convinced that Mannish's plans were ill-informed, she didn't doubt the pain the Wizard had created with such an order.

She couldn't see Mannish as he spoke, as she continued watching the Wizard stoke the small flames, but when he did speak, his voice was quiet.

"I'm well enough on my own. I just wish I could fulfill my parents' wishes for me." He chuckled. "You should have seen them the day I had my first vision." Then he paused. "They were *sure* I would save the world."

She lowered the spyglass and looked at him. He was giving her a soft smile, no longer watching the Wizard.

"I know, though, that life isn't about wishes or what we feel." He took a deep breath and let it out slowly. "It's cold and hard, and if that means–"

An explosion lit up the canyon. A cloud of pungent, yellow smoke filled the air, but before Eirin finished choking and coughing, Mannish grabbed the spyglass from where she'd dropped it.

"Isayas!" he shouted over the cacophony already rising around them. "He's unconscious!" He whipped around and began searching frantically. "Is Qeb here?"

"I'm here." Qeb appeared behind them, his hand on Eirin's shoulder. Nuru appeared on the other side, her furry shoulder rubbing against Eirin's left hip.

"Take her to her room!" Mannish shouted. "I'm going to try to help!"

Eirin wanted to argue that she wanted to go, too, but one look at her friends made it clear she wasn't going anywhere but with them.

Resigned, she let herself be pulled along with them as they shielded her from the rush of the crowd that now seemed to be stampeding toward the Wizard's chamber. As she did, though, she caught a glimpse of Drystan and Callispa's shadows as they soared overhead just below the canvases.

———

Qeb left Nuru with strict instructions to stay with Eirin in their room as he went to go see what had happened. Nuru wasn't overjoyed to be given instructions, but she grudgingly agreed.

"Not because I like listening to him," she clarified to Eirin after he'd gone. "But only because I agree that this happens to be the best course of action."

"Of course," Eirin agreed.

So they waited. And waited. And waited. Eirin tried to sleep, but she was only able to doze several times. Nuru, who stayed in her Atharrach form, remained by the window, her tail twitching as she looked out.

Hours later, as the day was waning, Mannish knocked on the door. He looked tired and was covered in what looked like soot when Eirin let him in, but before Eirin could ask any questions, he held up a hand and gave her a weary smile.

"The Wizard's alive." He walked in and ran a hand through his hair. "But he's in a deep sleep. And…" He frowned. "We can't seem to wake him."

Eirin froze. "We?" she whispered.

"Lady Phaidra, Karolus, the Nymphs." He shook his head. "Obviously, we don't know everything about the Wizard's ways." He slumped against the wall. "But I think…I think something went wrong with the magic. I don't think Lady Phaidra wanted me there, but she did let me see what had happened for your sake." He nodded at Eirin. "Then she told me to sleep a few hours, but I'm going to return and soon to see if there's anything we missed."

"What do they think happened?" Nuru asked. "And where were Drystan and his rider in all this?"

Qeb sighed. "Lady Phaidra kept me on the other side of the room from him, then conveniently sent me away as people started to leave. It seems as though one of the Wizard's materials might have been tampered with."

Nuru raised her thick cat brows. "Is that supposed to mean something to us?"

He gave Nuru a sardonic grin. "Sorry, I keep forgetting you weren't there for all the lessons Eirin and I had. Basically, Wizards take the raw magic from the world and manipulate it."

"Like Elves and Fae," Nuru said.

"Right," Eirin said. "But even more. There are certain elements that Wizards often carry with them to aid in their spells. Mannish showed me in one of his Wizarding books. They'll purify them and then turn them into powders to carry around with them."

Qeb nodded. "Tonight, he was using copper, sulfur, and nickel. But when Mannish examined the elements, he said it looked like someone might have changed out one of the elements for another. The copper was the wrong color." He drew his brows together as he stood. "Anyhow, that's the sum of it."

"Why can't I come?" Eirin asked as he made his way to the door.

He gave her a wry smile, his dark hair falling slightly over his eyes. "Eirin, I'm under no misconceptions when it comes to our abilities, and neither are you. Do you really think Lady Phaidra wants our most powerful Seer examining the scene where someone nearly killed a Wizard?"

Eirin huffed and sat down. "I know. But it's boring here."

Mannish let out a laugh. "I'm sure we'll remedy that soon enough." Then he paused. "I just...I ask that you please stay away just a while longer." His smile faded. "We can't lose you, Eirin."

54

Drystan and Callispa landed somewhat forcefully in the midst of the crowd that had gathered outside the Wizard's chambers. There were some uses to being one of the largest creatures in existence, Drystan thought sardonically as people were compelled to move back to make room for them. Callispa extinguished her flames, but Drystan waited to change back into his Human form until he was right in front of the building.

Like many of the other buildings on the mountain, the Wizard's chambers were built into the side of the mountain itself. Unlike Drystan and Eirin's room, however, it was large enough to have two levels. The first consisted of a cramped cooking and living space with a window that looked out over the canyon. Stairs then led up to the second floor into a bedroom that opened up onto a balcony that overlooked the city.

People gave him dirty looks as he pressed forward, forcing them to step back, but he didn't care. All he could think about was how he had come so close to getting Eirin what he had promised...only to possibly have lost it all here.

Who would do this? Drystan had to clamp down on the red that wanted to color his vision. Losing control in a place so filled with people was a bad idea. Even if he wanted to tear the head off of the person who had put Eirin's mission at risk.

481

And for once, he didn't even try to restrain the Dragon's desire in his head. Just its appearance.

Lady Phaidra was standing at the front of the crowd, where she was consulting Mannish and Karolus. Their heads were bent together, and they spoke in whispers. Qeb stood behind the lady. Drystan sent him a nod, which he returned slowly. The small room was too packed, however, for Drystan to continue pushing his way through. He had to wait close to the door.

Karolus looked up. "Would someone clear the room?" he shouted over the din. "We won't find a thing with half the city here!"

Drystan glanced back, but the crowd hadn't listened to a word Karolus had said. They were too busy talking amongst themselves.

"You heard him!" Callispa called, raising her hands and motioning for the others to move back. "They need the area clear to investigate!"

Still, few listened. Drystan rolled his eyes and stretched his shoulders as he concentrated on isolating his shoulder blades from the rest of his body in his mind. A few seconds later, he released. Wings wider than the room burst from his back, and he let his eyes blaze brightly.

"Anyone want to stay?" he asked, allowing some of the Dragon's growl to seep into his voice. Those standing in the front, many of whom he recognized as heads of their races, and some he'd knocked over with his wings, looked affronted but skittered backward down the stairs.

Callispa gave him an approving look before turning back to Lady Phaidra and the others, but Drystan lingered another moment to make sure no stragglers returned before joining them as well.

"What happened?" he asked as he joined the circle. "Where is he?"

Don't let him be dead.

"He's not dead," Lady Phaidra said gently. "He's already been taken down to the Nymphs."

"But?" Drystan asked. She was being far too careful with her words.

Lady Phaidra sent a look at Karolus, then Mannish. "He's…asleep."

"You mean resting?" Callispa asked.

Lady Phaidra grimaced slightly. "No, he's...he was that way when we found him." She finally met Drystan's eyes. "And he won't wake up."

Drystan felt as though someone had punched him in the gut. Of course, sleeping was better than dead. But if he wouldn't wake up... Was it really?

They continued to talk, but Drystan felt as though his mind had left his body behind, and he were now watching from a distance. He should be listening to all the details. How Mannish was convinced that someone had switched the Wizard's powders. What Lady Phaidra was saying about the blackened rings on the floor. What Karolus was saying about the likelihood of an accident. But all he could really think about was Eirin.

She had been so close.

A while later–Drystan didn't know how long–Lady Phaidra announced that they had done all they could do right now.

"He's safe with the Nymphs," she said with a sigh. "For now, let's all get some rest, and we'll come back soon and see if there are any changes." She looked at Drystan. "Especially you. I didn't realize how hard you'd been pushing last night when I asked you to take watch again. Otherwise, I would have let you sleep."

"I didn't mind," Drystan said. And he hadn't. If he couldn't guard Eirin, the next best thing he could do was guard her Wizard. Not that it seemed to have done any good.

"Nevertheless, you look exhausted. Enough of these naps you've been stealing here and there. Why don't you go get something to eat tonight, then I'll have one of the upper rooms in my house prepared." Her smile softened. "Hector built it for his students to rest there when they were over-tired. No one will bother you there."

The others agreed that sleep sounded like a good idea, and Drystan wanted nothing more than his own bed. But after the others had left, he remained. He wanted to see the scene of the accident for himself. So he knelt at the edge of the balcony.

The moon wasn't as bright tonight as it had been several nights before. Clouds floated across its beams, making the scene difficult to see well in the mottled shadows. As he studied the charred circles of powder, he tried to remember what Mannish had said about them.

Something about using the wrong powder, and how only someone with knowledge of Wizard spells or at least the ingredients' natural properties could have done this.

"You're still here. I would have assumed she'd sent you somewhere else by now."

Drystan nearly jumped out of his skin as a familiar figure stepped out of the shadows of the room behind him.

"Qeb, are you insane? I could have doused you in flames without knowing who it was." Then he looked around. "When did you leave?"

Qeb gave him a sardonic smile. "You're not that fast yet. And as you didn't notice, Lady Phaidra told me to go report to Eirin." He snorted. "Then to sleep."

Drystan rolled his eyes, but he was glad to see his friend. "Where have you been? I've tried looking for you, but every time I get a moment to search, you're nowhere to be found."

Qeb fixed him with a strange stare. "Odd. I was about to say the same thing about you."

Drystan held his arm out to the room from which Qeb had come. "I was asked to guard the Wizard again last night, and they've kept me in planning meetings or training ever since." He paused. "Eirin is all right, isn't she?"

"She is." Qeb's face remained impassive. "Thoughtful of you to see to her well-being."

Drystan sat back on his heels. "Excuse me?"

"You've been back for more than two days, and you couldn't even find time to visit her in person for five minutes." Qeb's voice hardened. "And she's noticed."

Drystan's face blazed hot, but his body had frozen in place. Qeb had never spoken to him this way before. Not even the time he'd accidentally broken Qeb's leg when they were roughhousing as boys in the Citadel after training hours. Now Qeb's words were cold and sharp. His best friend might as well have slapped him in the face.

"You know why I can't see her," he stuttered. "It's for her own safety."

Qeb gave him a reproachful look. "You've spent many small minutes in her presence in the past without setting the world on fire."

Drystan tried to swallow the lump in his throat. How could he explain it? How could he tell Qeb that if he went back to Eirin now... he might not be able to leave?

"And you've not only abandoned Eirin, but also–"

"I've done no such thing!" Drystan heard himself snap as he stood. "I asked you to stay with her so she wouldn't be abandoned!" Did Qeb think he had wanted to send him away? Did he think Drystan hadn't wanted his company?

"—in making allies with Callispa, you've further alienated Eirin in the process," Qeb continued as if Drystan hadn't spoken.

"What does Callispa have to do with any of this?" Drystan asked. "She's my trainer!"

Qeb gave him a look.

Drystan rolled his eyes. "You know all that was for show. And it's not as though I have a choice to be around her. Even if I wasn't trying to keep Eirin away, I'd still have to train with her." He shook his head. "What's with all of this taking sides? We're all trying to get Eirin through Solevar! Every one of us! I crossed half a mountain range and risked angering a Wizard to make sure she can! If I didn't care–"

"I never said you didn't care!" Qeb rubbed his neck and let out a gusty breath. When he spoke again, his voice was lower. "I'm not questioning your motives. I'm questioning your judgment."

"So am I," Drystan spat, the sting of Qeb's words still fresh. "Every day and all the time."

Qeb huffed. "I'm sorry. That's...this is not what I meant." He cringed and shook his head and began to pace.

"You mentioned Callispa," Drystan said, trying to school his voice into sounding somewhat less petulant. "What does she have to do with any of this?"

"Aside from convincing you to trick Eirin?"

Drystan opened his mouth to remind Qeb of why he had needed to trick Eirin, but Qeb went on.

"What I mean to say is that Callispa is close with Lady Phaidra. She adores her."

"What's wrong with that?"

Qeb studied Drystan for a long moment before finally saying, "While you were gone, Eirin and I made a discovery."

Drystan couldn't help the flash of jealousy that crackled through him like a lightning bolt, but he sought to stay on topic. If he should be annoyed at anyone for Eirin making discoveries with anyone but him…it was himself. "What did you find?" he croaked.

"Eirin thinks Mannish is planning on trying to find a Wizard's stone of his own," Qeb said slowly, his eyes on Drystan. "And we think Lady Phaidra might be sheltering him."

Drystan stared at him. "What?"

"At first, we thought Mannish was working on his own. But since you returned home, we've become convinced that Lady Phaidra…or someone near her is trying to keep you from us." His frown deepened. "Something she wasn't doing before Eirin made her discovery."

"That…that could be mere convenience," Drystan sputtered. "It's too coincidental."

"That's not all," Qeb continued. "After everything Eirin found—all of Mannish's secret studies on Wizards—I'm convinced tonight that Mannish is the one who put the Wizard in danger."

Drystan looked back down at the powder rings. "Mannish was convinced someone had switched one of them out. Who else could have known enough about a Wizard's materials to interfere undetected?" He went through the possibilities in his head. They had one Elf, but Drystan had no reason to think Vadik or any of the few Fae in their midst had any reason to cause injury to the Wizard. If Vadik had wanted to, he could have done so during the journey while the Wizard traveled right in their midst. And the few Fae they had with them were mostly new arrivals from the deeper parts of Solevar. They hadn't strayed far from their new quarters from what Drystan understood.

"You know for sure that Mannish was planning something?" he asked Qeb, who had been watching him quietly.

"Eirin is convinced of it." A sly smile crossed Qeb's face. "She even flirted with him a little to get more information."

Red flashed across Drystan's vision again, and this time, it was harder to dispel. He also had the sudden urge to slap the smile off of Qeb's face. This he also was just able to repress.

But only just.

"We went to Lady Phaidra with our discovery," Qeb continued. "And she asked us not to share our thoughts with anyone else until she'd had time to talk to Karolus after you'd returned." He nodded at the balcony. "Notice tonight who they called to touch the scene of the accident."

"Lady Phaidra said they wanted Eirin to remain hidden," Drystan said, frowning.

"Do you really think they would let any harm come to her up here with all of them surrounding her?" Qeb asked. "All of you?"

Drystan walked over to the bed and put his head in his hands. How had he not noticed this? How had he been ignorant of all of it?

"I tried to see you," he whispered, his face still in his hands. "But every time I went to where I thought you were, I couldn't find you. I thought..." He had thought Lady Phaidra had been trying to hide Eirin for her own protection. Apparently, he had thought wrong.

Qeb sat beside him on the bed, and Drystan felt a heavy hand land on his shoulder. They sat that way for a few minutes.

"I didn't realize it at the time," Qeb finally said in a quiet voice, "but I tied myself to you at a young age for a reason." He finally looked Drystan in the eyes. "Because I believed you were the right person to follow. I believed in you." He paused. "Eirin believes in you too."

"I don't deserve it," Drystan said, looking down. "I don't deserve either one of you. Or even Nuru, for that matter."

Qeb gave him a small smile. "I've been loyal to you all these years. I don't ask that you destroy yourself with shame, which is what I know you want to do." He hesitated, then went on. "What I'm asking for now is your trust." The remnants of his smile faded. "Because we need it now more than ever."

Drystan nodded, and when he spoke, it wasn't without difficulty. "You have my trust now because you always had it."

"Good." Qeb stood. "Then come and speak with Eirin yourself."

Drystan groaned. "You don't know what you're asking."

"I won't let you hurt her–" Qeb began, but Drystan cut him off.

"It's not that." He shook his head, then looked up at his friend, pleading with his eyes. "I can't say goodbye to her again, Qeb. I can't watch her plead for me to stay."

"Drystan—"

"Because she will," Drystan continued. "And I'll stay. And then in a moment of weakness…a lapse in control, I'll kill her the way I nearly did back with the Wyverns." He stood and went to the stairs. "I'll do what I can to find out about Mannish and Phaidra." He swallowed the lump in his throat. "But Qeb? I'm sorry. For ev—"

"I know." Qeb gave him a sad smile. "I know."

———

Callispa wasn't hard to find. She stood just outside the house on the bottom floor. Her red hair glowed in the moonlight, and a gentle smile of relief lit her face as he approached.

"Who were you talking to?" she asked, falling into step with him as Drystan left the house behind. Where he was going, he wasn't sure, but even as she spoke, he knew what he had to do. Coming to a stop, he turned to the girl beside him.

"You know Lady Phaidra."

Callispa giggled. "Obviously."

He nodded. "Do you think there's any possibility she might know more about tonight's incident than she's letting on?"

Callispa's smile melted. "What?"

"Think about it. Which Seer did they call to examine the accident that nearly killed the Wizard?"

Callispa blinked at him. "The one not critical to our next mission."

"I thought so as well. But think about it. Was Mannish able to See who had interfered with the Wizard's materials?"

"No. But Seer's can't See everything. And Mannish isn't as gifted as Eirin."

"Exactly." Drystan nodded. "What harm could have come from bringing Eirin to the place where the strongest Atharrachs in the city were gathered? How long would it really have taken her to See what happened?"

"Drystan, what are you implying?"

Drystan watched her carefully as he spoke his next words. "Do you think Lady Phaidra could have had anything to do with hurting the Wizard?"

Callispa's eyes narrowed. "Are you truly asking me this?" She seemed as though she wanted to go on, but seemed unable to find the right words. So she closed her mouth and walked in a circle before speaking again. When she did, her words came out in an angry whisper.

"I have known Lady Phaidra all of my life. She was there at my First Fire. She was the one who ultimately assigned me to you."

"Callispa–"

"She lost her daughter–my best friend–and her husband trying to help this cause. The same cause, Drystan. Your Seer's cause! But no matter how many Seers we get or how many journeys we make, people die. Lots of people. And it always ends the same way!"

Drystan tilted his head. "You think Eirin's cause is a lost one?"

"Lady Phaidra has been begging that Wizard to come down the mountain since before you were a toddler, hiding in your sheltered caves and blissfully unaware of all we were suffering!" Callispa was screaming now. Several other people down the street turned their heads to watch.

"So no! I don't believe she had anything to do with this!" Callispa shoved his shoulder. "For all we know, Isayas could be an incompetent Wizard and could have done this to himself!"

"Just…just consider the matter," Drystan said. "Please."

Callispa scoffed. "Go to bed, Drystan." Then she burst into flame and streaked off into the night.

55

$\mathcal{E}$irin knew better than to hope. But when Qeb returned, she still felt the bitter familiar waves of disappointment and anger crash through her as she realized he was alone.

"What happened?" Nuru asked before Qeb had even shut the door behind him.

Qeb held his hands up. "I did talk to him alone. He wouldn't come back with me, but I did warn him to consider his loyalties."

Qeb's words were even enough, but there was a look in his eye that made Eirin wonder at the nature of their talk. Had they had a disagreement? If they had, Eirin wanted to kick Drystan in the shins all the more. Qeb had been everything kind and protective. He didn't deserve to suffer pain at Drystan's hands too.

That's not really fair, a voice of reason whispered in Eirin's head. *You don't even know what they talked about.*

Eirin decided she didn't care. She could be mad for both of them.

"Was the Wizard's staff at least still there?" she asked in a huff.

"It is. Along with the rest of his belongings. I saw them in the corner as I went out."

Eirin frowned. "We should probably go get them and bring them to sit beside him at the very least."

"Drystan knows about Mannish then?" Nuru pressed. "And that we think Phaidra is keeping us apart?"

Qeb nodded. "I told him everything."

491

"What did he say?" demanded Eirin.

Qeb gave her a tired smile. "That's a conversation for another day. In short, though, he promised to think it over."

"But he's still staying away," Nuru said.

"He is." Qeb glanced at Eirin. "He's still worried." When she glared back at him, he smiled. "He wants to keep you safe."

Eirin rolled her eyes and threw herself back on her bed.

"While you were trying to talk sense into him," Nuru told Qeb, "Eirin and I came up with our own theories."

Qeb lowered himself onto a stool and broke a piece of bread off the end of their loaf. "I'm listening."

"Eirin thinks there are only two likely persons who could have pulled off what happened to the Wizard," Nuru continued. "Either Mannish or Rangvald."

Qeb tilted his head. "Interesting. Go on."

Nuru paused, but Eirin was too busy imagining how she'd like to bruise Drystan's annoying shins with her boots. So Nuru rolled her eyes and went on. "She thinks Mannish is a likely possibility because the Wizard doesn't want to include him."

"But Mannish was with Eirin when it happened," Qeb said. "And what would he gain by getting rid of him? This whole scheme was his idea?"

"The staff," Eirin said in a monotone voice. "And after listening to him go on about the different powders the Wizard was using, he left little doubt that few others here could know enough of the Wizard's ways apart from him. Who else would know how to switch them out or what to replace them with?" She finally looked at Qeb directly.

Nuru tilted her head thoughtfully. "That elf possibly, but he seems unlikely."

Qeb nodded slowly. "That makes sense. But why include Rangvald then?"

Eirin sat up to face her friends. "Because he didn't want the Wizard involved at all. He didn't even want them going to fetch Isayas." She frowned. "He might not have had all of the knowledge of a Seer, but he was alive long before the curse fell. He could have easily known enough about Wizards to have thwarted him."

"The question is now," Nuru added, "what we do about it all. Did you see anything new while you were there?"

Qeb brushed the crumbs off his shirt. "Unfortunately, no. Mannish did what you mentioned, jabbering on about the powders and whatnot. But he seemed genuinely confused."

Eirin sat up. "I want to go to the Wizard's room."

"Eirin," Qeb began, but Eirin held up a hand. "Mannish may or may not have been telling the truth. No, he doesn't seem to See as much as I do, so he might not have been able to discern the history of the room. But he could also be lying." She paused. "I think...I think he knows and Sees more than he lets on. But we'll never know if I don't go there myself to See."

Qeb and Nuru exchanged a glance. Eirin braced herself for all the reasons she shouldn't go and was plotting rebuttals in her head when Qeb finally looked at her and nodded.

"Wait...yes?" Eirin gaped.

"Yes." Qeb nodded again. "While I agree with the common desire to keep you safe, there's not going to be any safety left if we don't help you fix what's been broken. But we'll need to do it before Mannish wakes up and returns to the Wizard's room. They've all agreed to come back after getting some sleep. So we'd better go now."

"If we ever do get the best of these Time Stones," Nuru grumbled as they prepared to go out again, "I reserve the right to sleep for a year."

———

The room was still deserted when they arrived.

"I'm sure someone's watching," Qeb whispered as they made their way toward the stairs on the lower floor. "We'll probably have visitors in less than ten minutes."

"I only need a few," Eirin said breathlessly. "Is it hard to breathe in here? Or is that just my Humanity?"

Qeb and Nuru stopped their climb up the stairs and looked at her.

"I can't feel anything," Qeb said, and Nuru shook her head.

"Me neither."

By the time they got to the top of the stairs, Eirin was panting heavily. When she finally lifted her head from staring at her suddenly heavy feet, however, she knew why.

Magic floated through the air all around them. Eirin gasped as she watched it floating like sparkling dust motes around them. Magic of all colors, though some were brighter and more plentiful than others, coated the surfaces of the furniture and the floor. Most of it, though, lay dully in heaps of ashes that formed the blackened rings of powder on the balcony that Mannish had pointed out to her from afar.

"I'm going to keep a lookout below," Qeb said, still staring at the balcony. "Work as fast as you can."

But Eirin felt unable to respond.

"What is it?" Nuru asked, looking around, her tail swishing hard from side to side.

"It's magic," Eirin breathed. She held her hand out and let the floating magic motes caress her skin. "But none like I've ever seen before."

"Eirin, I'm sorry, but we don't have much time," Qeb whispered before turning resolutely toward the stairwell.

Eirin blinked a few times, then remembered what they had come to do. She leaned down and reached toward the rings of powder, but before she could touch them, Nuru swatted Eirin's hand away with her paw.

"I don't think that's a good idea," Nuru said. "If they injured the Wizard, think about what they could do to you."

Eirin looked longingly at the powder. She'd never seen so much raw magic in the world before, and it seemed to call to her soul. But Nuru was right. Caution would most likely serve here well.

"Um..." She shook her head. "The floor stones. Over there." She knelt beside the rings of powder and carefully placed her hands against one of the floor stones that wasn't covered in ash or powder.

Her mind was still so full of the recent events that it was somewhat difficult to focus on what she Saw. But eventually, her mind did find what it was looking for.

"I see the pavers," she said, laying these stones. And many people coming and going from the room. This must be when they built it."

"Can it go any faster?" Nuru asked, peering over the balcony edge. "Because I'm sure we're not going to be alone for very long."

Eirin frowned but kept her eyes shut. She had recently begun to learn how to speed and slow the visions, and she did so now until she saw a familiar face.

"He did the same spell the night before," Eirin said. "That one was successful."

"Obviously." Nuru snorted. "He didn't blow up."

Eirin continued to watch. The Wizard had been in and out several times.

"And so has Mannish," Eirin whispered. "Nuru, we were right. It was Mannish. He..." She continued watching. "He replaced the powder from one of the Wizard's jars with one of his own." She shook her head and opened her eyes. "We have our answer."

Without thinking, she moved her hand to the side so she could stand. And as she did, her fingers brushed the edge of the outermost ring of powder.

The heaviness that had lain on the room was nothing compared to the power that now engulfed her. Her skin seemed to buzz and sizzle, crackling and popping as the night turned white.

Through the assault on her senses, though, Eirin felt something even more potent. The stone which had rested against her chest for the last few months was no longer dormant. In a new blaze of color and light, colors for which she had no name, Eirin Saw what she'd been waiting for.

5 6

The vision Eirin now watched made all of her prior visions seem as though she'd been looking through muddy water. Crystal clear was the mountain below her and Solevar before her. But she wasn't in Mhaedin. Rather, she was above it, far removed as though she were an eagle above.

Without knowing why, she leaned forward and began to soar. Over and away from the mountain and the farms at its base. Over the forests and fields and hills and valleys. Rivers glittered up at her, blue and crystalline, and soon lakes, and then in the distance, what she could only assume to be the ocean.

Even more impressive than the land, however, was the palace that rose up out of a city that overlooked the ocean. It was a mix of gray and green stone. The green stones shone in the sunlight, and Eirin knew in her heart that it could only be one place.

"The Emerald Palace," she whispered. The home of the Blood Fire Throne. And even more importantly, of the Time Stones.

As if hearing her, the wind carrying her slowed. But rather than taking her to the entrance of the palace, she was taken through the window of the highest room of the tallest tower.

The room she landed in was larger than she had thought from the outside. It was also perfectly round, filled with books and scrolls placed carefully on shelves that seemed to cover every surface of the walls. There was one grand writing desk pushed up against the walls

497

in the only place with no shelves. And in the center of the room were what could only be the Time Stones.

As Eirin stared incredulously at the great circle of stones, she finally understood why Lady Seren and the books had struggled to describe them. An unfathomable number of small rectangular stones like the one that hung about her neck were placed in the circle. There were far, far more than she'd believed possible. All of varying colors, they lay perpendicular to one another. How they could move or be added to, Eirin had no idea. But they were here. And so was she.

As she studied them, her focus was moved without her permission, much as her flying had been, to the far right quadrant of the circle. She struggled to see what was being shown to her for a moment before it became clear.

A single stone with a piece that was missing.

Eirin knew instinctively that she never would have found it if she hadn't been shown. The stones, while all different, looked too much alike, and there were far too many of them.

"Eirin?"

At the sound of Nuru's voice, Eirin was yanked out of the vision. The fall was so hard that she moaned and grabbed her head as Nuru and Qeb rushed to steady her. But she pushed them away and stumbled back toward the inner part of the bedroom.

"Paper!" she moaned as she searched, her head still ringing. "I need ink and paper!"

Her friends stared at her stupidly as she blindly stumbled about the room, demanding something to write with. Finally, in the Wizard's bag, she found them. But by then, it was too late. The location of the missing stone was forgotten.

Eirin threw the paper down on the bed and let out a frustrated growl. "It showed me!" she cried. "It showed me where the missing piece of the stone was! And now I–"

She had reached into her shirt again to pull the stone out. But the moment her fingers brushed it, she was in the great tower again, and she could see the missing stone.

Eirin began to laugh with relief as Nuru and Qeb exchanged worried glances.

"I can still see it!" She looked excitedly from Nuru to Qeb. "The amount of magic in here must have enhanced my abilities!" She laughed again. "My mother was right! The stone will lead the way!" She touched it again and again, and every time, she was shown the Time Stones where the missing piece had been.

As she laughed, though, something else occurred to her. She looked around them suddenly and asked. "Where's the Wizard's staff?"

Qeb's eyes grew wide, and he cursed.

"What are we going to do?" Nuru asked.

Eirin felt the stone press against her chest, and she held her head high as she stood. "We're going to find Karolus. Phaidra might be working with Mannish, but he doesn't seem to be. And we're going to tell him why he can't listen to Mannish."

"Why can't he?" Qeb asked blankly.

Eirin smiled and pulled the stone out of her shirt. "Because we have this."

57

Callispa's words stung, but as fire burns away dross, Drystan began to see one blazing truth.

He needed to speak with Eirin.

Hang his heart. Eirin would die if they didn't get to the bottom of whatever was going on with Mannish and Lady Phaidra. Eirin's intuition had never led them wrong. And after talking with Qeb and seeing Callispa's reaction, Drystan was beginning to think that Eirin's theory was far more than intuition.

He had thought that Callispa's attachment to him had meant her loyalty. But it was obvious now that her loyalties lay deeper than what she felt toward him.

How had he been so blind?

He knew the answer to that. His desire to keep Eirin safe had become the driving purpose in his life. Seeing her clutch her burned hand to her chest had created a crack in his resolve. Watching her lie limp and burned on the hillside after the Wyverns' attack had broken him entirely. And even now, he hated the beast inside more than ever. But this wasn't the time for self-loathing. He could do that for the rest of his life. Right now, he had stumbled off the path and didn't know where he was going.

He needed to find Eirin. And he needed to listen to her as he had before. Eirin had been given the gift of Sight for a reason. And for somer reason, she seemed convinced that He was a part of her

501

future. Perhaps he might eventually have to leave once more to keep her safe. But with all that had transpired in recent days, he needed to find his direction again.

He made his way in Human form toward Eirin's room, but then he stopped. Phaidra had been doing her best to keep him away from her, it seemed. Even now, he saw shapes in the shadows that seemed to hesitate, just as he did at the fork in the road.

If he went straight to her room…

Before he could even finish the thought, Abrax stepped out from the shadows.

"Good evening, Drystan," he called in his deep voice. "I'd heard Lady Phaidra was offering the members of your journey special rooms in her home. Where are you headed?"

By every blasted rat, Qeb had been right.

"I'm going to see the Wizard," Drystan said, making his decision on the spot. "I was hoping to see if I could find any evidence on his robes. Or at least ask the Nymphs if they had noticed anything."

Abrax seemed to brighten. "Very good. When you're done, I believe Lady Phaidra hopes to meet in the Wizard's chamber before dawn. That is, if you're still not in great need of sleep."

Drystan was definitely in need of sleep, but his need to see Eirin far outweighed that at the moment.

"Thank you for telling me," he said, forcing a smile. "I shouldn't be long."

Under Abrax's watchful eye, Drystan made his way toward the Nymphs' healing room. The Wizard hadn't been his ultimate destination, but now he realized he would like to see him again. If he was awake, Drystan could ask him questions. If not, it would at least get him closer to the side of the city Eirin was on. If anyone asked him questions after that, he would need to say he was fetching something from his room.

His hopes of finding the Wizard awake had risen by the time he reached the Nymphs' healing room. Though he didn't know the man well, he felt that if there was anyone he could trust not to be under Phaidra's wiles, it was him.

And if anyone could help them get Eirin where she needed to be, Mhaedin's help or not, Isayas would be the one to do it.

"Can I help you?" the Nymph said politely.

"I was hoping to see the Wizard," Drystan said. "Is he awake?"

The Nymph's face turned to one of pity. "I'm sorry, but he is not." She glanced back into the room behind her and lowered her voice. "I'm not supposed to tell anyone, but I know you were the one to bring him…" She paused. "We're losing him fast."

58

$\mathcal{E}$irin, Qeb, and Nuru ran to Karolus's home. But they were informed by his housekeeper, a small Brownie with a trim beard, that Master Karolus was in the herb garden by the Annex, where he was supposed to be meeting with a few race heads.

"We don't have very long," Nuru muttered as she looked at the sky. It was still dark, and Eirin had no idea what time it was. She'd completely missed any tolling of the bells before this.

They reached the garden without any delay. But going through the entrance and making several twists and turns through the rows, it wasn't a man's shadow they encountered but a woman's. And though the light of the heart that Eirin could See was indeed a Dragon's, it wasn't that of a prince.

"Eirin!" Lady Phaidra exclaimed. "I didn't expect to see you here tonight. I thought you were safely tucked away in your room."

"We…we were looking for Karolus," Eirin said cautiously.

"What for?" Lady Phaidra asked.

Eirin glanced back at her friends, but their faces were hidden in the shadows.

"Does this have something to do with Mannish?" Lady Phaidra asked gently. "Because if so, I thought we'd discussed keeping this secret amongst ourselves."

Eirin hesitated a moment before answering. "You said you were going to speak with Karolus."

505

"Yes, I was. But I have't yet." She paused. "Have you found something new?" She flicked her hand slightly, and Eirin felt movement behind her. When she turned, she saw several bodies now blocking their way out.

"Well?" Lady Phaidra took a step closer.

Eirin hesitated a moment more. Her friends would not like this.

"I'll talk to you," she said slowly. "If you'll let my friends return to their rooms to sleep."

Lady Phaidra smiled. "Of course. Follow me." She motioned for Eirin to follow her, but Eirin didn't move until those guarding the garden entrance did as well.

"Eirin!" Qeb hissed, but Eirin said loudly, "Please get some sleep. I'll see you in the morning."

They stared at her, and though it was dark, Eirin could see the indignation on Nuru's face. Qeb looked dumbstruck. She needed them to stay behind. Right now, they were surrounded, and while Eirin had no doubt that Lady Phaidra had no intention of really letting them go, they would be able to fight better for themselves without worrying about hurting her as they did.

Unfortunately, Nuru didn't seem to have a mind to stay behind. When one of the guards moved closer to Eirin, Nuru sprang at him, knocking him into a stone wall. Shouts rang out, and magic flared as the guards took their Atharrach forms.

Eirin watched in horror as her friends, overpowered and enclosed, fought hard but to no avail. Before the fight was over, though, Lady Phaidra grasped Eirin's arm and pulled. Eirin twisted to get away, a move she'd learned well at the Citadel, but Lady Phaidra was too strong. Eirin could never hope to overpower a Dragon.

"You're coming with me, and we're going to have that little chat," Lady Phaidra said, pulling Eirin toward the building at the end of the garden. Eirin looked back behind her, but she couldn't see how the struggle was going in the dark.

"If I tell you everything willingly, will you let them go?" Eirin cried.

Lady Phaidra gave her a strange look. "You think you can bargain without leverage?"

Eirin felt a rebellious grin appear on her face. "Lady Phaidra, I grew up being intimidated every day of my life. Believe me. I can be very good at making things difficult."

Lady Phaidra studied her. Eirin wasn't sure the Dragon believed her, but eventually, she pursed her lips. "I can't let them go free, if that's what you're asking. They know too much."

"Let them go to their rooms and lock them in there." Eirin crossed her arms. "If nothing else, let them sleep in peace."

Lady Phaidra studied her a moment longer before nodding slowly. "Very well." She looked up and gave a shrill whistle. The grunts and growls and hisses in the garden quieted slightly, which Eirin knew meant her friends had been overpowered. Qeb would never stop a fight to listen to the enemy.

"Take them to their rooms. If they go peacefully, let them be. If they cannot, however, use bruthsi."

"Lady Phaidra!" someone from the shadows gasped. "You said we were never to–"

"I know what I said." She drew herself up to her full height. "Whether or not they receive it is up to them."

"Eirin!" Qeb shouted.

"Qeb, go!" Eirin cried. Then she did her best to calm herself. If she sounded distressed, he wouldn't listen no matter what she said. "We need to discuss this. It might as well be now." She glared at Lady Phaidra. "Because I know what she does not. And I think I can change her mind."

At least, she prayed she could.

Lady Phaidra's eyes glistened slightly in the dark, just a flash of amber before it disappeared again. "Follow me."

Eirin followed her through a side door into the building, which, of course, had been built into the side of the mountain. A number of twists and turns down tunnels, and Eirin found herself in a small room.

The room's walls had been painted a startling shade of red, and there were several candles lit. A small couch sat on one end and two chairs on the other. Lady Phaidra gestured to one of the chairs in the corner and then took the couch.

Eirin sat as she was bade, but she immediately regretted it. The chair was far too soft and cushy. Lady Phaidra hadn't put her there to make her comfortable. She had done it to incapacitate her. Getting out of the chair gracefully would be a feat of its own.

"So," Lady Phaidra spread her arms across the back of the couch, and her dress flared gracefully out. "You know what I do not."

Eirin nodded. "On more than one account."

"Well then." She lifted her arms. "Please enlighten me."

"I know that you're protecting Mannish," Eirin said cautiously. "And that you've been supporting his...examinations into the ways of the Wizard."

"And why shouldn't he? It is all there in the scholars' room for you, is it not?"

"Not just learning," Eirin said. "He's been making plans to find the Wizard's cave. And you've been keeping this from the others, haven't you?"

Lady Phaidra simply leaned back into the couch. "I'm hearing nothing I haven't heard before."

"I also know that Mannish injured the Wizard." Eirin lifted her chin defiantly.

"I know." Lady Phaidra gave her a small, strange smile.

Eirin felt her mouth fall open as she stared at the lady Dragon. "But...why then..."

"Why are you telling me all of this, Eirin? Usually, it's considered unwise to tell your enemy your secrets."

"Because you're not my enemy!" Eirin cried. "I never thought you were! We're working together! And I am trying to show you that you don't have to do this! There is another way to save Solevar, and it doesn't include stealing a Wizard's stone!" Her eyes narrowed. "Or his staff."

"What then do you suggest we do?" Lady Phaidra stood and looked down on Eirin. "The staff...the stones..." She paused and closed her eyes. After taking in a deep breath, she opened them, and when she spoke again, her voice was calmer.

"I'm well aware that of the two of you, you are without question the strongest. But while Mannish may not be as talented as you are at your ancient art, however, he is quite a clever boy." She leaned forward slightly, her eyes bright. "He's unearthed ways to give us the best chance we've ever had at reaching the Dragon's throne...with both of you alive."

Eirin tried to sit forward in the overstuffed chair. "I don't understand. He's not a Wizard. Everything we read about in the Wizards' lore was for Seers who had drunk from the sacred waters."

Lady Phaidra nodded and was quiet for a moment. "I...I know this might be hard to hear," she said slowly. "But I hope you will listen. Because all that Mannish has done, he's done for you." Her eyes held Eirin's. "He loves you, Eirin. After his parents died, you were like a light in his darkness. And he's desperate to get you to Iilaedin." Her eyes narrowed. "Alive. And now that he has the staff, he has a chance of doing just that."

Eirin frowned in confusion before it hit her. The words from the Wizard's journal.

FOR IT IS MY BELIEF THAT SO MUCH POWER HAS BEEN PRESSED INTO THE STONES AT THEIR CREATION THAT EVEN A SIMPLE SEER WOULD BE ABLE TO DIRECT THEIR PATH.

"I told you that won't work!" Eirin shouted. She leaped to her feet. "I warned you that if he tried to use the Wizard's stone, he could sink us into a deeper curse than we're in now! He could be the one who ends the curse with all our deaths! It's forbidden magic! Even if he had his own magic, it would be disallowed! That's why the other Wizards put Amrit to death!"

Lady Phaidra made a face. "Forbidden by whom, Eirin? The Time Keeper? How long has it been since He's chosen to grace us with His presence? When was the last time He chose to hear the cries of our hungry infants? Or watched the blood of His creatures flow?"

"I can't answer for Him!" Eirin shook her head. "But I know that if Mannish tries to go through with this, he will make everything worse! A Human a stone, much less a staff, that was meant for Wizards alone is just another example of–"

"If Mannish goes through with this, then at least he'll be doing *something*! It will be more than sitting here, watching my people starve. Or hovering above as I watch my daughter bleed out into the dirt! And then to arrive at the Time Stones only to lose Seer after Seer!"

She choked back a sob as she continued to rant. "Because I've done it! Done it so many times!" Lady Phaidra ran her right hand down her left arm over and over again, almost convulsively. "I've given away more than half of my scales to find that they do nothing for those who have put hope in my help." Lady Phaidra's eyes burned now with amber. "The Time Keeper has turned His back on us. His grace–that which you were so sure of–is gone. He's not sending help, nor does He care." She stood taller. "But there is still magic in the air. Don't deny it. You, of all privileged creatures, can feel it more than any of us. And we're going to use that power now to fix what the Time Keeper can't!" She sneered. "Or *won't*."

"I'm telling you!" Eirin groaned. "It won't work! He's not a Wizard! And even if he could draw magic from the Wizard's stone–"

"All Wizards were once Humans." Lady Phaidra stopped suddenly and drew in a long deep breath before letting it out slowly. When she opened her eyes again, they were free of the amber flame. "Mannish has my blessing to attempt to perform the rites that Isayas wouldn't." Her voice caught slightly. "Because it's better than doing nothing. Which in one hundred years of trying is all we've ever accomplished."

"This is madness!" Eirin pleaded, suddenly feeling as though she were on the verge of tears.

"If desperation to save my people is madness, then yes. Yes, I will choose madness any day."

Eirin searched for some way…any way to stop her. And as she moved, the slight pressure against her chest revealed her answer.

"You don't need to go to desperate measures!" Eirin said. "I just remembered something!"

Lady Phaidra studied her. "And what is that?"

"If you do as we planned… If you let Isayas lead us the right way, I know I can find the other half of the stone! Immediately! We won't have to wait because we know exactly where it is!"

Lady Phaidra froze. "And how do you know that? And why didn't you ever tell us?"

"Because I only found out today in the Wizard's room!" Eirin removed the stone from beneath her shirt and let it rest openly against her chest.

Lady Phaidra stayed frozen, staring with wide eyes at the stone. "Is...is that what I think it is?" she breathed.

Eirin nodded. "When I was on the Wizard's balcony, I accidentally touched one of his powder rings. The magic was so strong it activated a vision from this stone, and it showed me where the stone is! I know I can find it!" She clutched the stone in her hand as though it were a lifeline and she was drowning. "I promise, we can do this! I can remove it! But we can't go to the Blood Fire Throne the wrong way. We can't risk angering the Time Keeper any more than we already have!" She ended as suddenly as she'd begun, feeling breathless and slightly dizzy.

Lady Phaidra moved across the room as though in a daze. Slowly, she reached out to touch it, but Eirin jumped back. "It's still a piece of the Time Stone!" she said, shielding it with her hand. "No Atharrach can touch it!"

But Lady Phaidra didn't seem to be listening. She extended a single claw from her delicate Human hand and cut the cord from around Eirin's neck. Eirin cried out as Lady Phaidra carefully held it by the cord, drawing it closer to see. She must have heard Eirin, though, because she didn't touch the stone itself.

"This is the missing piece," she whispered. Then she gasped and began to laugh, tears running down her face. "I have it. I have it! Oh, Eirin, bless you!" She grabbed Eirin and kissed the top of her head. Eirin tried to snatch the stone back, but Lady Phaidra held it up high, letting it dangle over Eirin's head.

"Eirin, you brilliant girl!" She looked down at Eirin, her face radiant. "We don't have to go to Iilaedin!"

Eirin froze. "What?"

"We'll destroy this with the staff! And the curse will be broken!"

"No! Give it back! That's *not* how it's supposed to work!" Eirin threw herself out of the chair at the woman, but Lady Phaidra might as well have been in her full Dragon form. She was utterly immovable. "Please, please give it back!"

But Lady Phaidra simply beamed as she carefully dropped the stone into her reticule. "I'm sorry you can't see what a gift this is, Eirin. Because it's more than anything we ever could have hoped for!" Then she paused, her eyes softening as she took in the tears running down Eirin's cheeks. "I'm sorry it has to be this way. But you've just saved us all."

59

$\mathcal{E}$irin woke up to a throbbing head in a room she'd never seen before. The white-walled room had a high ceiling, at least twice what her ceiling was back in her room. Conical in shape, the floor was the room's widest point, the round walls shrinking as they made their way to the top, and there were no windows out of which to see, only a single skylight at the top of the soaring ceiling. There was no furniture, either, just a single blanket, which must have been spread over her as she slept, and a thin pillow placed beneath her head.

Eirin pushed herself into a sitting position as she tried to shake the fog from her head. How had she gotten here? And how long had she been unconscious? Only when she instinctively put her hand to her chest and felt nothing, however, did she remember.

The Wizard's explosion.

Lady Phaidra's confession.

And now the stone was gone.

Eirin searched frantically, hoping in vain that the cord had slipped and fallen into her clothes. But it was gone. Her memory hadn't failed her, for the stone wasn't there.

Eirin scrambled to her feet, squinting up at the skylight to see what time of day it was. From what she could tell, it was either dawn or dusk. The sky was a blueish gray, and no direct beams of light fell from the sky.

515

"Nuru?" Eirin screamed, her voice echoing in the empty room. "Qeb?" It was probably useless, but the tendrils of panic had set in. How had she been so stupid? Surely, there must have been a way to signal to Karolus that she wanted to speak with him without alerting Lady Phaidra.

Even more importantly, how had she missed Lady Phaidra's involvement? She should have known after Lady Phaidra had covered for Mannish all those times. But then, she recalled, she hadn't wanted to know. Lady Seren had promised them that if anyone could help, it was Lady Phaidra. And now, Lady Phaidra had betrayed them.

Another icicle of fear pierced her chest. Obviously, they couldn't kill her. She was too valuable. But what about her friends? Qeb and Nuru had been with her when she'd tried to bargain for their freedom. Yes, Lady Phaidra had given her word that they would be held in their rooms, but was there anything keeping her from killing them or putting them somewhere else? Perhaps Qeb's tie to Drystan might have some pull. Incurring the wrath of the third-born prince's descendant seemed like a terrible idea, and Eirin was confident that Karolus would disapprove. Still, Lady Phaidra had threatened to use the barbaric bruthsi root on them, shocking even her guards. Lady Phaidra had grown too desperate for sense.

It was foolish to hope he'd hear. But Eirin, too, was desperate. Angry tears welled up as she took a deep breath and shouted as loudly as she could,

"Drystan?"

But of course, Drystan wouldn't hear her. He was a Dragon, but who knew what kind of defenses this prison had? It was built to hold a creature far stronger than she was. She could see from the ground that the small, round skylight had multiple locks on it, locks which could only be opened from the outside.

She felt around her person for her weapons. She didn't carry many. But her sword was gone, and the dagger Drystan had given her back in Torbaine was also gone. For some reason, though she knew it was no fault of his, this made her feel as if he'd abandoned her again.

She did find the Elvish messenger still in her pocket, and she began to draw it out of her pocket to use it. But then she paused. This room was locked tight. There would be no way for it to escape even if it did fly up into the air. She put it back.

Of course, if Drystan had been with them, they never would have been overpowered that way in the first place. In fact, Lady Phaidra probably wouldn't have dared set upon them the way she had. Drystan might have left them for her good, but he was an idiot if he thought they were better off without him.

Not that he probably noticed, with as much time as he spent waltzing around with Callispa.

Calling Drystan all sorts of names under her breath, Eirin began feeling her face, wondering what they had used to knock her unconscious. She seemed bruise and bump-free, and as it was unlikely they would risk injuring their Seer, Eirin was sure they'd used some sort of herb or elixir. Most likely, one that would work within seconds, as she had no memory of being put to sleep.

What little light that did fill the room darkened, and Eirin looked up to see a face peering through the glass. She gasped.

"Thane?"

He put a finger to his lips and looked around briefly before motioning for her to move to the side. As soon as she had plastered herself against the wall, he shifted, and using one of his front hooves, smashed in the glass.

The shards glittered as they rained down, and Eirin wondered if they now had the attention of everyone within the next three streets up or down. But before she had time to worry, he used his hoof to clean off the rest of the glass that was stuck to the edges of the skylight and then lowered a knotted rope down inside.

For the first time in her life, Eirin was glad climbing had been a steady part of her training back in the Citadel. She shimmied up the rope, slowing only to make sure she didn't brush any of the remaining glass shards as she made it through the hole. Thane helped her climb out, then motioned for her to follow. She did this without question, pausing only to glance behind her and see that they were far north of the city. No one in the city would have heard her screaming even if they'd been listening for it. She'd been literally buried in the mountain. Which meant…

"How did you find me?" Eirin whispered as she followed him down the rocky path. "And I thought you weren't helping us."

Thane, who had shifted back into his Human form, gave her a guilty smile. "The sum of it is that after you visited, my conscience began to get the better of me. I was about to go ask my captain for permission to go find you when I saw him speaking with Lady Phaidra."

"You eavesdropped," Eirin said.

He nodded. "My name was mentioned more than once, and I heard your name several times. Qeb's twice, and though they never said Nuru's name, she was referenced as well." His voice hardened. "So when my captain called for me and told me he had some errands for me, I knew they wanted me out of the way for something." Thane turned and helped Eirin down a steep embankment. "So I agreed and went on my way."

"What about Nuru and Qeb?" Eirin asked as they knelt behind a boulder and peeked around at the nearest street.

Instead of moving down toward it, though, he motioned for her to follow him further north. "Oh, I've already freed them," he said. "They're waiting for us."

Eirin looked up at the sky again as she followed him into a shallow outcropping of rock. A small cavern became apparent, and Eirin nearly fainted with relief when Qeb and Nuru waved at her from the inside. Eirin ran and grabbed Nuru into an embrace.

"You're alive!" she whispered. For once, Nuru didn't shove her off but held her back.

"We wouldn't have been for long," Qeb sneered. "Lady Phaidra wanted us dead there and then, but her guards wouldn't do it. They agreed to lock us up until they could come to an agreement. That's when Thane found us." Then he smirked. "Notice how she has earned no Griffin ties."

Eirin noticed that Thane watched Nuru carefully, but Nuru refused to meet his eyes. She only sniffed. She wondered about how he had found them if they'd been locked up, but right now, there were more important things to discuss.

"Have I been asleep an entire day?" Eirin asked, looking back up at the sky.

Nuru nodded. "I didn't see it, but you reek of cadeliam."

"They must have dosed you heavily if you slept that long," Qeb growled. "Idiots."

"Have you talked to Drystan?" Eirin asked Thane.

He grimaced and shook his head. "I can't find him. But neither can anyone else. The powers that be have been carefully enquiring about him all day. No one seems to know where he is." He paused. "I haven't seen or asked Callispa, though. She would know if anyone would."

Eirin tried to ignore how much she detested that this was true.

"He must have ghosted them too," Nuru said with a smirk. "Of course, if he's hiding from them, that means we can't find him either."

Eirin's anger threatened to flare again. Maybe he had betrayed Callispa and Phaidra and all the others. But he still wasn't here.

She needed to focus on the task ahead.

"I need to get the stone back," she said. "I'm sure Lady Phaidra has it now."

"What stone?" Thane asked.

"Thane says the entire city has been called to the Bastion," Nuru said, ignoring him. "My guess is that whatever she's planning, she's putting into action now."

"Which means I have to get the stone back before she does something we all regret and destroys it." Eirin frowned.

"Eirin."

Qeb took Eirin by the shoulders and bent so their eyes were on the same level. His smile was kind. "Drystan may have been wrong about many things, but he believes we never went wrong in trusting your instinct." He paused. "Follow your instinct now."

Nuru gave her a dry smile. "And for better or for worse, we'll follow you all the way."

60

"This is going to be difficult," Eirin whispered as they peeked around the corner. People were walking to the arena in droves. Blending in should have been easy. Unfortunately, there were more than the usual number of guards stationed in the streets. From the corner in which they hid, Eirin could see three.

Their first target was to get Eirin's stone back. Lady Phaidra wanted to destroy it, and Eirin was convinced that she wanted to make it public.

"She wants everyone to see what she's doing," she had said as they'd planned. "She wants the whole city to know she's trying. There's no way she'd do something like destroy the stone in private."

"How will you get it from her there?" Nuru asked. "She'll be surrounded on all sides."

Eirin raised an eyebrow. "A distraction would be welcome."

But before they could make it to the arena, they had to figure out how to go unseen. And that was something Eirin didn't have a plan for.

"I would get you your cloaks," Thane whispered, "but as I completely disregarded my captain's orders and you three are missing, I'm guessing I'd attract some attention myself."

"Eirin!"

Eirin's body turned to ice briefly as someone behind them called her name. She turned slowly to find Madame Mayumi motioning frantically for Eirin to come. "Quickly!" she hissed. "In my shop! I have something to help you!"

Eirin looked at the others. This could be a trap, of course. But then, Eirin had seen Madame Mayumi's shop. It was pristinely kept with not so much as a pin out of place. Eirin got the feeling that Madame Mayumi would die before inviting four warriors into her sacred workplace so they could fight as they were ambushed. Slowly, Eirin stood and then darted over to the seamstress.

"Inside, quickly!" Madame Mayumi whispered as the others followed. "Someone will see!"

Once they were all inside, Madame Mayumi shut and locked the door. Because dusk was falling outside, the unlit shop was nearly black. But the dark didn't seem to bother their hostess. Madame Mayumi shifted quickly then scuttled between two rows of silk-wrapped bolts to a wardrobe in the back.

Eirin groped behind her until she found a chair to anchor herself to in the dark. But there was a brief burst of movements behind her, and when she glanced at the others, she found that they had all shifted and were watching Madame Mayumi with reflective eyes.

Eirin rolled her own eyes and returned to staring into the shadows.

"Hey, Eirin," Thane whispered. "Is it dark for you in here?"

"Yes. Why?"

"The Time Keeper must have a sense of humor."

She turned to glare up at him in the dark. "Why?"

"Just think. The Seer is the only one in here who can't see."

As he cackled softly, Eirin had made a fist and was wondering where his arm might be when Madame Mayumi came bustling back out. By squinting, Eirin could just make out that four of her eight legs were each holding a dark shape. Something silky and soft was shoved into Eirin's arms.

"Take these!" Madame Mayumi whispered urgently. "They feel delicate, but they are strong. I've sewn a thicker piece into the inside to keep you warm. And the silk should help keep you hidden at night." She paused. "It's of a...special variety."

Eirin hugged the fabric close. She opened her mouth, but Qeb beat her to it.

"We have nothing to pay you with—"

"Nonsense." Madame Mayumi waved a furry leg. "My son is in the guard that arrested you last night. He was quite distraught. In fact, he was going to free you today, but when he arrived at your rooms, you'd already disappeared." She paused, as though waiting for an explanation. But when no one spoke, she continued. "We hoped you hadn't left without rations or something to keep you warm. This is all I can give, I'm afraid, but it should at least provide some protection from the cold."

Eirin's eyes stung. "Thank you. So much. I wish we had a way to repay you."

Madame Mayumi tsked. When she spoke again, however, her voice wavered slightly. "Save Solevar, child. Save my son and his children, and I will have more thanks in my heart than you will ever know."

Eirin swallowed. "We'll do our best."

"Good. Now go out the side door here. You should be able to join the crowds without attracting too much attention. But go one or two at a time. Not all four."

They did as she told them to, each murmuring his thanks as they stepped outside. As they put their cloaks on, it was quickly decided that Nuru would go first, followed by Eirin, with Qeb and Thane close behind. So thirty seconds later, Eirin found herself alone, her head bent as she allowed herself to be jostled along with the crowd.

Slowly, she made her way toward the arena.

She hadn't been inside the arena since the mass funeral after the battle. And going now without Drystan or her friends nearby or even her knife made her feel naked and exposed.

Not vulnerable enough, however, to prevent her from changing course when she saw Callispa, who was standing a short distance from the arena's entrance. Thane's words flashed through her mind.

I haven't seen or asked Callispa, though. She would know if anyone would.

Unfortunately, Thane was right, and Callispa looked as though she were waiting for someone now. She could only be waiting for one person.

Eirin ignored the voice of reason in her head as she lowered her face and angled herself so that she would run right into Callispa. Callispa wasn't paying attention, so it was easy enough for Eirin to close one hand over her mouth while grabbing Callispa's shirt with the other and shoving her back into the rock wall behind her.

Callispa's eyes went wide when she saw Eirin's face beneath her hood, but Eirin angled her elbow into the girl's chest and kept her pressed against the stone. It was probably foolish, considering that Callispa could light herself on fire any time she wanted, and Eirin could not, but Eirin was done playing it safe. Lady Phaidra had pushed her too far.

"Where is he?" she demanded in a low voice. "And don't scream unless you wish him never to talk to you again."

"They're looking for you!" Callispa whispered. "They said you were missing!"

"Before or after they threw me into a prison cell?"

Callispa frowned. "Who threw you into a prison cell?"

"Lady Phaidra. And then doused me with enough cadeliam to knock me unconscious for an entire day."

Callispa shook her head and stood up straight, forcing Eirin back. "You're lying. She wouldn't do that."

"You're an Atharrach," Eirin hissed. "Smell me."

Callispa's frown deepened. But to Eirin's surprise, she did give a small sniff, and her eyes widened slightly.

"Now that you know I'm telling the truth," Eirin said, "I need to know where Drystan is!"

Callispa stared at her, and for a moment, Eirin thought she just might tell. But then Callispa pulled herself up to her full height, which was a whole handspan taller than Eirin's.

"There's a reason he won't see you. It's dangerous."

"So is getting drugged nearly to death. And yet, here we are."

But Callispa shook her head. "He set me on fire yesterday. Definitely not safe for—"

Eirin huffed. "This is important! Solevar will fall if Lady Phaidra has her way tonight!"

Uncertainty flickered along the torchlight that reflected in Callispa's eyes. But still she shook her head. "I'm sorry, Eirin. I can't. I just can't."

"You're sorry for me? Or for you?" Eirin began to turn. "And I'm not lying when I say that if you tell Lady Phaidra I was here, Drystan truly will never speak to you again."

Drystan might have abandoned her. And ignored her. And broken her heart. But Eirin was sure that had he known what was going on, he would be on their side.

At least, she hoped he would.

"He won't speak with you!" Callispa hissed to her back. "He's trying to protect you!"

Nevertheless, Eirin needed him. And she had no way of finding him. At least, not like this. So without any sudden gestures to attract the attention of those around her, she pulled the little folded white bird from her pocket and whispered into it. Then she watched in amazement as silver sparks began to emanate from the bird as its folded wings began to beat, raising it into the sky. As it rose, so did Eirin's prayer that help would indeed come.

61

Drystan's pulse had grown so fast he felt like he might choke on his own air. But it served him right.

How? How had he managed to lose every single one of his friends? Even Thane was missing.

After finding the Wizard still in a coma the night before, Drystan had set out to look for his friends. Their scents were all over the city, and they were familiar enough by now that Drystan didn't even have to be in Dragon form to trace them. But no matter how many trails he found, none of them led anywhere helpful. Most of them led to or from their rooms or their usual haunts. They weren't in their bedrooms, nor did they return at any time that first night nor any time during the next day. The scholars' room remained empty as well.

The closest he'd gotten was when he'd picked up Qeb, Nuru, and Eirin's scents leading to a small herb garden. These scents were fresher than any of the others. But once he was in the garden, they seemed to disappear. It was as if they had simply vanished.

Most likely, they had either flown out of the garden, or someone had flown them out, but the wind blew too much for any scent to linger in the air. The trails he'd been following had been on the ground, trees, and bushes or other objects they might have touched. But now they were just...gone.

After the disappearing trail in the herb garden, Drystan had gone to see Thane. Who was nowhere to be found either. His captain told Drystan that he'd sent Thane on a number of errands, but none of those brought him to Thane. In fact, the people Thane was supposed to interact with hadn't seen him all day.

What was going on?

"Is this some sort of punishment?" Drystan groaned as he made his way toward the swarming crowds. Still, even as he uttered the prayer, he knew better than that. He could have kept Eirin safe from afar without cutting himself off from her completely. Well, perhaps that's what he had meant at first, to get her to stop trailing him so he wouldn't hurt her again. But in the end, his motives had become self-ish, designed to protect his own heart.

He also wondered how he had been so blind to what Lady Phaidra and the others had been doing to him. He'd allowed himself to be manipulated like a puppet. All those meetings and all Lady Phaidra's requests that he guard the Wizard had simply been a ruse, a way to prevent him from speaking to his friends. And Drystan couldn't believe he'd needed Qeb to point it out to him.

Qeb, who was now missing too.

"There you are!"

Drystan was near the arena now, where every citizen of Mhaedin had been called, and Callispa was running toward him.

"I'm sorry for how I stomped out last night!" she blurted, wringing her hands. "I was upset and confused, but that was no way to answer your questions."

Such contrition might have softened Drystan on another day. But today, he didn't have time. "Have you seen Eirin? Or Qeb or any of the others?" he asked.

Callispa blinked at him, and a small furrow appeared between her brows. But then she cleared her throat and straightened. "Um, Eirin was here a little while ago. She was demanding to see you."

"Why didn't you tell me?" Drystan cried. "I've been looking for her all day!"

Callispa gaped at him. "How was I supposed to know you were looking for her? You've been gone all day!"

Drystan ran a hand through his hair and let out a groan. "Callispa, if I'm—"

"You're most likely to lose control when you're anxious," Callispa said in a lower voice, taking a few steps closer. "Which is now." She paused and took a deep breath. "Why don't you start from the beginning and tell me–"

"Where did she go?"

Callispa stared at him, mouth falling slightly open. After a moment, she huffed, and her shoulders fell. "Inside. With the crowd."

Drystan immediately made his way to the tunnel entrance. The crowds had dwindled somewhat, but he still felt as though he were crawling as he made this way inside the arena. He could feel Callispa following him, but he chose to pay her no heed.

Ignoring Callispa, however, didn't help him find Eirin. Or Qeb or Nuru or even Thane. With as much tact as he could muster, he did his best to push and shove his way down toward the platform. Knowing Eirin, if she was still in here, she would want to be in the middle of things. He had no idea what she was up to, but Eirin never did anything without reason. And if the others were smart...smarter than he had been, they were following her.

Before he could find any of them, however, the lights dimmed, and only Lady Phaidra was visible on the stage, surrounded by hundreds of lit candles. Karolus was standing at the edge of the stage out of the light. Drystan couldn't see his face well, but he was pretty sure his uncle didn't look particularly happy.

Lady Phaidra, however, wore a glittering smile and stepped forward. Gems glistened on her neck and ears and even in her hair, and her robe was finer than any Drystan had ever seen her wear, particularly since her husband had died.

"Friends," Lady Phaidra said, her Dragon voice sending her words booming through the arena with ease. "The last time we gathered here was to mourn those who bravely..." Her voice faltered, and several seconds passed before she seemed able to speak without difficulty again. "But now I bring news that should bring you all joy. In fact..." She paused again. "This just might mean the end of the curse."

A murmur that quickly approached shouting arose from the crowd, but Lady Phaidra simply raised her hands until it was silent again. "I know it's been discouraging with the Wizard's accident just days before we were supposed to set out for Solevar one more time. But this…I think this will change everything."

She reached into her robes and pulled out a small object dangling on a cord. When Drystan allowed his Dragon vision to take over his Human eyes, he easily made out Eirin's stone.

His heart sank into his chest. Eirin would never give up the stone willingly. She hadn't even wanted to speak about it with Lady Phaidra. So if Lady Phaidra had the stone, where was Eirin now?

"This," Lady Phaidra said, "was discovered by our Seer, Eirin. And she has given it to us so that we might please the Time Keeper."

Drystan nearly let out a burst of flame in protest, but he held himself back.

Lady Phaidra lowered the stone and looked around, her dark eyes glittering brightly. "You all know that a hundred years ago, Prince Kamon of Oreck's line attempted to change Solevar's fate. He convinced a Seer to place a new Time Stone in the Time Stone Circle so that he might try to change the way things were.

"And change the world he did. By bringing a dark curse upon us rather than adhering to the light. And ever since, we have suffered. Our Seers, the few who survived the venture into Solevar, have been unable to locate the foreign stone within. Most died before they even got the chance. But this…" She straightened her shoulders and stood taller. "This will change everything." Then she turned and looked to her left. "Mannish?"

The crowd broke into more furious whispers as Mannish climbed onto the stage as well. He wore white robes like the ones Eirin had shown him in the records of the Seers. And in his hands was the Wizard's staff.

So not only had Lady Phaidra protected Mannish in his schemes. She had been a part of them.

"Light shall, however, come from this darkness," Lady Phaidra said as Mannish came to stand beside her. She placed her arm over his shoulders and beamed up at the crowd. "For tonight, we shall give the Time Keeper what He has not yet seen. For we will destroy this shard of Time Stone. And then I am firmly convinced that He will grant us passage into Solevar to finish what we've begun."

Drystan stood. Those seated behind him protested that they

couldn't see, but he ignored them. He couldn't let them destroy that stone.

Looking around desperately, he was able to locate an empty parapet above. He could use that to shift, but he would have to be quick. Turning, he left his row and began running back up the dark stairs. When he got to the top, he swerved and grabbed a decorative silk braid that led up to the parapet. He knew by now that the guards were looking at him and had begun to converge. But he paused only when at the top of the rope to glance down once more at the stage.

Lady Phaidrahad laid the little stone in the middle of the stage and began backing up. Looking foolish as he handled the unwieldy staff, Mannish lowered its tip until it was inches from the stone.

Finally, in the parapet, Drystan let the fire consume him. But as it did, a small figure leaped onto the stage. Drystan had been coiled, ready to swoop down at Mannish, but he froze when he recognized Eirin. As she dashed across the stage, however, she wasn't the only one who gained attention. On the opposite side of the room, a Griffin stood and began to shout. Several rows back, a Centaur started breaking chairs. A Sphinx leaped up onto the other side of the stage and growled at Mannish, pushing him several steps back.

Lady Phaidra was so shocked that she seemed incoherent as Eirin snatched up the stone. Then, instead of running off the stage, she paused at Mannish's side and grabbed the staff from his hand before making her escape.

"Stop her!" Lady Phaidra screamed as Eirin sprinted down the steps.

Karolus, however, who was on the opposite side of the stage, didn't give her immediate chase. Instead, his eyes were on Drystan as Drystan launched himself off the parapet down toward the stage. By the time he landed, Eirin had escaped through a small doorway that led back out to the street.

"Karolus!" Lady Phaidra screamed, but Drystan didn't wait to hear what his uncle would say. He had to get to Eirin.

With a shout of frustration, he shifted back into his Human form, singeing Mannish's robes in the process and making him cry out.

Once he was fully in his Human form, Drystan charged for the door. He had to pause outside, however, to find her scent in the dark.

Left. She'd gone left down a small street. Drystan charged after her. As he ran, though, he began to sense something else. Or rather, someone else.

Drystan wasn't able to sense other Atharrachs the way Eirin could. He had found, however, that he could feel when other Dragons were nearby. And now he could sense yet another Dragon that was neither Lady Phaidra nor Karolus.

It was times like this he wished his father hadn't insisted on training her to run so blasted well. If Eirin had grown skilled at anything in the Citadel, it had been making an escape.

He could still smell her, but panic shot through him as he ran through the streets. The clouds had grown thick, and even with his improved eyesight, he couldn't see...

But no.

There.

Another Dragon was indeed flying nearby. A Dragon larger than Drystan had come to a stop beside one of the walls that edged a street-lined cliff, using its wings to hover. And there, a small figure in the dark leaped off the wall and landed on the Dragon's back.

"Eirin!" Drystan roared.

Eirin turned, and for a brief moment, their eyes met. And hers was not a look that begged him to follow.

"If you want me safe!" she shouted back to him, "then let me go!" Then she said something to the Dragon she rode, and they disappeared into the night.

62

$\mathcal{E}$irin shook with silent sobs as she clung to Rangvald's back. They cut through the trees, low enough that Rangvald's shining scales wouldn't be visible in the low light of the dim moon.

Eirin had cried for her family after leaving the mountain. More than once she had mourned their loss. During her flight out of Torbaine, however, there had been danger and then friendship to propel her forward. Now, though…

Now she was alone on the back of a near stranger, heading to a place she'd never been with only the wind whistling past her ears. Not even Nuru, who had once been her enemy, was with her this time.

Instead, she'd left everyone and everything behind. Everything except a small, broken stone and a stolen Wizard's staff.

Eirin couldn't recall many particular details from her daring plan. It had all happened so fast. She remembered making the sign for Nuru, Qeb, and Thane when Lady Phaidra had placed the stone on the floor. She'd known that if she hesitated, her stone might be gone forever, and the curse might become permanent. So spurred on by fear, she'd leaped onto the stage and snatched up the stone and the staff.

Now she looked at them through wet, blurry eyes. The stone seemed unharmed, much to her relief. She tied it around her neck again. She didn't even want the staff. But to see Mannish and Phaidra

535

use it that way had been unthinkable, so she'd wrestled it from a surprised Mannish as well.

Then she had ran. There was no plan, nor did she know where she was going. She had just run.

But the Time Keeper must have been listening because help had come just when she needed it most. She hadn't any idea that Rangvald had gotten her message until she heard an unfamiliar beating of wings just to her right.

"Jump!" he'd called.

Eirin jumped before she had time to rethink her course. Because Drystan was behind her, and if she paused even for a moment, she'd stop for him. Then he would leave again, and Lady Phaidra would have her in their power forever. Because there was no way they'd underestimate her after this. She would escape now, or she would never go. And even if she did, there was no way she would ever find the stone or the staff again.

She'd made her choices. And she didn't regret them. But that didn't fill the hollow space inside her when she remembered the way Drystan had looked at her, pain and confusion crossing his face.

But no, she couldn't feel these things. He had made his choices as well, and now he had to live with them.

She was shocked that he hadn't followed her. The Drystan she knew would have taken off after her no matter what she said. But, it seemed, he'd heeded her desperate plea. This was good, of course. It was what she needed to get away. She needed him to delay them, to stop Lady Phaidra from making chase. But it also made the hollow feeling inside her grow.

They flew until Eirin began to feel poorly. The familiar headache began to throb behind her eyes, and a strange sort of tingling rippled through her muscles.

"We're almost there," Rangvald called back in a low voice. As he spoke, a cluster of lights appeared ahead in the dark. Eirin gripped his spikes more tightly and forced herself to focus on them. She tried to remember if she'd felt so poorly this fast when they'd first attempted their ill-fated trek into Solevar, but her head hurt too much to think straight.

"The winds are strong tonight!" Rangvald called back again as if sensing her pain. "They're probably aggravating your reaction to the curse. Sometimes the sands of the southern dunes are stirred up and wreak havoc. You'll be safer inside."

Before long, towers came into view. Lady Phaidra hadn't been exaggerating when she'd called Rangvald's home a fortress. A great square wall ran around the entire city with a square battlement at each corner. The wall had a thin line of fire that licked the dark sky running around its entire circumference. Probably a line of oil like the one they'd used to protect their encampment in the mountain, Eirin figured.

The Dragon let out three short bursts of flames before swooping over the wall and down onto one of the battlements. Men standing guard on the wall helped Eirin down before Rangvald shifted back into a man. If any of them thought it was odd that she was carrying a Wizard's staff, none made mention, and for that, Eirin was grateful. She had tucked the stone back into her shirt during the journey, so that, at least, was safe.

For now.

Eirin was suddenly aware of her tear-stained cheeks now that she stood in the light of fire and the torches that lit the battlement. She tried hastily to wipe them away, but before she could successfully rid her face of her tears, Rangvald had gently taken her shoulders in his hands and pulled her into a hug.

At first, Eirin was too stunned to react. But once again, she found that Rangvald reminded her of her father, and then she sobbed into his robes.

"I'm sorry," he whispered above her head. "I know that was hard. Sometimes it's good to weep."

This only made Eirin cry harder until she felt as though all her tears were gone. But only when she loosened her grip did Rangvald loosen his as well. He stepped back and gave her a sad smile, wiping her tears away with his hands. In the firelight, she could better see the lines of age on his face, and it suddenly hit her how much suffering he must have seen in his time. Over a hundred and fifty years and a curse must have seen some very difficult times indeed.

"I want a room prepared," he told his servants when Eirin was finally able to collect herself. "Some new garments as well." He gave her a gentle smile. "And food."

Within minutes, a female servant appeared on the parapet, motioning for them to follow her. Eirin could tell from her magic that she was a Nymph. Eirin said nothing about this, however, as they followed the woman off the wall and down a set of steps into it. Then they turned and walked down a dark hallway until they arrived at a small, arched door.

"It's not greatly accommodating," Rangvald said apologetically as he held the door open for Eirin. "Just a bed, a chair, and a stand with a washbasin, I'm afraid. Nothing like–"

"This is fine." Eirin forced a smile. "I don't need anything out of the ordinary." She yawned. "All I really want to do now is sleep." Sleep and spend a few blessed hours out of this nightmare that had become her life.

"I'll leave you soon, of course," Rangvald said, standing at a respectful distance in the far corner of the room as several women came in and out bearing food and a fresh rug for the floor. "But I was hoping you could tell me–even in a brief form–what exactly happened."

Eirin frowned down at the plate of bread, cheese, and carrots she'd been given. She was sitting on the bed now with the plate in her lap. Then she opened her mouth to speak but chose to wait until the fire was lit and the room was empty.

"It seems," she said slowly, weighing how much to tell him, "that Mannish and Lady Phaidra never planned to take the Wizard to Mhaedin."

Rangvald's eyebrows rose. "Really?"

Eirin nodded. "They discovered the records of a Wizard named…Amrit."

Rangvald's thick brows now drew together. "The only Wizard ever to be put to death by his brothers."

"That one. Anyhow, it seems that Mannish and Lady Phaidra somehow believed Mannish could wield the Wizard's staff without him. Something in one of Amrit's texts convinced him of that." She shook her head. "Anyway, they staged an attack on Isayas and put him into a deep sleep. Then they stole the staff." She shrugged. "I took it before they could do any further damage." She thought about mentioning her Time Stone but then decided against it. There was no need to tell him that bit of information. Drystan might have been wrong about many things, but he'd been right in thinking the fewer people knew about her stone, the better. Stealing a Wizard's staff was bad enough on its own.

"I have questions, too, though," she said.

Rangvald laughed and seated himself in the chair. "Very well. Ask away."

Eirin nodded and broke off a piece of her cheese. "You've known Lady Phaidra longer than I have." Eirin frowned at the cheese as though it had been the thing to cause her troubles. "She's renowned for her leadership and intelligence. Everyone who comes to Mhaedin flocks there to live in the realm of the great Dragon lady."

"This is true," Rangvald said, steepling his fingers.

"So why did she do it, then?" Eirin asked. "She can't possibly have thought that stealing and misusing the Wizard's staff would work."

Rangvald gave her a tired smile then stared out at the dark window, unseeing. Female servants still flitted in and out to dust or refill Eirin's mug, but he didn't even seem to notice them.

"Phaidra has had a difficult life," he finally said. "We all have, of course, but her more than many others." He sighed and stared into the fire for a moment before shaking his head and seeming to remember himself. "Her parents were killed in the first wave of poison that fell with the curse. She was given a city at far too young an age, and when word spread that the mountains were safer than the low-lying areas, her city nearly doubled in size within just months of the time when the curse fell." He paused, and when he spoke again, his voice was quiet.

"Phaidra has held out hope far longer than most, to her credit. But she has lost both her daughter and her husband in a short span of time, and as the food dwindles, she grows desperate." He shifted his gaze to Eirin. "And desperate people do desperate things." Then sighed. "Did you have another question?"

"How did you find me so fast?"

At this, Rangvald gave her a guilty half-smile. "One of my informants had reported to me about the Wizard's accident. So I may or may not have been within the vicinity when I received your messenger."

"You have spies in Mhaedin?" Eirin asked.

"Of course. As Lady Phaidra has spies here as well." He shrugged. "It's expected. We can't live with each other, but neither can we live without the other. So each of us simply does our best to keep eyes upon the other." He shook his head and chuckled. "Anyhow, my informant told me what had happened, so I decided to pay a quiet visit of my own. Your messenger found me much closer than I usually am."

Eirin shivered.

"And that's a good thing, I suppose," he said, gesturing to one of the women passing by the door. "Fetch her a poultice for her head and tea. Then put her to bed."

"My head?" Eirin asked.

"You have a headache. I can tell because you've touched your temple three times in the last five minutes."

Eirin had been so focused on talking with Rangvald that she'd forgotten her pain. But now that he mentioned it...she did have a headache.

The woman, meanwhile, nodded and hurried away. When she was gone, he leaned forward. "You're here now. But what about your friends? Should I expect them as well?"

Eirin's throat grew tight, and she had to clear her throat twice to speak. "I did what I had to do. They know that."

"What about my young nephew, though?" He gave her a small smile. "I was under the impression he was more than just a friend, if you'll excuse my saying so."

Eirin sniffed. "He wouldn't see me. He made his choice, so I made mine."

Rangvald sighed and shook his head as he stood.

"I think, at this point, that the greatest healing you can seek is that of sleep." As he spoke, the woman reappeared with a potently scented poultice and steaming tea. She bustled around, pushing Eirin into a sleeping position and setting about preparing the poultice.

"I am glad, though, that you called me," he added as he went to stand in the door. "You're safe for now, and that's what's important."

He turned to go but then paused. Turning once more, he gave her a gentle look. "And Eirin?"

"Yes?" she asked.

He gave her a sad smile, then said quietly, "I'm sorry this is your burden to bear."

So was Eirin. But as she let her head rest upon the pillow, and the woman draped the poultice over her eyes, Eirin tried to simply be. For just a few moments, she wanted to escape to a world where she hadn't left her own world behind. For now, she just wanted to sleep.

63

"What was that?" Phaidra roared as she caught up with Drystan. She landed beside him, looking tall and fierce in her scales. Why did she look so tall? Drystan looked down to realize he had somehow shifted back into his Human form without even noticing.

"Why did you let her go?" Lady Phaidra screamed.

Drystan looked her in the eye, but instead of Lady Phaidra's glowing amber eyes, he still saw Eirin's eyes, wide and accusing.

"She asked me to," he said quietly. "So I let her." Then his sense caught up with his shock, and he turned to face her. "And now I'm wondering why she felt she had to flee. Because it wasn't from me!"

At least, he hoped it wasn't.

Karolus landed beside them both, also in his Dragon form. "Perhaps we should take this somewhere private," he said in a low voice, glancing back at the crowd that was gathering behind them.

But Drystan was done hiding. "No. No, we're going to do this here and now!" He felt his body beginning to heat and ripple, but for the first time, he had no desire to stop or control it. "All of this has happened because people have been keeping secrets!" he shouted. "But we don't have time to tiptoe around anymore!" He turned his glare on Phaidra. "Since you seem to know what's going on here, why don't we start with you?"

Lady Phaidra gasped. "How dare you? You didn't even have the sense to catch her before she got away, and—"

"No." Karolus turned to face her. "I think he's right. If we're going to discuss this here, why don't you tell us what you and Mannish were doing? Because you certainly didn't tell me." Karolus's eyes were also amber, but unlike Lady Phaidra's, they had also taken on a brilliant blue.

Lady Phaidra looked at them both before letting out a huff.

As she paused, Drystan's friends came to stand beside him. How good it felt to be surrounded by those he knew were on his side. How had he ever thought separating from them would be beneficial to any of them?

"Mannish and I knew the Wizard was unlikely to help," she finally said in a low voice. "But he had read enough of the Wizards' texts to know that he might be able to do something with the staff if he could only access it."

"So you sent us on a deadly mission not to get the Wizard, but his staff?"

Everyone turned to see Callispa. She was standing beside Qeb, and she looked like she was about to cry.

For the first time, Phaidra winced and looked down. "It was for the good of Mhaedin. I knew Isayas wouldn't hurt you."

"Then you and Mannish purposefully injured Isayas," Drystan said. "You may have even killed him. For what? A staff?"

"It's not *just* a staff!" Lady Phaidra snapped. "It holds one of the sacred stones. The very stone Isayas refused to use to help us. So when Mannish discovered that using the staff is possible–"

"*Might* be able to access," murmured Nuru. When everyone looked at her, she shrugged. "Sorry. That's what Eirin said. And I'm not seeing anything to the contrary."

"We were correct, though," Lady Phaidra said, emphasizing her words. "Isayas was being ridiculous, first refusing to help at all, then excluding one of our Seers. But with that staff, we had something we'd never had before."

"Which would be?" Qeb growled.

Lady Phaidra glowered at him. "Power untethered."

"If Isayas wasn't able to prevent our Seers from dying when he did come with us," Karolus said gently, "how was this boy supposed to do more?"

"He was willing to do what Isayas wouldn't!" Lady Phaidra thundered. "He was willing to use the stone to an extent Isayas was too afraid to try!"

"You mean to the extent that got a former Wizard executed," Qeb said with a frown.

"We don't have *time* for this!" Lady Phaidra cried. "The staff and stone are getting farther from us by the minute! And with Rangvald no less!"

"How did you find out about the stone?" Drystan demanded.

"She showed it to me! She thought it would convince me not to continue with Mannish's plan."

"So you stole it and tried to use what only a Seer should," Karolus growled.

"And wanted to kill us all," Nuru added casually.

"She was holding the key to breaking the curse the whole time, and she never said a word!" Lady Phaidra screamed, looking around at those surrounding her with disbelieving eyes. Mannish kept his eyes downcast. The crowd behind them murmured and whispered, but most stayed slightly back. "This doesn't bother you at all?" Large tears welled up in Lady Phaidra's large eyes, and steam hissed into the air as water met fire.

"You don't understand!" she growled at Drystan, her voice shaking. "You haven't taken thousands of people, young and old, to their deaths!"

Drystan couldn't help being reminded of his conversation with Isayas. But oh, how differently that conversation had gone.

"You haven't watched your daughter ripped to shreds by a pack of Fenris!" she continued, her words turning into wails. "And then your husband die slowly, his pain stretched out for days! And nothing you do ever changes anything. Because you *can't* do anything different. So you just have to go on repeating your mistakes over and over again so no one loses hope, knowing the whole time that you'll fail!" She swallowed, and her eyes flamed again. "But then I found something new. Two new objects that could create a new path! A Wizard's staff in the hands of a willing Seer and a piece of the Time Stone that started it all–"

"You don't understand at all, do you?" Drystan heard himself whisper.

Everyone turned to look at him. He hardly knew what words flowed from his mouth, but something inside of him was changing. It was finally making sense. He felt as though Eirin were speaking through him. Maybe in a way, after all those hours spent with her, she was. He felt suddenly as if he could see into her mind. And it was liberating.

"It was never about the stone. Or the staff." He shook his head. "It's all about the heart. It always was." He looked around, willing the others to meet his eyes. His chest swelled with relief and life as understanding washed over him like rain.

"It's the heart!" he cried. "It was always about the heart!"

Everything made sense now, from Eirin's faith that the Time Keeper would provide a way, to her insistence that he must embrace his place as prince. Her unrealistic belief in his purpose and her acceptance of the monster he'd always feared and hated inside…the monster he'd been fighting, trying to keep it separate from himself.

He looked back at Lady Phaidra and shook his head, red filling his vision. And for the first time, he welcomed it.

He welcomed everything. The lethality. The cunning. The raw strength. The fire and the wrath.

Drystan had feared being dangerous to Eirin. But Eirin had understood that he'd been created to be dangerous. She'd understood that he needed not only to allow the beast to appear, but for it to bleed into His precious Humanity, forging him into something new. The others had been trying to tell Drystan that, too, of course, in their own way. But Eirin…

Eirin had always known, from the first time he'd shifted and she'd placed her head against his. Eirin's touch, the hand of a gentle lamb, had sown the seed that probably not even she had fully understood at the time.

"She understood," Drystan said, struggling for words as the flood of comprehension washed over him, "that it wasn't about the technicalities of the magic of Wizards or the abilities of Seers. It was always about our hearts." He looked at Qeb and saw a grin spreading across his face. "That's why the curse fell to begin with! Kamon didn't trust the Time Keeper in his heart of hearts. His heart was determined to take that which wasn't his. And now," he looked back at Lady Phaidra, his gaze hardening, "you're trying to do the same thing. You're trying to cheat using forbidden magic. Eirin understood. And that's why she begged me to let her go." He looked to the people surrounding them, praying they would understand. "Eirin was confident this curse could be lifted because she studied the Time Keeper's heart by looking at what has been." He looked back at Lady Phaidra. "And having hope in what will be."

"Well, a lot of good that will do any of us," Lady Phaidra scoffed. "She's off with Rangvald now and has the stone and the staff as well."

"Unfortunately," Karolus said in a low voice, "Phaidra's right. Rangvald never does anything without his own purposes in mind."

"But you've asked him for help–" Nuru began, but Karolus held up a claw.

"I know. Because we had little choice." He frowned. "But there's a reason we've rarely told him everything. And now he has a Seer, her stone, and the Wizard's staff. And I'm afraid that puts him in a precarious place of power over all of us." He hesitated. "But especially over Eirin."

Drystan felt as though all the golden sunlight that had burst open in his heart moments ago was turning to ice.

"I'm going after her," he said.

"And so will I," Qeb said, stepping closer. How Drystan had missed seeing approval in his friend's eyes.

"I have nowhere better to be," Nuru said in a bored voice.

"And me." Thane stepped up beside them. Nuru gave him a look that was far from forgiving, but Thane just shrugged and gave her a crooked smile in return.

"Obviously, we need to go!" Lady Phaidra said. "But we need to get our priorities straight. Reclaiming the staff and the stone needs to be our–"

"No," Callispa said. Lady Phaidra looked at her in surprise, but Callispa just shook her head. "Drystan's right. Eirin was right." She gave Drystan an apologetic smile.

Various individuals, including Vadik the Elf, began stepping forward, announcing their intentions to join Drystan. Mannish took a step forward as well, but Karolus used a large, scaled wing to push him back.

"As little as you deserve to participate in any of this," he growled, "we're already missing one Seer. You're going to stay here where you're safe, and we know where to find you should we lose the Seer you helped chase away."

Mannish nodded at the ground.

A deafening roar shook the street they all stood on. Lady Phaidra had raised her wings in the air and was beating them furiously. The smaller individuals standing nearby had to grab onto their neighbors to keep from being knocked over.

"We've spent a hundred years dying!" she boomed in her Dragon voice. "And I'm not about to let you lose the one chance we have at saving our people!"

Drystan's vision flamed red again, and he felt himself beginning to rise. A roar sounded from his own throat that made even Phaidra cower. And for the first time in his life, Drystan relished the change. Raw power coursed through his limbs, and fire licked his body as it changed form. But for the first time, not a single flame went astray. Instead, the tongues of fire stayed within him, burning away his Humanity to reveal the beast within.

Death was within his grasp. Fear was his to give. He was what Eirin needed him to be.

He had been all along.

"Drystan," Karolus said, taking a step forward. "Wait. You're not going–"

Drystan turned and roared again, but Karolus just shook his head, and a slight smile tugged at the corner of his toothy mouth.

"What I meant to say was that you're not going alone."

64

*E*irin wasn't sure how long she slept, but she felt as though she'd just closed her impossibly heavy eyes when voices on the other side of the room were talking again.

"How badly did the ride tax her?" a familiar deep voice was asking. Rangvald had probably meant to keep his words to a whisper, but his Dragon's voice somewhat rumbled through anyway.

"Not as badly as I'd feared," a female voice responded. Eirin peeked over to see Rangvald standing by the door. The woman he was speaking to was in Human form, but Eirin could tell from her root-like lights that she was a Nymph. "The southern winds were blowing, but she seems more in need of rest than anything else." She paused. "Not that we can do much else without a Unicorn."

"I'm feeling better," Eirin croaked, pushing herself up in the bed. Both her visitors seemed startled as she did. The window outside was dark, and Eirin found a bowl of broth and some bread on the corner of the little table beside her bed.

"I'm sorry to wake you," Rangvald said as the Nymph excused herself. "I'd hoped you would sleep longer, but I wasn't sure what state you were in after our long flight." He paused. "That's why we can't simply fly straight to Iilaedin, you know. The southern dunes seem to have absorbed a large concentration of the curse, and on nights like tonight, the wind blows it northward."

551

"I haven't slept for an entire day, have I?" Eirin eyed the window suspiciously.

Rangvald laughed softly. "No, just a few hours." He studied her for a moment and came to stand at the foot of her bed. "I'll admit that I have a few questions I was hoping to ask you. I was going to wait until tomorrow, though. But if you don't mind while you eat…" He gestured to the food. "Our cook has a little trick she uses to keep it hot. One of the most talented Brownies I've ever met."

Eirin nodded as she pulled the food toward her. She had no idea how long it had been there, but it was steaming hot as if it had just been placed there. When she tipped the edge of a slice of bread up, she found a slight dusting of copper magic.

Instead of talking, however, Rangvald stood there, lost in thought, which gave Eirin a chance to look around the room. The stone was still hanging at her neck, thank goodness. And the Wizard's staff was where she'd left it on the ground beside the bed. This made her feel slightly better. No one had tried to steal what she'd abandoned her friends to preserve. While she by no means trusted Rangvald with all of her secrets, this did serve to raise him a level in her favor.

"You still wish to visit the Time Stones in Iilaedin, correct?" Rangvald finally asked.

Eirin nodded as she chewed.

He nodded as well. "Good. Because I think I know how to get you there."

Eirin put her bread down. "You mean other than the way Phaidra had planned?"

"Yes. Very different." He ran his hand over the ornamental bedpost that had been carved to look as though leaves covered it. "I brought it up to Phaidra and Karolus, but they weren't willing to follow my lead."

"Why?" Eirin asked.

Rangvald chuckled. "You're never afraid to ask the true questions. I like that. It makes talking to you easier." He pulled a folded map out of his cloak and carefully opened it, laying it between them on the bed. "You can see where we are here." He pointed to the bottom of the map where a small fortress had been marked. "Mhaedin is here."

He pointed to a marked city slightly northeast, hidden in a canyon. "Iilaedin is up here." His finger slid up the map to the far northwest corner, where the drawing of a tall palace stood.

"After most of our Humans died either on the way to or in Iilaedin, I began to wonder if there would be a way to cut them off from the elements of the journey. Something to protect them from the curse."

"Why didn't you try this before?" Eirin asked.

"The plan took myself and my advisers years to develop. We had to think of ways to bring in fresh air without exposing those on the inside to the curse. The Atharrachs would do well enough, but you Humans are..." He smiled slightly.

"Delicate," Eirin rolled her eyes, making him laugh.

"I suppose that's a way to put it. Anyhow, it took us a long time to create the plans. Then I needed years of cutting and sawing of wood to even begin the journey."

"Wood?" Eirin asked.

"Wood. We decided to create a wooden road. And it would be covered by wooden walls and a roof. A tunnel. We could do stone, of course, but that would take too long to construct. Wood is faster and easier to find." He traced a somewhat wavy line from his fortress to Mhaedin. "Essentially, it would be a long tunnel that the Seer could travel without touching the flora or fauna itself." He sighed. "We began construction, but we're not even a quarter of the way through."

Eirin blinked at him. "You've started already?"

"Boredom is not a good way to induce hope," he said with a sad smile. "So I set the plan in motion even though we had no Seer." He paused. "I'm going to be honest. While you seem like a very nice girl, you have to know that I was hoping all along that you would see the foolishness in Lady Phaidra's way and consider something new."

Eirin sat up straighter. "Why didn't you tell me all of this before?"

He raised his thick eyebrows. "Would you have listened?"

Eirin sighed. "Probably not." She paused. "But if you're less than a quarter done, is there any hope of finishing before the famines really set in?"

"Yes." He nodded and bent over the map again. "I've been

preparing for this since Mannish arrived. As soon as we heard that there was a Seer again, I told them to begin. You see, a great number of my strongest men and women are building the tunnel even now. And as they build it, I have others who go in and clean it to try and rid the wood itself of the residue of the curse." He stood. "It won't clear it all, of course. But it will be far better than tramping through the weeds. And at the speed they're going, it should only be months before they reach the capital." He met her eyes. "That is, if you'll make the journey."

Eirin hesitated. There seemed to be no other way. She needed to get to Iilaedin, or her family in the mountain would die, as would everyone she'd met in Mhaedin. But going alone…

She licked her lips. "What about…what about my friends?"

He gave her a small smile. "I guess we'll just have to wait a little longer and see what the Time Keeper has in store." Then he stood and folded the map once again. "Get some more rest. Whether we leave in a few days or a few weeks, you will need all your strength."

Eirin obeyed and laid her head down again. At the moment, she was feeling anything but strong.

65

_D_rystan locked the door and settled himself against the wall beside Qeb in the girls' room. The light coming through the window mocked him. Hours still remained until they could go after Eirin. This day already felt as though it had taken forever.

Thane sat on the stool, and Nuru was gathering her things onto her bed. Not that any of them had very much. A few changes of clothes. Their weapons. And Nuru had managed to glean an impressive pile of food as well.

"Why are you packing?" Thane asked Nuru. She didn't look at him when she spoke, punctuating her words with her movements.

"Because I get the feeling we won't be coming back."

Thane frowned. "I'd better get some food, too, then."

"First, we have to finish planning," Qeb said. Then he turned to Drystan. "What did Karolus tell you?"

"We'll be breaking the group into three," Drystan said. "Karolus will lead the main charge inside and do any talking that needs to be done. A second group will cause a distraction on the other side of the compound. Our job," he motioned to all of those in the room, "is to find Eirin and get her out."

"So he's planning on a battle?" Nuru asked.

"He doesn't want one, but he thinks it's inevitable," Drystan said. "It's why he wouldn't let us leave last night." He did his best to sound

557

calm as he spoke this, but inside, the Dragon hissed. Unfortunately, what Karolus had said made sense.

Drystan had wanted to leave as soon as he'd heard Eirin might be in trouble, but Karolus had grimly shaken his head.

"We'll have to make our attack under the cover of night," he had said. "And we'll need a strategy. Rangvald was always good at strategy, and now that he's got himself a Seer--a very gifted one at that-- he's not going to let her go easily."

"What if she wants to go with us?" Drystan asked.

Karolus had shaken his head. "I don't know what to expect. But we'd do best to be prepared." He looked around and lowered his voice. "I want to speak with you again before we go. But finish whatever it is that you need to do first. And don't worry about Eirin. She's a Seer. No harm shall come to her tonight. I can guarantee you that." Then he had studied Drystan a moment before putting his hand on Drystan's shoulder. "I am truly sorry I didn't get to know you sooner. I think my son…" His jaw tightened, and he had turned away.

"I still don't understand why we couldn't go after her last night," Nuru said. "We wouldn't have been that far behind. The trip would have easily been made before dawn."

"Karolus thinks we're more likely to find her this way and still have time to get back under the cover of night. If we'd gone in the early hours of the morning, we would have had to find a place to hide until nightfall." Drystan looked at Qeb. "Any thoughts?"

"I think we should wait to scale the fortress walls until after the fighting has begun," Qeb said. "Let the others distract them well first."

"They'll be looking for us," Thane pointed out. "A gigantic blue Dragon and his trusty Griffin are hard to miss."

"Just after they begin their attack then," Drystan said. "And I think you're right. We should scale the walls as Humans before shifting on the inside. We'll be less noticeable in Human form. They'll be expecting us as Atharrachs."

"Here's a question," Nuru said, raising her eyebrows at Drystan. "Have you thought about how you're actually going to convince her to go with you? Because it sounds like she didn't want to be followed."

Drystan felt his face and neck heat. "I will give Eirin whatever she wants."

Nuru's eyebrows stayed lifted. "Whatever she wants?"

His instincts told him not to, but Drystan nodded. "It's not as though we'll have much time to regret it after, no matter what she asks."

A knock sounded at the door, and Qeb answered. Outside were Callispa and Mannish.

"We thought you might be here," Callispa said with an apologetic smile, "so we came together."

"Can I ask what for?" Qeb asked icily.

Callispa's eyes flashed slightly up at him before she looked at Drystan. "I want to come with your group. I think I could be useful."

"We don't need–" Nuru began to say, but Qeb studied her for a moment, then looked at Drystan. "There's only four of us. And she can fly." He glanced at Thane and grinned. "Someone will have to carry Thane."

"I have experience carrying people over long distances!" Callispa said quickly. "And no one else but Drystan has that."

"No one needs to carry me!" Thane leaned back in his seat. "Just because I've been stupid doesn't mean I'm helpless." He looked at Drystan. "You can do it."

"I'll be carrying Eirin," Drystan said with a hard smile. "And only Eirin."

Nuru rolled her eyes, but Drystan nodded at Qeb. "All right. You're in, Callispa." Drystan was somewhat surprised at Qeb's quick acceptance, but at the moment, he wasn't in any position to be picky.

Well, too picky. Mannish was still standing at the door, studying his shoes.

"What about you?" Drystan turned to him, allowing some of the red to seep into his eyes. Mannish looked up and met them briefly, his own eyes widening before looking back down at the floor.

"Um, I just wanted to bring this." He put his hand in his cloak and pulled out a dagger. Drystan's throat tightened as he recognized his own handiwork. He took it and put it into his own boot.

"Thank you," he said coldly. "Now you can go."

"I also wanted to say I'm sorry!" Mannish burst out, looking up again. "I never wanted Lady Phaidra to do what she did. But she insisted it was for the best, and I couldn't stop her, and–"

"But you could have said no." Drystan stared him down.

Mannish shook his head, his whole body sagging. "Just…tell her sorry for me, won't you?"

"Goodbye, Mannish." Drystan said, closing the door. "And thank Lady Phaidra for the knife."

He was sure the knife hadn't been surrendered voluntarily. Lady Phaidra had been told by Karolus that if she knew what was good for her, she was going to stay in her home for now. She'd grown indignant, reminding him that this was her city, at which point he had reminded her that he was a son of Oreck.

Drystan smiled to himself. That exchange had been rather enjoyable to watch.

"Why don't you think we'll come back?" Thane asked Nuru once the door was closed.

"We're not coming back?" Callispa asked, her eyes widening.

"*You* can do whatever you want," Nuru snapped, closing her bag. "But he," she pointed at Drystan, "has said that he's going to promise Eirin whatever she wishes for if she comes with us. And I get the feeling that Eirin won't want to go anywhere but Iilaedin."

"You're going to give her whatever she wants?" Callispa asked Drystan.

"Yes." He met her gaze evenly. "I am."

———

After they had made their plans, the little group broke up so each could find whatever supplies he needed. Nuru had begun to pack for Eirin, but Drystan stopped her. "I'll get the rest," he said, nodding to Eirin's beloved map. Then he paused. "But could you find me her sword? Phaidra might still have it, but you shouldn't have an issue getting it back. Karolus has her under pretty tight watch."

Nuru gave him a feline smile. "With pleasure," she purred.

Then Drystan was alone. Carefully, he rolled up the map that Eirin's father had made and put it into the tube where she always kept it. Then he put some of the food he'd overstuffed his own bag with into hers. While he didn't particularly relish the idea of hunting in Solevar, he could survive as a Dragon on deer, wild swine, and other animals. But the more food grown in Mhaedin they could bring for Eirin, the better.

He glanced up at the girls' party gowns, which hung from pegs on the wall. His chest squeezed as he remembered how she'd looked that night, so soft and beautiful, as if she had a magical glow of her own. The gentle brush of her lips against his as he'd pulled her close. She'd felt so vulnerable then, like a perfect little glass doll.

She'd also felt vulnerable less than a week later, when he'd watched her limp, burned form lying still on the ground.

But neither wishful thinking about ball gowns nor shame over the past would help them now, and he would do best to keep his thoughts on the night ahead.

Dusk was finally falling when he made his way out onto the street where anyone who wanted to go with them was to gather. As he looked for his friends, though, he heard a deep voice calling his name.

Karolus was standing in a small corner by himself, and he gestured now for Drystan to join him. Drystan shouldered his pack again and did so.

"I didn't want to say it where the others could hear me," Karolus whispered, glancing out at the busy street. "But if you get the chance to talk with Rangvald tonight, don't trust him."

Drystan frowned. "You've trusted him. You've let him visit, and whenever you make plans for a journey to–"

"Because Phaidra said we had no choice." Karolus's face was grim. "And we really did have little." He paused. "I'm supposing you've heard of the disagreement between my father and Rangvald and Kamon?"

Drystan nodded. "Somewhat. But I don't know what it was about."

"No one does. My father never spoke a word of it after. He said they were too busy trying to keep their people alive to kindle an old fire. But he did tell me from a young age never to trust Rangvald completely. They worked together somewhat, much as we do today."

"And how is that?" Drystan quirked an eyebrow.

"With one eye open." Karolus gave him a wry smile. "He never even left me alone with him as a child."

"Then why did you say Eirin would be safe?" Drystan hissed. "She's far weaker than a Dragon! Even a child!"

"Because, as I said, she's a Seer. Rangvald would be insane to do anything to her tonight. She won't have had time to serve his purpose yet. Now we need to get there before he gets that chance." He paused. "Are you ready?"

Drystan let the Dragon within him roil, turning his vision red. "Never more."

66

When Eirin awoke again the next morning, she was alone. The fire was low, and she could see through her window that it was day. Similar to the ones in Mhaedin, canvases now blocked out most of the sky. They seemed to be hung from the city walls, the battlements, and the central part of the fortress within, though she couldn't see that part to tell for sure. Her tower was higher than she'd guessed it to be, high enough to look out over the walls into the forests of Solevar had the canvases not been there. The little she could see, though, told her that the morning was late, probably no earlier than the tenth hour. For a moment, Eirin couldn't help marveling at how at one time, she'd had a regular sleeping schedule.

That seemed nearly as impossible as fixing the Time Stones.

On the little table where she'd placed her empty dishes the night before, there was now a plate with a slice of bread and an egg. Eirin ate quickly, then washed her face and hands in the basin. Then, for want of something better to do, she decided to explore. Hopefully, they wouldn't mind her looking around on her own. She was weaponless, friendless, and stuck here until Rangvald was ready to make his way to Iilaedin. She might as well get out and explore while she was within the fortress walls and safe from the Wyverns.

Wyverns. She shuddered.

She peeked out of her door and found the narrow hall empty.

Silently, she closed her door and crept out. As she was staying in the battlement, which was part of the fortress wall, Eirin guessed there would be stairs set at regular intervals. Sure enough, she found one less than three minutes away, and she climbed down as quickly as she could.

The stairs were made of stone, as was the rest of the fortress. There were no rails, though, and the steps were narrow and steep. The place hadn't been built for comfort.

Eirin let herself out at the bottom of the spiraling stairs a few moments later. She had to blink several times in the indirect sunlight that made it through the canvases above before her eyes adjusted to the light. The room must have been darker than she'd thought.

Now that it was day, she could see the people milling about. They were tired and thin, even more so than those in Mhaedin. Small, drooping houses sat in rows in the fortress's courtyard. Many roofs were patched, and instead of glass, the windows were covered with some sort of oiled cloth. Of course, it would be harder to make glass out here. Back in the mountain, Torbaine had specialized in glass-making. There had been families whose whole lives were dedicated to pulverizing stone to make into sand that could be blasted into glass. There were many kinds of glass even. And in Mhaedin, Eirin had seen similar little workshops. But here, despite being at the foot of the mountain, Eirin guessed it was difficult for them to obtain large amounts of stone. The fortress itself, Lady Phaidra had once said, had been built before the curse. Rangvald had simply taken over. So leaving the fortress walls was most likely perilous.

Eirin stayed on the outskirts of the courtyard, keeping close to the wall. Part of her–the part that sounded annoyingly like Drystan–told her she should go back to her room. But no. She was here now. She'd made her decision. She wasn't about to hide until she either fixed the Time Stones or let the curse take her.

There were more homes squeezed into the fortress than Eirin had guessed could fit, and she was sure many more lived in the walls, as she was. She could see why Lady Phaidra and Karolus would call for Rangvald's help. His people might be hungry, but there were many.

Life here, however, was obviously harder than it was in Mhaedin.

According to Mannish, the fortress had never been built to house thousands of people. It had been meant as a military stratagem, a remnant of some ancient war. Changes had been made quickly to accommodate the many people who had fled there after the curse.

Changes, Eirin could see, that were probably never meant to last a hundred years.

She made her way now to a small grove of trees in the corner on the opposite side of the courtyard from where she'd descended the stairs. They were sickly and dry, but some fruit did hang on the vines. Eirin climbed beneath the trees and sat on the ground, inhaling deeply the smell of soil. There was a large open square nearby, one that looked the perfect size for town gatherings, complete with a large platform at the far end. Now there were only a few stalls set up, their wares sparse and their owners sad.

Hope was even drier here than it was in Mhaedin.

Eirin put her hand on the trunk of an apple tree to adjust her position when the familiar sensation of Seeing overtook her.

She was still standing at the edge of the town square. The sun was slightly brighter, meaning it must have been closer to late spring or early summer. Earlier, at least. She didn't have a Roc's knowledge of the heavens. What she could tell for sure, though, was that she recognized the voice that boomed out over the square.

She moved closer to the edge of the grove to see better. There were hundreds of people gathered on the dirt street, and they were looking up at someone. Eirin followed their gaze.

Rangvald stood on the platform in his Dragon form. In the light of day, she could see now that his scales weren't merely purple. They were black too. His scales were varying shades of the two colors, and they shone as he moved.

"Phaidra and Karolus," Rangvald's voice rumbled, "should touch the hills the first night of their flight. They're moving slowly, due to their numbers."

Based on these words, this vision might not have taken place so long ago.

"I've already talked to the Wyvern's captain," Rangvald continued. "Phaidra and Karolus are waiting to hear from our scouts before setting down for the night. Now, they're not telling me how they're transporting the Seers, but I can guarantee you that they'll be taking them by Dragon. At least in the beginning. This will make the Seers slightly harder to reach, but it also means Mhaedin's forces will be divided."

He nodded at a man in armor, a man whose light Eirin did not recognize on sight. "You take the scouts and prepare them as though you were giving them a report. The Wyvern's captain and the others will want some of you tied up. Do what they tell you to."

"My men won't take kindly to being bound by Wyverns," the man said. "They disliked working alongside the Basilisks enough last time. And that was with the luck of the blizzard intervening before we could finish–"

"I don't care what they take kindly to," Rangvald responded in a patient tone. "You need to convince the force from Mhaedin that we're scouting for them."

"Then what happens after the Wyverns come?" someone else asked.

"We want them to think we're rescuing them, so don't make your involvement known," Rangvald said. "Once the fight has begun, do as much quiet damage as possible. But only what will go unnoticed in the thick of the fight. Then return and meet me at the pond, as we discussed."

Eirin held onto the tree for support. Rangvald hadn't been their ally on that journey. He hadn't even saved them. He'd been the reason they failed.

Memories of the scars on Drystan's back and arms flashed in Eirin's memory, and she felt rage begin to bubble inside her.

"What happens if they overcome the Wyverns?" another man in armor asked.

"There will be two possible outcomes here," Rangvald responded, "but which one takes place will depend on several factors. We need those Seers. Or one, at least. And while my sources report that one of the Seers is far more gifted than the other, either will do." He paused. "I haven't told you this before, but I feel it's time now."

The crowd shifted but was silent.

"Ideally, Mhaedin will fall to the Wyverns. After they've deci-mated Mhaedin's forces, we'll swoop in and save the day. The remnants of their fighters will have no other choice but to join us, giving us a stronger force to finish the journey with. But if Mhaedin is too strong to be defeated by the Wyverns, we'll come to their aid in the end."

"Why can't we take them on directly?" someone called out.

"We can't afford them making a full frontal attack on us. Not yet. We're not ready, and they have too many. But if the Wyverns are doing well…" Rangvald said, then hesitated again, seeming to search the eyes of his listeners, "we need to bring down the Dragons."

A collective gasp went up from the crowd. Eirin was speechless.

"All of them, Sire?" one of the men in armor asked.

Rangvald arched a brow. "You didn't complain last time."

The man shifted. "Last time, it was only Karolus." He shook his head. "But this young one…it doesn't feel right."

"I understand." Rangvald frowned then sighed. "It grieves me that we must make such choices. I take no pleasure in ending the blood-lines of my brothers. But," his eyes sparked amber, "we are the sons of Oreck. Violence and fire run deep in our blood. If we don't stop them now, they will stop us. And if we wish to reach the Blood Fire Throne and restore not only the Time Stones but also peace to Sole-var, we cannot allow all three lines to flourish."

"Your Highness."

Eirin looked around for the small voice that had spoken up. After a moment, she found her, an old woman at the edge of the crowd. She held a basket on one arm and used her other hand to lean on the gentleman beside her. She was a Will-o'-the-Wisp. Eirin's heart tightened.

"Yes, madam," Rangvald said respectfully.

"What about the choosing of the kings?" the old woman asked. "The Blood Fire Throne–"

"I understand what you are saying," Rangvald said politely. "But considering the…circumstances that led to the curse being brought on in the first place, I'm afraid this is one tradition that will have to be put aside for the next generation." He stood on his hind legs, forcing Eirin to crane her neck back to see his face, and looked at the crowd again.

"If you have a clear chance to kill either of my nephews," he continued in a louder voice, "take it. It could mean the survival of your little ones." His face hardened. "Because if they are allowed to live, there will be a war."

Eirin stumbled. When she did, she let go of the tree, and the vision vanished. But she was unable to move for several minutes.

Lady Phaidra and Karolus had been right to be suspicious. Rangvald had been planning to turn on them all along. Karolus had been dubious about the outcome of their last attempted journey to Iilaedin. How many times had they been thwarted by Rangvald? And how long would it be before he was finally victorious?

She needed to get out of here. She needed to go back and warn Drystan and Karolus. She needed—

A man cleared his throat behind her, and Eirin jumped. Rangvald stood at the edge of the trees in his Human form. His brows were drawn, and his face was pinched as though he were in pain.

"I was afraid this would happen," he said in a strained voice.

Eirin swallowed. "What would happen?" He couldn't see her visions. As far as she knew, he might think she was simply lost.

But he shook his head. "I can read it on your face, Eirin." He gave her a sad half-smile.

"Read what?"

"The accusations. Shock. Anger." He chuckled slightly. "I've known Seers before this, you know. But before you make assumptions, be aware that you don't know everything yet. I have reasons for everything I've done."

"Trying to murder your nephews?" Eirin was surprised at the boldness in her own voice. But then again, he was talking about slaughtering Drystan as though he were putting down a lame horse. Eirin was angry with Drystan because he was her friend to be angry at. But Rangvald...

That Drystan was even related to this man seemed incomprehensible.

Rangvald sighed. "I see. Well then, I'm afraid you'll need to return to your room until I can explain it all."

———

Eirin was escorted by two very large Griffins in body armor. Rangvald followed. Instead of being brought to her room, however, Eirin was led to a much larger room. This one had two fireplaces, one on each side, several large reclining sofas, a long rectangular table, and various faded chairs spread throughout. Eirin could probably fit six of her little rooms in this one.

Rangvald made a motion to his Griffins, who let go of Eirin and left the room, closing the door firmly behind them. Eirin stood in the middle of the floor. She wanted very much to bolt for the door, but having grown up training around a Dragon, she knew she had as much chance of getting there first as she did sprouting wings and flying away. So she stood in place, wishing very much that she still had her dagger.

He couldn't kill her, but that didn't mean he couldn't make her life miserable.

"I can only guess what you saw," Rangvald said casually as he pulled a bottle of wine from a cupboard on the wall. Then he reached into the next cupboard and pulled out two crystal goblets. "And if I'm right, I understand your reaction. In fact, I value it. Anyone who would turn against her friend so easily would hardly be worthy of my own trust." He poured the wine and offered her a glass. She glared at it and shook her head. Seeming unoffended, he put the second glass with his on a small wooden table, then sank into the sofa beside it.

"We're going to be here for a while. You might as well sit." He gestured toward one of the chairs sitting across from him.

Eirin nearly said no on principle, but she was a Human, and while other races, as she'd discovered in Mhaedin, could stand nearly motionless for hours, she could not. So she marched over to the chair and plopped herself in it so hard it almost hurt.

"I...I don't suppose you know what caused Kamon to try his disastrous scheme?" Rangvald raised his dark brows as he took a sip.

"Not the particulars." Eirin kept her back straight and her chin high. "Only that there was a disagreement, and Kamon felt as though he had no other choice."

Rangvald nodded and took another sip of his wine. "That would be a way of putting it, yes. As brothers, we tended to keep our disagreements to ourselves. Unfortunately, this was one disagreement that we couldn't quite smooth over…" His words faded, and he stared, brow furrowed, into the fire. Then he shook his head.

"I was accused of some…less than legal scheming. Our father was dying, and we knew we would all be facing the Blood Fire Throne soon. When Kamon was made aware of the accusations against me, instead of talking to our dying father, he rightly called a meeting of the brothers…myself and Demitrius."

Eirin gave him a curt nod to show that she understood. But nothing more.

"This would have been good enough if he had believed me." Rangvald rolled his sleeves up as he spoke. The day, despite the closeness to autumn, was growing oppressively hot. "Unfortunately, I couldn't dissuade him."

"What were you accused of?" Eirin asked.

Rangvald hesitated. "I had been considering some changes to the structure of our fighting forces. As a Seer, you know the position and purpose of Dragons as given to them by the Time Keeper, yes?"

Eirin nodded. "To protect." She glanced at his skin, which was now just a shade darker than her own. "And to give of your magic."

"Right. We were made as overseers of all the others, Atharrach and Human. Unfortunately, our numbers had been dwindling."

Eirin shifted. "Even before the curse?"

"Unfortunately, yes. I'm afraid my kind are sometimes too generous with our scales. There had been locusts throughout the land a number of decades before, and many of the lower Dragons had given out far too many scales to citizens."

"So they could eat?" Eirin asked.

"That, and so they could regrow their crops at the end of summer. It took an exceptional amount of magic." He pursed his lips and stood. Then he walked over to the window and stared down at the forest. "Giving away all of that magic did save many people. But it came at a cost. Too many of our young Dragons aged far too fast. Their magic died far sooner than it should have. And as many of those Dragons hadn't yet married, within two decades, our numbers were lower than they had ever been without the Dragons needed to replace them." He paused, and when he spoke again, his voice was somewhat gravelly. "Just as everyone else was beginning to thrive again, we were dying out."

Eirin watched as several emotions crossed his face before he seemed to gain control again.

"Stop me if you know this, but the Time Keeper divided Solevar into very particular property lines with the express purpose of ensuring that there were Dragons assigned to protect those areas at all times. And if a line dies off, the king will award the land from the dead line to a younger Dragon, one that was second or third born." He put his empty glass down on the table.

"Because we had so many groups without protection, I chose to talk privately with a few officers from the king's guard about ways to ease the pressure our Dragons were experiencing, particularly the lower Dragons."

He met her eyes again, pleading. "Unfortunately, one of the officers shared my musings with my youngest brother. And when Kamon came to face me, he was so sure that I was breaking the law that he wouldn't believe anything else I said."

"And what about Karolus's father?" Eirin asked.

"Always the peacemaker, Demetrius tried to sweep everything under the rug and start again. He couldn't believe I'd betray them the way Kamon had been led to believe. And Kamon wouldn't believe me that..." Rangvald paused. "Unfortunately, I had done something proactive that to this day I regret. I think if I'd simply waited, Kamon might have believed me. And this whole thing would never have happened." He frowned at the window.

"What did you do?" Eirin asked, her heart thumping loudly in her chest.

He looked at her for a long moment before answering. "Instead of waiting for my brothers' consent, I had given the order for some of the measures I'd discussed with the officers to be put into practice. And in doing so, I accidentally convinced my brother that I was trying to take over the kingdom."

Eirin narrowed her gaze. "If this is meant to persuade me that you were right in trying to kill your nephews–"

"I don't want to kill them!" Rangvald boomed.

Pain shot through Eirin's ears as he shouted, his Dragon's roar unfurling in his words. She threw her hands over her ears and bent over to try and protect them. But there was no more shouting. Instead, Eirin looked up to see tears running down Rangvald's face.

"I'm sorry," he sobbed so hard she could barely make out the words. "I don't want to kill my nephews! I loved my brothers! I still love them! And I wish I could take it all back!"

"Then why try to kill them now?" Eirin demanded, her ears still throbbing.

"Because we are Dragons!" he cried. "And not only are we Dragons, but we're sons of Oreck! You're a Seer! You can See it! The fire that mingles with our magic gives us a bloodlust like you can never understand! And if that bloodlust is awakened… it's nearly impossible to stop."

"But Drystan–"

"Do you think he'll let me take you to the Time Stones? Do you think he wouldn't raze the rest of Solevar to keep you safe?"

Eirin opened her mouth to tell him that he was wrong. But then she shut it again.

"See?" He laughed, sounding slightly mad. "You know I'm telling the truth! What that boy did to himself…when he tore himself away from you…You have no idea how much pain he inflicted upon himself!"

Eirin stared at him. What was he talking about?

"You think he was being overcautious. You still do! I can see it in your eyes every time you speak of him. You resent him for what he did. But as a Seer, you ought to be the first to understand!"

Eirin shook her head. "I'm not–"

Rangvald slipped off the sofa and came to kneel in front of her. Eirin leaned back slightly, but he leaned in close. "In tearing himself away from you, that boy did one of the most painful things a Dragon can do!" Rangvald took her hand in his, his eyes too bright and his muscles too taut. "He burned a hole in his own heart to keep you safe!"

Eirin tried to form words, but none came. What was he talking about? She'd seen Drystan's heart. It was bursting with magic and blue fire, just as Rangvald's was. Just as Karolus's heart was. There was no hole.

"But maybe you can't See it." Rangvald's mad laughter turned into a sneer. He stood and reached back, grabbing the second glass of wine and downing it in one swig. Then he slammed the glass down on the table so hard it shattered. But he didn't even flinch. "Dragons love for life." He laughed. "There, a history lesson for the Seer. Another reason the Dragons weren't reproducing as they should. When the famine decimated our numbers, the ones who lost their mates couldn't go on. When their spouses died, they stopped trying to live and began waiting for death, giving their scales out as though they were sharing apples!"

"But we're not married," Eirin whispered. She stood as if in a dream, and leaned against her chair for support. "We never even said we loved–" As she spoke, though, her memory snagged on one moment, a moment that would be frozen in her mind forever.

Dancing under the stars, surrounded by couples who mingled their magic as they spun, Eirin had felt it. She hadn't understood it back then. Drystan might not have even understood it. But he had somehow moved the magic out of his heart...out of his being...and wrapped her in it as he'd held her tightly against him. She'd marveled as the golden and blue, magic and flames, had spun around them, weaving them together in a world of their own. The warmth of it had brushed her skin, and briefly, so briefly, she'd felt as though the magic were really hers as he bent down and wrapped her in a kiss.

"You remember!" Rangvald clasped his hands together and bent forward. "And now you know why it's more critical than ever that I make sure my nephews cannot follow us."

"He'll come with us if I ask him!" Eirin cried. Her bold facade was gone now, and she was shaking. If she'd had any idea of what Drystan had been through...

"No! No, he won't be satisfied to watch as I sit on the throne!" Rangvald hissed. "Just as Karolus won't trust me either! And don't think I don't know what he's about. Demetrius said he believed me. He said he knew I couldn't do such a heinous thing! But he never trusted me again. Not like we had before. Not like brothers!"

"But you can't know all of that!" Eirin tried to move out from behind her chair, but Rangvald let out another roar. His eyes glowed with rivers of amber, and he seemed to grow taller before her eyes.

"They will wage war on me whether you ask them to or not!"

"Prove it!" Eirin snapped, her own anger trying to rise up from the ashes of her fear. "If you're so sure about all of this, give me proof!"

"I'm so glad you asked!" He strode forward and grabbed her by the arm. Then he threw open the door so hard the hinges came off. Without a glance backward at his broken door, he dragged her down the hall until they reached her room again. Throwing her on the bed, he pointed at the window.

"They're on their way here tonight! All of them!"

Eirin's heart both leaped and fell at his words. Drystan was coming for her. The whole of Mhaedin was on its way, despite her abandoning them. But that joy was gone nearly before it had come. For Rangvald already knew.

"You see now," he said, grabbing the belt from her dressing robe that she'd cast off that morning. "They're coming to get you back, and they're willing to wage a war to do it." He leaned in close to her face where she could smell the wine on his sour breath. "This is why I tried to kill them before. Because I knew they would eventually bring bloodshed to my people. Unfortunately, we weren't strong enough in the forest. But we will be here."

As he spoke, he tied her hands behind her back. Then he yanked off his own belt and used it to bind her feet. When he was done, he stood back and drew in a deep breath. As he did, the mad smile melted from his face, and once more, he was the elegant, respectable gentleman Eirin had first met. Only his eyes still gleamed amber.

"Stay here like a good girl," he said, patting her foot. "I'm...sorry for what had to take place. I wish I could have spared you all of that. If you would have stayed in here, I would have." And with that, he walked out and locked the door behind him.

67

"I was glad clouds were out tonight," Nuru whispered as they stared at the wall towering before them. "Now, I'm not so sure. I can't see anything but their oil fires."

Drystan shifted to his Dragon vision. "There," he said softly, pointing. "There are three guards up there. They've ignored that strip there," he said, moving his hand to the right, "three times in their rounds. They must think it's not worth protecting."

"Or it's got some sort of protection we don't know about," Qeb said.

"Are we sure about this?" Callispa asked as they cowered in the shadows of the trees below the wall. "Scaling the wall in our Human forms?"

"You are going over in Human form," Nuru gave her a smug smile, "because if you didn't, you'd be a beacon announcing to everyone exactly where we are."

Callispa didn't look pleased with that answer, but she must have seen the wisdom in it because she gave a short nod.

"I'm going to carry you over," Qeb said, coming to stand beside her. He was in his Atharrach form already, towering over them all, including Thane. Callispa jumped a little when she noticed him, and Drystan had to smile. Qeb had crept up on him more times than he could count.

"Oh." Callispa nodded. "Very well."

"He's carrying everyone over," Thane said with a chuckle. "Nuru hasn't practiced flying with passengers yet—not that you'd want to be her first— and Drystan's the only other person with wings who doesn't light up like a bucket of oil. But he's too big and would get their attention for sure."

"Very good," Callispa repeated, straightening her clothes. Drystan exchanged an amused look with Qeb. It seemed there was someone who could shake the unflappable Phoenix after all. But then again, even Human Qeb seemed to have that effect on people.

"Listen!" Nuru hissed. Everyone froze. Sure enough, in the distance, they could hear Karolus's voice.

"...not here to make war, Rangvald. We're here for our Seer."

"She called me to come get her," Rangvald called back. Their voices were slightly muffled through the trees, but Drystan could just make them out if he shifted his ears.

"That's an...interesting look," Thane said, smirking.

Drystan rolled his eyes but kept listening.

"...let her tell us then," came Karolus's calm response. "Let us hear from her mouth that she wishes to stay."

"She doesn't wish to speak with you."

Was she hiding from them? Was he telling the truth? Drystan's chest radiated pain. He could feel Qeb's concerned eyes, but he did his best to ignore them.

"I'm sorry, Uncle," Karolus replied. "That's not going to be enough."

"You're willing to shed blood over this then? All for what? The disbelief that she may not want to go with you?"

"There was a misunderstanding at home, yes," Karolus called back. "And I will happily go on my way if she comes out and tells me to my face that she doesn't wish to return." He paused. "But I need to hear it for myself."

Drystan's heart lurched. That promise he could not abide by. He couldn't leave Eirin alone if he tried. Not again. He wasn't sure he could physically survive leaving her behind again.

"It's beginning," Callispa whispered.

Drystan's hair stood on end as they listened to the roars and screams that filled the air.

"Now?" Nuru asked.

Thane shook his head. "No. We need the second attack to come first from the other side. That should split their focus into two. Then we'll go–"

An explosion rocked the ground from the other side of the fortress.

"There it is," Thane said. He looked at Drystan. "Now?"

Drystan nodded to him and then to Qeb. Qeb grabbed Drystan by the shoulders and flew him up into the air and over the wall. Sure enough, they found the three guards manning their section of the wall.

"Let me," Qeb whispered. Drystan nodded and stepped back. He could take out the guards more easily than Qeb, but Qeb wanted this. If Qeb wanted to take out an army on his own, Drystan was more than happy to let him. It would give him a moment to scope out the area.

The thick stone walls of the fortress formed a large square with an open courtyard in the center. Karolus had guessed Eirin would be staying within one of the walls. The question was, which one?

To the south, fire already raged as the Dragons and their Atharrachs engaged. The north wall was also aflame, though this flame came from the explosion Karolus's men had created that had taken a sizeable chunk out of the wall.

As Drystan surveyed the fortress, Qeb strode forward, a sword in one hand and a battle axe in the other, his eyes gleaming in the dark. And as the guards turned and snarled, Qeb sent them a predatory smile that sent a shiver down Drystan's back.

"I don't wish to kill you," he told them. "But I will if you force my hand."

The guards attacked.

Drystan had seen Qeb fight before. They'd practiced combat together since they were small boys. They'd even fought side by side several times since Qeb's first shift. But Drystan had always been distracted during the battle, unable to really see his friend for the warrior he had become. Something in Qeb had been unleashed. And Drystan watched in awe.

The guards turned out to be a Fenris, a Centaur, and a Dokkaebi.

They would probably have been a decent match for the average Mhaedin soldier, possibly even better than most. But they stood no chance against Qeb. In addition to his size and strength, Qeb had excelled in strategy back at the Citadel, often surpassing Drystan with his understanding of thinking as the enemy did. No one had ever defeated him in the school's war games, and now the Fenris and Centaur fell within seconds.

The Dokkaebi was harder. He wasn't as tall as Drystan, but he was wider and heavier. Watching him fight was almost like watching a rock battle, if a rock had arms, legs, and a head.

But even with his strength and size, he was no match for Qeb. The whole fight was over in less than a minute.

When it was done, Qeb nodded at Drystan and went back to get the others, leaving Drystan to look at the bodies surrounding him. Part of him mourned. There had already been too much death. They didn't need more.

But then again, this was the only way to get Eirin. And he knew now that there was no distance he wouldn't go to get her back or follow her to the end of his days. He went back to scanning the visible parts of the wall for where Eirin might be hidden.

Five minutes later, they were all on the wall.

"We need to get off this wall to somewhere we can shift," Callispa whispered.

"You really aren't comfortable in your Human form, are you?" Nuru asked as they made their way to a set of winding stairs.

"Not all of us got hand-to-hand combat training with bruthsi from birth up," Callispa answered, nocking an arrow. "I'd rather use my own fire any day."

"That was fairly easy," Thane said with a grin.

"Here comes the hard part." Drystan nodded down to the scene unfolding before them.

His friends looked down at the fortress in dismay. It hadn't looked nearly as large on Karolus's map as it did now. Hundreds of windows looked out at them from the city wall. Then, of course, there were countless more cottages within the walls.

"Look at this!" Callispa called quietly. They followed her to the inner edge of the wall. She was squinting into the dark at the city gates, which were now on fire and hanging crooked. "Does that look like..."

"Mannish," Qeb finished.

Sure enough, the other Seer was also on the wall. He didn't appear to notice them, though, and he probably couldn't with his Human eyes. He was crouching in a corner, peeking over the edge of the wall at the chaos below. Fire had broken out in several parts of the city, and the screams were getting louder.

"We're not here for him," Drystan said, turning away. "We're here for Eirin. Now let's– Nuru, what are you doing?"

Nuru had shifted into her Sphinx form and was crouched down as though she were about to pounce. She turned around and grinned. "Finding Eirin." And with that, she bounded onto the nearby window ledge, peered inside, then moved on to the next.

"She could fly faster," Callispa said.

"She'll be harder for the enemy to spot if she stays close to the windows," Qeb explained.

"Well, if she's going," Thane said, "I guess we'd better get looking too."

"Let's find our way into the wall first," Drystan said. Karolus thinks she's probably being held there."

They all agreed and made their way down the nearest flight of stairs to the first door, which happened to open into the third story. The others moved into the hall, but before Drystan could follow, Callispa stepped back into the stairwell and touched his arm.

"This is a really small space. You're sure you'll have full control when you have to shift?" she asked. "Especially so close—"

He gave her a smile. "For once, I'm sure." Then, bursting into the hall, he knew he was telling the truth. Eirin would never be endangered by him again.

68

Eirin's backside still throbbed from where she'd banged it when she fell off the bed. It was harder to move around with her hands and feet bound than she'd expected, and she'd misjudged the distance from the bed to the floor, especially with the effects of the cadeliam still lingering in her head.

For all the Atharrachs liked to talk about taking care of their Seers, they were quite liberal with their use of it. For the second time in two days, Eirin had been put to sleep against her will, and now she was awake and ready to escape with a vengeance.

But even her awakening, which had happened after dark, had been hours ago. After falling off the bed, she'd done her best to search the dark floor for anything with which to cut her bonds. She'd even kicked over the furniture, trying to break one of her old dishes or the washbasin. Rangvald's people had been thorough, though, and it seemed everything fragile had been taken. Now the dark floor where she was stuck felt like a chasm, her only light coming from the ill-lit embers still glowing on her hearth.

There was also, of course, the terrible screaming and shrieking coming from outside. She could only guess that Drystan had come to find her. She had suspected...and hoped that he would. But none of that would do her any good if no one knew where she was. Since it had begun, she'd screamed herself hoarse. All to no avail.

She started once again to scoot toward the table, hoping perhaps to find something new that she'd missed in her earlier searches. It was a fanciful wish. No broken tea cups or plates were about to appear to save her.

Stupid, stupid girl. Why had she ever run to Rangvald? In the moment, when Lady Phaidra had taken everything, Eirin had felt as though it was her only answer. But now she was…here, tied up and useless. She had the stone at least, and the staff. Those wouldn't do her much good, though, unless she ever got free. And if Rangvald thought she would ever use the stone to help him get his crown, he was going to have another difficult lesson coming.

Still, for all her bravado, Eirin shook as she tried in vain to find something to free herself with. She'd been trapped in here all day now and was developing a desperate need to relieve herself. That, and she didn't particularly enjoy being anyone's prisoner.

Eirin rolled over for the hundredth time, it seemed, and tried to rub her aching hands against the rough spot on the edge of the small table she'd managed to overturn. But as with all the first attempts, she only succeeded in giving herself a splinter.

"Gaah!" She kicked the bedpost with her bound feet, which made the motion a lot less satisfying. But as she did, the sheet got caught on her foot, and as it fell, she got a glimpse of something shiny beneath the bed.

Eirin quickly bent, grabbed the sheet in her hands, and yanked. Unfortunately, she had to come up with some creative rolling and pulling before she could see under the bed again, but when she did, she nearly screamed for joy.

The shine she'd glimpsed was the stone in the Wizard's staff. She had been sure it had been taken. It looked, however, as though it had been kicked there by accident and forgotten, but Eirin blessed the Time Keeper's name anyway and used her new ability to roll to get close enough to reach it with both hands.

As soon as she had it out, though, she realized she had another problem. The staff might once have had sharp edges. But it had been used so much that the edges and corners had been worn down.

Eirin felt traitorous tears begin to form in her eyes, and before she knew what she was doing, sobs racked her body. No one would find her in here. There were too many rooms, even if they were searching one at a time. Why had she ever used that Elven–

A scratching at the window made her turn. Her eyes were so blurry from the tears that she had a hard time making out what the shadow was.

"Eirin!" the shadow hissed.

"Nuru!" Eirin cried. "I'm here! I'm on the floor!"

"Not so loud!" the Sphinx hissed, and Eirin smiled. She could just imagine Nuru rolling her eyes, even in Sphinx form.

Nuru batted at the window pane several times, but the window held fast. Eirin heard her let out a huff.

"I'll be back," Nuru hissed. "Stay here."

Eirin nearly laughed as her tears of sorrow moved to tears of joy. "I'll be here!"

Still, as her friend slunk back into the shadows, most likely to get help, Eirin sent up a prayer.

Let them find me, she prayed as she never had before. *And please, let it be on time!*

69

Drystan sheathed his sword and shifted to using his Dragon claws. His small group had run into multiple contingents of guards in the halls, and they were struggling to make headway. Rangvald was probably sending them out to prevent exactly what Drystan and his friends were doing. Drystan could cut most of them down as fast as they arrived, and his friends picked up the stragglers. But the enemy simply kept pouring in, and Callispa, who was supposed to be checking the rooms, kept having to stop and loose arrows at those who got too close.

"We'll never find her at this rate!" Thane called up to Drystan. "We need to come up with another way!"

"Thane's right," Qeb said. "This is taking too long."

Drystan paused briefly, wondering if he should take one full form or the other. The hall was nearly too narrow for him to fit, but he didn't need to remain in his Dragon form for long periods of time. Just long enough to send a blast of fire down the wall every time they got a new batch of attackers. It was easier to stay his Human size while retaining his Dragon claws when he could. Still, the fire came faster when he was a full Dragon.

"This would be a little easier if we could actually see to look for Eirin," Thane coughed as he waved the smoke away.

A figure emerged from the smoke on four legs, coughing as her

589

tail twitched. Drystan tensed, as did his friends, but a familiar voice came through.

"If you're done lighting the building on fire," Nuru said, glaring as she joined them, "I've found her."

Drystan shifted back into his Human form faster than he ever had before and was running before she finished the sentence. In her Sphinx form, Nuru loped ahead of him. They turned once before Nuru stopped in front of a door.

"This is the one," she said.

Drystan ran to the door and threw his shoulder against it, assuming it would be locked.

But it wasn't. The door opened easily, nearly sending him crashing to the floor. When he had righted himself, however, Drystan froze. The room was empty.

"Oh no," Thane said as they took in the signs of struggle. The single chair had been tipped, as had a little table. The bed was rumpled and messy. Drystan's heart nearly stopped when he spotted a small pool of blood on the floor.

Where was she?

A scream echoed down the hall, waking Drystan from his stupor.

He knew that voice.

He sprinted out of the room, the others on his heels. His newly improved hearing led him down the hall to a locked door. Without pausing, he ran through it, splintering it as it fell from its hinges.

Eirin and a tall figure were struggling. She was lying on a couch, her arms and legs bound. The tall figure was struggling to bind her with yet another rope when Eirin reached up with her fettered boots and kicked him in the face. The impact forced the tall figure back, and when he turned slightly, Drystan could see Rangvald's face.

Several violent emotions seized Drystan at once. First, overwhelming relief that the blood on the floor in the other room wasn't Eirin's. He knew this because there was a slight gash in Rangvald's left arm that still trickled blood. Now his nose bled as well from where she'd kicked him.

Drystan's second emotion was rage. Rage that burned white-hot through his whole body. He launched himself at Rangvald, shifting in the air as he went.

This room was much larger than Eirin's room had been, which was good because Rangvald shifted even faster than Drystan had. By the time they hit the wall, both Dragons were in full form.

Not waiting for Rangvald to make the first move, Drystan bit down hard on his uncle's shoulder. Rangvald let out a screech before slashing Drystan's face with his claws. The pain was so severe that for a moment, Drystan saw spots.

Rangvald took advantage of this, rolling his own weight onto Drystan's, making it difficult for Drystan to breathe.

He needed a better position.

Out of the corner of his eye, Drystan watched Qeb scoop Eirin up and deposit her on the other side of the room. Unfortunately, Rangvald saw too. He leaped off of Drystan's chest and charged. Drystan could sense Rangvald's fire building within his chest, even from behind him. Fearing for his friends, who he knew would stand in front of her, Drystan leaped at Rangvald from behind. This time, he crashed into his uncle at an angle, knocking him sideways off his feet.

So powerful was their collective fall that they smashed through multiple stone walls, falling hard on the stone floor at the base of the building.

Screams and shouts rang out as Rangvald turned and dove at Drystan again, pushing them out into the inner courtyard, away from the floors through which they'd fallen. Drystan barely missed Rangvald's teeth, but his evasion made recovery awkward. Rangvald struck again, this time digging his teeth into Drystan's back.

Drystan let out a roar and whipped his tail out as hard as he could. It struck Rangvald's legs ineffectively. So he threw himself backward, landing on Rangvald instead.

The longer the fight lasted, the more Drystan began to panic. They were terribly mismatched. Drystan had his youth, speed, and anger to fuel him, but Rangvald was far more skilled. He was also larger, larger than Karolus even. And the techniques Karolus had taught him might have worked more effectively if Drystan had been the size to carry them out.

"Your time with her is done!" Rangvald growled as he and Drystan faced one another again. Each was breathing heavily and bleeding in some capacity, but Drystan knew he couldn't last much longer. And he hated himself for it. "Let me take her to her destiny," Rangvald growled, "and she won't have to watch you die!"

Fury fueled Drystan's veins again, and he sent out a wall of flame. It was a good way, he had learned, to shield himself as he attacked. The enemy couldn't see him through it.

But the wall of flame was a mistake. For by the time he dove through it to reach Rangvald, Rangvald had moved as well. He lashed Drystan from behind with his tail. And as soon as Drystan was on the ground, Rangvald fastened his jaws around the back of Drystan's neck.

"No!" a shrill scream filled the air.

Don't let her see me die like this, Drystan prayed. He was powerless here. He had failed.

Before Rangvald brought his jaws crunching shut, however, he was gone.

Drystan rolled over to see Rangvald entangled with Karolus. Where his other uncle had come from, Drystan didn't know. But he was grateful.

Karolus had knocked Rangvald off Drystan, and now they were circling one another, rising in the air as they did.

The fighting around them seemed to have ceased as both armies watched. Everyone knew that their future would be determined by the outcome of this battle.

"This isn't between you and the boy," Karolus said. "This has always been between you and me."

"This was between me and my brothers!" Rangvald hissed. "But neither of you seems to be able to give that up. So it's between us all!"

"Go, Drystan," Karolus ordered, his eyes still on Rangvald. "Take her and flee. I will finish this."

"He'll do no such thing," Rangvald growled. In a flash, he turned and launched himself at Drystan again. But Drystan was ready this time. He slashed upward with his claws, and Rangvald fell to the ground with a serpentine scream.

Karolus took advantage of the fall and pounced, knocking Rangvald down before he could rise. As he tried to roll over, Drystan could see blood leaking down from Rangvald's eye.

Karolus landed on Rangvald once more, slashing Rangvald's chest. Rangvald screamed again. But Karolus continued, large wet tears running down his scaly face as he used his claws on the older Dragon faster than Drystan had ever seen him move.

"Go!" he shouted at Drystan again. "Take her now!"

Drystan hesitated for a moment longer. His instinct told him to stay near the scent of blood. But Karolus had bought them this time, fighting the uncle he had never trusted but never wanted to destroy. They might not get it again.

Drystan turned and flew up to where Qeb was standing at the edge of the broken building. Drystan took Eirin from Qeb's arms. Qeb, in turn, picked up Thane as Callispa and Nuru rose into the air as well. They were nearly all over the wall when a new scream pierced the night sky.

Drystan turned just in time to see Rangvald, torn and bloodied and still lying in the dirt, but with Karolus's neck in his jaws. Karolus's body hung limp as Rangvald let it fall to the ground.

"No!" Eirin cried.

"Go!" Drystan handed Eirin back to Qeb and turned to face Rangvald as the older Dragon pushed himself to his feet and stood over his nephew's body. Drystan braced himself for yet another fight as Rangvald lifted his wings and met Drystan's gaze.

But he was too injured. Drystan nearly collapsed with relief as he watched Rangvald fall back to the ground, where his people rushed to help him. Without waiting to see more, Drystan turned and followed his friends into the night.

70

The night air was unusually cool as they flew, but Eirin barely noticed. She felt frozen inside.

"We need to find shelter!" Qeb called in a low voice as they flew over the forest. He eyed Drystan with his slightly glowing eyes. "You need to rest, and the sun will be up in a few hours." Then he glanced at Callispa. "And we need to find some way to travel at night without lighting up the sky."

Callispa made a face at him. "It's not like I can help it."

"I didn't say it was your fault," Qeb said quietly. "Only that it's not wise to fly with fire when we're being pursued in the dark."

"I'm well enough," Drystan said. "But we should search for a place to sleep."

Drystan had taken Eirin back after he was sure Rangvald wasn't following them. Resting in his arms, feeling the rumble of his voice through his chest, was a torture Eirin hadn't known could exist. So far, she'd kept her arms and legs to herself as much as she could. Now she studied Drystan as well as she could in the dark. She couldn't see much from where he held her in his arms as they flew, but she tried peeking up at his face. If she squinted, she could make out dark spots marring the shine of the scales on his face. His neck.

All over.

She swallowed down the sudden turn in her stomach. She knew he'd been injured, but she hadn't realized the extent.

Eirin had been absolutely terrified when Drystan and Rangvald had gone after one another. She'd had no idea how badly Dragons could injure one another, and it had been difficult to make out the details of the fight amidst the smoke they emitted as they fought.

She resisted the urge now to order the others to land so she could inspect Drystan more closely. He would only resist. In the old days, she would have ignored his resistance. But now...now she wasn't sure that was her place anymore.

Callispa pointed to the northeast. "Mhaedin is only–"

"I'm *not* going back to Mhaedin."

The words came out louder than Eirin had meant, but she didn't take them back.

"Let's land down there," Thane called softly. "By that pond. Then we can talk."

Eirin felt Drystan change direction as they started to glide down. As they dipped low, she felt a twinge of jealousy. There were a million other things to worry about right now, but Callispa had gotten to fly with Drystan daily. If she hadn't been terrified that they would all be caught and killed, she would have loved that flight.

As soon as they landed, Eirin knelt at the pond to drink, but Callispa came to stand beside her. "What do you mean we're not going back to Mhaedin?" Her voice wasn't accusatory, but neither was it happy.

Eirin finished drinking her fill before standing to face the other girl. "Just what I said. I'm going to Iilaedin."

"Do I have to keep carrying this?" Nuru asked, holding out the Wizard's staff.

Back in the fortress, Eirin had been sure she was saved when Nuru had discovered her. But a minute after Nuru had gone, Rangvald had burst into her room and told her she was no longer safe. He'd tried to pick her up to take her with him.

And Eirin blessed the Time Keeper in her heart for her Human fragility. Because she knew as soon as Rangvald touched her that he wouldn't be able to treat her the way he would any Atharrach prisoner. He would have to be gentle.

He knew this, too, of course. Even with her wrists bound, she'd somehow managed to take the staff and stab him in the shoulder with its sharp tip.

He'd cursed and yanked the staff out of her hand. For a moment, he'd seemed ready to toss it away from her. But then he seemed to think better of it and took it along with them. Then he had brought her and the staff to the study she'd visited earlier, where he had attempted to bind her arms to her sides. She'd managed to get in one good kick to his face before Drystan and the others had shown up.

As soon as Drystan attacked Rangvald, Qeb had swept Eirin up in his arms and carried her to the opposite side of the room. She had watched his desire to stay with Drystan warring with his need to keep her safe. As he'd watched in frustration, Eirin had begged Nuru to pick the staff up for her where Rangvald had cast it onto the floor.

Bless her for not letting go.

"I'll take it," Eirin said, going over to Nuru. "Thank you for carrying it for me." What she would do with the thing was beyond her. All she knew was that it couldn't fall into the wrong hands. That lesson she'd learned well.

Although it would make a terrific walking stick. She planted it in the dirt beside her and faced the others. The time had come. She couldn't afford to play games anymore.

"None of you are obligated to come with me," she said, doing her best to sound utterly confident in her decision. "This choice is for me alone. But don't try to stop me, because I'm going to Iilaedin if I have to walk all by myself." She met Drystan's gaze boldly, daring him to stop her.

Instead, he bowed his head. "You won't be walking." He peeked up at her, his pale eyes glinting in the weak moonlight. "Because I'm going to carry you."

That...was not what Eirin was expecting. But before she could come up with words to answer him, Qeb took a step closer, a wry smile on his face. He said nothing, but really, nothing needed to be said. Wherever Drystan went, there Qeb would also be.

Nuru sniffed and squared her shoulders. "Well, I'm not about to let you make all these bad decisions on your own."

"Me neither," Thane said. For once, he wasn't smiling. "I made a terrible decision when I chose to listen to others instead of those I knew to be true. And I'm sorry." He glanced at Nuru again. "Sorry for it all."

Nuru gave him a cold look, but the corners of Drystan's mouth lifted. "Then it's good to have you back, Thane," Drystan said.

Nuru snorted. "You're one to talk." Eirin nearly snorted along with her. Drystan had been gone nearly as long as Thane. And while Eirin knew why now, it still didn't erase the hurt his absence had left behind.

"I'm coming too."

Everyone turned to look at Callispa. Her voice wavered, and she sounded as though she was about to cry.

"You'd leave your family?" Eirin asked. She should be grateful for any help they could find. Callispa would be a competent, reliable resource to have in Solevar. But it wasn't fair. This girl was the reason Drystan wouldn't speak with Eirin. Why did she have to be their help?

And now she was simply ready to abandon her family and leave it all behind?

Callispa gave Drystan a nervous smile and shrugged. "A trainer can't leave her Dragon before he's finished training."

Eirin wanted to gag, but she kept her jealousy to herself.

Even though she really, really wanted to.

"They'll be out here searching for us as soon as Rangvald is lucid enough to send them," Qeb said, scanning the sky with his eyes. "Neither they nor we can travel during the day, though, so we might as well get as far as we can tonight. Then we'll find a place to rest and hunker down where we'll be safe to sleep."

"What about Eirin?" Callispa asked.

Eirin scowled. "What about me?"

Callispa gave her an apologetic smile. "I mean the curse," she said in a softer tone. "You won't last very long out here. Not without protection."

Oh. Unfortunately, Callispa had a point.

As much as she wanted to deny it, Eirin knew all too well the headaches that came every time she ventured into Solevar. The only reason she didn't have one now, she was sure, was because the wind had died down, and they were still close to the mountain. "We're near the foot of the mountain. I'll survive for a night," Eirin finally said. "We'll figure out what to do in the morning."

"Climb on," Drystan said, shifting back into his Dragon form. He knelt, and Eirin took that as her sign to climb on his back. Awkwardly, she climbed his lowered wing. But riding on his back would be good, she reflected. He'd been carrying her in his arms earlier, and it had felt very…intimate. Eirin wasn't sure she was ready for that yet. No matter how much her heart wanted it. This was much better. It would also allow her to discreetly study him for more injuries.

They spent a few moments discussing how to proceed. Even if Drystan flew, carrying Callispa and Eirin, Qeb couldn't carry Thane for hours, as Thane was nearly as tall as he was. And Nuru had never trained to fly someone else for long distances. Besides, they had no idea whether or not Rangvald had sent out trackers. So in the end, everyone agreed that with Callispa's fiery wings and Thane's lack of wings, it would be best to travel on foot for the remainder of the night. Their entire group could walk in the shadow of the trees, virtually unseen from above.

Drystan walked in his Dragon form with Eirin perched on his back, and the others took care of themselves. Several times, they heard beating wings above them and dove down until the sounds were gone. They continued on undetected until just before dawn, when Thane discovered a small cave in the mountain's foothills. It was small and somewhat cramped, but there was a fresh stream trickling down from the heights nearby, and they could stay hidden for the duration of the day.

As their little party prepared for sleep, Eirin announced that she was going to the stream. It smelled fresh, coming from the mountain springs, and Eirin wanted to wash off the beginnings of the curse that she could feel coming on. No one objected, so she made her way down silently, believing they'd let her go the short distance alone. Not so.

"How are you feeling?"

Eirin nearly fell in the water. She put a hand on her beating heart and turned to see Drystan, back in Human form, standing behind her. How was such a big man so quiet?

When her heart calmed, she went back to washing her face and arms. It was rude to ignore him, she knew. But she found that suddenly she was at a loss for words. After everything that had happened, what could she even say?

"Well enough," she finally answered. "Probably because we're closer to the mountain still." Then, with a deep breath, she turned to face him. They stood there, staring for an eternal moment.

What was he thinking?

"I was never with Callispa," he finally blurted. Eirin blinked at him.

"It was just a way to get you to stay back," he continued in a rush. "She thought it might help you to stay away. But nothing..." He shook his head, his blue eyes staying welded to hers. "None of that was ever real. It was only ever for you."

Qeb had been right. Drystan had done it all for show. Eirin felt as though that should take away the pain. Everything should be right now. But for some reason...it didn't.

Why didn't it take away the pain? Then she remembered Rangvald's words.

In tearing himself away from you, that boy did one of the most painful things a Dragon can do! He burned a hole in his own heart to keep you safe!

Eirin sighed as her strength seemed to desert her. "I know what you did for me," she whispered, looking back down at the water. "And...I understand more now."

He really had been telling the truth all along. He had only wanted to keep her safe. Her own chest ached as she thought of the pain he had suffered for so long. And she had never known. "I'm also sorry it hurt. I never wanted you to hurt."

"I didn't want to leave you." Drystan came and knelt beside her. She wanted to look up at him, but if she did, she might get trapped in his gaze, and all of her self-control might leave her. "It was the only way I could think to protect you," he added softly.

Eirin looked up at him this time. "You don't seem to think I need protecting now."

"Not from me." He took her hand in his, making her breath catch in her throat. His large hand was rough and square. He traced its lines, sending a bolt of delight shooting up her arm. "Not anymore."

It was all she could do to resist him. "Drystan?"

"Yes?"

"I think…" She looked up and swallowed. "I'm glad to have you back." Her voice must *not* shake. "I worried so much." Focus. She had to focus. All of Solevar hung in the balance. She spoke as slowly and carefully as she could. "But I think for the duration of this journey that…" She willed her hand to pull away from his. Oh, it was hard. "It would be best," she continued, "if we focused on the journey alone. No distractions. No drama. Nothing that could endanger what we're trying to do."

There. She had said it.

The pain in Drystan's eyes nearly made her take it all back on the spot. But then he gave her a pained grin.

"Does this mean you want Qeb to keep towing you around instead?"

Eirin stood up straight. "I didn't say that."

His smile grew slightly less pained.

She took his hand and held it in both of hers. "A lot has happened to us since coming to Mhaedin. We both need to heal." Then she let his hand go and reached up carefully, unable to stop herself from tracing the path of his newest scar across his cheek. "Doing that as we run for our lives might be a bit of a distraction."

He couldn't know just how much of a distraction he was.

"Not for me." He shook his head. "Doing what you need. Helping you to be who you were made to be." He brushed her cheek with the tips of his fingers, and Eirin had to hold back tears. "It's all one."

Focus, Eirin. You have to focus.

"Then for me," she pleaded quietly. "Give me time for me."

Drystan stared at her for what felt like an eternity. Would he say no? Would he give up on her and really choose Callispa this time? Eirin didn't know if she could handle that again. But she would have to if that day ever came. For Solevar's sake. For the sake of her mother and father and brothers and the little sister who would be born if the world would just last long enough, she would have to persevere.

This was why she couldn't have distractions.

"Someone's coming!"

Eirin and Drystan jumped to their feet. Almost as fast, Drystan had shifted into his Dragon form. He moved in front of Eirin.

"Your sword and knife are in my bag," he said in a low voice without turning his head. "There, on the rock."

Eirin quickly ran to the large stone where Drystan had laid his bag. Sure enough, her sword and knife were inside. She resisted the urge to kiss them.

A weak Human she may be, but she would feel safer with a blade in her hand until the day she died.

After reclaiming her weapons, she grabbed the Wizard's staff again as well.

"They're so silent," she breathed after a long moment of nothing.

He jerked his head, and she took that as a sign to follow him. Softly they crept down through the brush. Whoever had called out the warning was now quiet. Where were their friends?

Through the early morning mist they walked and finally entered the clearing where their friends had set up camp. Then Eirin let out a small cry.

"Isayas!"

Sure enough, the Wizard was in their midst. The others crept out from their hiding places, their eyes as wide as Eirin's felt.

"But how…" Eirin began, but the Wizard just snorted.

"I'm a Wizard, my dear. Don't you think I know where my staff is?"

Eirin laughed, though she wasn't sure why. "I was keeping it for you."

"So have I heard." He gave her a stern look. "And why exactly is there blood on it?"

Eirin froze. "Um…I might have stabbed a Dragon with it."

The Wizard stared at her for a long moment before letting out a shout of laughter.

His laughter seemed to break the trance the rest of them were under, and a few minutes later, they were all gathered in a circle, eating a meager breakfast.

"But how did you wake up?" Callispa asked. "The Nymphs said you were nearly dead."

The Wizard scowled. "That idiot boy switched out my powders, which fed their toxic fumes back to me." He sat straighter. "But like porridge that's gone sour and sickened the one who eats it, bad magic must eventually leave the body." He chuckled. "A Wizard's at least." Then he looked around him. "You're a bit far from Mhaedin, aren't you?"

The others grew silent and looked at one another until Drystan cleared his throat.

"We're not going to Mhaedin." He looked at Eirin, who gave him a small smile and a nod. "We're going to Iilaedin."

Eirin held her breath. Would the Wizard be angry? Would he force them back to Mhaedin? Or would he simply leave them behind?"

To her surprise, the Wizard smiled. "Well then," he said, "it seems I've got one last adventure on my hands."

"You mean you'll come with us?" Eirin squeaked.

"That," he looked at her, "is exactly what I mean."

———

They slept in the cave that day, and in the evening, they made plans. To Eirin's great relief, Isayas promised that he could find a way to lessen the effects of the curse on her. At least temporarily.

"It won't be a permanent fix," he said, frowning slightly. He was pressing several plants together between two stones. Their oils stained the stones, and their scents filled the air as he worked. "But it should allow us to get deeper into Solevar without the worst parts of the curse affecting you."

"And you're sure there's no way you can help us fly?" Callispa asked longingly.

He gave her a small smile. "I'm sorry, but no. It's probably best this way, though. Rangvald will have most of Solevar out searching for you. As long as I can prevent Eirin from falling to the curse, we should have time to get her to Iilaedin before…" He let the words die and nodded down at the oils he was drawing. "Soon enough, by any means."

He didn't need to finish his sentence. Everyone knew what he was talking about. The summer had been an unusually long one, but it was waning. The curse was growing in strength, and Solevar couldn't hang on for much longer. They couldn't afford to make the mistakes of the past, and Eirin hoped they weren't making a mistake by walking to Iilaedin instead of flying.

She fingered the stone that hung from her neck nervously. Then she stopped. They weren't making the same mistakes of the past.

Isayas had sworn to help them, so now they had a Wizard. They were no longer encumbered by an army of hundreds or even dozens. It was just them. She was surrounded by her closest friends, and most importantly, she had the stone.

The power of a steady gaze drew Eirin's attention to her left. Drystan, in Human form, was filling his pack. But he was looking at her. Eirin watched him back.

More than ever, she was convinced that her choice to focus on the mission ahead of them was the right decision for both of them. That didn't mean, of course, that her need for him was any less than it had ever been. It would be right where it had always been.

Waiting.

Just like Solevar.

They set out as soon as darkness fell. Using her father's map and the Wizard's experience, they set a course due north. The night was once again unusually cool, and Eirin liked the way it felt against her skin. She also liked the warmth of Drystan's scales beneath her hands as she climbed up on his back. So long they had been waiting. But this…

This is where the end of their waiting began.

The Seer's Sacrifice
Legacy of the Time Stones, Book #3

Drystan began to jerk harder and harder at his bindings. Somehow, he managed to work his blindfold off, revealing eyes that were an alarming amber.

All of this happened just as a creature with skin as white as the moon appeared on the side of their boat opposite Drystan. She must have been beautiful...once. Her hair was as black as her skin was white, and her eyes had no whites in them at all. When she smiled at Eirin, it was to reveal perfect, pointed teeth. Then she turned her gaze to Drystan and let out a song much louder than any they had heard before.

At the same time, several other Sirens appeared in a circle around the boat, closing in slowly as they sang. Isayas continued to boom his own song as the end of his staff began to glow yellow. He swung the staff from side to side, his song never faltering as he walked from one side of the boat to the other. But Eirin could see beads of sweat dripping down his temples, and his hands shook slightly.

He wouldn't last much longer.

Drystan let out a snarl and swiveled his head from side to side like an animal.

"Isayas!" Eirin screamed, but it was Callispa who dropped her oar and ran to Drystan. She begged and pleaded for him to stay with them, using tones that were pleading and sweet, staring into his eyes, her face inches from his.

"Callispa!" Eirin called, letting go of the tiller. "Let me-"

"Stay there!" Callispa snapped. She turned back to Drystan, but before she could speak again, he struggled so hard to free his hands from the railing that he knocked her to the ground.

Looking stunned and confused, Isayas watched Drystan for a moment before grim determination settled on his face. Slowly, he raised his staff.

No. Isayas would not sacrifice himself this way. Eirin wouldn't let him. After throwing down the tiller once more, Eirin stepped over Callispa to stand before Drystan. His eyes still glowed amber, a hunger in them Eirin had never seen.

"Eirin, no!" Isayas shouted.

Eirin ignored him. Instead, she took Drystan's face in her hands, a face that was looking less and less Human by the second, and willed him to look into her eyes.

While Eirin knew less about Sirens than Callispa seemed to, and far less than Isayas, she knew how their songs worked and why they worked only on men. Their songs, though unintelligible to the female ear, were ones of seduction and temptation. They appealed to the darkest desires of the soul, charming the lusts good men did their best to subvert. They sang promises of pleasures and delight, of hopes and dreams fulfilled in the realization of those base desires.

And Eirin was not about to let them destroy the man she loved.

Read Seer's Sacrifice (Legacy of the Time Stones, Book #3) to find out how Eirin and Drystan's story ends!

Dear Reader,
Thank you for reading The Seer's Dragon*!*
If you'd like more of Eirin and Drystan, visit BrittanyFichterFiction.com*.*
By joining my email list, you'll get free access to exclusive chapters from the Legacy of the Time Stones Trilogy, sneak peeks, coupons and sales, and so much more!

Also, if you liked the book, please consider leaving an honest review on your favorite ebook retailer or Goodreads so other readers can discover this book, too!

ABOUT THE AUTHOR

Brittany lives with her Prince Charming, their little fairy, and their little prince in a ~~sparkling~~ (decently clean) castle in whatever kingdom the Air Force has most recently placed them. When she's not writing, Brittany can be found chasing her kids around with a DSLR and belting it in the church choir.

Subscribe: BrittanyFichterFiction.com
Email: BrittanyFichterFiction@gmail.com
Facebook: Facebook.com/BFichterFiction
Instagram: @BrittanyFichterFiction